Operation Ab

CW00502461

By

Robert Cubitt

Carter's Commandos – Book 1

Other titles by the Same Author

Fiction
The Deputy Prime Minister
The Inconvenience Store
The Charity Thieves

Warriors Series
The Warriors: The Girl I Left Behind Me
The Warriors: Mirror Man

The Magi Series
The Magi
Genghis Kant (The Magi Book 2)
New Earth (The Magi Book 3)
Cloning Around (The Magi Book 4)
Timeslip (The Magi Book 5)
The Return Of Su Mali (The Magi Book 6)
Robinson Kohli (The Magi Book 7)
Parallel Lines (The Magi Book 8)

Non-Fiction
A Commando's Story
I'm So Glad You Asked Me That
I Want That Job

Contents

Dedication

In memory of all the Commandos of World War II and in memory of one commando in particular.

The truth is often stranger than any fiction that can be written.

Author's Note On The Language Used In This Book

This is a story about soldiers and to maintain authenticity the language used reflects that. There is a use of swear words of the strongest kind. It is not my intention to cause offence, but only to reflect the language that was and still is used by soldiers. Apart from the swearing there is other language used that may cause offence. I don't condone the use of that language, but it reflects the period in which the story is set. While we may live in more enlightened times and would never consider using such words, the 1940s were different and the language used is contemporary for the period. We cannot change the past, we can only change the present and the future and I'm glad that our language has changed and become more sensitive to the feelings of others but we must never forget our past. We should, however, seek not to repeat it.

Abbreviations of rank used in this book (in descending order of seniority):

Lt Col – Lieutenant Colonel (often referred to simply as Colonel by their own subordinates)

Maj – Major

Capt – Captain

Lt – Lieutenant

2Lt – Second Lieutenant

RSM – Regimental Sergeant Major (Warrant Office Class 1)

CSM – Company Sergeant major (Warrant Officer Class 2)

TSM – Troop Sergeant Major (Warrant Officer Class 2) as used by the commandos.

SMjr – Sergeant Major (generic)

CSgt – Colour Sergeant

SSgt – Staff Sergeant

Sgt - Sergeant

LSgt – Lance Sergeant; a Brigade of Guards rank, but sometimes used by the commandos instead of Corporal.

Cpl – Corporal

LCpl – Lance Corporal

Pvt – Private

Tpr – Trooper, a cavalry rank equivalent to Private but used by the commandos.

Cdo – the abbreviation used when naming a specific commando, e.g. 15 Cdo.

Other military terminology is explained within the text where the narrative allows, or is explained in footnotes.

1 – Parachutes

Wiltshire, June 1941

The light lanced through Carter's eyelids and fought his efforts to remain asleep. Reluctantly he raised his head from the pillow and used his hand to shield his eyes while he identified the cause of this rude awakening. At the foot of his bed stood a soldier.

"Sorry, Sir. Orderly Officer's¹ compliments, but he says can you report to the Guardroom, fighting order². There's a bit of a flap on."

"OK. Tell him I'm on my way." Carter dragged himself out of bed and started to dress, his fingers fumbling with buttons and boot laces as his brain struggled to catch up with his body.

It was probably another drill, Carter thought. These things always were. He'd get to the Guardroom and there would be the CO, stopwatch in hand, timing the speed of his response to the summons. Or maybe it would be someone from Division HQ, sent to test the reactions of the battalion.

Just his luck to be in the duty company for the week. Not just the company, but to command the actual duty platoon that would be the first to be dragged out of bed. He consoled himself with the fact that now he had been woken, his fellow platoon commanders in B Company would also be being woken.

Grabbing his hat from the hook behind the door, he jammed it on his head and hurried through the corridors of the still slumbering Officers' Mess. Outside, the moon shone brightly, illuminating the barracks with a poor substitute for street lights.

As he jogged towards the Guardroom he caught up with some of his platoon, ambling towards the main gate, chatting and laughing.

"What do you think you're doing, walking during a drill. Get a move on, double march." He bellowed as he passed them. Taken by surprise by his sudden appearance, they broke into a run. Carter identified a couple of faces, he'd deal with them later.

Arriving at the Guardroom he pushed his way through the blackout curtain, past the Orderly Sergeant and into the rear office. The Orderly Officer was 'Gunner' Grant, one of the Platoon Commanders from D Company.

"Ah, Steven, I've had orders from Division. There's been a report of thousands of paratroops landing in the Salisbury area. I'll give you the details in a minute. The whole of the South Coast has been put on alert in case this is the start of the invasion.

The invasion again. Since September 1940 the likelihood of a German invasion had dropped dramatically, but still Division used it as the basis for drills such as this.

"OK, well, I suppose we have to go along with this."

The Orderly Officer was taken aback by Carter's reply. "This isn't a joke, Steven. This is for real."

"You mean it's not a drill?"

"No. This is a real report. As I said, the whole of the South Coast, from Dover to Penzance, is in a flap. The Orderly Sergeant will issue live ammunition to you and your men. I've got transport on the way. Your orders are to get down to Salisbury and carry out a reconnaissance and report back on what you find; numbers, apparent intentions, you know the sort of thing."

Carter did know the sort of thing. It was the usual things a defensive reconnaissance patrol would report on.

"OK. where are we going?"

The Orderly Officer pointed to a map of the area posted on the office wall. It showed the area around the barracks between the A303 to the north and Salisbury to the south. "The report was that there are paratroops close to the village of South Newton, about five miles from here." Carter made a note of the grid reference for the village. "The report said they were landing to the east of the village, so that would place them between there and the village of Lower Woodford. Your orders are to advance to South Newton and carry out a recce in an eastwards direction until you make contact. Then remain and report back. The rest of B Company will follow you, then the rest of the Battalion, once we've got them out of their beds."

It was a daunting task. His platoon was only twenty four men strong, plus himself and the Platoon Sergeant. On the plus side, if there were thousands of paratroops in the area, they wouldn't be hard to find. "Now, I've managed to get a map of the area for you." He handed Carter a neatly folded map, which Carter knew he would have to unfold and then re-fold so that it was displayed correctly in his map case. He'd often wondered why the Ordnance Survey and the War Office had never got together and agreed on the best way to fold maps for use by the military. For the moment he pushed it inside his battledress blouse.

"OK, I'd better get going."

He went out into the main Guardroom, where the Orderly Sergeant was doling out boxes of ammunition to the section corporals, fifty rounds per man. These were being passed out through the door to the waiting men. On the end of the counter were two boxes of point four five five calibre ammunition for Carter's Webley revolver. He scooped them up and pushed them into his ammunition pouches, one on either side of his webbing harness. He would load his revolver as they travelled. First, though, he had to brief his men.

Carter's Platoon Sergeant, Albert Liddle, was with the waiting men. "Platoon, 'shun!" he called, when he saw Carter appear. It was dark after the brightness of the Guardroom's interior and Carter's eyes struggled to adjust. He could only make out the shapes of his men, not any identifying features.

"At ease, men. OK, 4 Platoon." He started. "This isn't a drill, it's the real thing. There have been reports of enemy paratroops landing about five miles to the south of us and we've been given the task of going and taking a look to see what they're up to. Now, you've been issued with live ammunition, but you have to take care. That figure looming out of the darkness in front of you may be a Jerry parachutist, but equally it might be some old bloke staggering back home from the pub." This elicited a chuckle from his men. "Make sure you challenge first, loudly and clearly. If he shoots at you, you may shoot back; even if he is an old bloke on his way back from the pub." This brought more laughter.

"I'll brief you again when we get to where we're going." As he said it, a 3 Ton lorry pulled to a halt behind him with a squeal of protesting brakes.

"OK, men." Sgt Liddle shouted. "All aboard lads; chop chop."

Carter went around to the passenger side and climbed into the cab next to the Service Corps driver. He pulled the map out and showed the man where they were going. "I know it, Sir." The driver said. "It'll take about ten minutes to get there." A hand banged on the roof of the cab to tell the occupants that the Platoon were all on board. The driver ground the gears and they pulled away into the night.

As they travelled, Carter puzzled over what he had been asked to do. It made no sort of military sense. Not only had the risk of invasion been pretty much discounted since the end of the previous year, Salisbury was such an unlikely place for paratroops to land. It's main claim to fame was its cathedral with its four hundred and four foot spire, but that would only be of interest to tourists, not to Jerry paratroops.

Not only was there nothing of strategic importance in the area, it was too far inland. It must be nearly thirty miles to the nearest point of the coast. That was far too far for a relieving force to penetrate before the paratroops would inevitably be overpowered by the British troops in the area, troops like his own battalion. Even using *Blitzkrieg*[3] tactics a German relief force couldn't hope to make it that far inland so quickly. By the same measure, it was too far inland for it to be a raid. No airborne raiding force could hope to make its way back to the coast to take boats back to France. None of it made any sort of tactical or strategic sense.

As they approached their destination, Carter's eye was drawn to flickering lights across the fields to his left. "What the devil's that?" He asked, not really expecting a reply.

The driver stole a glance before returning his eyes to the road. "Looks like a fire to me."

"Yes, that's what I thought. But it's totally against blackout regulations to have a bonfire lit at night. Which means …" He let his mind join the dots. "… which means it wasn't lit buy anyone from around here. Stop the truck." He ordered.

The driver did as he was told. "Stay here, keep the engine running." Carter said as he climbed down from the cab. He jogged around to the tailgate.

"Everyone off." He ordered. "Four section, you stay here and guard the lorry, make sure no one tries to steal it. The rest of you form line abreast along the road. You see that fire?" he asked, He didn't wait for a reply. "We're going to take a look at it. Keep in line, if you see anything suspicious, call out and we'll stop and take a look."

He led the troops off the road and into the adjacent field. By his reckoning the fire was about half a mile away. Ten minutes' walk so long as they didn't encounter any obstructions, or any enemy paratroops.

The fire had started to dwindle; it had probably started to burn itself out some time before, Now it was just a few stubborn patches of flames in between the twisted skeleton of an aircraft. It was more like a burning dinosaur skeleton than something that might once have flown. In the darkness Carter couldn't be sure what type it had been. A Heinkel perhaps.

The blitz was long passed, but the *Luftwaffe* still paid regular night time visits to Britain's cities, though not with such large numbers of aircraft as in the Summer of 1940. From where it had crashed it had likely been somewhere like Bristol, Newport or Cardiff; Birmingham was an outside bet. It had probably been intercepted by a British night fighter, or maybe hit by anti-aircraft fire and made it as far as this before crashing.

If it was Heinkel then it would have had a crew of five. Was that the answer to the conundrum? Five parachutists, exaggerated into a force of thousands by multiple reports, fear and night time imagination. Carter couldn't be sure, but it was a more likely explanation than an invasion.

Across the fields drifted the sound of lorry engines. Carter turned to see headlights further back along the road. From the thin slits of their headlights he could tell there were at least three vehicles travelling in convoy. That would be about right if it was the rest of B Company. "Sgt Liddle, send a runner back to the road to intercept those vehicles. Pass my compliments to whoever is in charge and tell him what we found. Ask them to wait and I'll be there shortly."

To the rest of the platoon he said "OK, men. Looks like it's the crew of this aircraft that we're looking for. Up to five Jerries, if they all made it out alive. Spread out and search the immediate area. One section go to the left, two section go right, then circle around about a hundred yards out and meet up on the far side. Sgt Liddle is in charge, if you don't find anything, return to the road. Three section come with me in case I need you."

It would be unlikely that the crew would be around here if they had escaped by parachute. The aircraft would have descended at a steep angle, while nature would have blown the crew in whatever direction the wind was blowing, possibly miles from where the aircraft eventually crashed. Carter checked his watch; oh four thirty hours, perhaps another hour before the sun rose to give them any significant light to see by.

Leading three section back the way they had come, Carter made his way to the road. He was greeted by the Company Commander, Maj Congreve, who was standing beside Carter's lorry.

"A crashed Heinkel." Carter reported. "At least, that's what it looks like. It doesn't look much like a Heinkel now though. No sign of the crew but I've got my men doing a local area search. My guess is that they were blown ahead of the aircraft." He pulled his map out of his battledress blouse and spread it on the ground. Kneeling down he shone a torch on it. "We're here, Sir." He pointed to a spot on the line printed on the map that marked the road. "The wind is blowing from the south west, so …" he traced a line on the map leading towards Andover, "I think they'll be somewhere along this route."

"You're discounting the possibility of an invasion, then." The Company Commander's tone was light, not accusatory.

"Not discounting it totally, Sir, but thinking that the crew of a downed bomber is a more likely explanation for the sighting of parachutes. If there is a battalion of *Fallschirmjäger* out there, then that line of search is as logical as any other."

"If it was an invasion it would be more than a battalion, but I think you are probably right. Given the reports, that line is as good a search route as any. OK, I'll get the rest of the Company out of the trucks. We'll go line abreast from the left hand side of the crash, while your Platoon can extend the line to the right. We'll search for two miles, then we'll turn back. When we turn we'll split the line in the middle, two platoons to the right hand side and two to the left. If it comes to that we'll use runners to maintain contact.

One hundred and twenty men, advancing at five yard intervals, meant that they would cover a swathe of land six hundred yards wide. When they turned back, they would sweep two more sections of land on either side of the original track, each three hundred yards wide.

"I'm going to radio back to Battalion HQ and suggest they take the rest of the battalion to the far side of the search area, at Lower Woodford and do the same from that side, so we meet in the middle. If there's anything to be found, we'll find it."

Or the crew of the aircraft will slip sideways out of the gap in the middle, but Carter kept the thought to himself. They really needed forces on either side to close the box, but that wasn't his call. The Company Commander had formed his plan and it was Carter's job to follow it.

The two sections of Carter's platoon that had been searching around the aircraft wreckage returned to the road and he quickly briefed his Platoon on the search procedure.

"Keep the noise to a minimum and the chat to zero." He admonished. "If the crew are out there, we don't want them to know we're coming until we trip over them. Keep your eyes peeled on the ground between you as well as to your front, and if you come across any bushes or the like, make sure you give them a thorough examination. In fact fix your bayonets. The sight of those poking through the undergrowth will force anyone into the open." It was true that the vicious spike bayonets were frightening, held at arm's length on the end of a Lee Enfield rifle, it extended a soldier's reach by up to four feet.

He placed Sgt Liddle at the left hand end of the line, where it butted up against 1 Platoon, while he placed himself at the right hand end, the final man at the end of the six hundred yard wide advance. A whistle sounded a single blast and the line moved raggedly forward. They would take their pace from the Company Commander, some three hundred yards away in the middle of the line.

They hiked for a mile, the slow pace of the advance eating up time. The eastern horizon, diagonally to their left, was starting to lighten when Carter heard one of his men call out, stopping the line in a wave motion as the message was passed along it. Carter hurried to see what had caused the halt.

"Over there, Sir." The soldier, a Private by the name of Grimshaw pointed.

Straining his eyes, Carter peered into the early morning gloom. There it was, something rising and falling, shifting in the light breeze; sometimes large, sometimes smaller. A parachute, Carter decided.

"OK, Grimshaw, you come with me." Carter turned to see who the next man in line was, to his right. Pvt King. A reliable sort. "You come too, King. Keep spaced out on either side of me."

The object was about a hundred yards in front. They advanced slowly, expecting a gun shot at any moment, but nothing was heard except the rustle and snap of the parachute, louder as they got closer. From about fifty yards out they could see that there was something bulky lying at the end of the shrouds nearest to them, the parachute being blown away from them. At thirty yards distance Carter was pretty sure it was a man. He jerked as the parachute pulled at him but made no effort to defend himself. Unconscious, Carter thought. Or dead.

His latter suspicion was confirmed when they reached him. He was wearing a one piece flying suit, a leather helmet and goggles concealing most of his face and head. Well, the suit had been one piece. Now it had a great gash across the airman's body, through which internal organs were now poking. It was a wonder that he had made it out of the aircraft at all. Had he died before or after landing? Carter wondered.

He turned to Pvt King. "Go back and find the Company Commander and tell him what we've found. Grimshaw, you stay here until the rest of your section reach you, then make a stretcher using your rifles and gas capes⁴. Take him back to the truck. Be as gentle as you can with him.

Carter jogged back to the search line and detailed off Grimshaw's section to go and assist him with the body. The rest of the line closed up to fill the gap and Carter passed the word along that the line could advance.

There were curious glances as the Platoon passed the dead German. For the new recruits, Carter included, it would be the first time they had seen a dead body. The veterans of Dunkirk would have seen plenty.

They had gone another half mile, the daylight starting to increase rapidly, when a shot rang out. The veterans dived to the ground at once, but the newer recruits were slower to react. "Down!" Sgt Liddle bellowed, bringing an immediate reaction. Carter would reflect later that the men seemed to be more afraid of their Sergeant than they were of gunfire.

Raising himself up, Carter tried to see from where the gun had been fired. The long grass of the meadow defeated him.

"2 Platoon will advance by Sections." Carter called. "Four section first, followed by one and two." Three section was the one detailed to look after the German body. He raised himself onto one knee. "Four section, advance!"

He stood and ran forward with his men, racing about twenty yards before shouting "Down!" His men dropped obediently to the ground, then completed their manoeuvre by scuttling through the grass on their knees and elbows to confuse the aim of any German that had seen where they had gone to ground.

They had only been on their feet for a few seconds, but it had been enough time for Carter to see the humps of some bodies in the grass about fifty yards in front of them. Boots thudded through the grass as the next section advanced and more shots were fired from in front of them. "To your front, cover fire!" Carter bawled. His section let out a ragged volley. It wouldn't be accurate, but it would keep the German's heads down.

Two section went to ground to their front and left and immediately opened fire on the enemy. Carter heard Sgt Liddle shouting at the remaining troop to advance, as two section joined his own men in providing covering fire.

As one section hit the ground, Carter shout "Four section up!" at the same time as he launched himself to his feet. He was just about to order his men to go to ground again when a figure in front of him stood up and began waving its arms frantically. A second stood and he, too, waved his arms. Snatches of German reached Carter's ears.

"Cease firing!" Carter shouted, straining his voice to make himself heard above the cacophony of small arms fire. He had to repeat the order several times before the last rifle fell silent. Carter suspected that most of the rifle magazines were now empty and that was the main reason why his men had stopped firing.

"One section, circle left." He ordered, "and four section circle right. Two section with me. Advance to your front."

They got within ten yards before Carter brought his men to a halt. In front of them four aircrew now stood with their hands in the air. "Do any of you speak English?" Carter called.

"A little." The one on the extreme right said.

"Tell your friends to drop all their weapons. My men will search you."

Pistols were thrown to the ground, followed by knives that had been stored in sheaths stitched into the legs of their flying suits.

Carter detailed four men to stand in front of the prisoners, their bayonets poised just inches from their chests, while four others went around behind them to carry out body searches for more weapons, or anything that could be used as a weapon. The other two sections formed a ring around them, their weapons raised, daring any of the Germans to make a run for it.

"Our gunner, have you seen him?" The English speaker asked.

"I'm sorry. We found his body back there."

The German translated and there was some muttering from his fellow crew members, but they remained passive enough.

"What happened to you?" Carter asked the German who spoke English.

"We were returning from our mission. We got too close to Bristol and we were hit by *flak⁵*. We continued to here, but our aircraft ..." He used his hands to indicate the aircraft losing a dangerous amount height

Hearing sounds from behind him, Carter turned to see the Company Commander approaching, a section of men spread out behind him to provide an escort. Close by him was a radio operator, bending under the weight of a Type 18 set.

"Well done, Steven." Congreve said as he approached. "Are they all here?"

"Yes, Sir. With the body they're all present and accounted for, unless they had any passengers on board."

"I'll just report back and see what the CO wants to do now."

Taking the handset for the radio from the operator, Congreve had a lengthy exchange of radio messages, before turning his attention back to Carter.

"The CO wants us to return to the trucks and wait for him there. We can send the prisoners back to barracks in one of the trucks, under guard."

"I wonder why the CO wants us to wait?"

"We'll find out soon enough. Your men can have the honour of escorting the prisoners. Two sections should do it. The rest can wait with the rest of the company until the CO arrives."

[1] Orderly Officer – A duty officer who acts in place of the Commanding Officer at night and at weekends. He is authorised to take whatever action he deems fit to deal with an incident until relieved by an officer of more senior rank. Junior officers carry out the duty on a rota basis.

[2] Fighting order – the equipment that is necessary for a soldier to engage in combat. As well as uniform, helmet and a weapon it will include a webbing harness supporting ammunition pouches, water bottle, bayonet, respirator (gas mask) holder and a small pack containing shaving kit, spare socks and underwear, spare bootlaces, mess tins and, possibly, a small quantity of field rations. Marching order is similar, but the small pack is replaced by a big pack which is capable of holding spare uniform items, boots and other equipment so that the soldier can maintain himself in the field for longer periods. To the back of the pack will be strapped a 'trenching tool', a combined pick axe and shovel with a removable handle. Fighting order may involve burdens of up to 30 lbs (13 kgs) weight, marching order could go up as high as 60 lbs (27 kgs). Special forces, such as commandos or paratroops, would increase this to as much as 80 lbs (36 kgs).

[3] *Blitzkrieg* – a military tactic based on using highly mobile forces to concentrate firepower to achieve early breakthroughs and disrupt enemy defences. Used to good effect by the Germans in their invasion of the Low Countries and France in the Spring of 1940.

[4] Gas cape – a type of waterproof poncho. Invented during the First World War to keep chemical droplets from contaminating soldiers' uniforms, It was an easy garment to hose down after a gas attack. Mainly used as rainwear or to construct bivouacs during World War II.

5 *Flak.* – from the German *Fliegerabwehrkanone* meaning 'aircraft defence gun'. The word had its origins in World War I but was common to both English and Germans by World War II.

* * *

It was an hour before the rest of the battalion arrived, crossing the farmland from the other edge of the search area.

"No sign of the bastards!" The CO said as he arrived. Although it was still early in the day, the sun was now starting to climb high into the sky. "They must have gone to ground in the forest to wait for their relief force." He pointed towards the west where trees marked the boundary of a broad forested swathe. It wasn't a complete barrier. Over the years, patches had been cleared for farms and small holdings, but it was a still a large enough area to rival the New Forest, which lay further south.

The illogicality of the Germans landing so far inland seemed to have escaped Lt Col Neville.

"What if there were no paratroops, Sir? What if all there was is the bomber crew?" Carter ventured.

"Nonsense! The reports said there were thousands of them."

"But reports can be misleading, especially at night, Sir." Carter persisted. "There may have been duplicated sightings …"

"Division said there were thousands. Are you saying that Division has got it wrong?" The CO's face was starting to turn a dangerous shade of red.

"I think that what Carter means, Sir," The company commander intervening, his tone conciliatory, "is that with a lack of any sign of paratroops, it is possible that Division has been misinformed."

"Well I believe that the paratroops are hidden away in the forest. I can smell them, Congreve." The Colonel tapped his nose. "They're there alright. Now, I'm going to split you up by companies and allocate grid sections to you all. You are to search each grid section in turn until we find them. You, Carter," the CO turned his stern gaze on his junior officer, "you seem reluctant to believe they're there, so you can set up a road block here. Stop and question everyone who passes through the area and find out what they've seen. Someone must have seen some sign of them."

Only if there was a sign to be seen, Carter thought. This was a wild goose chase using men who were already tired after hunting across Salisbury Plain for a non-existent enemy. They had done well to find the German aircrew so quickly, especially in the dark. They should be allowed to return to the barracks for some well-earned rest. None of which Carter said out loud.

Instead he started to organise his remaining men into a road block, two men on either side of the road, with the rest in a defensive perimeter along the sides of the road. He sited Bren guns to fire along the approaches in both directions. All the trucks carried picks and shovels strapped to the outside and Carter now put them to use digging weapons pits. By heaping the soil up as walls they doubled the defensive height without having to dig too deep. It was a method used to construct defences since the days of the Roman legions.

Carter regretted putting his men to such unnecessary work and they would have to fill the pits in again when they were finally stood down, but it would only attract criticism from the CO if he ignored the basics.

Congreve, the Company Commander, crossed over to him and took him to one side. "You did well with that section attack, Steven. It was just the right tactical response against a small force like that."

"Thank you, Sir."

"Just remember, though, to set your Bren guns out on either flank, so they can fire ahead of your line of advance and keep the enemy's heads down."

Carter could feel himself blush slightly. Of course, he had forgotten that. Stupid! It was basic stuff. "Sorry, Sir"

"Don't get too upset about it. It was your first proper opposed action. It's easy to forget something in the heat of the moment. Just a learning point, that's all. Something to think about for next time."

"Yes, Sir."

"As for this, the CO seems to think that the Germans are still out there, so we had better go and look for them." He turned and walked back towards the rest of the company, who were standing or sitting about along the side of the closest field.

Carter went to the nearest weapons pit and took a hand at the digging. It was good for morale for the officers to be seen sharing the workload with the men, though not all his peers seemed to think that.

The day wore on, getting hotter. There was no shade along the side of the road and Carter could feel his skin start to prickle with sunburn. On this Sunday morning there was little traffic on the road, just a few farmers going out to tend flocks or herds before returning to eat their Sunday lunches.

Word was sent back by the Company Commander that the invasion alert had been cancelled. As dawn broke along the South Coast it revealed a sea totally empty of enemy shipping. Yet still the CO insisted in continuing the search through the forest. At noon Carter caught sight of him further along the road, accompanied by his radio operator and personal escort, climbing into his car and driving off in the direction of the barracks.

A short while later Carter saw a pair of cyclists approaching. As they drew closer Carter could see that one was a man and the other was a woman, no longer in the first flush of youth. Carter wasn't going to stop them, but they drew to a halt anyway.

"So, did you find those Jerries?" The man asked, a broad smile on his face.

"We captured a German bomber crew. Four survivors and one dead."

"But what about the others? There must 'ave been 'undreds of 'em." The man persisted.

"You saw them?" Carter asked.

"Course I saw 'em. Dropping out of the sky over that direction." He pointed towards the area where the Germans had been found.

"You waz drunk." The woman chimed in, a disapproving look on her face. "I said there was only a few, but would you listen? No, you and Arnold Fitchett wouldn't listen."

"Who rang the police?" Carter asked.

"That was Arnold. He ran to the phone box, while I watched."

"How did you know there were hundreds of them? Surely it was too dark to see clearly."

"Because of the battle." The man beamed. "Hundreds of guns going off all at the same time. Were you and your men involved?"

"Not in a battle. There were a few shots fired later, around five a.m."

"Yes, I 'eard them too, when I got up for milking. But the battle earlier was much bigger."

"What I think you heard was the exploding ammunition from the crashed bomber. The fire heats up the bullets in the machine guns and they go off like fire crackers." Carter explained.

"So there was no battle?"

"You can only have a battle if there are two sides to fight each other. Me and my men were the first to arrive on the scene after the alarm was raised."

"I told you it weren't no invasion." The woman scolded her husband. "Bloody Summer Festival."

"What's a Summer Festival?" Carter asked, curious now that he was able to corroborate his theory that the report of the bomber crew's parachutes had caused a false alarm.

"It's an old tradition around here." The man explained, cutting across his wife before she could speak again. "All the villages around here hold a summer festival, the weekend after Mid Summer's Day. So it was held last night.

"Is there much drinking involved?"

"There certainly is." The woman snapped, a sour look on her face. "This one was seeing double by the end."

"Treble more like." The man laughed.

Carter had always considered the saying 'seeing double' to be figurative, but given the reports of thousands of paratroops, where there had only been five, he now reconsidered his view.

"Well, thank you for your help. Rest assured that there are no more German paratroops in the area now."

"Good job too. I'd 'ave sen them off, don't you worry." He said as he climbed back onto his bike.

"You'd a done nothing of the like." His wife said, also getting back on her bike. "Silly old fool."

They cycled off down the road, bickering amicably.

An hour later the Company Commander returned, along with his men. "We've been recalled to barracks." He said. "The CO thinks we've been out on this 'training exercise', as he has renamed it, for long enough."

Carter recounted what the couple on their bikes had told him.

"Easy mistake for a civilian to make, I suppose. Better safe than sorry and it has done no harm for the Battalion's response capability to be tested."

It was Congreve's way of dealing with the situation without sounding critical of his superior. Carter ordered his men into a truck and they travelled the short distance back to barracks.

As the Service Corps driver steered them along the road, Carter thought about the morning's events. Notwithstanding the time wasted after the CO had arrived, he had actually enjoyed the hunt for the German bomber crew. It was the first time he had faced enemy fire, even though it was only a few pistol shots. It had got the adrenalin flowing and sharpened his reactions.

Unfortunately, it only served to throw the tedium of garrison soldiering into a starker contrast.

2 – The Volunteer

"Squad! Squad attention!". Carter tried not to wince as the Sergeant's shout hammered at his ear drums from just a couple of feet away. There was a crash of steel hobnails against wooden floorboards as twenty-four right feet slammed down next to twenty-four left feet.

"Room ready for inspection, Sah." The Sergeant reported.

Twenty-four figures stood ramrod straight at the foot of twenty-four bed spaces, twelve on each side of the hut, ready for inspection. He stepped across the threshold and marched to the first of them, turning to face the figure from just inches away. Private Parsons; a good soldier, if a little bit unimaginative. Every bit of his uniform had razor sharp creases, brass work gleaming so brightly it almost hurt Carter's eyes. He didn't have to look down to know that the toe caps of Parson's boots would reflect like a mirror. Carter stepped past him to examine the kit laid out on the bed. Looking along the room he could see the identical layout on each bed, positioned so precisely that he suspected that a length of string had been stretched the length of the room to provide guide lines.

He circled around in front of Parsons and moved to the next man. Grimshaw, probably the most untidy soldier in the British Army. But his pals had got to work on him and managed to make him look like something other than a sack of shit with a belt around its middle. He spotted a loose thread on the man's beret brim. Decision time. Did he have Grimshaw's name taken again, resulting in him being put on another 'fizzer'₁, or did he let it go. The effort that had been made, either by Grimshaw or by his friends, told him to let it go this time. He moved on to the next man.

Ryan; finest shot in the platoon, possibly in the battalion. He was going to Bisley₂ next month to compete for the regiment. There was never a problem with someone like him. He continued down the line: Wilson, Smith, King, Forester, Pond; each name something to remind him of the soldier's qualities. He got to Barraclough.

"Are you going to win next week, Barraclough?" he asked. It was the regimental boxing night and Barraclough was their big hope of bringing some silverware back to the B Company lines.

"I'm doing extra training, Sir. Just in case."

"Good man." He turned to the Sergeant. "Make sure Barraclough gets some extra time in the gym this week." He ordered.

"Very good, Sir." The Sergeant gave Barraclough what might have been a wink.

Carter moved on: Clancy, Munroe, Turner, Gough, Green.

Private Archibald Green. Nicknamed 'The Prof' by the rest of the platoon and given a less flattering name across the rest of the battalion. He was a bit of an enigma, should have enlisted as an officer, he had the education for it, but had turned down the chance. No one could work out why. But he was a good soldier and that was all that interested Carter for the moment.

"What's the capital of Nyasaland³?" He asked as he came to a stop in front of Green. It was a game they played. Carter would ask a question and Green would provide an answer. Carter sometimes had to go to the Officers' Mess library to check up on whether he was right. He usually was.

"Zomba, Sir." Green snapped without hesitation.

"Correct." Carter said. He'd overheard one of the other officers saying he had visited the place before the War.

"That was an easy one, Sir." Green grinned at him.

"Eyes front, Green!" the Sergeant snapped. Carter stifled a smile and moved on, to complete the circuit of the hut, finishing in front of Corporal Dyson.

"A very good turnout, men." He turned to the Sergeant. "What's next on the programme for today?"

"Route march, Sir, ending up at the rifle ranges. Ten rounds per man, then march back."

"Arrange for transport back from the ranges." He ordered. It was a small reward, considering how hard they had worked to prepare for the inspection but by providing trucks the platoon would get back earlier and get some additional time off.

"Yes Sir." He snapped up a parade ground standard salute, which Carter returned before turning on his heel and leaving the hut to return to his office in the B Company lines.

He threw his hat onto the stand in the corner, silently congratulating himself when it caught on one of the hooks and stayed there, swaying gently back and forth. He dropped into his seat behind his desk and looked at his in-tray. There wasn't much in it. There never was. Not enough to keep him occupied for an hour, let alone for the rest of the morning. He longed for something to interrupt the tedium of life in barracks.

The men were happy though. After the debacle of Dunkirk most of them would be content with the boredom. The battalion had seen a lot of action, as it had made up the British Expeditionary Force's rear guard for most of the retreat to the sea. But Carter hadn't been at Dunkirk. He'd been at University, studying to become an engineer. He could have stayed, of course, remaining to finish his degree before being conscripted, but hearing the news of the men being trapped on the beaches he knew that he couldn't stay in school while others fought and died. He sought an interview with his tutor, agreed a sabbatical until the end of the war and the next day he reported to the local recruiting office to volunteer. With his qualifications he was sent straight to an officer training school before being posted to the Second Battalion, The Huntingdonshire Regiment, where he soon found out that a soldier's life was far less exciting than he had imagined.

He picked up the first file from the small pile. A blue one, meaning it was something to do with personnel issues. He looked at the title: Special Applications. It told him nothing. He opened it and read the top entry.

It was a standard application form to do something that wasn't covered by the normal rules and regulations. At the top were the number rank and name of the applicant, followed by a pre-printed phrase 'Sir, I have the honour to request that …' followed by blank lines that allowed the soldier to describe what it was that he wanted to do. In this case, Private Green wanted to volunteer for special service under a specific Army Council Instruction. That rang a bell in Carter's memory. He got up from his chair and reached for the wad of Routine Orders that hung on a bulldog clip from a nail driven into the wall.

He leafed through until he found the one he wanted. Yes, there it was. A general call for volunteers for special service involving hazardous duties of an unspecified nature. It seemed that Carter wasn't the only one in the barracks who was hungering for something a little more exciting. He had heard of others, from different companies, volunteering but Green was the first from his platoon; at least, the first since Carter had arrived with the Battalion.

It must mean the commandos, he mused. Their raids across the North Sea and the English Channel were gaining a lot of news coverage as the nation became desperate for victories, even small ones. He recalled a newsreel item that he'd seen at the cinema recently, showing commandos raiding some islands off the coast of northern Norway. The islands were so insignificant that he couldn't even recall their names, but the newsreel had treated the raid as if it had been against Berlin itself.

Ollie Hansen, a friend from officer training, was up at Ringway, near Manchester, training to be a paratrooper with one of the commando units.

Well, if Green wanted to throw himself out of a perfectly good aeroplane, then Carter wasn't going to stand in his way, literally or metaphorically. Returning to his seat he scribbled a short recommendation on the application and signed his name. He closed the folder, crossed his name off the front and wrote in that of the Company Commander before dropping it into his 'out' tray for the Messenger to collect.

¹ Fizzer – slang for a 'charge' as in 'to press charges', the taking of disciplinary action against a soldier.

² Bisley – Located in Surrey, Bisley has been the home of the National Rifle Association (not to be confused with the similarly

named lobbying group in the USA) since 1890 and has hosted a wide range of military and civilian shooting competitions over the years.

[3] Nyasaland – This former British colony is now called Malawi. It gained its independence in July 1964.

* * *

"I'm getting damned sick of the commandos stealing all our best men." The Commanding Officer fumed the next day. In front of his desk, the regulation three paces back, stood Private Green. Slightly further away, and at an angle to the CO, stood Carter.

The summons had been unexpected. This sort of application usually went through 'on the nod' once the Company Commander had signed it off. It made Carter wonder what was so special about this one.

"So, Green, what is it that makes you want to volunteer for special service." The CO demanded. He was an old school officer who would probably have been retired had the war not broken out. Carter knew that he had served with distinction in France during the previous war, but his career had stalled afterwards, as the army shrank and there were half a dozen suitable candidates for every promotion. The sudden expansion of the army in 1938 had changed that, of course. With officers being posted to command newly formed reserve battalions, Lt Col Neville had found himself promoted to command of the 2nd Battalion when it returned from France, the previous incumbent having been seriously wounded.

"I want to kill Nazis, Sir." Green said, standing rigidly to attention, staring at a spot about two inches above the CO's head.

"You make it sound personal."

"It is, Sir. I spent my student years organising anti-fascist marches. Before that I went on ant-fascist marches with my father."

"Student years? Oh, yes, it says here you have a degree in Philosophy. Doesn't really go with that accent of yours."

"No, Sir. Got a scholarship." Green kept his face a blank, but there was something in his tone that resented the CO's reference to his accent.

"Still doesn't account for why you are so keen to volunteer. What motivated you march against the fascists in the first place."

Carter was getting nervous. This sort of questioning wasn't normal. Green's motivation was irrelevant. He was either entitled to volunteer under the relevant army instruction, or he wasn't. It was an open and shut case, as far as Carter was concerned.

"I don't like what they're doing to the Jews, Sir. All those laws the Nazis passed in the thirties, stripping the Jews of their nationality, confiscating their property, sending them to camps. It isn't right. They would have done it here if people hadn't stood up against them."

"You have sympathy with the Jews?"

"My Grandfather fled to Britain following Russia's pogroms against the Jews, Sir. My family name was Greenbaum, but my grandfather changed it so we would fit in better."

"So, you're a Jew, eh?" The CO could barely conceal the sneer in his voice.

"No, Sir. Jewishness is passed through the female line. My father may have been Jewish, but my mother is a gentile. That makes me a gentile in the eyes of Jewish law. Not that it matters, I'm an atheist myself."

"An atheist as well. The commies are all atheists. Are you a communist?"

"No, Sir. I am a Socialist."

"Just as bad, if you ask me. Well, I'm not going to have left wing agitators in my battalion, so I'll approve your application."

"Thank you, Sir." Green was an experienced enough soldier to maintain a mask that hid his true feelings about what had just been said.

"I doubt you'll be thanking me when you're lying on some beach somewhere being machine gunned by Jerry." The CO scribbled his signature on Green's application and handed the file to Carter. "Dismiss." He barked.

Green snapped off a salute, did a crisp about turn and marched out of the office.

The CO waited for the sound of his boots to fade along the corridor before he spoke again. "Sometimes I think that Herr Hitler has the right idea about the Jews. What do you think, Carter?"

Carter was horrified by what he had said. They were fighting this war to defeat fascism, but here was a senior officer in the Army suggesting the enemy leader may have a point. Carter wondered if he had been a secret Blackshirt[1] before they were banned at the outbreak of war.

"I try not to get involved in politics." Carter decided a non-committal answer was the best option. The CO's opinions had caused more than one junior officer to regret expressing his own feelings.

"He's a Socialist as well. One of those rabble rousers we had to deal with back in 1926[2]. We can do without his sort. Let the Commandos have him, eh? They'll soon knock that nonsense out of him."

"I know it isn't my place to ask," Carter said, "but I was wondering why you asked to interview Green. After all, this sort of application doesn't usually result in an interview."

"If I want to interview one of my men, I'll damn well interview him." The CO snapped. "Dammed impertinence. As it happens, I wanted to make sure you hadn't put the man up to volunteering. I know you think that garrison duties are tedious, but I don't want your views lowering the morale of the men."

Carter was just about to protest his innocence, when he realised that it would be futile and would only put him further into the CO's bad books.

"But that is a moot point now." The CO continued. "He's not the right type for the Huntingdons."

Given that Green was no different, in any significant way, from any of the other soldiers, Carter wondered what the 'right type' was.

It was pretty clear to him that it wasn't anyone who was either Jewish or a Socialist. It was time for him to go, Carter thought, before he did say something he would regret. While he held no strong political views of his own, if he really thought about it, he would probably consider himself to be a conservative with a small c, it went with his upbringing. But he hadn't yet had time to test that at the ballot box. The last General Election had been in 1935, when he had been just fifteen years old; far too young to vote. The next election probably wouldn't take place until the war's end, because of the need for national unity. But even considering all that, Carter was struggling to listen to the political views being expressed by his CO. They didn't even sound like large c conservatism. Perhaps it was time to stage a tactical withdrawal.

"I won't take up any more of your time, Sir. I know how busy you are."

"Eh?" Neville seemed to have drifted off into some sort of reverie, staring out of the office window and into the middle distance. "Yes, yes. You get along now."

[1] Blackshirts – the name given to members of the British Union of Fascists, founded in 1932 by Sir Oswald Mosley. At their peak they had a membership of about 50,000, though they will also have had some sympathisers. At the outbreak of World War II they were banned. Mosley and 740 other Blackshirts were imprisoned for the duration of the war to prevent them undermining the British war effort.

[2] 1926 – On 4th May 1926 the Trades Union Congress (TUC) called a General Strike in support of a million coal miners who had been locked out of the mines by their employers in a dispute over pay and working hours. Approximately 1.7 million people came out on strike, in addition to the miners who had been locked out. Troops were mobilised to escort food supplies and to assist in maintaining essential services. Tens of thousands of members of the public also volunteered to take the place of the strikers. The strike ended after 9

days without any concessions from the mine owners on the miners' case. The miners struggled on, but by November most were back down the mines working longer hours for less money.

* * *

Carter looked at the application form again, now with the CO's signature scrawled across the bottom. What he had heard disturbed him. He knew that the CO was a man of strong feelings. There had been plenty of Mess dinners where the CO held court over the brandy and cigars, extolling the virtues of Empire and the need for the British to lead the 'natives' out of the darkness. But the anti-Semitism he had heard expressed so openly was another matter. Someone who didn't regard all the population of the country as being equal in all things was someone that Carter couldn't respect. As far as Green's politics were concerned, they were his own business, not the CO's. And if he couldn't respect his commanding officer, could he serve under him?

And if he couldn't serve under him, what were his other options?

He looked at the form again, realising that the answer lay there. Not only did it provide a way out of the battalion, but it also provided a route out of his boredom. Dropping the blue file into the empty 'out tray'. He stood up and strolled along the corridor towards the Company Commander's office. He tapped on the door and obeyed the command to enter.

The Company Commander was barely older than himself. Major Jimmy Congreve had gone to France in 1939 as a Lieutenant and come back as acting Major when the previous incumbent had been killed in a strafing attack by a German Stuka on the road to Dunkirk. His rank had been confirmed later that year.

"Morning, Steven, what can I do for you."

"Erm, I …"

"Spit it out man. It can't be that bad."

"Well, the CO has just signed off that application for special service for Pvt Green and I was wondering if I should …"

"Oh, you want to be a commando, do you? Haven't you learnt the old Army adage about never volunteering?" He chuckled. "Or is there some other reason you might want to leave us?" Congreve gave Carter a shrewd look, "Don't answer that. Well, I can't say I blame you. It has been a bit dull around here for the last year, not withstanding that run-in with the German aircrew a couple of weeks ago. What makes you think you've got what it takes."

"I'm not sure I have, Sir, but the only way to find out is to give it a try."

"True enough I suppose. Have you ever done anything adventurous?"

"My father took me rock climbing when I was younger. Does that count?"

"I guess it does. OK, look, put something in writing and I'll send it up to the Old Man. He has the final say. I can tell you, though, he'll see it as a sign of disloyalty."

Carter didn't know what to say to that. If every CO took that attitude there would be no commandos. But he knew better than to voice his own feelings, they could only get him into trouble. Besides, Carter suspected that if the CO knew his real thoughts, being seen as disloyal would be the least of his problems.

"I realise that, but if I don't get out of here soon I'm likely to explode. Or die of boredom."

"I can tell you straight, when you're a soldier, boredom is far preferable to the alternative. But I guess you'll have to find that out for yourself."

"Thank you, Sir. I'll have a letter on your desk by lunchtime.

* * *

The company commander had been right. The Commanding officer had considered Carter's application to be a sign of disloyalty, but that worked in Carter's favour.

"I'll be damned if I'll keep you in the battalion now you've shown your true colours." He had raged. He scribbled a signature on the bottom of Carter's letter of application and threw it at him, before turning his back in dismissal. Carter's face went red with embarrassment. What would happen if they didn't take him, now that he had burnt his boats with the Old Man?

But first he had to have his interview. He stood outside a tea shop and examined the slip of paper in his hand. It was the right address, he could see that, but what was he doing at this location? Surely the man who was to interview him wouldn't be in a place like this. It was a perfectly respectable establishment, of course, but a tea shop? Oh well.

He pushed the door open and a bell tinkled. An elderly lady behind the counter looked up and gave him a smile.

"I'm looking for Lieutenant Colonel Vernon." He said with a hint of embarrassment, still certain he was making some sort of error which the old lady would have to correct him on.

"You're in the right place, my love." She said with a pleasant Devon accent. "Through the back." She pointed the way, "Up the stairs and he's in the room at the back."

Puzzled, but even more intrigued, he followed the directions until he found himself outside a closed door. Best to make a good first impression, he decided pulling his battledress blouse down to smooth out any wrinkles before wrapping his knuckles firmly against the white painted wood of the door.

"Come in." Came a voice from inside.

He pushed the door and entered what, for a moment, he thought was a bedroom. Well, it was a bedroom, but against the wall opposite the bed was a desk, with a chair in front in which a tall, slender figure was folded. He unfolded himself, rose and extended his hand.

"Lieutenant Colonel Robert Vernon, formerly of the Royal Fusiliers and now Commanding Officer of 15 Commando." He introduced himself. "And you must be Steven Carter."

Carter threw up a salute. "Yes Sir, that's me."

"At ease, Steven. Take the chair." He pointed to a bent wood item standing beside the bed. "Please excuse the surroundings. The commandos don't live in barracks. It's too restricting. Besides, there's too little room in barracks these days. We live in civilian billets and until I can find somewhere else, my room is also my office. Now, I said I was CO of 15 Commando, which is true. But it is also true that I am 15 Commando in toto. All there is, at the moment, is me. I've been promised men as soon as they can ship them out of Achnacarry, and I'll be getting some old hands in from a couple of the other commandos in a few days time, but today it's just me. And maybe you if I decide to accept you. How does that sound?"

"It sounds exciting, Sir."

"Good. Now, tell me about yourself. Where you were born, where you went to school, what you do in your spare time; that sort of thing."

Carter embarked on a potted history of his life, emphasising any aspect of it that might sound adventurous, which wasn't that much. The senior officer occasionally asked a question to clarify something.

"Never done any actual fighting, then?"

"No, Sir. I was too late for Dunkirk and there just hasn't been anything else since. My battalion is scheduled to go out to Malaya later this year. Apparently, the Foreign Office is worried the Japanese are after our rubber plantations."

"I wouldn't be surprised. I suspect they'll be in the war soon. That Prime Minister of theirs seems set on it. But they aren't our problem. So, why do you want to be a Commando?"

Carter had given the question a lot of thought as he had sat on the train to Ilfracombe.

"I want to do something that will make a difference. I'm not much use sitting on my backside in a barracks. I want to take the fight to the Jerries. This seems to be the way to do it."

"What do you think is the purpose of commando raids?"

"To destroy enemy installations, take prisoners, that sort of thing."

"That's is what we do, but that is not our purpose. Our purpose is to boost morale here at home. Mr Churchill knows that if we are to win this war the British people must believe that we can win it. So, we need victories to convince the people. Back in March numbers 3 and 4 Commando went all the way to the Arctic Circle to blow up some fish oil factories on the Lofoten Islands. OK, it will reduce the supply of fish oil for the German armaments industry, but not enough to do it any lasting harm. But when the newsreel footage was shown in the cinemas, people stood up and cheered. That was the purpose of the raid. To make people feel good about our country once again; to convince them that not only can we win this war, but it is inevitable that we will win it. Do you understand?"

"Yes, Sir. I get it, I really do."

"Good, just so you know, you might get yourself killed trying to blow up a cow shed that has no military value whatsoever. But you will become a hero in the process. That is what we do. We make heroes for the British people to admire and some of them, sadly, will be dead heroes."

"Are we talking about suicide missions?"

"No. We would never deliberately send men to their deaths. But what we do is dangerous. We've even had men die in training; that's how dangerous our work is. Are you still so keen?"

"Actually, you've made me even more keen." Carter was a surprised to realise that he really meant it.

"OK, well, you have the right background for the sort of people we want and your Company Commander speaks highly of you. Whether you actually make the grade is down to you. You will be sent to the training school at Achnacarry and you will undergo training so intense that not everyone makes it out the other end. We lose as many as ten percent of volunteers that way and you must bear in mind that they are already trained soldiers when they arrive. But we're looking for a different kind of soldier. Churchill said they must be men of the 'hunter class'. Are you that sort of man?"

"I have no idea, Sir. But I want to find out."

"That's a good answer. No fake bravado, because you'll be found out. Right!" he slapped his hands on his thighs, making his decision. "Get back to your unit and pack your bags. I'll ''phone ahead and get your posting order written. Ask your Adjutant for a travel warrant to Fort William and make sure you catch the night sleeper out of Euston. Got it?"

Carter looked at his watch. It was nearly eleven o'clock and he had a two hour train journey back to his unit, he had to pack all his kit and then there would be another train ride to London if he was to make the sleeper. It would be a busy day.

Vernon smiled at him. "It's your first test, Steven. If you don't make that train then you're not up to being a commando." He slapped Carter on the shoulder. "Now, the clock's ticking, so you'd better get a wiggle on."

* * *

The guard was blowing his whistle when Green and Carter threw their kit bags through the door and clambered onto the train behind them. The train gave a lurch as the locomotive took up the slack in the couplings, lurched again and then started to move slowly out of the station. Carter leant out, grabbed the door and swung it closed before letting out a whistle of relief.

"That was a close one, Green." He gasped. When the lorry had picked him up from the Officer's Mess he had been surprised to find Green already on board, his orders confirming that he, too, was bound for Achnacarry.

"First Class is that way, Sir." Green pointed towards the front of the train.

"If I'm going to make it as a commando officer, I think I'd better get used to roughing it. Shall we see if we can find an empty compartment?" Not only was he entitled to travel First Class, but Carter was also entitled to a sleeper berth, but he had found out that they were all booked, so unless someone had missed the train he would have to make do with sleeping in a sitting position anyway. But what he had learnt about the commandos was that there was a lot less formality between the officers and the men. Rank was observed and discipline maintained, but it was done in a quieter way.

By the time they found a compartment with empty seats it felt like they had walked all the way to Fort William. Green threw his rifle onto the luggage rack then pushed his kitbag on top of it, preventing the weapon from falling if the train made a sudden stop. As an officer, Carter was entitled to use a suitcase for his kit, but he had managed to scrounge up a kit bag as well. It seemed more practical and he felt sure that practical solutions would be preferable to ones of class distinction. He squeezed his bag in next to Green's and took the corner seat, opposite a matronly looking woman. She had a small boy sitting beside her, his finger engaged in a thorough exploration of his nasal cavity.

The boy looked up and spied the oak leaf emblem sewn onto Green's battledress blouse, just above the left breast pocket.

"Is that a Mention In Dispatches[1], Mister?" The boy asked, excitement in his voice.

"It is." Green replied.

"What did you get that for?"

"I cut the fingers off a German who was picking his nose." Green said. The boy snatched his finger out of his nostril. The matronly woman stifled a smile.

Carter knew the story of Green's MiD, having taken the trouble to look out the citation when he joined the battalion. He'd earned it for attacking a German armoured car in Belgium, throwing grenade after grenade at it until he had done enough damage to stop it, while the machine gunner inside the vehicle had directed automatic fire at him. If his actions had been witnessed by an officer it might have earned him a Military Medal, but Green had never mentioned feeling dissatisfied with the lesser award. In fact he had never mentioned it at all.

In the other corner the compartment's only other occupant, an elderly gentleman with a thick, bushy beard, gave a chuckle. "Got one of those me'self, back in the last lot." He said.

"Where was that?" Green asked.

"Hill 60. That were a rough one. Jerry was so well dug in we had to get him out like we was shelling winkles."

Green laughed at the small joke.

"Course, I'm too old for this one. But I'm in the Home Guard."

"They do valuable work." Carter said. The old man beamed with pride.

"We does what we can."

That seemed to exhaust his supply of conversation and he returned to the newspaper he had been reading. The matronly woman took some knitting out of a copious bag and the steady click-clack of the needles provided a counterpoint to clattering of the train over the rails. The boy pulled a comic from his blazer pocket and immersed himself in the adventure stories it recounted.

Green rested his head against the seat back and was soon letting out soft snores. Typical soldier, able to sleep anywhere, no matter how uncomfortable it was.

Carter took off his cap and placed it between his head and the side wall of the compartment, but he hadn't yet developed the knack of sleeping on demand. It took him until they clattered across the points at Rugby before he finally fell into a fitful doze.

The woman and the boy left the train at Birmingham and the old man at Crewe. Some noisy, no doubt beer fuelled, soldiers had looked into the compartment but they changed their mind about taking a seat when they saw the two shining 'pips'[2] on Carter's shoulders. With the carriage empty Green stretched out along one seat and Carter along the other, to get as much sleep as they could.

[1] Mention In Dispatches - As the name implies, an award for soldiers whose name is especially named in dispatches for their conduct, following action in combat. There is no medal, but the recipient receives a certificate and wears a bronze oak leaf badge above their breast pocket to signify the honour. The badge may be worn on the ribbon for the campaign medal for the relevant action, if one was awarded. It is one of only three awards that may be made posthumously.

[2] Pip – The small cloth or metal badges worn to indicate certain officer ranks. Their official name is "Bath stars", because they are a miniature version of the star that is the centrepiece of The Order of the Bath. Except for those worn by Guards officers, which are different designs depending on their regiment.

* * *

Bleary eyed, Carter hoisted his kit bag onto his shoulder and looked around the station. A Corporal was shouting and waving. "Achnacarry this way." He bellowed. "This way for Achnacarry."

Carter headed in the direction indicated, through a side entrance, where another Corporal was standing beside a three ton truck. "Kit bags in the back, Sir." He said, after saluting.

Carter threw his bag in, then made to climb in after it. "Oh no, Sir. You're not riding in this. If you could make your way round to the front and join the others, Sir."

Carter and Green did as they were told. In front of the station a small squad of men, no more than a dozen, stood in ranks of three. They were all dressed in full marching order, just as Green and Carter were, including their large packs. They also held their rifles, the butt resting on the cobbles next to the toe of their right boot, with the muzzle held loosely in their right hand. To one side were two officers, the shorter wore the trews and Glengarry of a lowland Scottish Regiment, while a tall, haughty looking one wore the cap badge of the Welsh Guards. A Sergeant marched over to Carter, saluted then consulted his clip board. "You'll be Lieutenant Carter, Sir."

"That's me." Carter confirmed.

"Please join the other officers, Sir." He turned his attention to Green. "Which makes you Private Green. Fall in on the end of the squad." He saluted Carter again before turning away and heading back inside the railway station.

As Green took his place in the squad and dressed himself into line, the Sergeant returned. "Squad! Squad 'shun!"

Feet slammed onto the cobbles of the station forecourt, sparks flying from the hobnails of their boots and gulls flew up from the surface of the loch, startled by the sudden noise.

A tall, muscular looking soldier emerged from the station, the emblem of a Royal Warrant on the sleeve of his battledress, just below the elbow. He wore a green coloured hat of a type which Carter had never seen before. He marched around to face the squad of men, stamping his feet into a parade ground halt, before standing himself at ease.

"My name is Sergeant Major O'Callaghan." He announced in a brogue that had been blown all the way from the Lagan estuary. "I am the Garrison Sergeant Major for the Commando Training Centre, Achnacarry. Everything that you will do over the next twelve weeks I have already done, not once, but several times over. You may have expected transport to take you to your new billets. You would be mistaken. There are only three occasions when you will get transport while you are here. Occasion one is if you need to get to a place where you will get even wetter and dirtier than you can get at Achnacarry. The second occasion is if you are dead, or so close to death that you may as well be dead. Occasion three is the worst of all. It is because you have failed to reach the standard required to be a commando and you are being brought back here to the railway station for return to unit. We call it RTU for short. For some of you, that could be today. Anyone who doesn't like the sound of that may fall out now and wait for the next train back to their unit. Any questions so far?"

"Does that provision about vehicles include officers, Sergeant Major." The tall guardsman drawled.

The Warrant Officer turned and gave the guardsman a look that suggested that he had just discovered something unpleasant on the sole of his boot. "Yes, Sir." He snapped. "To save you having to ask again, Sir, everything that happens at Achnacarry happens to everyone, including officers."

He turned back to address the squad again. "You will now march seventeen miles to Achnacarry. About four miles before you get there, you will march through the village of Spean Bridge. It is not unusual for the local populace to come out and watch you march through their village. So, when I give the order 'sing', you will sing to entertain the villagers. The first song you will sing will be 'Tipperary'. It is my favourite song and always brings a tear to my eye. If you fail to bring a tear to my eye, I will be certain to bring a tear to yours. The second song you will sing will be 'Pack Up Your Troubles'. You will alternate between those two songs until I give the order for you to stop singing."

The guardsman looked as if he was about to say something, then thought better of it.

"Squad, slope arms!" Hands slapped on the woodwork of rifles as they were hoisted in three crisp movements onto the soldiers' left shoulders.

"Squad, will turn to the right in column of route." O'Callaghan bawled. "Right turn! The squad obediently turned to the right, the cobbles echoing with the stamp of their feet. "Officers, take post." He called.

Carter and the other two officers marched up to the front of the short column. Although they were all of equal rank, the guardsman made sure he was in the leader's position, out in front of the centre rank. Carter looked at the Scotsman and saw a wry smile cross his face as they fell in on either side, half a yard behind. He didn't need to say 'wanker' out loud for Carter to understand the meaning of the smile.

"By the left, quick … march!" O'Callaghan commanded.

As one, the soldiers stepped forward. "Left, left, left, right, left". The Sergeant intoned from the rear of the column. "Left wheel" he ordered, as the squad reached the exit from the station forecourt and turned onto the A82, marching northwards.

As he marched, Carter was able to see the great bulk of Ben Nevis ahead of him. His father had climbed it several times and Carter wondered if he would get the opportunity while he was there. Had he asked the Garrison Sergeant Major, he would have been rewarded with a knowing chuckle.

They marched for an hour before they were called to a halt beside the road. The Sergeant told them they could have a five minute break and were given permission to smoke.

"We haven't been properly introduced." The Guards Officer made it sound as though it was a faux pas committed by Carter. "Gerald Llewelyn, Welsh Guards."

"Steven Carter, trainee commando." He replied, not wishing to get into a game of one-upmanship with the Guards officer over which regiment held seniority. Besides, Llewleyn could see his cap badge just as well as Carter could see Llewelyn's.

"Andrew Fraser." The Scotsman offered his hand to each of them in turn. "Royal Scots." Carter suppressed a smile. The Royal Scots were the oldest regiment in the British Army and centuries older than the Johnnie-come-latelies of the Welsh Guards, who were only formed in 1915. Llewelyn pretended he hadn't heard the comment.

"Didn't see you in First Class, old boy." He said to Carter.

"No, I stayed in Third[1] with Private Green."

"Slumming it with the troops, eh?" He turned his nose up as though smelling something unpleasant.

"I may need that man to save my life, one day." Carter retorted. "I'd rather he didn't have a memory of me not thinking him fit company for a train journey."

"He won't respect you for it, you know. His sort never do."

Carter was tempted to tell him that 'his sort' had a First Class Honours degree from a good university and Green's father was a baronet, but decided against it. Snobs like Llewelyn only looked at the rank, they never looked at the person.

"Fall in now. Jaldi![2]" The Sergeant's voice echoed off the sides of the nearby mountain. Carter wondered where the Sergeant Major was, then noticed him at the rear of the column, watching the men as they formed into rank. What was he looking for? Signs of weakness perhaps? Signs of fatigue? Carter took note though and straightened his back as he fell in at the front of the column once again.

The march continued, covering about four miles an hour with a five minute break at the top of every hour. During the second hour the men were permitted to loosen their rifle slings and carry the weapons over their shoulders. But they were not permitted to break the rhythm of the march. If they fell out of step the Sergeant would call the pace until they regained it again. The first soldier dropped out of the ranks just after they passed the eighth mile and the second went a mile later. Neither man was ever seen again; at least, not at Achnacarry.

At the second and third breaks Llewelyn pointedly ignored the other two officers, keeping himself apart. Carter spotted O'Callaghan watching the guardsman, though the man himself seemed oblivious to the observation. Carter and Fraser took the opportunity to chat with some of the men. They would be thrown together over the following weeks and it did no harm to find out a little bit about them. He spotted one wearing the same type of hat as the Sergeant major.

"I've never seen a hat like that before." He commented.

"It's a Caubeen, Sorr." He replied, his accent as strong as navvies' tea. "A lot of us Irish infantry wear them. It's a traditional hat, sort of t'ing."

"Are you from the same regiment as the Sergeant Major?"

"No, Sorr. He would be from one o' they proddie regiments; from the Six Counties. I'm a good Cat'lic. I'm in the Enniskillen Rifles."

"They're a northern regiment as well. Your accent isn't from the north, is it?"

"It isn't, Sorr. I'm from Mayo. I'm thinking Dev wouldn't be too pleased if he knew I was here."

Carter let out a chuckle, recognising the reference. Éamon de Valera, the Prime Minister of the Irish Free State was well known for his opposition to his countrymen joining the British Army, though thousands had. He had even managed to block the introduction of conscription into Northern Ireland.

"Dey keep us Paddies away from the Prods just in case we start to fight the Battle of the Boyne all over again, so we're nearly all Cat'lics in the Enniskillens." He laughed.

The conversation was cut short by the Sergeant calling them back into line.

Carter stretched out his hand to help the Irishman to his feet. "What's your name?" he asked, heaving the man up.

"O'Driscoll, Sorr."

"Good to meet you, O'Driscoll."

As they passed through Spean Bridge the Sergeant Major gave the order to sing, just as he had said he would and they obediently alternated between the two songs until they had passed out of the other side of the village and started to climb a long hill. Llewelyn didn't seem to be in any physical distress, but he had caught the attention of the Sergeant Major and in any man's army that was rarely a good thing.

As they rounded a bend at the top of the hill, Carter was sure he heard the rattle of a snare drum, but thought he was imagining it. But, no, there it was again, but this time joined by others. Then there was a great wailing sound that swept over them. As they crested the hill Carter saw a pipe band standing just off the road on an open piece of ground. As the squad approached, the Drum Major raised his mace and the band marched forward, wheeling onto the road to take up a position in front of the marching men.

And so, to the tune of The Black Bear, Carter marched into the Commando Training Centre at Achnacarry. His feet were blocks of pain and his shoulders protested at having to support the weight of his webbing harness and pack for so long, but he had crossed the first hurdle. The Sergeant called the orders to turn into line abreast and Carter marched around to stand in front of the front rank.

He was surprised to see a line of white painted crosses standing in a row opposite the guardroom. The sudden thought that he might die during training crossed his mind. Given the aches and pains he was feeling, the prospect of death didn't actually seem too bad. At least his feet wouldn't hurt any longer.

As the squad was dismissed he was pleased to see that Private Green was also still there and looking as fresh as a daisy.

"Officers to the big house." The Sergeant called, pointing the direction, as if they couldn't see the granite building that dominated the countryside.

[1] Third Class – Before nationalisation in 1945, Britain didn't have 'Second Class' carriages on its railways, because the train companies thought that the term was derogatory and people wouldn't use those carriages. Although Second Class had existed, it was abolished around 1890. Instead the rail companies had First Class and Third Class, the latter really being Second Class. Third Class was abolished in 1956 and nowadays it is referred to as Standard Class.

[2] Jaldi – an Urdu word meaning 'quick'. Words originating from the Indian sub-continent were often used as slang in the British Army as soldiers who had served there brought elements of the language back with them.

3 – Achnacarry

They were greeted at the door to the big house by an aged retainer dressed in a white steward's jacket.

"I'm John McAllen." He told them. "Most of the Mess members call me McAllen. I was sort of inherited by the Army when the family moved out of this house. I'll show you to your rooms."

He turned towards the grand staircase. Carter and Fraser hefted their kit bags onto their shoulders, but the guardsman made no move to claim his luggage.

"My trunk is by the door." Llewelyn told his retreating back.

"So it is, Sir, so it is." McAllen replied, not turning back.

"Aren't you going to arrange to have it taken up to my room?" Llewelyn was having to raise his voice to make sure McAllen heard as he climbed the stairs.

"No, Sir. I am not."

"Damned rude. I'll have that man's job." Llewelyn protested.

"I wouldn't advise doing any such thing." Fraser said quietly. "If it wasn't normal for officers to carry their own kit, I think that by now there would be someone carrying yours."

"I'll thank you to keep your opinions to yourself." Llewelyn snarled, grabbing at the handle of his trunk and dragging it across the floor towards the stairs.

"I think someone should have packed a little lighter." Carter whispered to Fraser as the Scotsman caught him up.

The two of them were shown into the room they were to share, as they heard the steady thump-drag of Llewelyn making his way up to the top floor of the house.

"The house is divided into two parts." McAllen advised them. "All the rooms on the first floor are given over to offices, except for the Commandant's private quarters. These were the servants' quarters, up here at the top of the house, and all the young gentlemen in training share rooms here. The library on the ground floor is the Adjutant's office. The Drawing Room is the Ante-room of the Officer's Mess and the Dining Room is the Dining Room. Now, the Commandant has asked for you to meet him in the Ante-Room at 7 p.m. for drinks. It isn't normal to dress for dinner, unless advised otherwise in advance. I have been asked to inform you that the rest of the day, until then, is yours." He lowered his voice. "I would suggest that a stroll around the grounds would be beneficial." He turned and left the room, calling to Llewelyn to follow him.

The room was spartan. It contained a single bed on each side, with two small lockers acting as a bedside table for each bed. At the foot of each bed there was a chair, and in the corners either side of the small window were two tall lockers. Apart from that there was no other furniture.

"I wonder where the bathrooms are?" Fraser asked.

* * *

The three officers entered the Ante-Room at five minutes before seven, their combined military experience telling them that they should always arrive early. McAllen stood to one side of the room holding a tray on which sat four whisky glasses, with a generous measure of amber liquid in each one.

"Whisky before dinner?" Llewelyn wrinkled his nose. "I think not. I'll have a dry sherry." He said to McAllen.

"It isn't normal, Sir." The retainer replied, the tone of resignation in his voice making it clear he didn't expect the Guards officer to listen to him.

"In my regiment it is entirely normal." Llewelyn dismissed the objection. McAllen bowed his head slightly and turned to leave the room through a well concealed service door. He returned a few moments later with a schooner of sherry standing alongside the two remaining whisky glasses. Llewelyn took his without acknowledging the old man's service.

As the clock on the mantelshelf struck seven, the door to the Drawing Room opened and a short, stocky figure strode in. He was about forty years of age and had a narrow face dominated by a clipped military moustache. His eyes glittered keenly. He seemed to take everything in with a single glance. Seeing the crown and single pip on either shoulder of his uniform, the three junior officers snapped to attention.

"As you were, gentlemen." The Lieutenant Colonel said, a trace of a country accent in his voice. "The Mess is your home, so we don't stand on formality." As the three men relaxed the senior officer took one of the remaining glasses from McAllen's tray.

"I am Lieutenant Colonel Vaughan and I am Commandant here at Achnacarry. Now, I'm sure that you have many questions about what you are going to experience here, so it is my normal practice to give you a short introduction to Achnacarry. So, to start with …" He paused, staring at Llewelyn's hand. "What the devil is that you have there, Llewelyn?"

"A glass of rather mediocre sherry, Sir." Llewelyn drawled in reply.

"I can see that. What I want to know is why you are holding it?"

"Sir, in our mess we always have an aperitif before dinner. Whisky is reserved for ... well, we rarely drink it in our regiment. A fine brandy perhaps, after dinner, but we leave whisky for the Scots to drink. They seem to like it." He beamed a smile, as though he had said something witty.

"This is a school for fighting men, Llewelyn, so you will take a drink fit for a fighting man. Get rid of that piss at once."

"Sir? …"

"I won't tell you again, Llewelyn. Get rid of the sherry and take a whisky."

Llewelyn placed the glass on the tray and rather reluctantly took the remaining whisky tumbler. McAllen did his best to hide his smile, but barely succeeded.

"Now, where was I? Oh yes, my welcome address. You will find that Achnacarry is different from anywhere else you have ever been. As officers you set the standard that your soldiers must reach. You lead from the front. When the ramp of your landing craft drops, you will be the first ashore. When you are told to run up a mountain, you will be the first to the top. You will never ask your men to do anything until you have demonstrated that you are able to do it yourself. The only time that you are ever last is when you re-embark onto your landing craft. Then you will be the last man to leave the beach. You will leave no man behind, not even the dead.

In the morning you will be introduced to the troop that you will command. Let me make it clear that your command is only nominal. You will have one of my training Sergeants attached to you and he is your Oracle and your Bible. He and the other instructors will teach you everything you and your men need to know. Listen to them, learn from them and do as they tell you and you stand a chance of seeing the end of this war. If you don't listen to them, then you may pay the price with your life, but worse than that, your men may pay the price for you. If you fail to achieve the standard that is required of you, you will be returned to your unit. Your rank will not protect you.

Later you will meet some of our specialist instructors. They will teach you more skills to help keep you alive. I especially recommend that you pay attention to lieutenants Sykes and Fairbairn. They know more about how to keep yourself alive in a fight than any other soldiers in the British Army.

At the same time you will be required, in conjunction with your training Sergeant, to assess the performance of your men. If you do not consider them to be making the grade, it will be your decision that sees them RTU'd. There are no second chances, either for you or for your men. And just to make sure you understand the consequences of your decisions, you should remember that the man you go soft on, may, one day, be the man who you need to save your life, or whose life you may have to save. You have to have total confidence in your men and they have to have total confidence in you. Now, are there any questions?"

"Well, Sir." Llewelyn said, "I know it isn't something that I should be bothering you with, but I don't seem to have a batman assigned to me."

"Why, young man, do you think you should have a batman?" The quiet tone of the Commandant's voice should have been a warning to Llewelyn, but if he had noted it he decided to ignore it.

"Well, Sir, a gentleman doesn't clean his own kit or his own room. Officers always have a batman assigned."

The Commandant turned to face Fraser. "Well, Fraser, what do you think of that?"

"I'm capable of cleaning my own room and my own kit, Sir. Though I did have a batman in my previous unit."

"What about you, Carter?"

"Similarly, Sir, I had a batman, but I don't need one. Besides, everything our men have to do, we also have to do and I guess that includes cleaning our own kit."

"What do you think now, Llewelyn?"

"I think that we should be maintaining standards, Sir. As I said, a gentleman ..."

"Where were you based, Llewelyn?" The Commandant asked, looking into his whisky glass as though seeking the answer there.

Llewelyn seemed to be taken aback by the sudden change in direction of the question. "W ... Windsor, Sir."

"Very well. At oh eight hundred hours tomorrow, you will report to the Adjutant and ask him to issue you with a travel warrant to Windsor. You are dismissed."

"But Sir, I ..."

"I said, you are dismissed, Llewelyn. Now get out." The menace in the Commandant's voice was palpable.

Llewelyn's face went bright red as he turned and stormed out of the room. He managed to resist the temptation to slam the door.

The Commandant relaxed his shoulders and took a sip of his whisky. "I must apologise for that little display, gentlemen. I must say it was an unusual situation. I have had to RTU officers in the past, but never on the evening of their arrival." He drained his glass and McAllen appeared at his elbow, offering the tray so that the empty glass could be placed on it. The Commandant clapped his hands and rubbed them together, as though warming them. "Now, I understand that there is a fine haggis waiting for us in the dining room, so perhaps we should now go and join your colleagues and see if we can do it justice." He led them towards the double doors at the far end of the room. As he left he turned back to address McAllen. "Have one of the kitchen staff take something up for Mr Llewelyn to eat. But make sure it's cold when it gets there."

"What does haggis taste like?" Carter asked Fraser in a whisper, hoping that the Scotsman would know.

"Like shit, but don't tell the Colonel I said that." Fraser whispered back with a wink.

The dining room was full of junior officers, most of whom Carter guessed were trainees. The Colonel waved everyone back into their seats as they tried to stand, then took his place at the head of the long table, between two majors. He sat down and McAllen appeared at his elbow to put a plate of food in front of the Commandant. Some young women appeared through a service door, carrying so many plates they seemed to be defying gravity.

Carter found himself sitting next to an older officer, another of a similar age sitting across the long table from him. He introduced himself.

"Eric Sykes." The man replied.

"William Fairbairn." The man opposite added.

"The Colonel just mentioned your names. Said that you would be able to teach us how to stay alive."

"The Colonel is too kind." Sykes said. "But we do have certain, shall we say, specialist skills we can teach you."

"What sort of skills?"

"Have you heard of martial arts?" Fairbairn said, with a grin.

"Vaguely. Isn't it some sort of wrestling?"

"Yes it is. Call it eastern wrestling if you want. It comes in various forms, most of which have religious origins; monks who didn't carry weapons but who still needed to be able to protect themselves without killing. But it's totally useless. We teach a different sort of martial art, in ours your enemy doesn't get up again."

"Where did you learn it?"

"We were in the police in Shanghai. It was a rough city and you had to be able to take care of yourself. So we learnt how to fight like the street gangs. Eric and I even wrote a book about it, didn't we Eric?"

"We did."

"So, how does it work?" Carter couldn't help his curiosity.

"Just about anything can be turned into a weapon. You see this?" Sykes held up his fist.

Carter nodded.

"With this you can give a man a black eye." Sykes said. He fished in the pocket of his battledress blouse and produced a stub of pencil. "But do this." He inserted the stub between his knuckles so that the sharp end was protruding about an inch, "and you can put his eye out. Believe me, he isn't going to be troubling you too much when he's stumbling around half blind."

"Doesn't seem very gentlemanly." Carter observed.

"I'll tell you what, you fight by the Marquis of Queensbury rules and I'll fight by Shanghai street rules, and we'll see who's still alive at the end." Fairbairn chuckled.

"What are Shanghai street rules?" Carter asked.

"Rule one is that there are no rules. There isn't a rule two." Sykes laughed at his own joke and Fairbairn gave the sort of chuckle that suggested that he he'd heard the joke before on more than one occasion.

"I guess you could kill me with that fork then." Carter indicated the item of cutlery in Sykes' hand.

"Young man, if I had to, I could kill you with a teaspoon."

It was time to change the subject, Carter thought, before Sykes warmed to his theme of blood and gore. "So what were British police doing in Shanghai?"

Sykes chewed on a bit of haggis before answering. "Shanghai had a large international community. Under a set of laws granted by the Chinese, it was given some self-governing powers, under what was called the Shanghai Municipal Council, including the right to police itself. We British formed the original core of the police force until local Chinese were allowed to join in 1864. Later there was a Sikh and a Japanese contingent. Unfortunately the troubled politics of China made Shanghai attractive to former revolutionaries who set up as criminal gangs and most of our work consisted of keeping the streets safe for people to walk down. That's how we learnt all about street fighting.

"Was it a big police force?"

"Nearly five thousand at its peak."

"Must have been interesting." Carter observed.

"In its way. Certainly better than pounding a beat in London, which is what we were both doing before we went out there."

"The pay was a lot better, as well." Fairbairn said.

"Well, I look forward to learning all about it, the street fighting bit I mean."

"We'll see if you're still saying that after I've put you on your backside a few times." Fairbairn chuckled.

* * *

As McAllen had advised, Carter and Fraser had walked the grounds of Achnacarry House in the late afternoon sunshine. To the south of the house stood rows of Nissen huts, where the soldiers were accommodated and beyond those a wide, well trodden grassed area which was being used for various activities. On one side a group of soldiers were doing bayonet practice, running at sacks of straw, stabbing them, withdrawing their rifles then running on to repeat the action on the next row of dummies. On another part of the field another group seemed to be engaged in some sort of wrestling contest.

They carried on walking until they found themselves standing on the shore of a loch. Out on the water were several boats, each carrying ten men, eight using paddles to propel the boat, one at the rear holding a steering paddle and one at the front manning a Bren gun which was resting on the prow. To the left some landing craft bobbed at anchor.

"Those are Goatley boats." Fraser observed, nodding towards the ones being propelled across the loch.

"They look pretty flimsy." Carter replied. A burst of automatic fire rang out and Fraser threw himself to the ground. Somewhat slower, Carter followed suit.

"If they were shooting at us you'd be dead by now." Fraser observed dryly. He raised his head. More fire rang out.

"Bren guns, firing on the boats. Look!" Fraser pointed.

Carter raised his head to look. Sure enough, a series of spreading ripples showed where the bullets had struck the water in front of the leading boat. Realising that it wasn't them that was being fired at, Carter and Fraser clambered to their feet. Another burst of fire echoed across the loch, this time disturbing the water behind the rearmost boat.

"They seem to play for real up here." Carter said.

"Did you see those crosses at the entrance gate?" Fraser asked.

"I did. I suppose those must be the ones who got it wrong."

They followed the bank of the loch until they reached the mouth of a small river, then turned back towards the house following its route. They saw a group of NCOs standing next to some sort of large A frame and stopped to watch what was going on. A rope angled up from the frame, disappearing into the trees on the far side of the river. As they watched, a man flew across the river, suspended beneath the rope. He was caught at the bottom by one of the NCOs, releasing whatever he had been hanging onto. At once he unslung his rifle from his back and went into a crouch, ready to engage an imaginary enemy. A second man flew across the river, landed and went to join him. The first man regained his feet and the two of them ran off towards the bayonet practice area.

The two officers watched for a while, as a whole troop descended the aerial slide and ran off across the training ground. One of the NCOs spotted them and walked across. He saluted and grinned at them.

"New arrivals I'm guessing. The Death Slide always catches the eye the first time you see it."

"It looks quite frightening." Carter admitted.

"You get used to it … or you don't." The Sergeant said meaningfully.

"I'm Lieutenant Carter and this is Lieutenant Fraser." Carter introduced them both.

"Sergeant Chitty." The Sergeant replied. "I'm one of the training Sergeants. You're assigned to Ten Troop, Sir." He said to Fraser. "Your Sergeant will be Alex Cameron. He was born and raised locally. You're lucky; he used to be a ghillie on the estate and he knows every inch of the land around here. You, Sir, will have Eleven Troop and you'll have to make do with Bob Harkness. He's a cockney and had never seen a mountain until he came here. But he's a good man."

"Well, thanks for the information, Sergeant."

"No problem, Sir. But I'll have to leave you now or my lot will probably be back in their billets before I can catch them up and stop them." He grinned to show he was joking, then jogged off across the training area.

"I guess that's what we've got to look forward to." Carter observed, eying the rope slide with some suspicion.

"That's the sort of thing that I came for." Fraser replied with a smile. "Shall we see what else is going on?"

* * *

Carter took his place in front of Eleven Troop as Sgt Harkness completed roll call.

"All present and correct, Sir". He reported.

"Thank you, Sergeant. So, what have you in store for our first day?"

Each troop was supposed to be made up of twenty soldiers, but the sudden departure of Llewelyn had meant that Twelve Troop had to be merged with Ten and Eleven to put thirty men into each. Now they stood to attention on the training ground dressed in their regulation PT kit. Well, almost regulation. Instead of plimsoles they wore boots and gaiters[1].

They had each been issued with a new pattern of boot, with moulded rubber soles instead of hob nailed leather. The boots may have had a softer sole, which made less noise when they walked and therefore were more suited to the needs of the commandos, but their uppers were as stiff and unyielding as all new military issue boots. They would need hours of attention with polish and brush before they would start to soften. But the more they wore them the sooner they would be broken in. Though Carter had never done PT in boots before, he knew it wouldn't take long for blisters to start to form.

"Today, Sir, we take a little ride." As the Sergeant spoke three 3 ton lorries rolled onto the training area and came to a stop behind the two troops.

Carter recalled what Sgt Major O'Callaghan had said the previous day. If you are given transport it will be to take you somewhere where you can get wetter and dirtier than you would at Achnacarry. This didn't look too promising. But no one said it would be easy, Carter reminded himself.

"Right men, fall out and split yourself into three groups of twenty, then get on board the trucks." The Sgt called. The men took a quarter turn to the right, stamped their booted feet and broke up, looking for friends with whom they could travel.

"Sir." The Sgt addressed Carter. "If you'd like to take a seat in the second truck."

"You seem to know where we're going, so why don't you take the front seat. I'll travel in the back with the men."

"As you wish, Sir." The Sgt said, but he seemed to approve of the decision. Carter made his way to rear of the second truck and put one foot into the foot hole in the tailboard. He offered his arms up and they were grabbed from above, hauling him upwards and into the rear of the lorry. He looked to see who had assisted him and was unsurprised to find that one of the pairs of hands belonged to Green. The other belonged to O'Driscoll. He seemed to have made, if not a friend, at least an acquaintance. There were no seats, so Carter sat himself on the floor with the rest of his troop.

The Sgt lifted the tailboard and slammed it into place. One of the good things about working with trained soldiers was that they didn't have to be told what to do all the time. The men nearest to the tailboard operated the latches that held it in place.

The lorry lurched away, turning through one hundred and eighty degrees to exit the camp by the Guardroom gate.

"Right, who's for a song?" Carter called.

"Not fucking Tipperary again!" A voice from the front of the truck called, given anonymity by the bodies in front of him.

"No. I think we'll have 'Roll Me Over In The Clover'." Carter replied. This received a cheer. Its bawdy lyrics, Carter had discovered when he joined his previous battalion, were always appreciated by the soldiers.

"Right, everyone has to sing a verse and all join in the chorus. Pvt Green, start us off!"

Green took a deep breath then bawled out the words of the first verse. The men joined in with enthusiasm.

The song came to an end and someone else started the next one, unbidden. "Where do you think we're going, Sir."

Carter looked out the back of the truck and saw the houses of Spean Bridge receding behind them. That meant they were heading back in the direction of Fort William. He tried to imagine why soldiers in PT kit would need to go to that town to exercise and couldn't think of a reason. The only other feature of note he'd seen the previous day was … oh no, it couldn't be Ben Nevis could it?

Time to be the reassuring officer. "I think we're going to climb Ben Nevis, Green. Should be a bit if a lark."

"But why are we doing it in PT kit, Sir?"

"What is your degree in, Green?"

"Philosophy and Logic, Sir, but what's that …" He stopped mid-sentence, seeing what his officer was implying. Apply some logic to the problem. "We're going to run up the mountain, aren't we, Sir".

"In the absence of any evidence to the contrary, I would agree."

"You mean that feckin' great mountain we saw yesterday, Sorr?" O'Driscoll interjected.

"Yes, O'Driscoll, the mountain."

"Oh Jeez, me mammy never mentioned mountains."

"You don't have mountains in Mayo, O'Driscoll?"

"We have some beautiful mountains in Mayo, Sorr, but we don't run up the feckers. We have Croagh Patrick, the most holy mountain in Ireland and we walk up it barefoot, just as St Patrick himself once did. But we don't run up the fecker!"

Carter decided it would be a good idea to get O'Driscoll off the subject of mountains. "What made you join the British army, O'Driscoll. You Irish fought a war to get rid of us."

"Ah, Sorr, it wiz nothing personal. Yez are all OK so long as you stay your side of the Irish Sea. But that little fecker Hitler, he's a different breed of animal altogether. I reckoned that if he invaded England, then he'd not stop when he got to Holyhead. He'd just keep right on going until he got to the Dingle Peninsula and I couldn't be havin' that. Then he'd probably keep right on going until he reached America. I've got an auntie in America and I wizn't having some Nazi stormtrooper raping her."

"Not much chance of him invading now."

"Ah, sure, Sorr, I'm having too much fun now to be wantin' to go home."

"But volunteering for the commandos, that's beyond the call of duty."

O'Driscoll gave a mischievous grin. "Well, Sorr, they say that if a commando trips over in the street there'll be a lassie under him to break his fall before he reaches the ground. You don't get that in Mayo, I can assure you."

Carter couldn't help but laugh. "Is that why you volunteered, Green?"

"No, Sir. It was the pay and the working hours that attracted me." He grinned, the irony heavy in his voice.

Further conversation was forestalled by the truck turning off the main road and onto a bumpy lane. They grabbed hold of whatever they could to prevent themselves from being bounced right out the back of the truck. After a few minutes of this the truck came to a standstill. The tailgate dropped open and the Sgt's shouted orders got them out of the trucks and into three ranks.

"Right men." He shouted. "We'll just wait a few minutes to give Ten Troop time to get out of the way, then we'll move off. We are going to run to the top of that little hill over there ..." he pointed towards the bulk of the mountain looming to their right. " ... and the last two men to the top get the honour of carrying me back down."

"What if you're the last?" Some wag in the rear rank called.

"I can assure you, laddie, that I will not be last. Now, move to the right in column of route, right turn!" The troop turned to the right. Carter moved up to take his place three paces in front of the foremost man in the centre rank.

"By the right, quick march!" The troop stepped obediently off. "Into double time ... double march!" They stepped up a gear, changing to a jogging pace, the Sgt calling the step so that their feet made a rhythmic thumping on the packed earth of the track.

Carter saw an open gate ahead of them and knew that the three ranks couldn't all get through it together, but the Sgt knew his business.

"Double mark time!" he ordered, bringing the troop to a halt, though their feet still pounded up and down at one hundred and eighty paces per minute. "Left rank, forward!"

The left hand rank of ten men moved forward while the remaining twenty men kept the pace going without actually moving. The centre rank followed and then, finally, the right hand rank. That meant that Carter was now in the middle third of the troop and he remembered the words of the Commandant the previous evening. He increased his pace, gradually passing the men in front of him until he reached the front again. He found that he was running alongside Sgt Harkness, who had come up from the rear on the other side of the ranks of men. Carter was starting to breath heavily, but the Sgt didn't seem to be affected. But he no longer called the cadence as he accepted that it was almost impossible to keep the troop in step over the increasingly broken ground.

Carter could only feel his feet in terms of their pain. His boots felt like lumps of lead hanging off the ends of his legs and he felt a blister growing on his right heel and another on a toe on his left foot. He did his best to block out the pain.

Carter had been a cross country runner for both school and college and knew how to counter the tedium. Don't think of how far you have run and don't think of how far you still have to go. Think of something nice, something soothing. Go into your own little world and concentrate all your thoughts on that, not on the agony of your body. He dug deeply and found a memory. Him, his sister, his mother and his father. A picnic on the Lincolnshire coast when he had been, what, it must have been ten years old. He focused his mind on that day, all the things they had done and the happiness it had brought them.

At the end of his daydream he returned his attention to the mountain. The peak was closer, but still distant. He turned and jogged backwards, working out where his troop were and how they were performing. Not bad, he thought. A little bit strung out along the path, but still all in contact with each other. He needed to appoint a second in command to bring up the rear and chivvy along any stragglers. Was that within the rules? He would have to ask Sgt Harkness. His slower pace while running backwards had allowed the Sergeant to gain ground. He put on a spurt to close the gap then settled back into his steady rhythm once again, his breath coming in deep lungfuls. In through the nose, out through the mouth; in through the nose, out through the mouth; he kept the rhythm going, in time with his strides. One breath every four strides, just as he had been taught at school. The thought of school triggered another memory and he turned his mind inwards again.

His reveries were broken as he heard the thud of boots approaching. It was Ten Troop, returning down the mountain having completed their climb. For some reason he was pleased to see that Fraser looked as tired as he felt. The two troops passed each other without exchanging the normal greetings and banter. There was no breath to spare for that sort of thing.

Just as he thought he was going to collapse with exhaustion, Carter saw how close he was to the peak. Sgt Harkness was already there, standing admiring the view as though he had been on a gentle stroll along the sea front at Clacton. A hundred yards to go. Carter dug deep into his reserves. Fifty, forty, thirty, twenty, ten and he was there, drawing in deep breaths, his hands on his thighs, his feet and his calves screaming in agony.

The first of the troop to join him was O'Driscoll.

"I thought you didn't do mountains." Carter observed, between gasps.

"Ah, sure, Sorr, 'tis nothing much after you've done Croagh Patrick a few times." The Irishman said, taking in a huge mouthful of air before starting a coughing fit.

"Sounds like you should cut out the fags though."

"Maybe you're right there, Sorr."

"Some of the men are struggling a bit, Sir." Harkness said, pointing back down the path.

Carter looked up. While the majority of the men were still bunched up, jogging stolidly onwards, there were a few strung out along the track. Two were walking and one, still at least four hundred yards from the peak, had stopped moving altogether. Carter didn't need to be told what to do. He took a deep breath and set off back down the path.

"Well done." He said as he passed each man. "Keep going, not far now."

"You two." He addressed the two men who were walking, chatting and laughing. "If you've got the breath to talk then you've got the breath to run. Now get moving."

They broke into a run again. "And don't stop running till you get to the top." He shouted at their retreating backs.

He reached the man who was standing on the path, bent over, drawing in huge gasps of air. "Are you OK, lad?" The man was probably the same age as Carter, maybe older.

"Will be in a moment, Sir. Just give me a few seconds."

"What's your name and unit?"

"Glass, Sir. First Royal Tank Regiment."

"More used to riding than running then, eh Glass?"

"That's right, Sir."

"OK, well, you've got to get used to this if you want to stay. Try and walk a little."

The soldier did as he was bid, his legs moving jerkily. "Now try a little faster, just keep up with me."

Setting a gentle pace, Carter coaxed the man the rest of the way up the hill. At the top the troop stood waiting. As they got within fifty yards the men started to applaud. Carter wasn't sure if it was ironic or well meant, but it seemed to help Glass and he put a spurt on to cross the finish line.

Sgt Harkness didn't keep to his threat to make the last two men carry him down the mountain, but he did tell the last three, Glass and the chatty pair, that they would report for extra PT before the evening meal every night for the rest of the week. They went back down at a more gentle pace, the need to control their momentum paramount in order to prevent them falling and rolling all the way down the four thousand feet of the mountain. The climb had taken them over two hours.

Back at the track at the base of the mountain they found a Bedford utility truck waiting, dixie's[2] of water on the ground beside it with tin mugs lined up in a row. They were allowed to drink their fill before Sgt Harkness ordered them back into ranks of three and they started the run back to Achnacarry. It was shortened by taking a route across the fields, moors and forests of the region, but it was still a long way after such an exertion.

Staggering through the door of his room, Carter fell onto his bed, every muscle of his legs screaming at him in protest. On the opposite bed Fraser was also laying supine.

"I think I might have made a mistake coming here." Fraser said, his voice barely audible.

"You know what they say. If you can't take a joke you shouldn't have joined." Carter responded.

"And never volunteer for anything." Fraser said, before falling silent. It was only seconds before the sound of snoring filled the room. By succumbing to sleep they would have to sacrifice lunch, but the thought of eating at that moment wasn't something that Carter gave serious consideration.

[1] Gaiters – These were thick webbing wrappings worn around the ankles that held the trouser cuffs in place, preventing them from snagging on barbed wire and other sharp objects. They also concealed any actual damage that might occur. The bottom of the gaiter went over the neck of the boot, preventing the ingress of stones etc. They replaced the long puttees (from the Hindi word *patti*, meaning bandage) that had been worn during the First World War and which were wound around the legs from knee to ankle. Gaiters went out of use in 1960 and were replaced by ankle length puttees until the 1980s, when high topped combat boots were introduced after the Falklands War.

[2] Dixie – From the Hindi word degchi, meaning a small cooking pot. A large cooking vessel with a swivel handle across the top that allows two to be carried at the same time. It holds 3 gallons of water and the lid could be removed to use as a frying pan or roasting tin. Widely used in the British army as field cooking equipment. Also widely used in the 1950s and 60s by the Boy Scout movement as camping equipment, as they were cheap to purchase after the war.

The training varied from day to day, with new subjects being brought forward as each new skill was mastered. The only thing that didn't vary was the daily conditioning regime. On the second day the troop was introduced to the pine logs. Six men to a log, they ran everywhere with them. They threw them back and forth, raised them and lowered them over their heads and they ran with them, the rear man letting go and sprinting to the front and the log moving forward to rest on his shoulder as the next man took his turn. Carter soon felt the chest and sleeves of his shirts start to tighten as new layers of muscle were added to his frame

They carried out navigation exercises by land and by sea, by day and by night. They learnt how to use the Goatley boats before practicing beach assaults from both the boats and the school's own fleet of landing craft. Live ammunition was fired at them and thunderflashes simulated grenades, mortar fire and artillery rounds.

They tackled the fearsome Tarzan course. This was a series of obstacles that forced men to climb, crawl, and swing across gaping chasms high in the trees. One length of rope had to be 'cat crawled' across a vertiginous drop between two trees, while another crossed the River Arkaig by toggle rope bridge.

The toggle rope was a standard issue item for the commandos. Each rope was six feet long with a small loop spliced in one end and a wooden toggle, similar to those used to fasten duffel coats, attached at the other. By inserting the toggle into the loop of another rope, they could be joined together to make longer lengths. If you used enough of them you could build a bridge that spanned a river. Crossing it was never easy, but it was made harder by live Bren gun rounds fired at them on either side and lobbing pyrotechnics at those crossing, sending a spray of cold river water skywards.

Then there was the Death Slide. It ran fifty feet across the river, starting up a tree at a height of forty feet and descending at a steep angle to ground level. Close to the bottom an inverted V of rope straddled the slide to act as a brake. To descend, a soldier joined the ends of his toggle rope to form a circle, then folded it over the rope of the Death Slide, leaving a loop dangling down on either side. Inserting his hands through these two loops and gripping for all he was worth, the soldier said a silent prayer, kicked off against the trunk of the tree, and placed himself at the mercy of gravity and the inadequate looking braking mechanism.

Carter had been terrified the first time that he had done it and was still terrified the final time he did it.

A more traditional assault course, known as the Dark Mile, meandered through the woodland for a distance of five miles. It was designed so that it couldn't be completed by one man on his own. The men had to work together in pairs to conquer it and they would stay in those pairs for many of the other techniques they had to learn. The system was called 'me and my pal' and formed friendships that would last a lifetime.

The most enjoyable skill Carter learnt was demolition. A stern-faced Sergeant of the Royal Engineers taught them to lay charges, insert detonators, measure fuses and fit timers, so that they could blow up most sorts of installations. They were also taught how to set booby traps, so that they could continue to hurt the Germans even after they had withdrawn from the beaches.

Fraser found out that The Laird, as he was called, had a tree in front of the cottage he was occupying for the duration of the war. It was blocking the light to his small lounge, so Carter and Fraser volunteered to remove it with the use of explosives. Unfortunately, they misjudged the amount of explosives they needed and not only did they remove the tree, they also removed every pain of glass in the cottage.

* * *

Wildlife teemed across the estate and formed a constant temptation for the soldiers. Their food was filling, but bland in the extreme. Anything that could be found to vary the diet was welcomed.

Carter was out with Fraser and another officer by the name of Cullen, doing a cross country map reading exercise, when they came across Sgt Cameron, Fraser's training Sergeant, lying in the heather. He hushed them with a finger to his lips and signalled that they should take cover.

Once they were lying in the grass Cameron pointed to something in front of them. Carter raised his head to see a deer, silhouetted against the skyline. It was a young buck, only two prongs on its antlers.

"That would make a nice meal." Fraser whispered into Carter's ear.

"We can't go shooting The Laird's deer." Carter protested.

"That would be true," Cameron's broad accent joined the conversation, "if that were a deer."

Carter gave him a puzzled look. "What is it if it isn't a deer?" he asked.

"That is a Highland ferret." Cameron said, a smile playing around the corners of his mouth. "As such it is vermin and may be shot."

Cameron had been a gillie on the estate before the war and knew as much about its wildlife as any man alive. If he said it was a Highland ferret, Carter wasn't going to argue. "Fifty-fifty." Carter said.

"That wiz whit I wiz thinking, Sir."

"Who's the best shot?" Carter asked.

"I got three bulls the last time I was on the range." Cullen said.

"That's two more than me." Fraser confessed.

Carter decided he wasn't going to own up to not having scored a bull in recent visits to the range. "OK, Kenneth. It looks like it's your shot."

Cullen rolled onto his back and removed the empty magazine from his rifle. The officers all carried rifles when training because the other ranks had to. They also all carried full magazines of ammunition, just to add weight to their equipment, which required them to exert more effort. Blank ammunition would only have been half as heavy. It also meant they were always ready for surprise trips to the rifle ranges, which were made usually when they were breathing their heaviest. But they kept an empty magazine actually fitted to the rifle, as a safety precaution.

Cullen inserted a full magazine of ten rounds into his rifle and rolled back onto his stomach. Nestling the butt of the rifle into his shoulder he pressed his cheek against butt. "Range?" he asked.

"I'd say four hundred." Cameron answered. Knowing Cameron's experience, no one thought to argue.

Cullen adjusted the rear sight of his rifle and then pulled the cocking handle to the rear, before sliding it carefully home, quietly forcing a round into the breach.

"You're sure this is a Highland ferret?" He asked, without taking his eye from the rear sight.

"Sure as I've ever been aboot anything." The Sergeant replied.

Cullen's finger whitened on the trigger as he applied pressure, squeezing, not jerking. The quiet of the moor was shattered as the rifle fired, crows rising squawking into the air at the sudden sound.

They leapt to their feet and ran forward to the place where they had seen the stag. They found it lying in the heather, quite dead.

The enormity of what they had just done hit them all at the same time, not least Cameron.

"You can be sent to prison for poaching." Fraser said. "You must have caught poachers on the estate before, Sgt Cameron."

"Aye, I have that Sir."

"If the Colonel finds out …" There was no need for Carter to finish the sentence.

"But there's nay point in letting the beast go to waste now its deed." Cameron reminded them.

"Well, we agreed. Half to the Sergeant's Mess and half to the Officers." Fraser reminded them. "But what will the Colonel say when he finds prime venison on his plate?"

"There's only one way to find out." Cameron said.

"That's easy for you to say, Sergeant. He won't assume that you have anything to do with it, but us three … he knows we're out on the moor today and he's bound to ask questions."

"Maybe he won't." Cullen said.

"Why not?"

"Maybe he'll think The Laird had it sent over. I've heard it said that he does send game over, in season. Last autumn I believe they had pheasant in the mess and there's usually grouse in August, or so I've been told. Maybe he'll just think it was a gift for the Mess."

They looked at the young stag, their mouths watering at the thought of a meal of venison. They also had to consider what to do with the animal now it was dead if it wasn't eaten. To just dispose of the carcass would be a sin in these times of food shortages.

"OK, we take it back and see what happens." Carter said, the other four nodding their agreement.

The exercise was cancelled on Sgt Cameron's authority. The reason he had been out there was to monitor their progress and no one would challenge them if he didn't. They used their rifle slings to suspend the animal from their rifles and carried their burden back towards the Big House. Stopping about a mile short, Cameron sent them on ahead. "I'll get it butchered and your half sent to the back door of the house. I know the Service Corps cook and I'll see he knows what to do with it. The next time you see this beastie he'll be on your plates."

Dinner was a tense meal that evening as Carter, Fraser and Cullen waited to see what would happen when the meal was served. The Colonel's plate was set in front of him by McAllen, as usual and the Colonel raised his fork, picking up a morsel of gravy-soaked meat. Carter was so distracted that he didn't even notice the woman who placed his own plate in front of him, but his nostrils twitched at the savoury smell.

It seemed to take an age for the Colonel's fork to reach his lips. He inserted it and then withdrew it, chewing on the meat. A smile came to his lips. "A fine piece of venison." The Colonel said.

Carter tried not to make a sound as he sighed with relief. He caught Fraser's eye first, then Cullen's. winking at them both. The Colonel was now an 'accessory after the fact' in their criminal activity.

Carter allowed himself to enjoy the best meal he'd had at Achnacarry and the best he would have before he finally left the training centre.

* * *

They set ambushes by day and by night, and were ambushed in turn either by one of the other troops or by the Demonstration Platoon. The weeks passed without being noticed. The only variation to the routine was at the weekend. Saturday afternoons were devoted to sport: soccer, rugby, boxing or swimming in the freezing cold of Loch Arkaig. Sunday meant church parade for everyone, regardless of religion or belief. Only Sunday afternoon was left idle, but then only to give everyone time to carry out essential repairs to their kit.

Carter used Sunday afternoons to write up his assessments of his men, in consultation with Sgt Harkness.

They lost their first man at the end of the first week. After staggering in from the first timed speed march, Gunner Merchant requested an interview with Carter and told him that he wasn't cut out to be a commando. Carter respected his admission. It was better to find that out now than when attacking a beach in France under a hail of German machine gun fire.

Three others from the troop were to depart over the following weeks. Private Patterson broke an ankle in a fall and would have to wait for that to heal before he could return to training. Private Ecclestone fell out on a speed march complaining of a twisted ankle, but when the troop returned to camp Sgt Harkness saw him engaged in a kick about with members of another troop. His deceit earned him an immediate RTU. The final casualty was one that Carter had to agonise over.

Private McClean tried hard at everything he did, but he just wasn't making the grade. On the rifle ranges he couldn't hit a barn if he was inside it. Training in unarmed combat he was more of a danger to himself than he was to his opponent. The unarmed combat instructors, Lieutenants Fairbairn and Sykes, told Carter that he fought more like a little girl than a man and there was nothing more they could do with him. The final straw came when McClean was standing sentry one night when the troop were taking part in a night exercise. He issued a challenge to a figure emerging from the darkness but didn't wait for the reply and Carter would have been killed if McClean had been using live ammunition instead of blanks. Not only that, but it gave away their position to Ten Troop, who were hunting them.

Carter had thought long and hard but had to admit that McLean wasn't cut out for the commandos. Reluctantly he wrote the three dreaded letters on his report, next to Mclean's name. RTU.

The biggest challenge, however, were the speed marches. These were the test of progress when it came to fitness, carried out while wearing full fighting order and carrying their rifles and a hundred rounds of ammunition. At the end of the first week they did a not too demanding five miles in an hour. They were breathing heavily, but they made the time.

"The Commandant always expects an improvement on that pace, Sir." Sgt Harkness advised. It was O'Driscoll that told them how to get faster times.

"You only tire yourself out by runnin', Sorr." He said. "In the Rifles we use a different technique altogether. Let me show you."

He went fifty yards along the track before turning back to face them. He marched ten paces at the Rifles' standard of one hundred and forty paces a minute, then broke into a jog for ten paces, then back into the march again, alternating between the two until he was standing in front of Carter once again. "Sure, it fair eats up the miles, Sorr, and it doesn't wear you out."

The troop adopted the technique for all their speed marches and found that they finished comfortably within the target time, earning Sgt Harkness's approval. As the weeks progressed, so did the distances. Seven miles, then nine, then twelve and, finally, seventeen. At the end of each march, just as they were starting to relax, they would be given another task: dig a defensive position; undertake range firing practice; do half an hour of drill and, after the final march, complete the five mile assault course then do more range practice.

One of the things that Carter noticed very quickly was the lack of grumbling. Soldiers always grumbled about something, he had been told at Officer Training School. The time to worry was when they stopped grumbling, the old cliché went, because it probably meant they were planning to desert or to start a mutiny. But these trainees were a different breed, or at least they were trying to be different.

There was always plenty of banter, but never any complaints. After getting soaked to the skin the men found it hard to get their clothes dry, but they just pulled them on the next day and got on with it. The food was filling, but monotonous in its lack of variety, but they wolfed it down as though it was ambrosia sent by the gods. They marched for mile after mile in all weather conditions and then stood chatting in the rain instead of rushing back to their huts. Carter heard only one complaint all the time he was at Achnacarry. It came during a boxing match when one of the combatants objected to his fight being stopped, despite the fact that his knees had turned to jelly under his opponent's onslaught. It was the only time he heard the words 'It's not fair'.

It was possible that there was some grumbling when he wasn't present, but a chat with Green suggested that wasn't the case either. "We're always too busy to moan." He said. "And if we don't like it, we can always go back where we came from."

It was true. The only thing keeping the men there was themselves.

* * *

"OK, change of plan, men." Carter said, as the landing craft wallowed on the gentle swell out on the loch. The moon provided just enough light for him to make out the black and white striped faces of the men under his command. "We're not going in to the beach by the standard route. Everyone does that and everyone ends up getting shot to bits by the defenders. We're taking a different route. Now, you're all familiar enough with the ground not to need maps and models, so I want you to imagine the route we're going to take."

"Are you sure this is wise, Sir?" Sgt Harkness whispered in his ear. "it's never a good idea to switch plans late in the day."

"It's risky, I know, but as commandos we have to be flexible. Circumstances change all the time and we have to be ready to adapt to the situation. In my mind I'm imagining the enemy having reinforced the landing beach with tanks, and we're not equipped to deal with those, so I have to either cancel the operation, which I'm not going to do, or I'm going to have to change the plan."

"It's your decision, Sir." Harkness's voice displayed his reluctance to support the change in plan.

"I know, and I'm willing to accept the consequences if it goes wrong. Now, men. What we're going to do is go further out into the loch, until we're a thousand yards from the beach. That is the limit of the prohibited line, along which the Bren guns will be firing live ammunition. We will then turn west for one hundred yards before turning back towards the shore."

"I'm not sure that's allowed, Sir." Sgt Harkness tried to object again. "I'm not sure it's in the rules for the exercise."

"Is there anything in the rules that says I can't do that?"

"Well, Sir, the rules say you can't cross the Bren gun lines."

"Yes, but the rules also say that the line only extends one thousand yards into the loch. They say nothing about what I can do at the one thousand and first yard."

"But there are other rules, Sir."

"Tell me which one applies in these circumstances."

Harkness fell silent, trying to recall all the information that had been imparted when the task had been briefed earlier in the day. "I can't think of one, off the top of my head but …"

"But nothing. If there is no rule, then we can't be breaking it. I didn't set the rules, I'm just using them to my advantage, just as I would on the sports fields."

Harkness fell silent, though the stiffness of his body told Carter he wasn't very happy. It was almost unheard of for an officer not to follow the advice offered by his training sergeant.

"Now, we will aim for a landing point just to the east of the junction with the road to Spean Bridge. You know the one, where the road along the loch side meets the one that takes us to the Guardroom. From their we'll march about a hundred yards into the weapons training area, before we turn back towards the loch and attack from the rear. Everything else is as briefed, with the same teams attacking the same defensive positions. The only difference will be that you'll be facing the opposite direction, so the teams that should have been on the left will now be on the right and vice versa. Any questions?"

There was some muttering, suggesting that there were questions, but they probably related to whether or not Carter had gone insane, so no one actually asked them. If Carter wanted to break the rules, that was his look out. It was his commando career that would go down the Swanee.

Carter struggled through the ranks packed within the confines of the landing craft until he reached the rear, then he issued a new compass bearing to the craft's Cox'n. There was an attempt at an argument, so in the end Carter had to order him to just get on with it. The Cox'n shrugged his shoulders. As with the commandos, it wasn't his career that was on the line.

They were about half way to the beach when the Bren guns started firing, one at each end of the landing beach. The twin streams of tracer shot across the loch to land with small unheard splashes about five hundred yards out into the loch. The thousand yard prohibition was just a 'belt and braces' precaution. Carter checked his watch; bang on schedule. The Bren gunners wouldn't have been able to see the landing craft even if it had been on its pre-planned course. They were firing because, according to the exercise plan, it was time to fire.

The landing craft changed course and followed the route that Carter had ordered. Thirty minutes later the ramp dropped and the commandos ran ashore, crossing the road and taking up defensive positions on the far side. Carter heard, rather than saw, the craft withdrawing from the beach and heading back out into the loch.

With the landing completed, unopposed, Carter waited until it was clear that their unexpected arrival on a different part of the beach had gone unremarked. They were about half a mile from the place they had been expected to land and it was possible that the noise made by the landing craft had travelled that far, but no alarm was raised. The Bren guns were still firing, but that was to be expected.

Carter led them inland the one hundred yards that he had predicted, then turned across to lead them parallel to the road. The tracer rounds fired by the Bren guns gave them a good idea of their position in relation to the defenders. When Carter estimated that he was mid-way between the two guns, he turned to face the loch and stretched his arms out to either side, indicating to his men to take up line abreast formation. They were too far away to mount a charge yet, so Carter led them forward at a slow walk. All the signs were that the enemy were still looking out towards the loch, wondering where Carter's landing craft was. According to the plan he was now late.

Someone got impatient and a Very Pistol coughed, sending a parachute flare into the night sky. As it popped into life it illuminated everything beneath it, especially the empty loch. Voices rose in surprise, and Carter distinctly heard one ask "where the fuck are they?"

It was time for him out find out. "Charge!" Carter yelled at the top of his voice, running forward, firing his rifle from the hip,

Pulling the bolt to the rear and jacking another round into the chamber in smooth, well-practiced movements. Ahead of them Carter could see the enemy force trying frantically to turn their machine guns and Brens around to face the threat from behind. The riflemen were quicker, but still too slow to react to the onslaught. Carter's men fired downwards into the weapons pits, 'killing' the occupants, then continued through the line to take up defensive positions beyond.

A whistle blew, three short blasts, ending the exercise. A voice rang out through the night. "Carter, where are you?"

"Over here, Sir." Carter rose to his feet, signalling to Maj Neale, the Senior Training Officer at Achnacarry and the 'umpire' for the night's exercise.

"I don't know what you think you were playing at, laddie, but you're in deep trouble. How did you get behind us?"

"We landed behind the eastern Bren gun line, Sir, then marched inland from there."

"So, you cheated. That means the end for you. Report to the Commandant first thing in the morning." There was no mistaking the fury in the Training Officer's voice. In the darkness Carter couldn't see the major's face, but he could imagine it being crimson.

"But Sir …" Carter started to protest.

"But nothing, young man. You are dismissed. Now get your men back to camp."

* * *

Carter stood to attention in front of Lt Col Vaughan's desk. The Old Man was examining him as though through a microscope, wondering what sort of creature he was looking at. This was it, Carter knew. This was him about to get his marching orders out of the commandos and back into the Huntingdons. He shouldn't have done it, he acknowledged to himself. It had always been risky; now he would have to pay the price.

Of course he could throw himself onto Vaughan's mercy, but he doubted that would impress the Commandant. It would be to plead for a second chance and you didn't get those at Achnacarry.

"So, you deliberately took your men into the beach by a route that circumvented the boundaries of the exercise." Vaughan said at last. "Where I come from, that is called cheating."

It was difficult to know how to handle this, Carter conceded to himself. If he was too belligerent he would make Vaughan angry, or would that be angrier? That would be the end of his commando career. It was the mistake that Llewelyn had made on his first day at Achnacarry. But on the other hand, if he didn't offer a credible defence of his actions, the same result would occur. Somewhere between the two lay the fine line that he must walk in order not to get RTUd.

"I concede, Sir, that I did stretch the rules of the exercise to the limit, but I don't agree that I cheated."

"Oh, and why not?"

Time for the three point defence. It was something that he had learnt at university, in the debates that were held at the Student Union. If you had less than three arguments, it sounded like your case was weak. More than three and it was like you were trying to batter your opponent into submission. But of course, they still had to be the right three arguments.

"Firstly, Sir, the boundaries of the exercise area are poorly defined. I was told that for a distance of one thousand yards out into the loch, I was not permitted to stray outside two imaginary lines. That was for safety reasons, of course; those two lines were the ones the Brens would be firing along, using live ammunition. However, nobody said that I couldn't go outside of those lines at a distance of more than one thousand yards, which is what I did."

Carter waited, trying to see what sort of reaction his first line of defence would get. Vaughan said nothing, he just maintained his gimlet stare.

"Secondly, Sir, I was following the rules set by our unarmed combat instructors. Rule one is that there are no rules in a street fight. There is no rule two." Carter saw the corners of Vaughan's lips twitch as he tried to suppress a smile. He would be very familiar with Syke's and Fairbairn's favourite saying. Carter decided it was a good sign; his point had hit home. "The commandos are street fighters, Sir, so there are no rules. I would never disobey an instruction that is aimed at preventing an accident, so I wouldn't cross the Bren lines within the thousand yard limit, but I believe that out with that, there are no rules in an exercise. The objective is to defeat the enemy and we can be sure that the enemy won't respect any rules that we might try to set."

He paused, taking a metaphorical breath before proceeding with his final argument, the one he felt was his most powerful, but which also carried the highest risk.

"Finally, Sir, the commandos are an unconventional force. We fight using unconventional methods and tactics. If we are to be bound by convention during training, only using the tactics that conform to conventional warfare, then we end up becoming conventional soldiers, the enemy will be able to predict our tactics and, eventually, they will learn to counter them. If they learn to do that it will come at a great cost to us.

By behaving in an unconventional manner, as I did, I believe I was working within the spirit of the commando ethos. It isn't possible for a commando to defeat the enemy by force of arms as he is the defender and the defender always has the advantage. So, to defeat our enemy with minimal casualties, it is necessary to deceive him and use his weaknesses against him. By using the undefended flanks of the exercise area, I was able to deceive my enemy and use my enemy's weakness against him."

His argument made, Carter fell silent. If he said any more he would probably undo any good that he might have done.

Vaughan said nothing, almost willing Carter to blunder into the silence and make matters worse. But Carter held his nerve. He had made his move, it was now up to the Commandant to counter attack.

Vaughan said nothing for a long time. Instead he stood up and turned his back on Carter, hands clasped behind his back, staring at a giant painting that dominated the room from above the fireplace. It was of a cavalry charge made by a Scottish regiment during the Crimean war. It had been a conventional attack and had resulted in high levels of casualties amongst the cavalrymen. The only saving grace had been the routing of the enemy.

"What if you had run into Bren gun fire anyway, by taking the line that you did?" Vaughan asked at last.

"Well, Sir, first of all, we were in landing craft and the ramps at the front are thick enough to stop point three oh three bullets, so there wasn't too much risk to life. But if we had taken fire I would have fired the emergency signal, Sir. A red flare would have stopped the gunfire at once.

"And your plan of attack would have then failed." Vaughan grunted.

"And I would already be on the train back to Wiltshire, Sir."

He couldn't be sure, but he thought the Commandant's shoulder might have vibrated a little, as though he was suppressing a laugh. He turned, suddenly his expression a little softer than it had been. "This is a school, Carter and at schools we learn. I have just learnt a couple of things. The first is that I had better draft better rules for exercises if I want to prevent young whipper-snappers like you from, to use your expression, stretching them to the limit. The second is that you actually have a point. We are unconventional soldiers and our strength comes from going against accepted military doctrine." He paused, clearly weighing something up in his mind. "Very well, Carter. You have persuaded me that you didn't cheat. You only stretched the rules. But be warned, don't try it again or you really will be on the homeward train and I won't bother to give you a chance to explain yourself first. Now, get out."

Carter snapped off a salute and got out, just in case the Commandant changed his mind.

* * *

Then, finally, they were nearing the end. The Privates and the Guardsmen, the Fusiliers and Gunners and Signallers could all call themselves Trooper, the rank used by the commandos. After the last speed march was completed they were awarded their Commando Dagger[1] and given their postings.

A week earlier, Lieutenant Colonel Vernon had arrived unexpectedly, seeking out Carter. "The Commando is almost up to strength, I've got all the officers except for you and one other, but I'm still short a few men. I wondered if you might have any suggestions. You've seen them training, so I thought that you might have spotted some talent."

"They're all pretty good for different reasons. I've some names I could suggest." Carter replied. "Green and O'Driscoll, for starters."

Vernon had started writing down the names but paused. "O'Driscoll, is he Irish?"

"He is, Sir."

"Hmm. Terrible reputation for drink, the Irish."

Carter knew that the reputation was well earned, in England if not in Ireland. The navvies who'd built Britain's canals and railways, and were now heavily engaged in building Britain's defences, were well known for their alcohol consumption. But Carter liked O'Driscoll and knew him to be a good soldier.

"Well you have nothing to fear from O'Driscoll, Sir. He signed 'The Pledge' when he was thirteen and has never touched a drop in his life." It was a bare faced lie and if O'Driscoll ever blotted his copy book it was likely that Carter would fall with him, but he wanted him in 15 Cdo.

"OK, I'll take him on your say so. Anyone else?"

Carter gave him the names of another dozen of his troop and a couple more from Ten Troop that he thought would meet his Commanding Officer's needs. The remainder were pretty good as well, but Vernon had made it clear that he only wanted the pick of the litter.

"Any suggestion for an officer?" Vernon asked.

"How about Andrew Fraser?" Carter had introduced his roommate when his CO had arrived, before Fraser had made himself scarce.

"The Scots usually go to 11 Cdo." Vernon replied thoughtfully. All the commandos had been given recruiting areas and 11 had been given Scotland, just as 12 had recruited in Northern Ireland and 15 in the South West of England.

"But he doesn't have to. Besides, with transfers and reinforcement drafts that seems to have gone by the board, hasn't it, Sir? He's very good. Better than me in some respects. You'd be lucky to get him."

"I'll give it some thought, but if he's reluctant then I won't push it." He stood up from where he had been sitting on Fraser's bed. "I had a word with Colonel Vaughan when I got here. He told me he's been very impressed with you. Well, what he actually said was that you were a little unconventional in your approach, but that it worked for you."

"That's good of him to say, Sir." Carter decided against explaining what Vaughan had meant.

"It isn't just good, Steven, it's excellent. The Commandant is very sparing with his praise, so if he says you're good, then it is the highest accolade. I look forward to you joining us at Troon." During the weeks that Carter had spent at Achnacarry, 15 Cdo had moved to Scotland, as had the other commandos based in the south of England. It moved them further from prying eyes and closer to parts of the country that allowed them to train in the harshest conditions. By locating all the commandos in Scotland, it also made best use of scarce resources such as ships and landing craft. "You'll be going in at the deep end."

"Oh, why is that, Sir?"

The senior officer tapped the side of his nose knowingly. "Can't say too much at the moment, but you'll be seeing action before the end of the year. Now, I've a train to catch." He stood and extended his hand for Carter to shake. "I look forward to buying you a drink in The Clansman." Seeing Carter's puzzled look, he elaborated. "It's the pub we've sort of adopted as our Officers' Mess."

[1] Commando Dagger – Officially designated the Sykes-Fairbairn fighting knife, it was designed by the two unarmed combat training officers named in this chapter. It was first issued to the commandos in January 1941. It became the symbol of the commandos, with the image of a red dagger embroidered onto a black triangular shoulder patch (see book cover). It remains so today with the Royal Marine Commandos.

4 – Troon

On leaving Achnacarry the troop, including Carter, were told they had earned themselves some leave and were given a week before they had to report to their new units. Carter returned home to Lincolnshire to spend some time with his parents and younger sister. It didn't go well.

The atmosphere was strained. He hadn't told his parents where he had been for the previous twelve weeks, partly for security reasons and partly because he hadn't wanted to disappoint them if he hadn't made the grade. Their reaction on seeing him with the red-on-black Commando shoulder flashes and the triangular sleeve patch with its stylised commando dagger, was neither what he had expected nor hoped for.

Carter's mother, already fearful for his safety because he had joined the Army in the first place, was beside herself with worry about what might happen to him now that he was a commando. This made Carter senior angry for making his mother worry so much. It didn't help that his sixteen year old sister, Abigail, wouldn't stop asking him questions about what he had been doing and how dangerous it was. Both parents had lost family members during the First World War and knew the cost of combat. His father had served in the trenches with the Huntingdonshire Regiment, the same regiment Carter had joined and had seen the human cost at close quarters.

Carter's father distanced himself for the duration of the week, busying himself with his solicitor's practice and the Home Guard, of which he was the local platoon commander. Mrs Carter fussed around her son, breaking down in tears frequently for fear that she might never see him again. By the end of the week he was glad to get away and insisted that his family didn't accompany him to the station to say their farewells.

The train had to pass through the city where he went to university, so Carter took the opportunity to visit his old college chums. That visit went no better. Although Carter hadn't intended it, his uniform came between them, a silent condemnation of them remaining in the safety of academia while others did the fighting. They were due to graduate the following year and all of the four that Carter met up with in the pub had applied for work that would see them in reserved occupations, safe from the threat of conscription. Carter hadn't said anything, but he felt disappointment for friends that in 1938 had campaigned against the scourge of fascism so hard while at university but were now uninterested in bearing arms to rid Europe of it.

But they drank beer together and exchanged university gossip as Carter told them some of the more risqué jokes that he had heard since they had last met. At the end of the evening they accompanied him to the station, taking turns to struggle under the weight of the kitbag that Carter hardly even felt to be a burden anymore. They waved him off from the platform, shouting ribald remarks about his future prospects with the ladies now that he wore the coveted commando flashes.

* * *

Troon is a small coastal town in Ayrshire, famous mainly for having hosted the British Open golf championship in 1923. Apart from its small harbour, it wasn't a good location for the commandos, having none of the rugged countryside close by that some of the other Ayrshire towns benefitted from. To the south, the town of Ayr provided a more enticing seaside atmosphere, while to the north Ardrossan and Largs offered better training facilities. But 15 Cdo had been the last to form so they got what was left over after the older commando units had taken the choice locations.

Lieutenant Colonel Vernon had established his HQ in a disused sweet factory, which had been forced to close due to the wartime shortage of sugar, the principle ingredient of its product. The factory floor, once cleared of its machinery, provided an indoor assembly and training area for the troops, while the office spaces and store rooms accommodated the small administration staff. Carter made his way to a door bearing a handwritten paper sign saying 'Adjutant', which was held in place with drawing pins. The door stood open. A harassed looking Captain was shuffling paper from one side of his desk to another.

In response to Carter's knock, the occupant said "Come in, you must be Carter I'm guessing." The Adjutant's paper movement became more agitated until he found the document he was looking for. "Yes, here we are. Formerly 2nd Battalion, Huntingdonshire Regiment, now confirmed as posted to us." He extended his hand across the desk. "Welcome, I'm Richard Bird, nicknamed Dickie for obvious reason, or just Adj if you feel that way inclined. As they probably told you at Achnacarry, we've been reorganised into six troops of sixty men. It's a good number to split between two landing craft. Each troop is commanded by a Captain, with two Lieutenants or Second Lieutenants, each of whom leads thirty men. As well as being Adjutant, I also command 2 Troop. Although you are senior in terms of your commissioning date, you will be the junior officer in 4 Troop. I wouldn't argue over that, as it's commando experience that counts here and Molly Brown came to us from 4 Cdo with oodles of that."

"Molly?"

"Yes, it's actually Ranulph, but you know how nicknames stick in the Army. Something to do with some woman that survived the sinking of the Titanic. Anyway, your Troop Commander is Martin Turner. He came in from 6 Commando, so he also has a lot of experience, so sorry, but you're the new kid in the class. Now, the men you trained with have nearly all arrived from leave, we're just waiting for a couple. I've got five spaces in your half troop, so would you like to stake your claim on any of them?"

"Yes, if I may I'd like Green, O'Driscoll, and Glass." Despite his initial struggle with the physical demands of the course, Glass had turned out to be very good at field craft and had taken to unarmed combat like a duck to water. If you wanted someone to creep up and dispose of a German sentry, Glass would be your first choice. "Apart from those I'd be happy with any of the others."

"OK, I'll make sure they're detailed to your troop. Now, that's all I have for you for the moment. If you report to the QM's office he'll sort you out with your billet."

Dickie Bird went back to shuffling paper, so Carter considered himself dismissed. He stepped back into the corridor and went looking for the door marked Quartermaster. All the doors in the corridor were left standing open so he had to stop at each in turn and peer inwards until he found the one bearing the right word. Inside was a stocky, florid looking Major. Carter thought that any attempt to undertake the commando training would be likely to induce a seizure, until he saw the blue and white ribbon of a Military Cross on the man's chest. He was too young to have earned it during the Great War and the ribbon looked brand new, so it must be a more recent award.

The Major looked up. "Come in, come in, don't stand there in the doorway like a nervous schoolboy." He said in a mild Scottish accent. He stood and extended his hand. As Carter was still wearing his peaked cap, he threw up a salute before shaking it, which the Major acknowledged with a nod. "Major Trent, but I'll answer to QM. We don't do a lot of Sirs around here, except for the CO and the 2IC, of course. Welcome to 15 Cdo … what's your Christian name?"

"Steven, Sir."

"Welcome, Steven." He was much better organised than the Adjutant and had his papers arranged in three trays; in, out and pending. From the latter he picked up a piece of paper and handed it to Carter. "That's your billet, 25 Gillies Street, which is also where Martin Turner and Molly Brown are billeted." He picked up a brown coloured booklet from the pending tray and handed that across.

"Your ration book, which you give to your landlady so she can buy your food. There are a few things in there that the civvies don't get, so if you want your laundry done for free or an extra lump of coal on the fire, you'd do well to share some of it with your hosts. Last but not least." He took a key from his pocket and unlocked a drawer in his desk and took out a small cash box. Carefully he counted two ten shilling notes and a half crown, which he pushed across the desk to Carter, before following it with a receipt book. "One week's subsistence allowance to pay for your keep. Please sign the receipt. It's up to your landlady how much of that she actually takes off you, but bear in mind that when you go off on exercises or operations lasting more than twelve hours you lose the relevant amount per day, so if you want to keep her sweet I would advise handing the lot over each week if you want a warm room to come back to. I hand out the allowance to officers on Monday morning at oh seven hundred sharp, unless we're away, in which case it's the morning after we return. Got all that?"

"I think so, Sir."

"Good. Now, one more thing and keep this to yourself. We are entitled to an alcohol allowance for the Officers' Mess. We don't have one of those, so we buy the bottles and sell them on to the landlord of The Clansman at cost. He then sells the drinks back to us at Mess prices. Any profits are shared fifty-fifty and we pass our share on to the landlord of McNeil's Bar on Jubilee Road. He then uses it to subsidise the price of drinks for our boys because they don't have a canteen. That encourages the lads to all drink in the same place which makes it easier for the Regimental Police[1] to keep an eye on them. The CO will give you a great speech about keeping the local population on-side and that's one of the ways we do it. But we have to keep it quiet because if the locals find out they can get cheap drinks in McNeil's they'll jam the place and that will have the opposite effect."

"Do the men know about the arrangement?"

"Officially no, but they're not stupid so I guess that some of them have worked out that the beer in McNeil's is cheaper than elsewhere and they'll be wondering why. Now, if you'll excuse me, I've got bullets to go and count."

He picked up his hat from the corner of the desk and a clipboard from its hook on the wall and came round the table towards Carter. Carter stepped to one side to let the Major pass him, then followed him out.

Outside the factory he asked an ARP Warden[2] how to find Gillies Street. He was greeted at the door of number 25 by a woman in her mid-fifties who bestowed a generous smile on him.

"I'm Moira Bliss, Lieutenant." She said, shaking his hand. She was smartly dressed in a tweed skirt and a sweater that looked as though it might be hand knitted. Around her neck was a strand of pearls. She looked as though she was dressed for an outing, but Carter was to find out that she always took great care of her appearance, at least when her 'gentlemen', as she called her tenants, were around.

"Should I call you Mrs Bliss?" Carter asked. The ARP Warden had told him that she was a widow, having lost her husband in the First World War, so Carter avoided any questions about him.

"I'm happy for you to call me Moira. I don't stand on ceremony. I'll show you to your room; you're sharing with Lt Brown." She led him up the stairs to the first floor and along a short corridor. "That's the bathroom," She pointed towards a door at the rear of the house, "and that's Captain Turner's room." She indicated a door. Carter guessed that the room faced the front of the house. Right opposite was another door. "This is you, here." She said, pushing the door open for Carter to enter.

The room was bright and airy and had a single bed on either side of the door, each with a bedside table with a reading lamp on it. Beneath the window stood a dressing table and diagonally across the corner was a large wardrobe, in the other corner it was mirrored by a chest of drawers. Above each bed was a framed print, one featuring sailing ships at sea and the other showing the Charge of the Light Brigade.

"This was my sons' room, before they went off to the Navy." She announced, a tinge of sadness in her voice. "I used to use Captain Turner's room, but now I occupy what was the front parlour."

"Where are your sons now?"

"I don't know exactly, but one of them is serving on a corvette on convoy escort duties and the other is serving on a battle cruiser, I think he called it, in the Far East."

Carter knew not to ask any more. "Shall we sort out the administration?" He said, cheerfully. "Here's my ration card." He handed the document over. "And here's the money for my keep." Moira folded the two notes into her hand and returned the coin back to him.

"I don't keep alcohol in the house, so you'll need something with which to buy a drink." She smiled at him. "I know you commandos have a bit of a thirst."

Carter knew better than to argue and later they developed a ritual in which he would hand over his full subsistence allowance for the week and she would give him back a portion, as though she was handing out pocket money to her two sons.

"Now, I'll leave you to settle in. The other two gentlemen will be back at six, they told me, so I'll serve dinner at seven. We eat in the dining room, which is to the left of the front door." She left the room, closing the door behind her.

Carter checked the wardrobe and found Brown's uniforms and shirts hanging neatly on the left hand side, leaving the right hand side for Carter. The chest of drawers had two drawers of the four empty for Carter's use and the right hand drawer of the dressing table was also empty. It seemed that there would be no issues over sharing. A book lay on the bedside table next to the bed on the left of the room, so Carter assumed that was the one occupied by Brown. He glanced at the cover and saw that it was an Agatha Christie mystery. That was good, nothing too high brow.

Carter had no idea where Turner and Brown were, but he knew that wherever it was the Troop would be with them, so there was nothing he could do until they returned. He unpacked his kit and stowed it in the space that Brown had left for him then removed his boots and settled onto the bed for a snooze. Once again there had been no sleeper berths available and the train had been crowded, leaving sleep hard to come by. But over the previous weeks he had become better at snatching a few winks whenever he could. It was, he had soon found out, an essential skill for a commando.

[1] Regimental Police – Members of a unit who serve in a role similar to that of a Special Constable, to maintain discipline. Not to be confused with the Royal Military Police (RMP or, more commonly MP) who are trained police officers and are under independent command.

[2] ARP Warden – Air Raid Precautions Warden. Volunteers who patrol an area during the night to keep a look out for breaches of the blackout regulations. In the event of an air raid they directed people to the nearest public shelter. They also reported the landing places of bombs so that unexploded ones could be dealt with, as well as incendiary and delayed action bombs and summoned the fire brigade and ambulance services when required.

* * *

There was a gentle thumping behind Carter's eyes that told him he should have been more sparing with the whisky the previous evening. With his Troop Commander and roommate, after dinner they had adjourned to The Clansman. Dinner had been a good, solid Scottish meal of mince and stovies, with Mrs Bliss making a small amount of meat go a long way.

The evening had been a convivial one, with Carter meeting most of the other junior officers including his old roommate, Andrew Fraser, who had accepted the CO's invitation to join 15 Commando. "If I wanted to stay with the Jocks I wouldn't have joined the commandos." He quipped. "I was rather hoping for a stint down South, but here I am still in Scotland!" He had been assigned to 3 Troop. Carter noticed that he'd exchanged his tartan trews for standard khaki battledress trousers.

The CO was away in London which, everyone told him, was significant in terms of the Commando's prospects for undertaking an operation in the near future. If it was true it would be their first. The 2IC, or Second in Command, was deputising for the Old Man, as he was affectionately referred to even though he had yet to turn thirty, at a dinner with the Mayor.

Turner was alarmingly fresh looking and showed no signs of the previous evening's drinking. Carter found him in a large room identified by the piece of paper pinned to the door as the 4 Troop office. There was a large, square table in the centre, with a map spread out on it. Seats were arranged around the wall. It wasn't the sort of room where a lot of paperwork was done, but it would be big enough to be used to provide briefings for the officers and NCOs of the troop.

"Good morning, Steven." Turner greeted him. "Did you sleep well?"

"Like a log, Martin." It was a tradition that junior officers, which included the rank of Captain, didn't address each other as 'Sir' even if one of them outranked the other. The use of the honorific was only applied to majors and above.

"Good. I'll take you along and introduce you to your Sergeant in a minute. He's doing PT with the rest of the troop right now. Strictly speaking we should both be with them, but I thought I'd set you a little task this morning. It will give you a chance to get to know your men."

And for you to get to see what I'm made of, Carter thought.

"Take a look at the map. Do you see this farmhouse here?" he pointed his finger at a small square mark on the map that had a long, winding track leading to it from the main road. Carter reached into the breast pocket of his battledress blouse and withdrew his notebook and pencil. He did a quick calculation of the farm's grid reference and jotted it down.

"That's Hamilton Farm. It's derelict, has been for years, apparently." Turner nodded in approval at Carter's action, then continued. "I'd like you to conduct two patrols there. The first, this morning, will be a reconnaissance patrol. Assume for the purposes of this exercise that it is occupied by Germans soldiers, let's say half a platoon in strength, so you can't approach too close."

Carter guessed that part of the exercise would be to see if he could get close enough to study the location without giving himself and his men away. Turner would probably station a man, or men, inside the farm to keep a lookout for him.

"Take a close look at it, come back here and formulate a plan, then take your men out tonight as a fighting patrol and attack it. How does that sound?"

"Like it might be fun, Sir."

"I hope so." The look Turner gave Carter suggested that it would be fun, but not necessarily for Carter.

They were interrupted by the entrance of a Major. The two junior officers snapped to attention.

"As you were." The major boomed. He was a big man with a big voice and Carter wondered how he managed to do anything covertly, which was a necessity in the commandos. The Major extended his hand. "I'm Couples, the 2IC. As you've probably already heard, the CO is away for a couple of days, so it falls to me to welcome you to 15 Cdo. As part of my role I'm also the Training Officer, so when you're up to your neck in the Kyle of Bute in the freezing cold it was probably my idea to put you there." He laughed at his own joke. "What has Martin got planned for you for today?"

"A recce of a place called Hamilton Farm, followed by a night attack, Sir." Carter replied.

The corners of the 2IC's mouth twitched, as though he was trying to suppress a smile.

"Ah, Hamilton Farm eh? Well, good luck with that. I'll leave you to get on with it then." With that he was gone as suddenly as he had arrived.

Turner watched him leave, then turned to Carter, "You study the map, Steven, while I'll go and get Sgt Chalk. He's a good man, you can rely on him. He's a regular who came to us from the Middlesex Regiment via 3 Commando, so he's got plenty of experience."

Turner left the room and Carter leant over the map and started to study it. The 2IC's suppressed smile had worried him. The map's contour lines showed him that it sat in a sort of lopsided bowl, the lower, northern, side of it providing passage for a river. There was marshland marked between the river and the edge of the track that led to the farm, so there was no hope of approaching from that side. Behind the farm the contour lines were massed tightly together, showing a steep climb, or descent, depending on which way you were travelling. Boulders were also marked, suggesting that it was more of a cliff than a slope. At the top was a triangulation point, or trig point as it was more commonly known.

That left the south and west as possible approach routes for an attack, one of which, Carter suspected, he was expected to take. The map indicated that it was open farmland, flat and featureless.

There was a tap on the door and a Sergeant stepped through. He was dressed in PT kit so didn't salute, but he came to ramrod attention. "Sgt Chalk, Sah!"

"At ease Sergeant." Carter said, extending his hand to be shaken. "How did the PT session go?"

"Pretty standard, Sir. A five mile run followed by some calisthenics." Carter suppressed a smile at the use of the word. He normally described those sorts of things as 'physical jerks'. "Most of the men do a lot of their own physical fitness work, if they have time. You won't find any unfit men in 4 Troop, Sir."

"Good to hear it, Sergeant. Now, tell me about Hamilton Farm."

"Is that what Capt Turner has in store for us today? It's a tough one, Sir. We've been up here what … ten weeks and no one has ever managed to capture it. It's pretty easy to defend, as you've probably seen from the map. There's only really two lines of approach." He leaned over the map and pointed. "You can get across the river and up to the farmhouse here. There's a narrow footpath through the boggy ground, but a defender would put a machine gun at the top of the rise and just mow you down. The rear is a cliff, as you can see, which only leaves the fields, and they're as flat as a witch's tit."

"Yes, that's pretty much what I had worked out. Have you defended it?"

"Oh yes, Sir. A couple of times. Once against 1 Troop and once against 3 Troop. Neither of them got close."

"Do all the defenders tend to use the same plan?"

"Oh yes, Sir. The firing positions are pretty obvious if you want to provide overlapping arcs of fire."

"OK Sergeant, well, I hope we can do better than the other troops that have tried. Get the men changed into fighting order and assemble here in one hour. I'll brief them and then we'll go and take a look."

"Shall I draw blank ammunitions?"

"Yes, please do. Fifty rounds per man and as much Bren ammunition as they can carry. We may as well try to make some noise when we attack. Get some pyrotechnics as well; oh, and Very pistol with some flares."

The Sergeant sprang to attention once more and then turned on his heel and marched out.

* * *

Using his elbows and knees, Carter crawled to the edge of the tree line. To one side was the remains of a stone wall, barely more than a heap of rubble, but it provided the sort of jagged outline that would prevent his silhouette from attracting attention from any watchers in the farm. Not that he should have a silhouette. They had approached from the north, so the October sun was low on the opposite horizon and the bulk of the stand of pine tree behind them should mean that they were dark shapes against more dark shapes; almost invisible.

There was a scuffling sound beside him as Sgt Chalk took up position alongside Carter. Behind them the troop was arranged in a circular defensive ring, ready to repel any attackers that might discover the patrol. There was no real risk of that; Carter would have had to have been second guessed about his route or they would have to have been followed, neither of which seemed likely. But routines such as these saved lives when they were operating in enemy territory, so it was essential to maintain the troop's fieldcraft and tactical discipline.

* * *

It had been a long morning so far. After returning to his billet Carter had dressed himself in his 'fighting order' and returned to the factory, where the Sergeant had assembled the troop ready for inspection. They were wearing 'caps comforter', their issue balaclavas folded and stitched into a woollen hat, over which their steel helmets would fit if they had to be jammed on in a hurry. Compared to the motley selection of headgear that the commandos normally wore, the caps at least gave them an air of uniformity, while also being very warm at night.

For months there had been talk of providing the commandos with a form of head dress of their own, to foster some air of esprit de corps, but so far it had come to nothing. 2 Commando had a QM who had somehow managed to get hold of a load of tam-o'shanters, the beret like hats with pom-poms on, worn by highland regiments. Others had scrounged up enough brown berets to kit out all their men, but overall the commandos, when assembled, looked like they belonged to different armies.

The troop all wore camouflage cream, smeared over their faces and hands in random patterns. At first the commandos had mixed soot or soil with water so they could apply it, until a former employee of a well-known pharmaceutical company contacted his old employers, who had agreed to produce a bespoke product based on women's 'cold cream'. It worked well and the company had now agreed a contract to supply the whole of the army. In daylight the stripes worked the same way as they did for a tiger or a zebra, breaking up the shape of the soldiers' faces, making them harder to recognise as being that of a living creature. At night it did the same, while also dampening any shine off of cheek bones or forehead.

Unlike the brass work of his old battalion, the commandos had painted the buckles and tabs of their webbing a matt black, to prevent light from reflecting off them. Carter wondered how his old RSM, who was rumoured to be able to spot a bit of smudged brass from a hundred yards, would react if he saw it. If the soldiers had been wearing cap badges they, too, would have been painted black. Finally, to reduce noise, the soldiers' rifle sling swivels had been strapped with bits of hessian torn from sandbags, to stop them rattling. The commandos believed that every small thing that could give them an advantage should be used. Bullshine was for the parade ground, not the battlefield.

Walking up and down each rank, Carter carried out an inspection of his men. It wasn't necessary in terms of their turnout, any decent Sergeant would have already made sure they were correctly dressed. But it was necessary for him to start to get to know his men. He stopped in front of a tall, thin soldier with corporal's stripes on his sleeves.

"What's your name, Corporal?" he asked.

"Franklyn, Sir." The soldier snapped back, "F Section". The twenty-eight other ranks, or ORs, of his half troop were further sub divided into seven man sections, each led by a Corporal. He had a Lance Corporal as his deputy who also looked after a two-man Bren gun team. The sections of Carter's half troop were designated E to H, while Molly Brown's were A to D.

"Which regiment did you come from, Franklyn?"

"Coldstream Guards, Sir. Then 4 Commando."

"Good turnout, Franklyn." Carter said before moving to the next man along.

After the inspection came the briefing. The men forming a half circle around a blackboard on which Carter had sketched a map showing their approach to the farm. They would leave the town on the A78, heading south before joining the A77. After a mile they would turn east off the road and continue inland until they reached the stand of pines that sat across the shallow valley about half a mile to the north of Hamilton Farm, the river running between the two positions. From there Carter would carry out his reconnaissance, before returning to Troon by an alternative route, just in case they might have been seen and an ambush set for them.

* * *

The march had taken two hours but none of the troop had even broken sweat. Pulling his binoculars from inside his battledress blouse, Carter started to draw a sketch map in his notebook. The maps could tell him a lot, but not the fine detail, such as the tumble down garden wall with a gate in it, nor the heap of rusting farm tools stacked along one wall of the farmhouse. There were also some ramshackle outbuildings that weren't marked on the map.

It was barely a farmhouse any longer. The roof was missing entirely and the window frames devoid of any windows and the doorframes stood empty. It was no more than a shell. About forty yards behind the farm loomed the cliff. Not vertical, but very steep with boulders protruding from it. Smaller rocks littered the bottom, having been washed out by the heavy Scottish rains.

As he watched, Carter became aware of the sound of engines, labouring in low gear. Around a bend in the track two three ton trucks appeared, lurching and swaying along the broken surface. They disgorged their passengers before turning and returning along the track. The passengers were also commandos, no doubt a defending force sent to prevent the capture of the farm by Carter's men.

He raised his binoculars and focused on two men standing apart from the crowd. Carter handed the binoculars to his Sergeant.

"Wally Hammond." Chalk whispered. "One of the two Sergeants from 3 Troop. Don't know the officer though." Chalk was no longer calling his officer 'Sir', which was standard practice in the field; he also wouldn't be saluting Carter. No point in identifying the leaders for the benefit of enemy snipers.

"I do. He's the bloke I shared a room with at Achnacarry: Lt Fraser."

So that was the plan. Pit the two new officers against each other and see who came off best. It wasn't really a surprise; the commandos turned just about everything into a competition. It kept them performing to their highest level.

"Is he any good?"

"Good enough to be here." Carter replied.

The Sergeant started pointing and Carter could tell that he was shouting orders, even though the sound didn't carry across the valley to them. The cluster of soldiers started to break up into smaller groups. They slipped off their webbing harness and laid them on the ground. Unbuckling their entrenching tools from the back of their packs they started digging, the occasional clang of steel against stone ringing out.

"That soil is coming up pretty easily." Carter observed after a few minutes.

"They'll be digging in the same place as before."

"You mean they always dig their positions in the same places?"

"They pretty much have to. In some places the rock is only a few inches below the surface. You can't dig a slit trench there. So they dig where everyone else has dug before."

"And you know where those positions are."

"Of course. I've defended the farm twice before."

Carter pushed his notebook across to the Sergeant. "Mark them on there."

The Sergeant did as he was bid then returned the notebook to his officer. Carter examined the sketch map carefully. The majority of the positions were on the south and west of the farm, the side that an attack normally came from. The north and east had far less protection. As well as rifle and Bren gun positions there was also a square marked 'mortar pit'. Each troop had a two inch mortar, which was small enough to be carried by one man. A second man carried the weapon's bombs.

Sited above the river crossing was a Bren gun which would be able to fire along the narrow path up from the river between the boggy ground on either side. Two more slit tranches were placed either side of the approach track, also with a Bren gun allocated.

Along the back wall of the farm, forty yards from the foot of the cliff, there was a long empty stretch, devoid of defences.

"No defences here." Carter whispered, pointing to the sketch map.

"No." Sgt Chalk replied. "Under the grass the rocks of the cliff extend to the back wall of the house. There's no way of digging. You'd have to build sand bagged emplacements and no one has ever felt the need to do that. You'd never get down that cliff in the dark. You'd be slipping and sliding all over the place. Someone could break a leg or worse. Then there would be all the noise."

Slit trenches extended almost to the base of the cliff at the southern end, anchoring the flank, preventing any infiltration along the rear wall. Attacking across the fields it would be unlikely that anyone could break through that way. The river and its boggy banks protected the northern flank.

"OK. I've seen enough, I think. Let's get back to the factory and the men can have some lunch and a kip. We've got a long night ahead of us."

* * *

The evening briefing was attended by Martin Turner, wearing an armband with the word 'UMPIRE' stencilled on it. "Don't mind me." He said, "I'm not here."

Like buggery, you're not here, Carter thought. But after twelve weeks at Achnacarry he was used to being under constant observation. He called his men forward to huddle in a semi-circle around him while he told them what his plan was. The essence of it was that they would attack the right flank of the farm's defences, where the last slit trench sat close to the base of the cliff. If they could break through there, he told them, then the rear of the farm lay undefended.

"We attack at midnight exactly." He concluded.

There was a sharp intake of breath from some of the soldiers and some whispering.

"Silence." Sgt Chalk bellowed. He did, however, offer Carter a quizzical glance. Carter saw, too, that Martin Turner was frowning. He could understand why. Sentries spent two hours on duty and four hours off. If the normal timings were observed, midnight would be when the sentries were being changed, meaning that there would be twice as many men in the defences. It also meant that there would be less of a delay in the defences being reinforced, because two thirds of the defenders would already be in position. Carter suppressed a smile. The announcement of the attack time wasn't for the benefit of his men, it was for the benefit of anyone else who might be listening.

Twice during his preparation of the chalk boards, on which he had drawn his maps, he had seen Andrew Fraser strolling past the office door. By rights he should still have been with his men, out at the farm, which suggested some ulterior motive for being back at HQ. Fraser might not even know that Carter had seen him at the farm, so he might think that his presence wasn't considered out of place. But a change of timing for the attack was the least of the surprises that Fraser could expect that night.

Sgt Chalk chivvied the men out of the warmth of the sweet factory and into the drizzle of the night. Good, thought Carter, the weather had turned in their favour. Soldiers on sentry duty didn't like the rain. It soaked into their clothing and trickled down their necks. They tended to pull their gas capes, poncho like waterproofs, over their heads and that restricted both vision and hearing. If Carter was really lucky the rain would get heavier to provide a constant splattering background noise that interfered with the men's hearing even more. Every solider knew that at night, hearing was a far more important sense than sight.

The men formed up in their sections on both sides of the road. They were spaced at least five yards apart, a precaution against grenade and mortar attacks. Just because they were right outside their own HQ the Sergeant wasn't going to allow his men to ignore the basics.

As he left the building, Carter gave a small signal to the NCO, calling him across, but not in an elaborate manner that an unseen observer might notice. When he got close enough Carter leant forward to whisper directly into the Sergeant's ear. "Forget everything that you just heard in there. It's a complete load of bollocks. You remember the route we took this morning, we passed a Dutch barn?"

"Yes, I know it."

"I'm taking the men there and then I'll brief them again, this time with the real plan."

"You think someone might have been spying on us?"

"Let's be polite and call it 'intelligence gathering'. I think it's possible. I'm not complaining, I'd have done the same myself if I was in charge of the defences. Now, let's get this show on the road."

E Section were in front on the left hand side of the road, with F section behind them. Carter slotted himself in between them while the Sergeant took up a similar position between G and H Section. Carter tapped the man in front of him on the shoulder. "Move off." He instructed in a hoarse whisper. The man passed the message forward and the formation moved off through the night, if not silently then at least quietly enough for them not to be noticed by the inhabitants of the houses along their route out of town. In the middle of the road Martin Turner, the 'umpire', walked quietly along. He was the only one of then that wasn't dressed for combat, though he had streaked his face and hands with 'cam cream'.

When they reached the point on the A77 where they left the road, Turner came across to Carter as he waited for his men to climb the stile into the fields. "This isn't the route you briefed, Steven". His tone was curious, but Carter also sensed a challenge in his voice.

"Just a little subterfuge on my part, Martin. Walls have ears; careless talk costs lives and that sort of thing."

"So you aren't going to attack where you said."

"No. And I'm not attacking at midnight, either. There's a barn up ahead and we'll lie up there for a couple of hours before I re-brief the men on the real plan."

"Don't you trust your fellow officers?" It sounded like a reproof.

"I would trust them with my life, Martin. But I wouldn't play poker against a single one of them."

Turner chuckled. "OK, well, it's your show. As I said, I'm not here."

* * *

Satisfied with what he had seen, Carter wriggled backwards. He found his Sergeant waiting for him.

"Nothing to be seen." He reported, having to raise his voice slightly to be heard above the hiss of the rain. "No lights showing and no signs of movement. Not that I could see that far even if there was any."

"Are you sure about this? In the dark, with rain making everything slippery?"

In an ordinary infantry battalion Carter wouldn't have thought twice about reprimanding his subordinate for challenging his orders. But this wasn't an ordinary battalion, it was the commandos. Everyone was permitted to voice an opinion. A good commander would take those opinions into account and use them to revise the plan where necessary. All that mattered was that they supported the decision, his decision, when the time came.

"It's the only chance we've got. Besides, it's a little bit late in the day to change the plan again."

"Ok. I'll get the men started." He crawled away into the dark and Carter was just about able to hear his whispered voice as he gave his orders. Ten minutes later he was back.

"We've got the rope secured to the trig point. Ready to go when you are."

Carter checked his watch. He could go whenever he wanted, but he had told his men the attack would commence at oh four hundred hours. There were still three minutes to go. He watched the sweep second hand crawl round the dial at the same time trying to suppress the butterflies that were holding a carnival in his stomach.

'A commando officer will never ask his men to do anything that he hasn't done himself.' So said Lt Col Vaughan, the Commandant at Achnacarry. The words rang in Carter's head as he crawled back to the edge of the cliff. Back in the barn he had demonstrated the technique, just as his father had shown him all those years before. Straddle the rope, grip tightly with both hands and walk backwards over the edge. The 'rope' was in fact thirty toggle ropes joined together to make one long one, one hundred and eighty feet in length. Carter hoped it was long enough; a lot of its length and been wasted in tying it to the trig point, which was several yards from the edge of the cliff. In this rain the toggles would be useful, stopping his hands from sliding down and falling all the way to the bottom if he lost his grip. But it would have been better if he'd been able to provide the men with some practical experience, but that couldn't be done without giving the game away to the opposition. Fortunately the cliff wasn't sheer. If he slipped and fell there was some chance that one would actually kill themselves.

Carter suffered from a fear of heights that his father wouldn't accept, making him climb mountains no matter how terrified he had been. At least in the darkness Carter couldn't see the drop below him. It removed some of the terror. Slowly he lowered away, taking one small step backwards before relaxing his grip enough for his hands to follow, before tightening his grip again. About a foot of movement every two or three seconds, with an estimated fifty feet to the bottom. It should take about two minutes. It seemed like an age. Unable to check his watch, Carter tried counting the sound of his heartbeats thudding in his ears, to gauge the passage of time but it was no good. His heart was pounding at such a rate that he couldn't keep up. After what seemed like a lifetime Carter felt the ground start to level off beneath his feet. He was at the bottom. Relaxing his grip one final time, he jerked the rope twice to indicate that he was safely down.

His hands free, he was now able to draw his pistol, one man against half a troop if the alarm was raised. He had six blank bullets in the cylinder of his Mk VI Webley, it would be enough to make sure that he made some noise before he 'died' and that was about all.

A body nudged against him as the next man arrived. Carter indicated to the left where the man should take up his position. "Don't stumble into the trench'" He whispered into the man's ear. He thought the heard a stifled laugh, but it may just have been the man's boot sliding on the sodden grass.

One by one the men arrived and Carter directed them left and right to form a skirmish line. They were coming down more quickly than he had anticipated. Clearly some of the men were less nervous about the descent than he had been, or they were less aware of the danger. He was surprised that the men had been so quiet. He had expected at least one to slip and let out a curse, but it seemed that they were all as sure footed as cats. The last man arrived; Sgt Chalk.

"All ready up above." The Sgt breathed in his ear. Carter held out his hand and the Sergeant rooted around inside his battledress blouse, pulling out a clumsy, thick barrelled weapon.

Carter pulled back the hammer, cringing at the harsh click as it locked into place. Pointing the weapon skywards, Carter pulled the trigger. After the silence there was a deafening bang and the flare streaked up to explode in a bright green light at the zenith of its arc. At once the four Bren guns positioned along the top of the cliff opened fire. Carter passed the Very Pistol back to the Sergeant, who reloaded it and fired it again. This time a bright white light lit up the sky, illuminating the whole area. It hung there, apparently immobile, held aloft by its tiny parachute. It was only an illusion, of course. The flare had to obey the laws of gravity, but by firing flare after flare the Sergeant was able to keep the farm lit up for the Bren gunners to maintain their fire on the slit trenches. With the guns firing downwards into them the strength of the defensive position became their weakness, turning the six foot by three foot rectangles into death traps.

At the base of the cliff the rest of the commandos leapt forward screaming blood curdling battle cries. Carter took E section straight forward to the farm's rear door, while the other three sections split left and right to attack the defences from the rear.

With the Bren guns pouring simulated death from above and the assault from the rear the defenders had no option but to surrender. Captain Turner ran from trench to trench calling out 'dead! dead!' to each man as he reached him.

Carter reached the rear wall of the farm, pressing himself up against it next to the gaping doorway. He pulled a thunder-flash from his belt, twisted off the cap and struck the fuse before throwing it through the door. "Grenade!" He yelled, pressing himself back against the wall.

There was a pause then the flash and bang of the pyrotechnic going off. E Section's Corporal stepped into the room and started to hose down the walls, floor and ceiling with his Thompson sub machine gun. The off-duty soldiers who were inside the farmhouse were unable to escape. It was the Sergeant's weapon but had been swapped so that Chalk could fire his Very Pistol. Carter fell through the door under the weight of the rest of the section piling in behind him.

Another Captain appeared in the light, his features being alternately lit then cast into shadow as the flares swung beneath their parachutes. Like Martin Turner he also wore an armband identifying him as an umpire. "All dead." He shouted as the men inside the farm scrabbled for their weapons. "Too slow, you're all dead." Carter recognised the officer as 3 Troop's CO, Gerald Mullen.

Fraser appeared from another room. Carter levelled his Webley at his old roommate's chest. "I'll accept your surrender, Andrew." He yelled above the clatter of small arms fire. Fraser pasted a rueful grin on his face and raised his hands.

"Cease fire." Carter called. "Cease fire." The order was relayed from man to man until silence returned to the farm, the explosion of a final thunder-flash punctuating the end of the short battle. From the firing of the green flare to the last shot had taken less than three minutes.

"Where have you been. We expected you hours ago." Fraser said as he crossed the room. He offered his hand for Carter to shake. Magnanimous in victory, Carter did so.

"I know, I'm rotten for keeping you waiting."

"But how did you get past the defences?"

"We came down the cliff." Carter grinned.

"But no one comes that way. It's too dangerous."

Carter laughed. "No. No one has come that way before tonight."

"You're a mad bugger, Carter."

"Maybe. But I'm the mad bugger that kicked your troop's arse."

Fraser laughed. "I'll get my revenge, one day."

"You'll have to get up earlier in the morning than this." Carter said.

Outside the building Carter's men were disarming their 'prisoners' and herding them into one of the outbuildings. Carter went outside, going from man to man, congratulating them on their efforts. "Start setting up a perimeter to defend against a counter-attack." Carter told Sgt Chalk as the latter sought him out in the darkness.

"No need for that, Steven." Martin Turner interjected. "Well done. I have to say that was quite a novel approach in more ways than one."

"Fortune favours the brave." Carter replied. Or the stupid, he didn't say out loud.

"Well, it certainly favoured you tonight. By tradition the winners of these little contests get a ride back to HQ, while the losers get to walk. So if you'd like to get your men down to the end of the track you'll find transport there waiting for you. The CO is back from London and there to be a briefing for the whole Commando at sixteen hundred, so your men are stood down until then."

"I'll let them know when I dismiss them."

* * *

Carter felt that another hour's sleep wouldn't have gone amiss, but an order to assemble with his troop couldn't be ignored. When he arrived, he found the sweet factory jammed to the rafters with the commandos. He took a moment to congratulate his men once again on their success, then led them through the door and into the HQ. There was hardly space to squeeze a lemon, let alone another thirty men, but somehow they managed to find themselves a spot on the floor where they could stand. The officers were all assembled along the wall at the far end of the room, behind a makeshift lectern. The air of anticipation could have been cut with a knife, the expectant hum of muted conversation forming an almost solid background.

The 2IC stopped Carter as he squeezed past to join the other officers of 4 Troop. "Congratulations on your operation last night." He said with solemn sincerity. "I'm going to ask you to show all the troops how to do that trick with the rope. Do you have any other ideas like that you can share?"

"I'm strictly a beginner when it comes to rock climbing." Carter said modestly. "My dad's the expert." He paused, trying to decide if he had established enough credibility to make another suggestion. Well, the 2IC had asked, so why not give him an answer? "Actually, Sir, it occurred to me while I was at Achnacarry that we always landed on beaches. They're the obvious place and the enemy would know that as well, so they'd defend them. What if we were to land in places that they wouldn't expect and so wouldn't defend? Places like the foot of cliffs. If we taught a few men how to climb properly, they could reach the top and lower ropes. Then the rest of the troop could pull themselves up after them.

They were interrupted before the 2IC could answer, by the Sergeant Major's voice cutting across the hubbub.

"Parade! Parade 'shun!"

Despite being packed in like sardines, the commandos were able to straighten up and stamp their feet into the ground in a ragged attempt to come to order.

"At ease, men." Lieutenant Colonel Vernon said, as he strode across the floor to take his place behind the lectern. He faced them, taking his time to pick out faces in the crowd. The expression on his face was neutral, not giving away anything about why he had called his command into the HQ.

Feet shuffled as some men started to become impatient. A couple of coughs rang out, but the CO wasn't going to start speaking until he was ready. He was enjoying this moment. He let the silence drag on for a few more seconds, then spoke.

"I think it is no secret that I've been visiting HQ Combined Operations for the last few days. There have probably been rumours flying around as to why that may be. Well, I can now tell you that 15 Cdo has been put on notice to carry out its first …" He got no further as the whole room erupted into one massive cheer. The whole building seemed to shake as the men stamped their feet and yelled their approval. This is what they had been waiting for. Two thirds of the commando had come straight in from Achnacarry. This would be their first operation; it was what they had volunteered for.

Vernon let the men enjoy themselves for a full minute before raising his hand in an attempt to restore silence.

"Silence!" The Sergeant Major's bellow cut across the noise. Like a ripple, from the front of the room towards the back, the men stopped shouting and cheering and fell silent once again.

"You seem happy about that." The CO quipped. The men laughed.

"As I was saying. 15 Cdo has been put on notice to carry out its first operation. For security reasons I'm not at liberty to tell you where it will take place, or when, but I can tell you that it has been designated Operation Absolom. Please do not bandy that word around the town. Although it has no meaning in itself, if someone were to hear it and put it together with some of the other activity that will be associated with the operation, it could lead to Jerry being ready for us when we strike and I'm sure we don't want that."

"We'll give 'im a good 'iding." A voice called from the anonymity of the back of the room. Others joined in, agreeing with him.

Vernon raised his hand for order again.

"I'm sure we will give him a good hiding, but it will be even better if we can catch him napping when we do it.

Now, the operation is still some weeks away, but as of now we start training for it. Each troop will follow a particular training programme aimed at improving and enhancing your skills. Later we will start to join the troops up to work together in larger groups until, eventually, we will start to work as a full commando and rehearse the operation just as it will be carried out on the day. By that time you will each know what you have to do, how you have to do it and when you have to do it," Vernon smiled. "You'll even will be able to do it backwards, blindfolded, and in your sleep."

He paused to let the men chuckle at his little joke.

"Now, once we start training the only thing we will stop for is sleep and food. If you thought Achnacarry was intense, you ain't seen nothing yet." He paused again to allow the men to chuckle at the Al Jolson reference.

"So, with that in mind, I'm granting you all a forty eight hour pass to go out and enjoy yourselves."

This brought renewed bouts of cheering. which the Sergeant Major had to use the power of his voice to quieten the men once again so that the CO could be heard.

"I know it won't give you time to go home, unless you are one of those who originates from north of the border, but it will give you time to go to Glasgow or Ayr and let off a bit of steam. However …" he let the word hang in the air, "that does not give you licence to run amok. Any man who gets into trouble with the police, however minor, will find himself RTU'd. Do I make myself clear?"

There was a loud "Yes, Sir" from the assembled throng. Carter knew the threat would do no good. Someone would get too worse for wear and end up in a police cell, he suspected. It's what soldiers did when they were let loose for a few hours. But perhaps he was pre-judging the men. They had a lot more self-discipline than the average solider.

"Right, men. Off you go and I want you back on parade, sober and ready for a speed march at oh seven hundred hours on Saturday."

"Parade! Parade ''shun." The Sergeant Major bellowed once again, as the CO marched from the room and back to his office.

As Carter left he was intercepted by the 2IC once again.

"I've just got to go and have a chat with the CO, but pop by my office in about half an hour. I'd like to hear more about that rock climbing idea of yours."

5 – Operation Absolom

Carter decided to spend his forty eight hours of freedom catching up with his correspondence. He wrote a long letter to his parents and another one to his sister, the tone of that lighter and more relaxed. He followed that up with letters to his college friends and to a couple of friends he had made during his time at the Officer Training School. The letters would have to go via Martin Turner to be checked to make sure that Carter hadn't given away any secrets, but that was an accepted fact of life during wartime. By the middle of the second day, however, Carter was starting to get bored.

He had already run ten miles that morning, but he felt restless, too much pent-up energy coursing through his body, caused by the excitement of the impending raid. It was weeks away, he knew, but it was like waiting for Christmas when he had been a child, caught up in the anticipation of the big day.

He decided that a long walk might be beneficial, perhaps taking his mind off the Op. Following the A77 southwards he found a footpath that led into a range of low hills. The fields were dotted with grazing cattle and the late autumn sunshine bathed the scene in a golden glow. He turned off the road and started to climb the gentle upward slope. Reaching a high point he turned and looked back the way he had come, glimpsing the sparkling waters of the Firth of Clyde, the bulk of the Isle of Arran dominating the horizon.

It was a fine view and one that he hadn't had much time to appreciate since his arrival, less than a week before. He doubted he would get much more time before they departed to carry out the operation. And then? Afterwards, would he ever stand here again? He pushed the thought from his mind. That's not the way commandos think, he scolded himself.

He wondered where Operation Absolom might be taking them; what sort of landscape might he encounter. The most likely destination was Norway. If they were going to raid France or the Low Countries they would be moving south so as to train on terrain similar to that which they would land on. The fact that no mention had been made of moving suggested that more rugged terrain was required, such as that found in Scotland. Well, they would find out soon enough.

"I never tire of this view." A female voice came from behind him. Some commando he was, allowing someone to get that close without him knowing it. Complacency got people killed. It said so on one of the crosses at the entrance to Achnacarry.

He turned to see an attractive young woman of his own age approaching. She was dressed in the clothes of a working farmer, a waterproof jacket hung open to reveal a thick sweater and her legs were clad in heavy tweed trousers. Her skin was wind beaten to an attractive shade of brown that matched her hair, which was held back in a pony tail and covered with a peaked cap. On her feet were wellington boots. A black and white border collie dog trailed at her heels.

"Sorry. You took me by surprise." Carter smiled. "I'm not trespassing, am I?"

"Technically, yes, but don't worry about it. It would be wrong to prevent anyone from seeing this." She swept her arm to take in the vista. She held a horn handled walking stick in her hand.

"This is your land?"

"My father's. Our family have farmed here for generations. Father's health isn't too good, so I'm pretty much running things these days. It's a tough job with so many of the men in the army."

"I thought farming was a reserved occupation."

"Yes, but the men lie about that when they go into the recruiting office to volunteer. If every man who said he worked in the sweetie factory had actually worked there, the place would have been too crowded to make a single sweet." She laughed. "I've got a couple of Land Army[1] girls, but they're townies and I spend most of my time showing them how to do things. It's often quicker to do it myself." She laughed again, a pleasant, almost musical sound. Carter was reminded that he had hardly spoken to a woman for many months, at least, not one that wasn't related to him.

She examined the insignia on his uniform. "So, you're one of those commandos that keep us awake at night with your banging and crashing."

"I'm sorry. Yes, we can be a bit noisy."

"There's a war on, so I guess we have to put up with it, but it does scare the animals."

On the night he had arrived, drinking in The Clansman, stories had been told of rapacious farmers claiming compensation for cows that weren't giving milk or hens that were laying eggs without shells. The Colonel sent the claims off to HQ South West Scotland to be dealt with, annotated with comments regarding whether or not they had been making any noise on the days or nights in question. What happened then the commandos neither knew nor cared. Carter decided not to mention his fellow officers' opinions of the local farming community.

It was pleasant standing on the hillside talking to this attractive young woman, but it was starting to get late and Mrs Bliss would be none too pleased if he wasn't back in time for his dinner. "Which is the best way to get back to town?" He asked.

"Past our farmhouse, probably. That's where I'm going, so we can walk together."

The idea wasn't entirely repulsive, so Carter followed the young woman across the fields. He tried to make small talk, but he had never been any good at it. They did manage to get into a more in-depth chat about a film they had both seen and had differing views on.

"You don't have a very strong Scottish accent." Carter observed.

"The result of an expensive boarding school education. But don't be fooled. When I need to I can swear like a Glaswegian shipyard worker in language a Sassenach like you would never understand." She had broadened her accent considerably to demonstrate her mastery of the local dialect.

At last they reached a large stone-built farmhouse standing at the corner of a yard, surrounded by outbuildings.

"I'm sorry, where are my manners." Carter blurted. "I haven't even introduced myself. I'm Steven Carter." He extended his hand to compete the formality.

"Fiona Hamilton." She replied, shaking it.

"Is that old farm up there anything to do with your family?" He pointed in the general direction of Hamilton Farm.

"It belonged to my great uncle. He died without any heirs, so it came to my father as his closest relative. We farm the land, but we never used the house, so it fell into ruin."

"That was where we were making all the noise the other night." He confessed.

"I know. The land girls spent several hours picking up your cartridge cases." She frowned.

"Are they a problem?"

"Not around the farm buildings themselves, but if they're in the fields and the animals stand on them they can get them lodged in their hooves. It can hurt them quite badly and their feet get infected. The vets bills can be astronomical."

Carter began to get the feeling that he was being told off. "I'm sorry. I'll let the Colonel know. I'm sure he wouldn't want to cause unnecessary suffering to the animals." Nor would he want relations with the local community to become strained, Carter knew.

Fiona seemed to relent a little. "Sorry for going on about it." She paused for a moment, considering something. "Would you like to come for supper tonight? If you're not busy, of course."

It was a tempting offer. Though Mrs Bliss did her best with the food she was able to get with the officers' ration cards, it was hardly gourmet standard. Fiona must have sensed what he was thinking.

"I'm able to offer a few things that aren't readily available in the shops." She had lowered her voice, sharing a confidence. "We rear a couple of pigs up in the woods where they won't be seen by the Ministry men. The ham we get from them is home cured."

That swung it for Carter. It was a long time since he'd had ham. The curing took too long, so most pork went straight to the shops. "What time shall I arrive?"

[1] Land Army – the Women's Land Army (WLA) was established during the First World War to provide labour for farms in the absence of men serving in the armed forces. Known colloquially as Land Girls, they were reactivated during World War 2. While the government handled the recruitment and postings for Land Girls, they were paid by the farmers themselves. The minimum wage was 22 shillings (about £44 p.w. at current currency values), from which up to 14 shillings could be deducted for board and lodgings. By comparison, a Private in the army was paid 14 shillings per week but didn't have to pay for food and accommodation. While the majority of Land Girls had a pleasant experience, conditions varied considerably from farm to farm and some, the author's mother included, had a less than happy time. By 1944 there were 80,000 women serving in the WLA, of which 22,000 lived in hostel accommodation rather than on the farms.

* * *

While the evening he'd spent with Fiona and her parents had been very pleasant, it had been all too brief. As he had left the farmhouse he had extracted a promise from Fiona to go to the cinema with him, then rather spoilt the invitation by warning her that it might be several weeks before he could deliver on the promise. But she had agreed and that was the main thing and it was something he could focus on during the challenge of the next day's speed march. It was the longest he had ever done in a single day, from Troon to Irvine, inland to Kilmarnock and then back to Troon; a total of twenty five miles. While he was physically fit enough for the task, the tedium of it was another matter. He allowed himself to fantasise a little about Fiona Hamilton and what the future might hold for them.

But for the future to hold anything, he must first survive Operation Absolom, which would be no simple matter.

The days started to blur into each other as the training intensified. One of their regular exercises was to board one of commando landing ships, usually the Prince Leopold, sail up the considerable length of Loch Fyne to land on the west side, close to Inveraray. They would storm ashore and run up the steep hill to Dun na Cuaiche monument, close to the Castle, before running back down to the shore again. By that time the landing craft would have withdrawn from the beach in a simulation of the tide having changed. That meant wading out to them through the freezing waters of the loch. They did that by day and by night, often not having time to dry their uniforms between assaults.

On an uninhabited island in the Hebrides a mock up of a village was created using tents and wooden packing cases, which the commandos had to assault. Local Home Guard units often provided the defending troops and on some occasions soldiers would be brought in from one of the garrisons on the mainland. The commandos would never act as defenders; their role in Operation Absolom was purely offensive. On one occasion troops from 14 Cdo made up the defenders but disputes over who had 'won' the engagement resulted in the two sides exchanging blows and it was decided that pitting commandos against each other wasn't a good idea. The inter-commando rivalries were too strong.

Great emphasis was placed on demolition training with the commandos being given the opportunity to blow up several structures that local landowners wanted rid of. Explosives were all but impossible for civilians to get hold of, even for bona fide demolition companies, so the training allowance granted to 15 Commando was put to good use.

As Lt Col Vernon had predicted, the commandos started working in ever larger formations, learning to co-ordinate their attacks with the units alongside them until they found themselves spending more time at sea than on land.

It was on the 4th December that the whole commando was paraded once again in the cramped sweet factory. The CO stood in front of them.

"The time has come, men, for you to leave Troon for the last time until Operation Absolom is concluded. Tomorrow we will board transport to take us up to Port Glasgow where we will embark upon the Prince Leopold and the Princess Beatrix. They will become your home until we return here again. There are still a couple of weeks more of training to go, but we will be doing that in locations that make it impractical for us to return here to Troon, even for a couple of days. On board you will be told the location of our objective and the date on which the operation will take place. Once you have heard that you will not be allowed to leave the Commando for any reason. That includes compassionate grounds such as family funerals."

That attracted an intake of breath from some of the men. It was an unwritten rule that a soldier would be allowed home for the funeral of a close relative if it was humanly possible for them to arrive in time. Soldiers had even been allowed out of military prison to attend a funeral. But the needs of operational security overrode even that. There was too much risk that a solider might inadvertently reveal some small detail which an enemy agent might send back to his masters in Berlin.

"If you are injured or fall sick you will be treated on board ship. You will receive incoming mail, but you won't be allowed to send any letters. While you are on board you may write letters, but these won't be posted until the ships return to port, or you can take them back and replace them with new letters if you wish."

The thought was a sombre one, writing a last letter home, letting your loved ones know that even as you were going into battle, you were thinking of them. Would such a letter be a comfort? Or would it be a reminder of the loss of the husband, fiancé, son or brother that had written it? Carter hoped that his family would never have to find out. He might not even write a letter of his own.

"Those of you who have not already done so will also be able to make your Will."

Well, that certainly lightened the mood, Carter thought. But these things were important and the men needed to know that every eventuality had been considered. Most of the men didn't have much to leave behind, but they had to be given the chance to pass it on to the right people. The army even provided blank Will forms, so the soldiers only had to fill in the details.

"Now, the officers have put money behind the bar at McNeil's."

Oh, have we? thought Carter. He chuckled inwardly. By the time the men got there the QM will have held a collection from the officers to replace whatever money had already been deposited.

"So, I suggest that you go and drink it up. Parade in your troops with full kit at oh six hundred in the morning."

* * *

HMS Prince Leopold had barely slipped her moorings and set course into the drifting fog of the Clyde when the CO summoned the officers to one of the large rooms which, in more peaceful times, had served as the First Class lounge for the fare paying passengers. Once their troops were on board the two ships the officers had been directed to sail aboard the Prince Leopold, which had been selected as the CO's floating HQ. They would be reunited with their men when the ships docked later in the day. Each officer held a notebook in his hand, ready to record the detail of what they were about to be told.

In the centre of the room stood a table, about six feet square, covered with a blanket. The officers had seen similar arrangements before. It was a scale model of their objective, to be revealed when the CO arrived. Carter felt tempted to lift one corner of the blanket and take a peek, but it probably wouldn't tell him that much. Any place names would be meaningless to him. The Sergeant Major arrived with an easel, which he quickly set up, before returning a few moments later with a blackboard which was also covered with a blanket. That would be a larger scale map, so that they could get a feeling for the general geography of the location and compare it to the finer detail of the model.

They stiffened to attention as Lt Col Vernon arrived, a wad of notes held in one hand and a long, thin wooden pointer in his other.

"As you were, gentlemen." He drawled. "No doubt you have already worked out why you are here. This will be the first time you see the target for Operation Absolom. As well as the maps and model that you see before you, we also have some aerial reconnaissance photographs that the RAF has obtained for us, at considerable risk. You should know that men have already died on this operation, just obtaining those photographs."

He paused for a moment to allow that information to sink in. "Everything you see here will be replicated on board the Princess Beatrix, so you will have access to it without having to come over to this ship every time. Each troop will be allocated plenty of time with the model, on a rota basis, so you can brief your own men."

Vernon scanned the faces of the expectant officers. "Our mission, gentlemen, is to attack the small town of Kirkesfjord in Norway." He removed the blanket and uncovered the map with a flourish, like a magician revealing his assistant fully restored. having previously been sawn in half. "This, Gentlemen, is Kirkesfjord, population approximately five hundred if you include a couple of outlying hamlets. There is a resident garrison of about fifty German soldiers."

As Carter had expected, the map showed the coast of Norway, from the Skagerrack in the south to Trondheim further north. A paper arrow pinned to the board pointed to a location about half way between the two extremities.

The men leaned forward for a closer look as the Lt Col continued, "If you have never heard of it I'm not surprised, it is not the sort of place you would have visited unless you are very keen on fish and their associated products."

He flipped the map over to reveal a second one, which was of a much smaller area of land, providing more detail.

"As you can see, it is a fjord approximately ten miles in length, which is a dead end. At the eastern end is the town of

Groening, which is the nearest significant garrison. Intelligence suggest a garrison of about a hundred troops, with no armour or artillery. The seaward end widens out, and this island here …" he pointed with the stick he had brought with him, "called Moyland, acts like the cork in a bottle. German coastal shipping will often harbour up behind the island during the day, so an artillery battery is mounted on the inland facing side of the island to provide protection against seaborne attack. There are three guns pointing north and another three pointing south. The gunners on the island number about thirty. There is also an airfield here …" he pointed again, some way inland from the fjord, "at Holmvik, which is home to a *Staffel* of Me 110 fighters. Their main purpose is to provide air cover for the convoys as they pass along this section of the coast, but we can expect to attract their attention."

He turned away from the map to face the assembled officers. "The plan is for us to join up with a flotilla of warships who will support our attack. We will also be provided with air cover from the RAF. With all three armed forces engaged, this will be the first fully fledged Combined Operations effort since the commandos were founded and we should take great pride that we have been selected as the Army element of the force." He paused again, mainly for effect.

"The ships will be the Cruiser HMS Reykjavik and four destroyers: the Orbit, the Orinoco, the Orion and the Orchid. The Reykjavik will bombard the artillery battery on the island at the same time as the RAF will carry out a bombing raid on Holmvik, hoping to close down the runway for a few hours and prevent the Luftwaffe from intervening. However, that is a slim hope. Two of the destroyers will enter the northern channel while the other two enter the southern channel, preventing any interference from any German naval vessels that aren't already inside the fjord. We won't know what is in there until we arrive, but it isn't likely to be more than a couple of armed trawlers or perhaps a couple of E-Boats and then only if they are escorting merchant vessels. The Prince Leopold and the Princess Beatrix will follow the destroyers into the fjord via the southern channel and launch their landing craft."

Vernon stepped forward and with another somewhat theatrical move, uncovered the table with another flourish, to reveal the model of the fjord. Pointing with his stick he continued the briefing.

"1 and 2 Troops will launch from the Princess Beatrix and attack the artillery battery and silence it. Prisoners will be sent back to the Princess Beatrix, while the rest of the troops return to the landing craft and join in the assault on the village of Kirkesfjord itself."

Carter could see that the village was a straggle of houses lying along the side of the fjord, with a road running behind. Alleys ran between some of the houses, leading down to the water's edge. At the western end the road was terminated by a jetty. Labels on the roofs of the little model buildings told what they were. Carter picked out the Post Office and the Town Hall as well as three larger buildings marked as fish oil factories.

"By that time Troops 3 to 6 will have landed here ..." He tapped a strip of sand paper that represented a beach, lying to the northern side of the jetty, "and will be advancing through the village. 3 Troop will take the centre, 4 Troop the left flank and 5 Troop the right. 6 Troop will act as demolition team and will blow up the three fish oil factories in the village which are here, here and here." Vernon pointed to three larger structures on the model, spaced out along the side of the fjord with a short jetty in front of each one. Houses and other buildings lay between them. "The rest of you will engage and neutralise any German troops that are in the village. There are also some known Quislings who the Norwegian government would like us to arrest and bring back, along with any Norwegians who would like to volunteer for the Free Norwegian armed forces. Each troop will be accompanied by a member of the Norwegian troop of 10 Commando, who will act as interpreters. In a couple of days we will also be joined by two troops from 16

Commando who will act as our floating reserve, to be used as I see fit. Any questions so far?"

"When do we go, Sir?" Martin Turner asked.

"We thought we would deliver Jerry a nice Christmas present, and as we all know Santa visits on Christmas Eve." This brought a laugh, easing the tension somewhat. "We will be a little earlier than is traditional." The CO continued. "The attack will start at dawn on the 24th, which in those latitudes will be oh nine hundred hours. The landing craft will hit the beaches at oh nine thirty hours precisely. Sunset is fifteen fifteen hours, but I want us to start embarking on the landing craft by thirteen thirty and be clear of the fjord by fourteen thirty. That gives us approximately four hours ashore to complete all our objectives."

"Do we know anything about the defences?" Carter asked.

"The aerial photographs show some pre-prepared positions which are probably set up for machine guns or mortars. There are two down by this jetty …" he pointed to the short structure which was to one side of their planned landing area, "and another two on the road to Groening. As you can see, the landward side of the village is a steep cliff, so there is no way the enemy can get up there to fire downwards. Neither can we, for that matter, so I don't think you'll be able to repeat your trick from Hamilton Farm, Steven." That brought a laugh from the rest of the officers.

"The soldiers are billeted on the local population, which means they are scattered about which works in our favour. When the bombardment starts the alarm will be raised, but it will take time for the garrison to assemble and take up their defensive positions. Probably not half an hour though, so be prepared for a hot reception on the landing beaches. With so many civilians in the village we can't risk a naval bombardment, so the first priority must be neutralising those machine gun pits, which will be 4 and 5 Troop's job."

He paused while the officers from the two troops noted that down.

"You mentioned air cover, Sir." Martin Turner said.

"Yes, I was just coming to that. We'll have a squadron of Beaufighters overhead and their job is to keep those Me 110s away. We'd prefer Spitfires or Hurricanes, but the range is too great. They'd run out of fuel after a couple of minutes. Even the Beaufighters will have to work in relays throughout the day so we won't have any more than a couple at a time above our heads. The Navy will give us some anti-aircraft cover though, which will help. In addition, there will be a squadron of Hampdens dropping smoke pots into the water in front of the landing craft. That will provide cover for the approach and should put the machine gunners off their aim. The landing craft will also be fitted with Lewis Guns to provide counter-fire."

The briefing continued for another hour with more questions being asked and answered until the officers could think of no more. Carter relaxed a little. The greatest fear is fear of the unknown and the briefing had put an end to that.

* * *

It was 9th December and the commandos on board the Prince Leopold had been summoned to the main lounge. Having just returned from a practice landing, 4 Troop were soaking wet and very cold, all anxious to get to their hammock spaces on the lower decks and change into some dry clothing. But the CO had been insistent, so they stood dripping and shivering. Fortunately the CO didn't keep them waiting for long.

He stood the troops at ease, his face serious. Carter wondered if the operation had been cancelled. Many had been before, some as late as the day the ships were due to sail.

The CO wasted no time with preamble. "Men, it is my sad duty to have to inform you that at dawn on 7th December, the Japanese bombed Pearl Harbour in the Hawaiian Islands. No declaration of war had been made in advance of the attack."

There was a gasp from the assembled troops. Few of them knew where Hawaii was, or even that it was part of the USA, but they knew that Japan had assembled a massive army and navy over the previous decade. They had conquered most of China and now seemed intent on expanding their empire even further.

The CO continued. "The United States of America has declared war on Japan. However, the Japanese have also crossed the border from China into Indochina. French forces are opposing them. They have also attacked our colony of Hong Kong."

Carter's thoughts went to Sgt Chalk and the other members of the Middlesex Regiment that were in the commando. Their regiment was part of the Hong Kong garrison. It was several thousand men strong, but that wouldn't be enough to keep the Japanese at bay. But worse news was to come.

"The Japanese have also landed troops on the coast of Malaya." The colonel continued.

A lump came to Carter's throat. The Huntingdons were now in Malaya and would be defending the colony. His old friends were in grave danger while he was here, playing soldiers in the North Atlantic. Why had he left them? He was such a stupid idiot.

He scolded himself. He was going to be doing his bit in a just a couple of weeks' time. It wouldn't matter where he was being shot at, in Norway or in Malaya. The danger was likely to be the same. He re-focused his attention on the CO, who was speaking again.

"Although that fighting is taking place a long way from here, it does have an impact on the war in Europe. With us facing the Japanese it is going to stretch our resources. Troops that might have been available to invade Europe and beat Germany will now be needed in the Far East. That makes our work even more vital, as we must keep the morale of the British people high in the face of this new threat."

"Will the Americans declare war on the Germans as well, Sir?" A voice called out.

"A good question. All I can say is that we don't know. The Japanese signed a treaty with Italy and Germany last year, so technically the Germans are as much an enemy of the USA as the Japanese. But, to the best of my knowledge, as yet there has been no official declaration of war against Germany. That's all I have for you at the moment. If I hear anything else I'll place bulletins on the notice boards. Now, I suggest you all go and get dried off.

The troops filed out in a sombre mood.

* * *

On 11th December the CO informed the commandos that America had declared war on Germany, an announcement that brought a cheer and lightened the mood. With America now in the war and committed to fight against the Germans, the victory was now inevitable, at least as far as the gossip on the lower decks was concerned.

The training continued relentlessly, with the two landing ships moving further north each day. Storms forced the cancellation of some exercises and delayed the two ships as the Princess Beatrix started to take in water through a split in her bow plates.; They had to put in at Stornoway to allow the ship to be repaired. The men spent these idle days either repairing and preparing their kit, or in front of the model table, going through each phase of the operation until it could be recited word perfect.

The more experienced soldiers knew that it would make no difference. The enemy would react to whatever the commandos did and their reactions would be unpredictable, so the plan was bound to change. No plan survives first contact with the enemy, as the old cliché went, but by knowing what they were supposed to do, the men could keep their minds focused on the task.

When someone asked "What do we do if the enemy does this?" the answer was always the same: "We counter it and we keep going forward."

They reached the Royal Navy anchorage at Scapa Flo in the Orkney islands where, on the night of 13th/14th October 1939, a German U Boat had sunk the battleship Royal Oak. Here they joined up with the cruiser Reykjavik, and the four destroyers, allowing the ships to practise their manoeuvres and make sure that the signals plan worked correctly.

Radio equipment was something that was still in short supply with the commandos. Lt Col Vernon was able to borrow a Type 18 radio set from the Royal Marine detachment on board the cruiser and a soldier, a former signaler, was found in 5 Troop who knew how to work the set. He found himself attached to the CO like a shadow.

Using this set the CO could communicate with the cruiser and the cruiser could communicate with the other ships and the landing craft to relay any requests that the Colonel sent through. It was a cumbersome process but when they tried it out during a mock landing they found it worked. The troops on the ground would communicate with shouts and hand signals, as they always did.

The tension mounted and the troops had to be kept busy. On the 22nd December they carried out a final landing exercise on the island of Unst in the Shetlands, before turning east towards the Norwegian coast, about 200 nautical miles away.

* * *

Almost silently the commandos lowered themselves down the scramble nets and into the landing craft, cramming themselves in between the marine plywood sides. They were still some miles offshore, but sound carried a long way at night and the clatter of a dropped rifle or a steel helmet banging against the side of the craft might be all that was needed to announce the presence of the flotilla to the enemy.

Ahead lay the reassuring bulk of the cruiser, with the four destroyers arranged in pairs on either side. From inside the landing craft the commandos couldn't see the single white light on the horizon that was being displayed on the top of the periscope of the submarine HMS TomTom, which had been sent ahead to mark the entrance to the southern channel. The distance between the cruiser and the pair of destroyers on the port side increased as they peeled off to find the entrance to the northern channel.

The flotilla slowed as they approached the channel, the cliffs starting to rise in front of them. Above the throb of the marine engines and the rush of the sea beneath them, the commandos heard the sound of aircraft engines. The bombers were heading for the airfield at Holmvik.

Carter felt his stomach start to knot. He unholstered and checked his Webley again, to make sure it was loaded. He had done it a dozen times already but he felt the need to keep his hands occupied. He could feel the press of his men against his back and to either side. In front of him he only felt the cold reflecting off of the metal ramp of the landing craft. He was the centre man in the front rank, the one who would be first to run down the ramp and put his feet on Norwegian soil. Well, the first apart from 1 and 2 troops who would be landing on Moyland twenty minutes earlier to seize the artillery battery.

Above his head Carter could make out the snowy white peaks of the cliffs which formed the flanks of the fjords. There was a lurch as the landing craft began to be lowered down the sides of the Prince Leopold. They would be suspended inches above the sea's surface until the very last moment before being launched. Carter checked his watch. The bright green dot of the sweep second hand was creeping towards the hour mark. Ten, nine …..; He stood on tip toe to look over the front of the ramp … five, four, … He turned to look at the commando nearest to him, the man's jaw clenched with either fear or concentration, possibly both … two, one.

A thunderous roar split the dawn sky as the six forward guns of HMS Reykjavik opened fire on the artillery battery. There seemed to be an interminable wait until six explosions lit up the sloping sides of the hill that formed most of the island of Moyland. If the gunners were awake, which they should have been at that hour, it wouldn't take them long to react. As the echoes faded Carter could hear the sound of more distant explosions, carried to them along the funnel of the fjord. That would be the bombs dropping on the airfield.

The cruiser fired a second time, pouring more death onto the island. No counter fire had been heard. Perhaps the gunners were in their air raid shelters, sent there when the Blenheim bombers had passed overhead.

The landing craft lurched again and there was a loud splash as it hit the water. A naval rating, perched above Carter's head, released the forward falls and then ran nimbly down the narrow walkway on the port side, back to the tiny wheel house at the rear of the craft. Carter felt vibrations beneath his feet as the Cox'n increased the revs on the single engine, powering the landing craft away from the Prince Leopold's side. The landing craft would proceed in two lines, just as they had been launched from either side of the landing ships, until they were about half a mile from the shore, when the cox'ns would bring them into line abreast, so that all the landing craft could hit the beach at the same time to release their human cargo in a single wave of armed fury.

Within the protection of the cliffs to either side, the waters of the fjord were relatively calm. They hit the occasional larger wave, which caused the landing craft to buck, but generally the ride was a smooth one, untroubling to any but those most prone to sea sickness. Carter was lucky to have good sea legs, but not all his companions was so fortunate. From further back he heard a sudden retching and then cries of disgust from those standing closest to the unfortunate and weak stomached commando.

"Silence back there!" Sgt Chalk bellowed. Carter wasn't sure why, because there could be no doubt that the enemy now knew they were there, but he refrained from commenting on the order, or the volume at which it had been delivered. The Sergeant was probably as nervous as himself and shouting orders would help him to ease the internal tension.

Time ticked by slowly for Carter. Each time he looked at his watch the minute hand hadn't seemed to have moved.

"You'll wear that out, Sir." Sgt Chalk said from behind him.

Carter tried to think of an excuse for his sudden keen interest in his watch but the only one he had was his nervousness, which he didn't want to admit in front of his men. The light was increasing as the sun started to climb above south eastern horizon. It would hardly get any higher than the surrounding hills, but it would illuminate the attacking force, allowing the enemy to anticipate their landing area.

An aircraft, one of the Blenheims, skimmed low over the peaks, smoke streaming from one engine. It seemed to give up its struggle to stay aloft and dropped out of sight. Oh nine ten hours. 1 and 2 Troops would be landing on Moyland. It was rumoured that the QM, who was leading the attack, would play the bagpipes as he went ashore. That would scare the shit out of the Germans, Carter thought.

As though to confirm his thoughts, Carter heard the distant popping of small arms fire drifting across the fjord, with the occasional louder crack of a grenade exploding. He checked his watch again, still fifteen minutes to go.

Carter wondered if all soldiers felt like he did, the first time they went into action. Were some able to dissociate themselves from the thought of being torn limb from limb? They would have to be made from sterner stuff than himself if they were. Most of the men around him would have a relative that had served during the Great War. The stories of death and destruction would be well known, filling the minds of those prone to worry. Stay calm, remember your training and find cover quickly, he reminded himself.

He felt the change of direction as the landing craft turned to move alongside the one ahead. They were now on the left flank of the attacking force, the northern end. To their right was Molly Brown's half troop with Captain Turner on board, then 3 Troop's two landing craft, those of 5 Troop and finally 6 Troop. Although they were the demolition troop they would still hit the beach alongside the others, then fall to the rear after the beachhead had been established.

An aircraft dropped out of the cloud base, flying low over the fjord heading north. From its belly an object dropped, landing in the sea with a splash. At once it started to belch a thick white smoke which billowed between the landing craft and their destination. A second aircraft repeated the manoeuvre, dropping its smoke float further north, extending the smoky barrage.

They were Hampden bombers, old aircraft, distinguishable by the narrow tadpole shape of the fuselage. A third, then a fourth, flew across in front of the line of landing craft. As Carter watched he saw the sixth turn for its bombing run. Behind it a lean, twin engined aircraft approached from the east and swung in behind the Hampden. It was an Me 110, faster and nimbler than its prey. Lights twinkled at its nose as it fired its two cannons and four machine guns.

The Hampden lurched to the left, putting it closer to the flotilla below. The bomb aimer must have been in the process of releasing the smoke pot because it flew downwards. Carter looked on in horror, anticipating where it would land; the middle of Molly Brown's landing craft.

He wasn't mistaken. The missile crashed into the centre of the craft, sending a burst of burning phosphorous up into the air and spreading more around within the tight confines of the craft. Across the water Carter could hear the sounds of screaming men. A hubbub started behind him as his own men reacted to the disaster that was unfolding only yards away.

"Silence!" Bellowed Sgt Chalk, this time with some justification. Men started to heave themselves up on the starboard gunwale, trying to see what had happened. "Get down, you stupid bastards!" He yelled again. "Do you want your fucking heads shot off by a Jerry machine gunner?"

A figure hauled itself onto the gunwale of the burning landing craft, totally enveloped in flames. The stricken soldier threw himself into the waters of the fjord and sank. The landing craft surged on too quickly to see if the man had returned to the surface, but it was unlikely. The weight of the soldier's equipment would have dragged him down to the bottom.

The neighbouring landing craft started to pull ahead of the rest of the line. Carter saw what the Cox'n was trying to do. The only way to save any of his passengers was to get them out of the inferno and the quickest way to do that was to get them to shore and drop the ramp. But there was a danger in that as well. If the craft beached without any support, the injured and panicked men would be a sitting target for any Germans close enough to open fire on them.

Carter turned to face his own men. "Pass it back to the Cox'n. Speed up and keep abreast of the other landing craft."

There was a hubbub of voices as everyone tried to pass on the message at once and Carter had to hope that it wasn't misinterpreted, Chinese Whispers style. But he felt the vibrations under his feet increase as the engine responded to the Cox'n's command.

Bullets started to buzz in the air above their heads as the enemy machine guns fired blindly through the smoke. One struck the ramp in front of Carter's face and set the metal ringing. Carter reared back instinctively, but he couldn't move far against the press of men behind him. From the rear of the boat came the answering chatter of fire from the Lewis guns as the two Royal Navy ratings fired their weapons.

Risking a quick look, Carter saw that 3 Troop's landing craft had also speeded up and were keeping pace; he wasn't able to see the remaining four craft carrying 5 and 6 troops.

"Stand by." The loudspeaker mounted in front of the wheelhouse squawked.

The order was given by the Cox'n when they were fifty feet out from the beach, so that the commandos could brace themselves. Suddenly the vibrations beneath his feet ceased as the Cox'n throttled back the engine. The landing craft would coast into the beach, rather than drive itself home. The grinding of the flat bottomed hull on the shingle threw Carter hard against the landing ramp and the shock rippled its way to the back, forcing the commandos forwards until they could regain their balance. Grabbing the top of the ramp Carter pulled himself upright and was almost wrenched off his feet as the ramp was released to fall open. This was it; this was what he had been training for.

The ramp sent a splash of water sideways then settled onto the rocky shoreline. Carter was already moving, feeling the men on either side of him surge past, screaming their battle cries. He ran directly forward, not pausing in case he was trampled by the men behind. He heard the crack of a bullet passing close, then almost immediately the bang of the weapon that had fired it. He dived for cover and came to rest at the line of small rocks that formed the landward edge of the beach. It offered a temporary sanctuary as he was below the line of fire of the enemy weapons. His men were fanning out to the left and right, just as they had been trained to do.

6 – Kirkesfjord

Carter counted to ten in his head, allowing time for his brain to catch up with his body and start to clear itself from the effects of the mad dash he had just made. He took stock of his senses. There was a hammering, coming in short, controlled bursts. The direction was in front, so it was an enemy machine gun. The bullets were passing harmlessly above the heads of him and his men, but it was also keeping their heads down and the men in cover, risking losing the momentum of the landing. He listened for a few seconds longer and sensed it coming from his right. That made it the weapons pit that was positioned to the left of the road that ended at the jetty.

Looking around him he located Sgt Chalk, who was pointing, directing the fire of a Bren gun. He wriggled his way across to him and tapped him on the arm to gain his attention.

"You hold George and How Sections[1] here and lay down covering fire. I'll take the other two sections and attack from the flank. Got it?" There shouldn't be any lack of understanding. It was the manoeuvre they had practiced over and over again, ready for this day.

The Sergeant nodded his understanding and Carter wriggled away to where the other two sections were lined up along the edge of the beach, bobbing up to fire on the enemy then ducking down again as fire was returned. There must be riflemen out there as well as the machine gun, Carter realised.

The two Corporals, Franklyn and Porter, saw him coming and crawled across to meet him half way. The German bullets could clearly be heard cracking above their heads, but the men were lower than the machine guns could be depressed because of the rocks, leaving Carter nervous but not able to be hit.

"OK, lads. I want your Bren guns out on the left flank, where they can fire at that MG without hitting us. Then we do an advance by sections. I'll be with you and Easy section, Franklyn. Fox Section will provide covering fire while we advance, then we'll do the same as you bring your men forward, Porter. Twenty yard dashes, so as not to keep the men exposed for too long. When we get close enough I'll give the order 'grenade' and every man is to throw one bomb. As soon as they've exploded, we're on our feet and charging. Any questions?"

Both men shook their heads. It was a standard military manoeuvre and one that the men would have been used to even if they hadn't been commandos. The fact that they were, just made it less likely that anyone would go to ground and refuse to advance again, which was always a danger when attacking an enemy position head on. Once one man did it, it seemed to grant a licence for others to do the same and the attack stalled.

"OK. Give the order to fix bayonets and Easy Section will advance on my whistle blast."

In the tightly packed belly of the landing craft bayonets were a hazard, so they couldn't be fitted to rifles until after landing. The men would have preferred to take their chances and they had tried it once, but a scratch across the face of one commando, close enough to an eye to risk the man being blinded, had persuaded the CO that it was a bad idea.

The two corporals slithered back to their sections and quickly told their men what to do. Carter saw the men draw the wicked spike bayonets that added another eight inches to the length of their Lee-Enfield rifles. The Bren gunners worked their way to the side, finding cover in a jumble of rocks at the far end of the beach where they could fire diagonally across the line of advance of the two sections and keep the enemy's heads down. Or so Carter hoped.

The two guns started sending out short, three round bursts of fire, which told Carter that the gunners could see their target. Chips of rock started to fly up in front of the Bren guns as the enemy retaliated.

Carter pulled his whistle from the breast pocket of his battledress blouse and blew a single long blast, then stood in a crouch and ran forwards for ten yards before dropping to the ground once more. As he hit the hard, smooth rock he realised that he hadn't drawn his Webley. He rectified that as the five remaining men of Fox section dashed past him and ran on for another ten yards. Rifle fire crackled from Easy section, providing covering fire.

As soon as the first shot rang out from Fox section he shouted "Up!", clambering to his feet as he did so and dashing forwards once again. This is where it got tricky. The enemy knew where they were and what they were trying to do. As they rose they would open fire. Only the covering fire from the two Bren guns and the men under Sgt Chalk's command would keep their heads down. Even then the Germans might fire blindly, pointing their weapons over the top of their cover and pulling the triggers in the hope of hitting something.

But not only did Carter have to run ten yards to catch up with Foxtrot section, he also had to lead Easy another ten yards further forward, leapfrogging past the other section. They would be exposed for only three or four seconds, but it was enough for well trained soldiers to aim and fire.

The sonic shock of a bullet cracked past his ear so close that he flinched. Don't let it bother you, Steven old man, he told himself. It missed you. You're still alive. It's the one you don't hear that will get you. Just keep going. Don't give in to the fear! Don't let your men see how afraid you are.

He dropped again, his body jarring against the rock, a sharper edge digging into his thigh. They must stand out like a fly on a pane of glass, he thought. But in the mad dash he had seen how far away the machine gun nest was. Two more dashes would do it. Fox section thundered past once again, but one of their number fell and lay still. There was nothing that could be done, not in the middle of an attack like this. For anyone to stop and help would mean certain death.

"Up!" he shouted again, hoping that his men continued to follow him. During their training they always did, but during training they knew that no bullets would ever strike them. Even during live firing exercises the 'enemy' made sure they fired only on the fixed lines that had been marked out in advance; designed to make sure that no one was hit accidentally. But above the pounding thud of his heart in his ears and the thumping of his boots on the ground he could make out the more ragged thrum of the boots of Easy section.

"Down!" he yelled, throwing himself onto the hard rocky surface once again. In that dash he had seen that the machine gun nest was made of sandbags, not dug into the ground. Of course it wasn't! The ground was solid rock. He pointed his revolver forward and loosed a couple of rounds. He realised that his Webley wasn't a good choice of weapon. Officers carried a hand gun so they could hold a map case or a compass in their other hand. But here he didn't need a map case or a compass. A Tommy gun or a rifle would be far more use to him than this pop gun. Too late to rectify that now, but a lesson to be learnt for future operations.

He thrust the distracting thoughts from his mind as Fox section rumbled past again, threw themselves down and started firing their rifles. The volleys were getting more ragged as some soldiers had to pause to change magazines.

This was it. This was the one. He braced himself. Not so big a dash this time, just far enough to draw level with Fox section. Ten yards perhaps, exposure for just a couple of seconds. Still his flesh cringed in anticipation of being ripped apart by a German bullet. He braced himself.

"Up!" He shouted, then almost immediately "Down!" followed by "Prepare grenades." He half rolled onto his side so that he could fumble a grenade from a loop on his webbing harness where it hung. He was leaning on his left elbow, so he used the index finger of that hand to hook through the ring of the grenade's safety pin. "Throw!" he shouted, at the same time as he pulled the grenade away from his left hand, drawing the pin out, before he pulled back his arm and then threw the missile in a high arc. As he watched he saw the safety lever spring away from the grenade and heard its tinkle as it bounced off the rock in front of him. At once he lowered his head, resting his face on the back of his hands so that any shrapnel would hit his helmet. There was a staccato clattering sound as the grenades landed, then a long pause. What was happening?

Were they all duds? No, that was imp …. The air was spilt by the bangs of the grenades going off in a ragged series. Shrapnel thrummed through the air above Carter's head and he felt a bit pluck at his back pack.

Speed was of the essence now. The enemy mustn't be given the chance to recover from the explosions.

"Charge!" He shouted at the top of his voice, simultaneously leaping to his feet. He was running on pure adrenalin now. He must make that work for him. He paused, levelled his Webley at the sandbagged position and fired it again, two rounds, then run again. The distance to the machine gun post was short, barely twenty yards. Two of Fox section were already closing on it. As Carter watched they leapt the sandbag parapet to land inside and started stabbing downwards with their bayonets. To the right Carter saw a wounded German trying to crawl away, smearing a streak of blood in his wake.

A grey clad figure seemed to rear out of the ground in front of Carter. He raised his Webley, about to fire, when his brain registered that the German's hands were raised. Carter continued his forward run and switched to a roundhouse swing, the butt of the Webley clanging against the German's helmet, knocking the man sideways. He ran on, through the defensive line and into the clear ground beyond. There was no more cover there than there had been on the stretch of ground they had just crossed, but he went down on one knee and surveyed what was in front of him. Commandos arrived on either side and threw themselves down, their weapons trained on the houses at the edge of the village, which was where the next threat lay.

"Porter, send a man back to deal with your wounded." Carter called to the men on his right. Time to deal with the things that couldn't be dealt with during the attack. For all Carter knew, Porter might have been the man that had fallen, but so long as someone obeyed, that was all that mattered. "Franklyn, two men to secure and search any prisoners."

Without waiting to be ordered, Green and O'Driscoll were on their feet and trotting back to the nearest German, the one that Carter had left dazed.

The thud of boots made Carter turn. Behind them Sgt Chalk was bringing up the other two sections, their duty of providing covering fire having been discharged. The two Bren gun teams that Carter had ordered into the rocks were also jogging forward. "Sgt Chalk, set up a defensive perimeter." Carter called as he arrived. The sections fanned out and sought whatever cover could be found.

Weapons were still being fired from the other side of the road and Carter turned to see 5 Troop pressing home their own attack on the other defensive position. He checked his watch; only eight minutes had passed since the landing craft ramp had dropped.

"Good job, Steven. I knew I could rely on you." Carter looked back over his shoulder to see Martin Turner arriving. He was accompanied by about a dozen men from the other landing craft, the one that had been struck by the smoke float.

"Molly? Is he …"

"He's fine. I left him in charge of the wounded until the medical team can come ashore. He'll catch us up later."

"How many …"

"Two dead. One likely to die, a couple that won't ever fight again. The rest are minor injuries. Could have been worse."

That was as close to despondency as a commando ever got. If a commando got his leg blown off he would probably say 'It could have been worse', Carter thought.

"OK, get your men ready to move out. Col Vernon is bringing 3 Troop forward and as soon as they get here we advance on the village."

Carter could see that 3 Troop were indeed making their way along the road, two lines of men, one on either side. Vernon himself was walking down the centre of the road, making himself an attractive target for any Germans sniper. It was a show of bravado for the benefit of his men.

Carter started to form his own men into a lengthy skirmish line between the base of the cliffs and 3 Troop's left flank. On the far side of the road 5 Troop were already strung out between the road and the edge of the fjord. Three prisoners were being led away, back to the beach and a lengthy spell in a PoW camp.

As Vernon drew level with 4 Troop he gave Carter a nod of congratulation before moving on. There would be time for fine words only when they were safely back on the landing ships. Carter gave the order to advance and his troop moved forward to keep pace. This would be the difficult part. The Germans would set up firing positions in the houses and factories that lay ahead of them and each one would have to be cleared before the commandos could move on. It was tedious but nerve-jangling work. But they couldn't afford the risk of a German being left in their rear, to pop out and shoot someone in the back. At the same time, they were under orders to minimise the damage to civilian property, which was a bit of a joke among the men. The Norwegian population still had to live in those houses after the commandos departed, they knew.

But the safety of his men was Carter's highest priority, after the achievement of their objective, of course. He would order his men to do what was necessary and hope the Norwegians understood.

[1] The phonetic alphabet in use here is that used by the British army in 1941. To confuse matters, the RAF used a different phonetic alphabet and didn't adopt the Army one until 1943. The present phonetic alphabet wasn't introduced into the British armed forces until 1956 as part of a standardisation exercise with the rest of NATO.

* * *

They had gone only a few yards before the sniper struck. A member of 3 Troop fell, writhing in agony, blood pulsing from a wound. 4 Troop went to ground, one of the Bren guns opening fire.

"Cease fire! Cease fire!" Carter bellowed. Unless the gunner had, by some chance, seen the muzzle flash of the sniper rifle or the puff of smoke after it fired, it was a waste of ammunition.

"Easy section!" Carter called to attract their attention. He pointed left, directing them to the rear of the nearest house. "Fox section!" he directed them straight ahead, where they could take cover behind the same house and fire along the main street. On the far side of the road 5 Troop were continuing forward. That made sense. The trooper that had fallen was on the left of the road, which meant that the sniper was probably firing from the right hand side. 3 Troop were crawling to that side as well, putting buildings between them and the enemy.

But that meant that the remaining members of 4 Troop were probably at risk. The two sections that he had sent forward hadn't caused the sniper to fire, which meant that they had already been shielded by the first house on the left. Some of the remaining sections may also be screened, but others weren't and there was no way of knowing how many of each. But he had to get them out of there. "Go left." He shouted, getting to his feet and pointing. As they rose and ran towards the house, one of them ran in front of Carter. There was the bang of the sniper rifle and the man stumbled and fell back into Carter's arms. Without thinking Carter grabbed hold of the man's webbing and dragged him along with him. The man had stopped a bullet meant for him; he didn't even know who it was yet.

The weight of the casualty slowed Carter down, but willing hands took the injured man and laid him gently on the ground. Carter saw that it was Thompson, one of the men from his training troop at Achnacarry. His breathing was laboured. There was only a small hole in the side of his battledress blouse, just below his armpit. No sign of an exit wound, so the bullet was still in there. One of the men ripped the injured man's battledress blouse open and tore his shirt before applying a field dressing to the wound. They would have to deal with the sniper before they could risk evacuating him to the beach for the attention of the Navy medics.

Carter made his way to the corner where a trooper was taking a careful look to see if he could identify the sniper's location.

"Anything, Vardy?"

"I think I got his muzzle flash. Third house along on the right, bottom left window."

"Let me take a look." Vardy slid backwards and Carter took the vacant space. He dropped to the ground and moved far enough so that one eye could take in the house that Vardy had indicated. There was the window, in total darkness. The southerly sun meant that no light could reach inside. A sniper could certainly sit back in the gloom and wait for a target to appear. Carter wasn't going to risk a man's life by presenting a target; but he could risk his own.

"Keep an eye on that window, Vardy. I'm going to cross the street."

Vardy's eyes widened, but he didn't say anything. If his officer wanted to get himself killed, that wasn't Vardy's problem.

Carter got to his knees, as though he was about to start a sprint race. But he couldn't run fast, that would defeat the object. Instead he went forward in a loping crouch, fast enough for it to seem like he was really trying to cross the street, but slowly enough to make himself a target. After three paces he threw himself forward and down. The timing had been perfect. There was a crack as the sniper's bullet flew above him, followed by the bang of the sniper's rifle being fired. Carter jumped up and sprinted back into cover while the sniper jacked another round into the barrel of his rifle, a second bullet hastening him on his way.

"Got him!" Vardy said. "Just where I said."

Carter turned and looked for the nearest Bren gun team. There, four men back, standing chatting as though they hadn't a care in the world.

"You two! Over here." Carter commanded.

They trotted up, taking care not to expose themselves.

"OK, target third house down on the right. Bottom left window. Take a quick look."

The gunner did as he was told, sticking his head out a fraction then withdrawing it. A splinter flew from the wooden wall of the house as the sniper tried to hit the briefly presented target.

"Got it, Sir."

"Don't call me Sir in the middle of an Op." Carter growled, but not too harshly. There were some habits that were hard to break. "Right, get down on your bellies and when I give the command, give that window a couple of magazines."

"Right, Si … er, right."

Carter sprinted to the rear corner of the house and found Franklyn and his men sheltering in the garden at the back. He briefed him on what was to happen. "As soon as the Bren opens up, I want you and your men to get down the back of these houses as quickly as possible and get yourself opposite the sniper's house. When the Bren gun stops firing for the second time, cross the road. The sniper won't be able to see you from his angle. Throw a grenade in through the window, then go in after it. Signal when he's no longer a threat." Carter wondered why he had used the euphemism. There was no way the sniper would end up in any condition other than dead.

Carter trotted back to the Bren team, who were already lying prone. They needed only to shuffle forward a couple of inches to be able to fire.

"OK, fire now."

The gunner dragged himself forward on his elbows then pushed his gun forward on its bipod legs. Lowering his eye to the rear sight the gunner made a tiny adjustment to his position then squeezed the trigger. Carter risked a look. Splinters were flying from the frame around the window, but some of the bullets would be entering the room, keeping the sniper from firing again. He might even be dead already, but that would have to be a lucky shot.

The gun fell silent and Carter heard the click and clatter of the empty magazine being removed and a full one being inserted by the gun's loader. The gunner wrenched back on the cocking handle and started firing again. The gun's thirty rounds were soon gone and the gun fell silent.

"Reload, but hold your fire." Carter snapped. He heard the sounds of his order being carried out. Ahead of him he saw Franklyn and the other six men of his section crossing the road and flattening themselves against the front wall of the house. Carter cursed. They were exposed to any weapon that might be fired along the street from deeper within the village.

Franklyn's arm went back and then forward. Lobbing the grenade through the window without exposing himself to anyone inside. It was quite possible that the sniper had a spotter with him and he would be armed with something like an MP40 Schmeisser sub machine pistol.

The grenade went off with a loud crack, shredding the room's curtains and wafting them out through the windows to flap around. Franklyn's Bren gunner stepped forward, firing his gun from the hip to empty it into the room, hosing down the walls and ceiling. There were no shots in reply.

When the Bren fell silent Franklyn clambered over the window sill and into the room. He appeared a moment later, waving Carter forward. There was an instinctive surge from the men behind him, but Carter called them to a halt. "Not so fast. We still have the three houses on this side of the road to clear." He pointed to the three between themselves and the sniper's position. On the far side of the road 5 Troop were already working their way through the second house. Given a few more minutes they would have come across the sniper for themselves.

Two firefights and two casualties from his troop so far. Could have been worse. He waved a section of men forward into the main street and they kicked in the door of the first house.

* * *

How Section moved on to the next house, but before their Corporal could use his size nine key, the door swung open and a wizened old man shuffled out in his carpet slippers, his hands held above his head. Corporal Mills stepped back, lowering his rifle to a safe position. The old man placed one finger to his lips and pointed upwards with his other hand. The Corporal nodded his understanding.

Silently he detailed two men to stand guard at the front and sent two more to the rear of the house, while he led his other two men through the open door.

A boom echoed across the fjord, causing Carter to turn to identify the source. Sitting out in the middle of the channel he saw smoke drifting away from the muzzles of the forward guns on one of the destroyers. It had fired eastwards, towards the town of Groening. Part of the plan. Artillery fire would crater the road between the town and the village, preventing reinforcements from being sent. It also meant that movement had been seen on the road. Two birds, one stone.

As he watched the destroyer's forward guns fire again, he saw a flotilla of four landing craft chug by between the ship and the shore. The floating reserve was being committed. Another part of the plan. They would land at the far end of the village and seize the defensive positions there in the hope that with the commandos both in front and behind, the enemy might see sense and surrender.

There was a clatter of boots behind him and Carter saw a bareheaded German prisoner being forced out of the house at bayonet point, his hands folded on his head.

"Found him up in the front bedroom, priming 'potato mashers'." The Corporal reported.

"OK. There should be a prisoner handling point set up near the first house by now. Get him back there then come back and continue the 'house to house'." Prisoner handling was another task assigned to 6 Troop, who wouldn't need all of their men to blow up the factories. Carter breathed a sigh of relief. If the prisoner had started lobbing the Model 24 *Steilhandgrenaten* out of the bedroom window it could have created carnage amongst his men.

Carter gave the German a dismissive glance, then looked again. There was something different about him.

"Wait." He ordered the Corporal, stepping forward to take a closer look. He pulled back the collar of the German's Greatcoat and gasped at what he saw. What the hell was he doing here?

"Corporal Mills I need one of your men to carry a message to Col Vernon."

Mills called forward one of his troopers while Carter scribbled a note in his pad then tore out the page, folded it and handed it to the man.

"The Colonel is with 3 Troop, they're just across the road." With the centre of the street being so dangerous, Vernon had pushed his men to the right, in amongst the houses on that side of the road, while 5 Troop were now working their way along the thin strip of land between the rear of the buildings and the edge of the fjord.

The trooper crossed the road in a crouching run, slipping between the two closest buildings in search of the CO.

"Anyone seen Capt Turner?" Carter asked the world in general.

"He's a couple of houses down, I think." One of the men called back.

"OK, Mills, get that Jerry back to the prisoner handling point. The rest of you carry on with the house-to-house." Carter turned back to run down the side of the house and then into the rear garden. Two more troopers were escorting German prisoners to the rear, using the houses as cover. Carter jogged forward, crouching and sprinting as he crossed the gaps between the houses. He found a knot of men huddling in the shelter of one of them. At the street end he saw the lanky frame of the Troop Commander, directing fire at an unseen target.

"Martin!" Carter called, attracting his attention.

"Oh, hello Steven. A bit busy here right now."

"Yes, sorry about this." He apologised. He was struck by the ludicrousness of them carrying on a conversation more suited to a busy bank branch. "But I thought you should know. We've got SS in the village."

That caught Turner's attention. "You're sure?"

"He was wearing *feldgrau*, but the SS wear that as well these days. But I saw his collar badges with my own eyes. He was a *Sturmann*." It was a rank roughly equivalent to a Lance Corporal.

"Any idea if there are any more?"

"No, but it's unlikely that he was here visiting relatives."

"OK, well, thanks for letting me know. You've told the Boss?"

"Yes, I sent a runner."

"Good man. Now, if you don't mind, I have another sniper to deal with. He just took down Tpr Griffiths"

"Anything I can do?"

"I don't know. He's up in the church tower. Take a look for yourself."

Carter edged towards the corner of the house and peered round. The church was about a hundred yards away along the main street, just past one of the big factory buildings. Carter could see a cluster of commandos laying demolition charges along the nearer side of it, in readiness for its destruction.

The church was of typical Nordic style, a white painted wooden building with pointed arched windows along its side. The door was at the front, nearest to the street and above it, on the roof, there was a stubby bell tower supporting a short steeple topped by a weather vane. It looked as though the bell had been removed, but it was hard to see because of the all the sandbags that had been stacked around it. The sniper was using loop holes between the bags to fire without risking himself being exposed. It must have been a pre-prepared position because there was no way the Germans would have had time to lug the sandbags up to the tower that morning. But from above, the sandbags wouldn't have been visible in the aerial reconnaissance photographs that Carter had studied.

"Looks like the best way of getting at him is through the inside of the church." Carter said. "Up the stairs and take him from below. If you can lay on some covering fire, I reckon I can make it."

"It's a big risk, Steven. If he sees you he'll know what you're doing and he'll target you."

"The closer I get the harder it will be for him. He can't lean out to shoot downwards without exposing his whole body. The worst that can happen is that he'll try to escape. I'm guessing he'll have a bolt hole out the back, to stop himself being trapped in there."

"You should take a couple of men with you."

"No. I think it's safer on my own. He might not see me, but he'd hardly fail to spot a gang of us."

Turner thought about it for a moment. "It's mad, but that's what you do, isn't it Steven, mad things?"

"I do seem to have a reputation for it."

Turner laughed, an incongruous sound in the middle of all the small arms fire and the whip crack of exploding grenades. "Very well. I'll get Bren gun teams working on the tower while you make your way around. Which way will you go?"

"Down the back of the houses until I get level with the church, then straight across. He'll lose his firing angle on me within a few yards, so I won't be exposed for long. Besides, he's aiming down this way. He'd have to turn through ninety degrees even to see me."

"He may have a spotter with him." It was normal practice for a sniper to have a second man with him to identify potential targets, using binoculars as a substitute for the sniper's high-powered telescopic sight.

"But he's probably looking this way as well. They think they have us pinned down." Looking at the cluster of troopers behind the house, Carter knew that they were pinned down. Forty or so men being halted by a single man in a well-prepared position, armed only with a bolt action rifle. Something had to be done before the Germans spotted the weakness and exploited it with a counter attack.

"OK, Steven. I'll give you five minutes of cover fire, then we'll cease firing to allow you to cross the road. But be careful. The houses between us and the church haven't been cleared yet."

"Thank you. I won't go in through the front door. It's probably barricaded anyway. I'll go down between the church and the factory and try to find a back way in, or I'll go in through a window."

"OK, synchronise watches."

That had already been done before they boarded the landing craft, but there was no harm in doing it again. "We cease firing at ten thirty five precisely." Turner stated.

"Got it. Wish me luck." Carter didn't give his Troop Commander time to say anything more, as he jogged away to the rear corner of the house.

* * *

Carter dodged from cover to cover along the backs of the houses. It wasn't just the sniper he had to think about, he reminded himself. Any of these buildings could be harbouring German defenders and he was armed only with his Webley. Too late he realised that he should have borrowed a Thompson gun. Well, he wasn't going back now. But if there were any Germans in the houses they were concentrating on the street side, not on the rear, so he made the short journey unscathed.

He came to a halt when he spied the church on the other side of the main street. From this side on view he could see the long barrel of the sniper's rifle protruding between the sand bagged defence of the bell tower. He saw the puff of smoke that announced another shot, but the sound was drowned out by the other noises of the battle that was ranging, not least that of the destroyer's guns as it continued to rain artillery shells on the road connecting Kirkesfjord to the larger town of Groening, or maybe on enemy shipping.

Carter checked his watch. Ten thirty four. A minute to go. Splinters flew from the structure of the bell tower as the Bren gunners maintained their fire. Sand trickled down the front of the building as a sandbag was holed.

The second hand crawled around the dial of Carter's watch. As it approached the ten he braced himself, flexing the big muscles in his legs that would drive him across the road. A knot of fear grew in his throat and his skin crawled in anticipation of the bullet that might end his life. As the hand of his watch hit the twelve, Carter launched himself across the road, the pounding of his heart drowning out the thud of his boots until he was able to flatten himself against the front of the church. Rifle fire from further along the street tried to pick him out, but the church's tiny porch offered some protection. But it served as a warning and he hurried to get around the corner. There was a twenty yard wide gap between the church and the fish oil factory that was its neighbour. Carter could hear shouts of command within the factory. English voices, probably laying more demolition charges. He'd better hurry. The rear of the church might offer some way in to the building, so he eased himself along the side, ducking his head below the level of the windows in case there were more Germans inside.

That was a point. What if there were more defenders inside? The six rounds in his Webley wouldn't last long against a determined defence. He fingered his one remaining grenade, hanging from his webbing harness. That should even up the odds a little. Was it sacrilegious to throw a grenade into a church, his over active mind wondered? Surely it must be. Well, he wasn't too sure he had a mortal soul to endanger, so it was an issue he would have to defer until he had time to consult the padre who, at that moment, would be back on the beach giving comfort to the wounded.

Carter froze as a figure came around the corner of the church. The German saw Carter at the same time as Carter saw him. The race started. The German's rifle swung towards Carter as the commando raised his hand to fire. The range was close, barely six feet, neither of them could miss.

Carter won by a fraction of a second. As the German's finger whitened on the trigger of his rifle, Carter's Webley spat once, then again. The German managed to fire his weapon and Carter felt the snap of air past his check and the crack of the supersonic sound it made, simultaneous to the bang of the weapon. But it was too late for the German, who collapsed in a heap, dead before he hit the ground.

Carter released the breath he had been holding and gulped in fresh supplies. Close. He felt his hand shaking. He'd just killed a man, snuffed out his life in an instance. It was the first he knew he had killed personally. The others, back towards the beach, any of his men might have killed, but this had been him. The fact that the German would have done the same to him didn't seem to matter. He had killed a man. How did he feel about that?

He felt that if he didn't do something quick, the next German might kill him. Snap out of it, Carter, he told himself. Time for philosophising later. Right now you've got a job to do. You're a soldier, a commando. It's what we do. He took another deep breath while he struggled to get control of his nerves.

Calmer now, he crossed the gap to the shadow of the factory where some abandoned oil drums lay rusting. They would provide some cover. He surveyed the bell tower as he used the respite to replace the two spent cartridges in his revolver. Splinters flew again as the Bren guns resumed their fire. Was the sniper still up there, or was he even now making his escape? The answer came in the form of another puff of smoke.

There was no sign of any more Germans behind the church, from where the dead man had appeared. OK, now was the time. Carter emerged at a crouch. It was probably what saved him as the world exploded behind him and he was lifted and thrown around like a rag doll. Before being dropped unceremoniously onto the ground.

6 Troop had blown up the first of the fish oil factories.

* * *

He coughed the dust from his throat and blinked several times as his vision began to clear. He could feel himself pinned down by rubble, but it wasn't crushing him. He moved his arm and something slid off, giving him more freedom. A kick of his leg produced the same result. Gradually he was able to release himself from the pile of broken planks and other loose debris. He scraped dust and splinters from his face, feeling the wetness of his own blood as he did so. Not much, probably no more than scratches. His head hurt. Probing gently, he found the seat of the pain; an egg sized lump on the side of his head. That must have been where he hit the ground.

Now that he knew why he was hurting, he had to work out what had caused the hurt. Smoke tickled his nostrils and his rapidly returning hearing recorded the roar and crackle of flames. It was quite close by, he guessed, because he could feel the heat.

There was a rapid popping sound. Ammunition cooking off. He ducked. It wasn't aimed at him, but exploding ammunition went in all directions. It would be a shame to die from a random bullet. How did he know it was ammunition? How did he know what exploding bullets sounded like?

He struggled to sit upright, the pain in his head protesting. To one side he saw the soup bowl shape of his steel helmet. He dragged it towards him and jammed it back on his head, wincing as it pressed hard against the tender lump. He felt nauseated and had to wait for the feeling to pass. Looking around him he tried to work out where he was.

There were several buildings on fire and others damaged by blast and gunshots. A few yards away a dead German lay, also half covered by debris, blood seeping from two small holes in his *feldgrau* greatcoat. A tug at his own neck made him look down at his chest. It was a lanyard. He followed it to its end and saw the standard issue Webley revolver lying beside him. He picked it up and checked the load. Two bullets fired. What's the betting that the diameter of the wounds in the German's coat matched the point four five five calibre of his weapon. He pushed the revolver back into the holster at his waist.

But that didn't solve the mystery of how he had got here, or even where 'here' was. He scanned the length of the single street, flanked on either side by houses and other buildings. At the end it finished abruptly at a stone jetty. Beyond the jetty lay the expanse of a fjord.

'Fjord'. That was a Norwegian word. Why had he used it? Because he was in Norway, he concluded. Once triggered, the memories flooded back. Operation Absolom, Kirkesfjord, Norway.

That made it Christmas Eve. They'd been sent to give Jerry a Christmas gift; one he wouldn't enjoy.

The whoop-whoop of a naval vessel's siren broke the silence, sounding a farewell and echoing across the expanse of water, sending the sea birds aloft, screeching in protest. He craned his neck and saw the stern of a destroyer disappearing around a bend in the steep cliffs. That would be HMS Orbit. She had been detailed as rear-guard for the flotilla of landing craft that had brought them there and would also take them back to the mother ship, HMS Prince Leopold. Too late for him to jump up and try to attract their attention, even if his aching head had allowed it.

So that was the where; now for the what. A German sniper. That was it. He had just taken out young Private Griffiths. Good chap Griffiths; handy in the boxing ring. Great shame. That was it. He'd seen the sniper's position and directed fire onto it as he sneaked down the side of a fish oil factory to find a back way into the church where the sniper had set up shop.

There it was, just a few yards away, the white painted wooden building with a red roof. Every window had been broken by the blast that had sent Carter flying and covered him in debris.

He'd been close to one of the fish oil factories, the reason they'd been sent there. The fish oil factories that the demolition teams had been tasked with blowing up. He must have been too close. Damned lucky to be alive.

He looked up to the front of the building, towards the sniper's position in the stubby bell tower. The bell tower was no more, just a ragged wooden stump and the remnants of the sandbags that had protected the sniper, sand dribbling down the wooden tiles of the roof. The blast from the demolition couldn't have done that. It must have been artillery fire, directed from the destroyer that had stood out in the fjord. A bit over the top, in his opinion. He'd have got the sniper if … But he hadn't and someone had taken the decision to use a sledge hammer to crack a nut rather than risk another man.

How long had he been out cold? He checked his watch, noting the cracked glass, but the second hand was still sweeping steadily around the dial; fourteen thirty hours, give or take a couple of minutes. Dusk starting to creep in at these northern latitudes. They'd been scheduled to start re-embarking on the landing craft at thirteen thirty. The disappearing destroyer suggested they'd been bang on time.

The only sounds he could hear were the crackling flames and the odd rumble of collapsing walls as the fires did their work. He looked around again. The Germans would be back, those that had fled rather than face the commandos. With them would come reinforcements and they would search the town, seeking out stragglers. Seeking out him. He couldn't afford to sit around here feeling sorry for himself.

The German's rifle lay close to his body. He stood up and crossed the few feet to pick it up. He worked the bolt action of the Mauser Gewehr 24, ejecting a spent cartridge and ramming another home from the five round magazine. It was a good rifle, reliable and had been in service with the Wehrmacht since they had seized hundreds of thousands of them when they invaded Czechoslovakia, but this one seemed new, so was probably of German manufacture. He rooted around in the dead German's ammunition pouches and found several blocks of bullets, the rims at the bottom of the cartridge cases held on metal strips, five rounds to a strip. He pushed them into his own pouches above his spare Webley ammunition.

The German didn't seem to have any grenades on him, which was a pity. Maybe he would find more dead Germans. There was no doubt about it, really. The commandos were good shots, spending twice as much time practicing on the rifle ranges as regular infantry.

He stood stock still, listening. A sound had come from behind him. What was it? He tried to identify it. Even with the continuing noise from the burning buildings he could recognise the creaking of a hinge.

He dived right, his head protesting at the sudden movement. His helmet flew off once again. He must remember to tighten the chin strap, he scolded himself, even as he crawled on knees and elbows to find some cover. He pushed the rifle ahead of him and pressed the butt into his shoulder, then carefully raised his head, seeking out the source of the noise.

There, slightly right of his eyeline. A head appeared, projecting through a trapdoor, next to a house, two down from where he had woken up. No uniform, no helmet and no visible sign of a weapon. Must be a local; a civilian.

But the commando didn't relax. He couldn't be sure. Through the aperture of the rear sight he lined up the blade of the foresight on his target, dead centre of the figure's chest. The man climbed higher, exposing his body, holding his arms above his head. He waved one of them, calling the commando officer forward.

Steven Carter checked both sides of himself to make sure that he wasn't being lured into a trap. He craned his head around to check his six o'clock. No sign of any enemy behind him. Cautiously he rose to his feet and approached the man.

The man continued to beckon, his arm waving frantically, trying to get Carter to hurry.

"Down here." The man said in heavily accented English. "Hide, before Germans come."

No point in looking a gift horse in the mouth, Carter decided. He descended a ladder into the cellar of the house that loomed above him. The man followed him, dropping the trapdoor into place as soon as his head was below the height of the low ceiling.

The cellar was lit only by a single oil lamp, the warm glow from which illuminated the faces of the other occupants of the room.

"My wife, Helga." He indicated an attractive woman standing in the middle of the room, her hands folded protectively around the shoulders of two small, blond haired boys. "My boys, Eirik and Nils." He added. "My name is Olav." He extended his hand to allow Steven to shake it.

Steven introduced himself. "I'm Lieutenant Steven Carter. Call me Steven, please. We seem to have made a bit of a mess of your town."

The man shrugged, as though it was of no account. "You kill Germans. That is all we ask."

"We destroyed your factories." Carter was having difficulty understanding how the man was so forgiving for the carnage that had come storming out of the sea to destroy his home.

"The Germans need fish oil. They will re-build them. Meanwhile, we have boats and nets. We can fish. We will not starve."

"Am I the only British soldier you found?"

"The only one we have seen. But only because we heard you moaning."

"I was moaning?"

"Oh yes, for several minutes. We didn't go to help because we thought you might be a German. Then I saw you sit up."

"You were very brave. I could have shot you."

Olav shrugged again. "But you did not."

The woman turned and gently ushered her two sons up a flight of stairs to the upper level of the house. "We were hiding down here when you were fighting, it is safer. Better you stay down here, in case you are seen through windows. My wife will fix food for you."

"Hang on, I can probably contribute." He undid the heavy buckle of his webbing belt and shrugged his way out of his harness so that he could reach his pack and open it up to search inside. They had all been issued with a day's rations, which had remained untouched. He took out a tin of bully beef and a small packet of tea leaves, offering them to the woman. She took them from him with a smile, before following the boys up the stairs.

"You are commandos." It wasn't a question, it was a statement of fact, announced clearly on the shoulder of Carter's battledress blouse. "We have heard of you. You have raided other places in Norway."

"Yes, the Lofoten Islands and Floss. I'm surprised you have heard. The Germans don't broadcast news of what we do, do they?"

"We listen to the BBC; in secret of course. King Hackon broadcasts to us and encourages us to resist the Germans. There isn't much we can do, but I can help you."

"If the Germans find me in your house they'll probably shoot you."

"I know. Tonight we'll get you out of the village. I have a small boat. We'll cross the fjord to the other side. There is a place you can hide until I can contact the Osvald Group, the resistance. They're communists, but they are fighting the Germans so we co-operate with them. They can put you in touch with people who may be able to get you home. If not, they will get you to Sweden."

There was a hissing sound, like steam escaping and they turned to see what it was. The woman, Helga, was standing at the top of the stairs, waving her husband towards her.

"*Hva er det?*" he asked.

"*Det er en annen soldat utlenfor.*" She replied.

"My wife says that there is another soldier outside. I'll go upstairs and take a look." He moved quickly, gently easing his wife to one side so that he could get past her. He was back a few moments later.

"It is getting dark, so he is hard to see, but I think he may be one of yours. Can you take a look?" He gestured to the trap door at the top of its short ladder.

There was no room to use the long German rifle, so Carter drew his Webley and climbed the ladder, holding on with one hand. He used his helmeted head to nudge the trapdoor open a few inches, a shot of pain reminding him that he still had an egg sized bump. He could see the soldier, hunched over, creeping carefully along the side of the road, trying to stay in the deeper shadows, but he was being defeated by the flickering glow of the flames. The gathering dusk wasn't quite complete, but it was dark enough to hide everything but his general shape and the occasional glimpse of skin turned orange by the fire's glow.

The shape of the helmet was right, the inverted soup bowl shape easy to distinguish from the German type. He was holding a rifle at the high port, angled upwards across his body. But there wasn't enough light to pick out any other detail. The figure edged forwards again, coming a few yards closer.

Carter climbed one more rung of the ladder, so that his body was clear and his arm able to aim the Webley, with the trapdoor resting against his back and shoulders.

"Halt! He hissed. The figure obeyed, turning slightly towards him, but keeping the rifle pointed safely skywards. "Witchcraft." He hissed again, issuing the challenge word for the day.

"Cauldron" came the muted reply.

"OK. Come here and get inside." Carter ordered. He slid back down the ladder and backed across the cellar a few paces. As the soldier started to descend backwards, he kept the Webley pointed at him, just in case it was a German ruse. Just because the reply had been correct it didn't mean that a commando couldn't have been forced to give up his uniform and provide the password for the day. Under duress, of course. It was a scenario they had played out at Achnacarry.

The soldier reached the bottom and turned.

"Trooper Green! What the fuck are you doing here?" Carter snapped, recognising the man.

"Lieutenant Carter, I was looking for you. Aren't you just the sight for sore eyes." He beamed.

7 – Holmvik

"Well, technically, Sir, I think I may be absent without leave." Tpr Green replied to his rather astonished officer, a grin plastered on his face. "I came looking for you."

Helga came down the internal stairs carrying a tray on which sat two steaming bowls of soup. It smelt delicious and was far more enticing than the bully beef Carter had been expecting.

"This is our hostess, Helga. And, of course, her husband Olav." Carter made the introductions. "Olav speaks very good English." This raised a smile from the Norwegian, "But I'm afraid Helga doesn't. Now, you'd better tell me the story of how you got here, from the start."

"Well, the last time I saw you was when we assaulted those Jerry positions just beyond the landing beaches. Paddy O'Driscoll and myself took a couple of prisoners back to the beach, then we went forward again, looking for the Troop. We came under a bit of fire, which slowed us down and we had to work our way around the backs of the houses. When we found the Troop they were doing house clearances, so we joined in with our section and just got on with it. Eventually we cleared the village and the factories had been blown up, so we were all recalled to the landing craft, ready to go back to the Leopold. That was when I noticed you weren't there.

I asked around the lads, but no one seemed to know where you were, so I reported you missing to Sgt Chalk and he told the Captain. The Captain came across and told me he thought you were dead, killed when the first factory was blown up. Just a stupid accident, he said. Well, I said to Paddy that I didn't think you were dead. They don't call you 'Lucky Carter' for nothing."

"I didn't know they called me that at all." Carter interjected, not sure if he liked the nickname or not. It was the first time he had heard it attached to himself. He decided he could live with it. He'd heard of officers being given far worse nicknames than that.

"Oh yes, ever since Hamilton Farm. Everyone thinks you got lucky that night. So many things could have gone wrong. Anyway, long story short, me and Paddy were just having a chat about what we should do when Molly Brown … begging your pardon, Lt Brown, told us to get on our landing craft. But I told Paddy I was going to find you and so I legged it. Next thing I know, there you are, popping up out of the ground like a bleedin' rabbit."

"How were things on the beach? Were there many casualties?"

"I heard two officers were killed and fifteen of the lads, then there were the ones on the landing craft that got hit. There were more wounded. The snipers took a heavy toll."

"House to house work is always dangerous. And there were SS in the village as well, that we didn't know about." Carter turned to Olav. "When did the SS arrive?"

"Two days ago. They were sent here to spend Christmas. They just turned up and started issuing orders. We were to cook them a big Christmas Dinner and provide them with alcohol. They said they wanted women, too. If they wouldn't co-operate voluntarily they would take what they wanted. Our wives and daughters were very frightened. We complained to the senior Wehrmacht officer of course, the garrison commander, but he just said that if we knew what was good for us we would do as we were told. I think he was afraid of the SS as well. Your coming here saved us from the SS."

"Anyway, Green, how did you plan on getting away once the landing craft had gone, regardless of whether or not you found me?"

"I hadn't thought that far ahead, Sir. All I knew was that if you were wounded, not dead, then I wasn't going to leave you for the Germans."

"Well, I'm alright. You shouldn't have come back."

"That lump on your head and the blood on your face and hands says you're not alright and whether I should of come back is a moot point right now, beggin' your pardon, Sir. So how come you speak such good English then, Olav?" Green asked, changing the subject and spooning hot soup into his mouth to prevent himself from having to answer more questions.

"I work for eight years before the war on your Cunard ships. I start in the galley where one of the cooks is Norwegian. He got me the job. But I see that the First Class stewards make lots of money in tips, but they all speak English. So I learn English and I spent two years as steward in First Class. But then the war came, so I came back to look after my family."

Helga was back at the top of the stairs, gesticulating to her husband again.

"Det er lastebiler som kommer. Tyske soldater, tror jeg." She said.

"She says that she can hear trucks. She thinks it is German soldiers." Olav translated.

"Turn the lamp down." Carter instructed, before setting his bowl aside and climbing the ladder. Once the cellar was in darkness he lifted the trap door a fraction and peered out into the night. Flickering flames still provided a little illumination, but not much. He could hear the noise of the lorries, they seemed to have stopped at the far end of the village, the end closest to Groening. Probably setting up new defensive positions for the night. But more significantly he heard the squeal of tank tracks and the throaty roar of a heavy diesel engine that was getting closer.

The Germans weren't known to have any armour in the area. But then again, the SS weren't supposed to be there, either.

The tank crunched over debris, but nothing could drown out the rumble and squeal of its tracks. Against the skyline Carter could make out its silhouette. It was the right size and shape to be a Panzer III, but its type wasn't really important. It was armour and therefore immune to just about anything that he and Green could do against it. Behind the tank, soldiers followed in files on either side of the road. Their rifles were unslung and they seemed alert. Did they think that the commandos were still there? Well, technically they were, in the form of himself and Tpr Green, but the Germans wouldn't know that.

Probably just a precaution; closing the stable doors after the horse had bolted. What was important was that they weren't making any attempt to search the buildings, at least, not yet.

"I think they're just securing the town for the moment." Carter reported.

"Will they search?"

"I don't think so, not yet. They'll be worried about booby traps."

"What are 'booby traps'?" Olav asked, puzzled.

"It's a trap that stupid soldiers blunder into if they aren't careful. They pull open a door and there's a grenade lodged in it, for example. When the door is opened the safety clip flies off and the grenade explodes and kills the soldier."

A look of alarm spread over the Norwegian's face as he considered the implications for his children. "Are there any traps like that?"

Carter gave what he hoped was a reassuring look. "No. There would be too much risk to your people to leave traps like that, so we didn't set any. But the Germans wouldn't have been so fussy, so they'll assume that we did lay traps. I don't think they'll start searching until the morning."

"In that case I will get you out tonight, as planned. The soldiers will make it more difficult, but it can still be done."

"Good man. We don't want to put you in any danger by staying here."

* * *

They waited until after midnight, Green and Carter taking it in turns to sit at the top of the ladder, the trapdoor propped open a fraction to allow them to hear any sounds of approaching soldiers. But after the tank had reached the jetty, silence reigned once again. Sentries would have been posted and would be changed every two hours, but the rest of the reinforcements would be trying their hardest to get some sleep. The whole force wouldn't be roused until about an hour before dawn, when the order to 'stand to' would be given, calling on the Germans to be ready for an attack that wasn't coming.

Olav came down the stairs from the house, his wife remaining at the top, wringing her hand with worry. He pushed open one half of a double door at the rear of the cellar. The slope on which the house was built meant that the ground outside was below that of the cellar floor, so a long ramp bridged the gap. "This allows me to bring my boat inside for repairs." Olav informed them. "But at the moment it is tied up at the water's edge."

Carefully they picked their way over the rocky ground. On the other side of the street there had been sufficient soil for the houses to have small gardens, but on this side the terrain was slabs of water smoothed rock right up to the edge of the fjord. The house was supported on brick stilts that had been mortared straight onto the natural rock foundation.

They found the boat bobbing on the ripples of the fjord. It was about twelve feet long and five feet wide at the middle, large enough to carry the three of them across smooth water. At the rear was an outboard motor, tilted forward to raise the propeller. But half way down two oars rested in rowlocks. That was how the boat would be propelled that night.

"Can either of you row?" Olav whispered. "We can go faster with two."

"I did a bit of rowing." Carter admitted, remembering the three months of agony he had put himself through in his first term at university. After the Christmas break he had joined the rugby club and never sat in one of the university's racing shells again.

"Good. You get in first and take the right hand oar as we look at it. Then I'll get in. You, Trooper Green, untie the boat, push us off and them climb in."

"Typical, always the bleedin' junior rank that has to get his feet wet." Although it was said as a grumble, Carter could see Green's toothy white grin.

Carter clambered aboard and took his seat on the starboard side of the little craft. He placed his captured rifle in the bottom of the boat but kept his webbing harness on. Olav climbed in after him and took his seat alongside. They unshipped their oars and dipped them into the water, taking care not to make a splash. Green untied the boat's painter from the metal spike that secured it, dropped it over the transom and then gave the boat a shove. There was the grating of the boat's keel across the rock, then it wobbled free as it found deeper water. Green clambered over the back and sat himself down next to the outboard motor, his rifle held across his lap in readiness.

"Slowly now." Olav instructed. "It will make less noise. Carter pushed his oar forward, dipped it into the blackness of the water and pulled slowly back towards his chest. The boat slid forward with only the tiniest of rippling sounds. They quickly established their rhythm and it wasn't long before the silhouettes of the houses had merged into the general background of the high sides of the fjord.

When Olav considered they were far enough from the shore, he allowed them to increase the pace, but not so fast that they risked losing their rhythm. "You see the high peak against the skyline?" Olav asked.

"Yes, I see it."

"I keep that directly above Trooper Green's head and then we are sure to find our landing place."

"What's there?"

"A path will take you up into a high valley, perhaps a two kilometre walk. It is used in the summer for cattle and there is a hut there for the herdsman to stay the night if he needs to. It is kept stocked with firewood and water. You will be able to keep warm and to make hot food. The Germans have never been there, so they probably don't even know about it. There is no reason for them to go to that side of the fjord to look for you even if they found out you were in the village."

That was good, Carter thought. They could light a fire at night when the smoke wouldn't be seen. With the nights eighteen hours long, they wouldn't freeze to death.

"I will pass the word to trusted friends and it will reach the Osvald Group. I will tell them where to find you. They will probably want some sort of repayment from your government for helping you; weapons most likely."

"I can't speak for my government," Carter replied, "but they will want to encourage resistance groups. The Osvald Group may be communists, but they are also the enemies of Germany and that is good enough right now."

They rowed on in silence. With no way of gauging distance across the dark fjord, the time seemed to stretch out interminably. But at last Carter became aware of the bulk of the cliffs above them once again. Finally the boat grounded itself in the shallows and Carter could rest his shoulders, weary from the repetitive and unaccustomed action of rowing.

"We are about fifty metres to the left of where we should be." Olav informed them, still keeping his voice low, even this far from the village. "Follow the beach in that direction," he pointed, "and you will find the bottom of the path. It isn't very steep, it can't be if we want to get cattle up it. When the path starts to flatten and the grass gets thicker, you are in the valley. The hut is about another fifty metres on the right of the valley floor."

"Thank you, Olav. We owe you a great debt." Carter took his hand and gave it a firm shake.

"All I ask is that you get back to England and then come back and kill more Germans."

"I think that might be arranged." Carter grinned.

"Thanks mate." Green added, shaking the Norwegian's hand. "You and your misses keep your head down and don't do anything stupid.

"Like helping British commandos." Olav grinned back.

"Yeah, well, maybe don't do it again then."

Olav clambered back into his boat and Carter and Green pushed it back into the fjord. They heard the gentle slap of oars as Olav turned the boat and then he was swallowed up by the darkness.

There was no moon, but the millions of stars provided a little bit of light to allow them to pick their way across the shingle of the narrow beach until they found the path. Carter led the way as they climbed gently up the hill. After climbs like the ones they experienced at Achnacarry and Inveraray, the gentle slope offered them no challenge. Only the need to take care where they put their feet, so they wouldn't turn an ankle, slowed them down.

Less than an hour later they were pushing open the door of the herdsman's hut. They could see the gleam of snow on the sides of the hills above them, but it hadn't yet reached this lower altitude. The hut smelt damp and stale, but beggars couldn't be choosers. Carter checked his watch. It was only two o'clock, so plenty of time for them to warm themselves before they had to douse a fire.

Green struck a match.

"Idiot!" snapped Carter. "We haven't checked where the sight lines are yet. For all you know, that flame could be lighting us up like a beacon." Green quickly blew out the flame, plunging them into darkness once more. Green should have known better, Carter mused. They had all seen carelessly lit matches that were visible from miles away on a clear night. Light and sound, the two could be a commando's best friend when operating at night - or his worst enemy.

"We can't light a fire without lighting a match, Sir." Green protested.

"I know, but we check the place out first. If we need to, we can cover windows to prevent any flames from being seen across the other side of the fjord." He started to feel his way around the walls, moving slowly so that he could feel any obstructions. To the left of the door, as he faced the wall, he found the first window. It wasn't just windows facing the fjord that would be a problem. Any shaft of light that went out through a window would be reflected off the side of the valley. Even if it wasn't strong, it might still be seen. Carter began to think that the idea of lighting a fire wasn't a good one. Olav wouldn't have thought twice about it, but Olav had never been hunted at night by a determined and skilful enemy.

Below the window was a table and Carter could feel the layer of dust on its surface. He also stumbled against a chair. Working his way past the obstructions he reached the corner of the hut and turned to continue his investigation. Yes, there was a window in that wall too, probably to allow the herdsman to keep an eye on any animals that were on that side of the hut. Any light from there would probably be seen on the other side of the fjord. Here he found a low bed, the bare springs rattling as he bumped against it. He turned the next corner and found a metal stove next to the chimney breast above a hearth, beyond which was a stack of cut wood. The final wall revealed another window, with a book case to one side and a long sideboard of some sort below. Beyond the window was a tall cupboard that swung open to Carter's touch and which he couldn't close again, unable to find the securing catch in the darkness.

Returning towards his start point he found a final window before he reached the door once again.

"I'm wondering if those windows are fitted with shutters, Sir." Green mused.

"I'll go outside and check." The hut was raised up on rocks on one side, keeping the floor level, with a short flight of steps leading down from the doorway. It meant that Carter had to stretch to reach the windows, but yes, there did seem to be shutters on the outside. But what sort of condition were they in? It only needed one of the angled slats to be broken for light to escape.

No, they wouldn't light a fire that night. They would check the hut over properly in the morning and see what needed doing. In the meantime he would assume nothing, including an assumption that they hadn't been followed. He had learnt at Achnacarry that assumptions were dangerous and that in the field they could be lethal.

But it didn't mean they had to go without something warm inside them. They both carried little stoves, fuelled by hexamine[1] blocks, that could boil a mess tin full of water to make tea. Carter no longer had his stock of tea leaves, but Green had his.

Returning inside, he ordered Green to try to get some sleep while he took first watch. They would have to do two-on-two off, which was tiring, but they had done it before often enough.

Carter moved the rattling bed away from the wall and took up a position to one side of the window, where he could see but where his silhouette wouldn't be easy to identify. Behind him Green's snores soon filled the hut.

[1] Hexamine – a solid fuel, white in colour, similar to that used in firelighters. The stoves in which they were burnt were about the size of a tobacco tin.

* * *

Dawn broke, grey and heavy with thick clouds over the fjord. Slowly the light improved enough for Carter to make out the wisps of smoke at the chimneys of the houses in the distant village. The occupants of Kirkesfjord were starting their day once again. Merry Christmas, he thought.

Most of the Norwegians would be spending the festive season trying to repair the damage that had been done to the houses the previous day. At least two had been burnt to the ground, several had suffered serious fire damage and others had broken windows, smashed doors and bullet or shrapnel holes. Even from this distance Carter could make out the heaps of debris that marked where the fish oil factories had once stood. He had studied the village for hours during their briefing sessions and now, even to him, the town looked incomplete.

He opened his pack and pulled out his binoculars. Raising them to his eyes he surveyed the village. The tank was still standing by the jetty, it's short fifty millimetre gun pointing impotently along the south channel. Half a dozen soldiers stood around it.

At the far end of the village stood three Mercedes-Benz trucks that had brought the soldiers to the town. They were parked beside the road and more soldiers milled around them. The weapons pits were manned, though, and Carter could see the machine guns pointing back towards Groening, as though they were expecting an imminent attack.

The houses prevented Carter from seeing what was happening in the village itself, but making a crude calculation of the numbers of soldiers that could be carried by the trucks told him that about two thirds were unaccounted for, which probably meant they were carrying out a house to house search.

Carter's stomach rumbled. It was more than twelve hours since he had enjoyed Helga's delicious fish soup. Far nicer then the bully beef he had given …

Alarm bells rang in Carter's head. The bully beef! What had she done with it? If any German soldier found the obviously British rations they would know at once that a commando had been in the house. Carter dreaded to think what might happen after they found it.

"What's up, Sir." Green asked, passing him a mess tin a quarter full of steaming tea. He had used his small hexamine fuelled stove to boil enough water for a brew. The small regulation issue device didn't give off any smoke that was worth mentioning. "You look as though you've seen a ghost."

"It's worse than that. I think we might have caused Olav and his family some problems. I gave them a tin of bully beef and some tea. If the Germans find it …" He didn't need to complete the sentence.

"We'll know soon enough if they do." Green observed. "All they have to do is threaten his wife or kids and Olav is going to talk."

"And I wouldn't blame him." Carter said. No man could be expected to place the lives of strangers ahead of those of his loved ones. A soldier might resist interrogation, but Olav wasn't a soldier and, more importantly, neither were his family.

They didn't have to wait long. Just after midday a boat pulled away from the jetty. It was a small fishing boat, its deck crammed with soldiers dressed in *feldgrau*. Turning across the south channel it headed diagonally towards them.

"They're coming, Sir." Green told Carter, who was sitting at a dusty table examining his map. He hadn't needed to use it since the landing, but a thorough knowledge of it would now help them.

"OK, well, we can't stay here. We could probably defend it for a while, but all they have to do is send enough troops up to overwhelm us or just starve us out. Pack up your kit and let's go."

"Already packed and ready, sir."

"You don't need to keep calling me 'Sir'. Tell you what, I'll call you Prof and you call me 'Lucky', at least till we're back with the commando." Carter strapped his steel helmet onto his pack and withdrew his cap comforter from inside it, pulling it down over his head until it covered the top half of his ears, which gave him some warmth without restricting his hearing.

"Suits me, Lucky." Green replied, pulling his webbing on and buckling his belt. "Where are we going?"

"There's no way inland across these hills, especially with all that snow. As far as I can see this valley climbs for about another five hundred feet before crossing a saddle between two peaks, then we can get down the other side. There a hamlet called Sansig that lies on a bay. Maybe we can steal a boat or something."

"Do you think they'll follow?"

"Oh yes. But they'll also radio back to HQ and try to get troops down the other side to box us in. Hopefully we'll be a long way away before they can do that."

Carter led them from the hut and up the valley, heading south. It wasn't long before they reached the snow line, which slowed them.

"It'll slow the Germans as well." Carter said, putting his foot into snow that reached his knees.

"They'll be able to track us as well." Green observed.

"They'll know where we're going. It's the only place we can go."

They fell silent again, reserving their strength for the walk. Their fitness paid dividends and they could only hope that the garrison troops that were following them had gone soft and would find the going tougher to manage. Night fell, but it didn't stop them. They were passing through the 'saddle' between the two hills, which didn't require a map and compass to follow, though Carter could have employed them if necessary. Around midnight they started to descend. The going got steeper and more slippery, even when they dropped below the snowline again and into a patch of pine forest that was clinging to the southern slopes of the hills. They found it easier to slide down on their backsides in several places, jamming their rifles into the ground to acts as a brake.

Even from a distance they could tell that Sansig was deserted. It had that abandoned look to it. No lights showed and there was the irregular banging of a door on the night breeze which no occupant would allow to continue in case it kept them awake.

Carter and Green carried out a cursory inspection of the group of half a dozen houses but it was too dark to see if there had been anything left that might be of any use. A search of the waterline did reveal a boat, but it was half sunk, which suggested that even if they were able to drain it, it wouldn't get them far. Besides, it had neither engine nor oars to propel it.

"Are you sure you want to keep calling me 'Lucky'?" Carter asked, as they squatted inside one of the houses, brewing tea. Time was a luxury they couldn't afford to waste, but it was better that they get some sustenance while they could. They would need the calories. Green opened his tin of bully beef and a packet of 'hard tack' biscuits and they shared that as they waited for the water to boil.

"It could be worse." Green observed. Carter stifled a groan. He was starting to hate the platitude. "We could be sitting in that water, freezing our bollocks off."

Carter decided not to comment. If German soldiers appeared along the track that led to the village, the bay was about the only place they could hide. But he decided not to share that thought right at that moment.

"We'll head inland, for the airfield at Holmvik. The Germans will expect us to steer well clear of anywhere that they have forces, so they won't expect us to take that direction. Then we'll turn north and pass inland of Groening."

"Heading for where?"

"Alesund, or Molde, or even Trondheim. There's a lot of smaller coastal villages as well. We must be able to find a boat somewhere. Maybe even a friendly Norwegian to take us across to Shetland."

"Why not Bergen? It's south of us and a lot closer." Green handed over a steaming mess tin.

"Because we're heading south already. The Germans will expect us to keep going in that direction, so they'll continue to search that way. The whole coastline will be alert and out looking for us." He took a sip of his tea, careful not to burn his lips. "Besides, between us and Bergen is Sognefjorden. It's over a hundred and twenty miles long and riddled with smaller fjords along its sides. It would be a nightmare trying to get around it and even harder trying to get across it. No. North will be a little easier and also unexpected from a German perspective."

"Where would we end up if we turned right here and followed the cliffs the other way?"

"If there's a path, which there isn't so far as I can make out from the map, it would just take us around the headland and back into Kirkesfjord. We'd end up back at the place where Olav put us ashore last night."

"Not so much as out of the frying pan, but back in the frying pan again." Green said, with a wry chuckle.

They finished their tea in silence, washed the mess tins in the icy water of the bay, hid their rubbish and started along the narrow track that was the sole access to the hamlet from the coastal road.

Carter was well aware that there might be enemy soldiers coming the other way along the track, so they paused frequently to listen, but heard nothing. They had travelled for an hour before they heard the tell-tale crunch of boots against frosty ground, accompanied by the jingle of rifle slings and the hushed voices of ill-disciplined soldiers. Carter glanced to his left to see that they were alongside a steep cliff. It could be climbed, but not quickly enough. "Into the water!" he whispered, sliding off the side of the track, not even looking to see if Green was following. Gripping the smooth rock as best he could with one hand, he allowed his boots to slide downwards until they hit the surface of the water. It seemed to slope quite gradually out towards the deeper water. He allowed gravity to continue to pull him downwards until he was submerged up to his neck. Taking hold of his rifle in both hands again he aimed it back up the slope and eased the safety catch off.

Maybe he really was lucky, but the night had remained cloudy and there were no stars to give even the minutest amount of light. So long as they didn't make any noise there was no reason for the Germans to even look their way and certainly no reason for them to risk the slippery rocks at the bay's edge.

Carter shivered enough to set up small ripples. The water was so cold that he soon lost the feeling in his limbs. He knew they couldn't stay there for long before their core temperatures started to drop and their bodies started to draw blood in from the extremities to keep heart and lungs working. If that happened, frost bite would be inevitable. His teeth started to chatter and he had to clamp his jaw tight to silence them. He was glad he wasn't wearing his helmet, because his violent shivering could have easily caused it to clang against the rocky shore.

The Germans weren't making any effort to hide their presence. Why would they, after all? They were the masters of this country now. They were the hunters. But hunters moved silently, lest they disturb their prey and send it fleeing to safety. These men just stumbled along in the dark. A German voice said something and a couple of others laughed. Then they were gone along the track.

Carter allowed them five minutes to get clear, before they crawled shivering from the water. "Right!" he hissed through chattering teeth. "We've g…g…got to w…warm up, so we'll j…jog."

"O … Ok!" Green chattered back.

There was a risk, Carter knew. There may be more Germans waiting along the track, waiting for just this eventuality. But if there was no one in front of them they would now have at least an hour's head start and possibly two. An hour if the Germans had a radio and reported back that Sansig was empty, two hours if the Germans didn't have a radio, reached Sansig and turned back to follow them. Would they wait for the other patrol to come down the side of the hill to meet them, proof that Carter and Green were already past them and heading inland?

There was no way to second guess this. They would jog to warm themselves up and maybe get rid of some of the icy water from their clothes. If there were Germans on the main road then Carter would fight. He would tell Green to do as he pleased. He couldn't order the man to fight to the death, even if he was willing to die himself. But if there were no Germans they would head inland towards the airfield before turning back towards Groening.

Dropping his rifle to his side, gripped in just one hand in what was called a 'long trail', Carter broke into a gentle loping run. His boots squelched water at every step, accompanying each thud of boot against ground. Their breath billowed around them in clouds of condensation and soon steam started to rise from the thick woollen serge of their battledress uniforms.

The line of the water started to arc away from them as it curved round the bay and Carter realised they must be near the end of the shallow bay and close to the road that headed south from Groening. He drew them to a halt, their breath coming in gentle gasps. For fit men the two or three miles they had run had barely raised their pulses. Carter dropped into a crouch and they waddled forward. There was a little bit of cover, in the form of stunted frozen grass, but if they got the lighter sky behind them they would be seen. The silence was deafening, Carter's heart thumping in his ears with a regular beat. He started to feel cold again, his clothing only just starting to dry on him.

"I'll go." Green mouthed into his ear, then crawled forward. Carter had no idea how far away the road might be, but it couldn't be very far. He was looking along the end of the bay almost at right angles and, according to the map, the road ran right along the very edge of the water.

Green was gone for nearly thirty minutes. "Couldn't see any signs of Germans." He whispered. "If they've set an ambush it's very well concealed."

If all the local troops were as poorly trained as the ones that had passed them on the track, then it was unlikely that they could have set an ambush that Green couldn't detect. Or was it a double bluff? Had the soldiers deliberately made a noise in order to lull Carter and Green into a false sense of security, encouraging them to blunder into a trap.

Carter silently scolded himself. He was getting paranoid. The Germans knew they were hunting only two commandos. They didn't need to indulge in any trickery. They just had to be competent in their approach which, it seemed, they weren't. Besides, there were only supposed to be a hundred soldiers in Groening. Even with hastily sent reinforcements, they couldn't swamp the whole area. If Carter had been the hunter, he might have set an ambush there, rather than sent troops along the track, but the Germans hadn't.

"What's on the other side of the road?"

The map indicated forest, but forests could be cut down for timber, so the terrain might have changed since the map had been drawn.

"Pine forest, quite dense. I don't think we could get through it in the dark."

"OK, we'll head towards Groening and turn off the road as soon as we find a break in the trees. According to the map there is a long, gentle valley between us and Holmvik. At the top is a bit of a plateau where the airfield has been built. We turn back north before we get to the airfield itself and see if we can find a route inland behind Groening and try to get around behind the Germans without being spotted.

* * *

Carter re-focused his binoculars as the light steadily improved. The cloud was starting to break up, giving more wintery sunshine. The airfield was already alive with activity. A line of Me 110s was receiving attention, being made ready for take-off. Further away Carter could make out the burnt-out wreck of one of them, no doubt a relic of the Blenheim bomber attack of two mornings earlier.

Had it only been two days? It seemed more to Carter. But they'd had hardly any sleep and that played tricks on the mind. It reminded him that they needed to find somewhere to lay up and rest before too long. They needed to be alert if they were to survive in this hostile territory. Hunger and fatigue were as much enemies as the Germans.

The airfield was about a mile distant, at the top of the valley that they had spent the rest of their night working their way along. It hadn't been easy. Away from the road a lot of the forest had been cut and the ground was littered with pine branches and tree stumps. It would have been slow going even during the day, but it was considerably slower in the dark.

There was a buzzing above Carter's head, like an angry wasp and he turned to look at the fragile shape of a small plane descending towards the runway.

"Spotter plane" Green whispered, as though Carter needed telling. "Do you think it's been sent to help find us?"

"Quite probable. It means we're going to have to stick to cover."

"But we'll know it's there, because of the noise."

"Not if it climbs high enough. The wind up there will blow the sound away from us. The observer can watch the ground through binoculars, and we won't even know if he's there."

"But he can only work by day."

"That's true. We own the night." It had become something of a motto for the commandos, if only an unofficial one. The powers that be preferred 'United We Conquer'.

"Well," Carter continued, "they'll have to turn the aircraft round and brief the crew, so we have a little bit of time. We'll probably hear it take off, or maybe see it." Carter studied his map. "There's a building here." He tapped the location to show Green where he meant. "It has a track marked to it, connecting it to the road, but nothing to say what it is. Maybe it's another one of those herders' huts. I think we'll head for it and see what's there. Maybe we can hole up there until it gets dark."

They retreated into the tree line a little more, then crept along, keeping a close eye on the open side of the patch of trees to make sure they hadn't attracted any attention from the airfield.

Between two lines of trees they found a track that wasn't even marked on the map. "Logging road." Carter whispered. "Cleared so they can drag trees away and get them to a place where a truck can get in." he studied the map again. "Looks like it leads to the place we're heading for."

With the rutted track to help them, they were able to pick up their pace a little. They were almost at the hut when they heard the sound of the spotter plane taking off from the airfield. They melted into the trees and saw the flash of its wings as it passed low overhead. "Looks like it's heading for the fjord area." Carter whispered.

"They must think we're still out there somewhere."

"Suits us." Carter grunted as he led them back onto the track and on towards the spot on the map that he had chosen.

They spotted the roof of the building through a gap in the trees that marked the end of the track. It was a much bigger building than the herder's hut and more solid looking. They crept quietly forward, close enough for Carter to examine through his binoculars.

In front of the hut was a large area of cleared ground. Stacked along one side were cut logs, each about twelve feet long. They were arranged in organised piles with different diameter logs in each pile. There were no vehicles visible, neither trucks to haul the logs away, nor cars to transport a workforce. Not so much as a push bike. Although the hut was wooden, it had a stone chimney. No smoke was visible from it and Carter couldn't sense any lingering on the air.

"Looks deserted." He whispered to Green.

"Do you want me to take a closer look?"

"Yes, but be careful."

Green bit back on a retort, thinking better of it. He picked his way forward until he was almost at the rear of the hut, then slipped into the trees on his right, choosing his route so that he wouldn't have to pass around the front of the hut, which was where any occupants might emerge. Fifteen minutes later he was back.

"There's two huts, a smaller one on the other side. Both have got big padlocks on the doors. The big one also has shutters across the windows, but the smaller one doesn't have windows at all. Looks like it might be an equipment shed of some sort. No sign of life though."

"Are the padlocks new?"

"Looks like it. No signs of rust. The one on the big hut locks a sliding bolt. But the screw heads are intact. I reckon I could probably unscrew it and then we could get inside." It was an old burglar's trick and Carter wondered how Green knew it. It would save them having to smash the lock off the door, which would be a giveaway if anyone came up to check on security.

"OK, lead the way."

Green took Carter by the same route that he had taken, emerging in a gap between the larger and the smaller hut. Carter sniffed diesel fumes from the smaller hut. Probably where they kept the tractor that hauled the logs to this collection point.

Close to, it was apparent that the hut was well maintained. The paint was sufficiently fresh for it not to have seen a full winter and there was no sign of rot around the door frame or the shutters. Green took a penknife from his pocket and opened up one of the blades, inserting it into the screw head. It took some effort, but he was eventually able to turn the screw enough to allow him to do the rest of the job with his fingers. A few minutes later all four screws were lying in the palm of Carter's hand as Green slid the whole assembly to one side, removing the bolt from the U shaped retainer fixed to the door frame. The door swung open under its own weight, the well-oiled hinges not making a sound.

They stepped inside. The shutters were closed but enough light was getting through the slats for them to see what was there. Six pairs of bunk beds provided sleeping space for a dozen people. Each bunk had a mattress, but there was no bedding. Between each pair of bunks were lockers, the doors standing open to reveal that they were empty.

Green spotted a key hanging in a hook just inside the door. He took it and went outside. Carter continued his examination of the bunk house. At one end was a wood fired stove, which probably also heated the hut. To one side were cupboards containing plates and cutlery and, Carter's mouth began to water, an assortment of canned food. He couldn't understand the Norwegian labels, but the pictures showed soups, stews, fish, vegetables and fruit.

He turned as he heard a footfall behind him. Green hung the key back on its hook. "There's a tractor in the shed and a whole load of lumberjack equipment: axes, chainsaws, you name it, they've got it."

"Not the sort of thing we're interested in. Look at this." He pointed to a framed photograph hanging on the wall, showing thirteen figures. Twelve were dressed in heavy boots, knee socks, thick trousers and woollen shirts. They could have stepped out of a film about the Canadian Rockies. In the middle stood a stern looking figure wearing a suit and a bowler hat. His face was dominated by a drooping moustache, which made him look very sad.

"Probably the workforce." Green observed. "Bloke in the middle looks like he's lost a shilling and found a tanner[1]."

"Probably the manager. What do you make of this place?" Carter asked, seeking confirmation of the conclusions he had already drawn.

"Well, pretty obvious those twelve geezers in the photo aren't local, or they wouldn't need beds here. So they're brought in when the trees are ready to cut. The beds aren't made up, so they haven't just popped into town for a Christmas drink. There's no sign of fresh food, and nothing that's going stale. Either they've been very careful about throwing out the rubbish, or there's been no one here for a while. The manager is probably the guy with the tash, so he probably re-stocks the tinned stuff after they leave, then comes back with the fresh food when they're due back. I reckon they've gone home for Christmas, wherever home is and aren't due back for a while."

"That's pretty much what I thought. OK, we'll lay up here for tonight, get some hot food inside us and try and get some of our gear dry. We can't undress though, just in case we have to move sharpish. We'll also try and get some sleep. If all goes well we'll move on tomorrow night, so the spotter plane can't find us."

"How long do you think they'll keep looking?"

"Hard to say. If we were ordinary soldiers, they would probably scale down the search after a couple of days and hope to pick us up at routine checks points, like bus terminals, ferries or railway stations. But they know we're commandos, so they will probably keep up the search for longer. After all, what would we do if we had a couple of commandos lurking around in Epping Forest?"

Green nodded his understanding.

"Soon as it gets dark we can light the stove. It's closed in so we don't have to worry about the flames being seen. Then we can cook some food. We'll keep all the shutters closed except the one at the end that overlooks the access road. If there's going to be any trouble, that's where it will come from. I'll take first watch while you cook the food, then we'll go two on, two off for the rest of the night."

[1] A shilling was five pence in present day coinage and a tanner was the nickname given to a sixpenny piece, or two and a half pence today. In 1941 a shilling would have had the spending power of about £3.40 in today's money.

* * *

Carter was being shaken awake, Green's voice hissing in his ear. "Wake up, wake up. We've got company." It was one of the tricks that Carter had learnt, to be able to go from a deep sleep to a state of full alert in seconds. Danger doesn't give you time to gather your senses and work out where you are.

"What is it?" he may be fully awake, but his tongue had yet to catch up and he slurred his words.

"An engine. Sounds like a motor bike. It's getting closer though."

Carter grabbed his webbing and picked up his rifle, before taking the handful of steps from the bunk on which he had been sleeping, to the window where Green had been keeping watch. Carter eased the catch open and gave the window frame a push. If they needed to use their weapons, he didn't want to have to break the glass before he could fire.

There was no mistaking the high revving of a motor cycle engine, getting louder and then quieter by turns as it passed between the trees that flanked the approach track.

It reached full volume as it swung into the open space in front of the bunkhouse. A letterbox shaped strip of light from the headlamp marked its location as it slowed and came to a standstill, the engine noise dropping as it was allowed to idle, then the head light was extinguished and the engine noise died.

The thinnest sliver of a sickle moon provided the smallest amount of illumination. Enough to show that the vehicle was a motorcycle combination. The driver climbed off the bike while the passenger rose in the sidecar and stretched. They weren't taking any precautions. That meant they were just a routine patrol, probably ordered to stop in at the loggers' camp just to make sure there was no one there.

If it was really suspected that the two commandos were hiding there, the force would be much larger. At least a dozen men. The approach would also have been silent as the hunters hoped to take their prey by surprise.

The next question, however, was what to do about them? Both he and Green were good shots with a rifle, by day or night. They were less than a hundred yards away, more like fifty, so taking them down wouldn't be a problem. They would be standing at the gates of Hell before they even knew that they'd been shot. For Carter it helped to think of the enemy as being evil, though they were probably just a pair of conscripts who were obeying the orders they had been given.

Moonlight glinted off metal on the chest of one of the men. Too big a flash for it to be from buttons. It must be the gorget of the *Feldgendarmerie*, the German military police. Even more reason to think that this was just a routine patrol.

"Don't fire unless I give the word." Carter whispered in Green's ear. "If you do fire, you take whichever is on the right." If they both hit the same target, the possibility was that the other target would have time to take cover. "We only shoot if they start to get too close."

If they were a routine patrol, it was better for them to leave unmolested. If Carter and Green killed them their absence would be noticed after a while and would draw the hunt to the last place the Germans had been sent, which was this hut. Even that assumed that the shots weren't heard by other hunters. Carter preferred it if the Germans thought he and Green were still out on the hills south of Kirkesfjord.

"The fire." Whispered Green. "They'll smell the smoke."

Damn! Carter had forgotten that. But either his luck was holding or the gentle breeze was in the wrong direction, because there was no sign that the Germans were aware that a fire was burning within the bunkhouse. Perhaps it had burnt so low it was no longer producing any smoke.

The Germans held some sort of discussion, not loud enough for Carter to make out any words, not that he would have understood them anyway. One of them lit a cigarette and gesticulated towards the hut. That made him a much easier target, thought Carter. The second one wandered forward a few yards closer, perhaps to get a better look. He now stood in the wan moonlight. Carter squeezed his rifle a little tighter into his shoulder, bracing himself for the recoil when he pulled the trigger.

There was a squawk, like a parrot that was being strangled, then some electronic chatter. The bike had a radio installed behind the seat of the sidecar. Probably a short-range VHF set. The smoking soldier went and answered the call, exchanging a few words. Then he called to his comrade *"Willi, Komm hier. Sie wollen dass wir am kontrollpunkt sind."*

The second soldier didn't need another invitation. He turned back and made his way to the motor bike once again, clambering into the sidecar. The first soldier crushed his cigarette on the ground, kick started the bike and turned it around in its own length, sending it back down the track in a spray of dirt.

"Close call." Carter breathed.

"Still calling you 'Lucky', Lucky!" Green grinned at him.

"Right, we can't stay here in case they come back. So we're off now. Fill your pack with as much of that tinned food as you can manage. I'll do the same."

"That's looting, Lucky."

"That's survival, Prof."

8 – Ålesund

Dawn found them several miles from the logging camp, still tracking along the high end of the pine forest, just below the snow line. The air was slightly warmer close to the fjord, keeping the snow at bay unless very severe weather set in. Carter hoped that wouldn't happen before they found a way out of Norway. The days were cold and the nights colder, but they had managed so far. But there were limits to what even a commando's body could endure and Carter had no desire to find out what they were.

Through the trees they caught occasional glimpses of the small town of Groening, until it fell behind them and the road below turned more to the west, running behind the range of snowy hills that flanked the Kirkesfjord.

"There's a small town called Fondheim, about fifteen miles away. It had been considered as the target for the operation, but the harbour there is quite well defended and the beaches are open to the sea, which would have made landing tricky. But where there's a harbour, there's boats. Perhaps we can sneak in and steal one."

"Anything big enough to cross the North Sea will probably be guarded." Green replied.

"And guards get sloppy. We're trained to sneak up on guards and deal with them."

"We could do with Danny Glass for that." Carter mused.

"I'll remember that next time I get stuck behind enemy lines." Carter said, instantly regretting it. Green had come back to look for him; he hadn't needed to do that. Now his life was as much in danger as Carter's own. By rights Green should be sitting in McNeil's Bar swapping stories of the raid with the rest of the Troop, not hiding in a freezing ditch while his officer dragged him around Norway in the middle of winter.

"We'll continue to follow the line of the road so long as we have tree cover." Carter continued. "If the trees run out we'll stand out like a pimple on a pretty girl's face."

"I didn't know you'd met my girl." Green quipped.

Rising out of the ditch, Carter led them up the slope a little way before turning parallel to the road and continuing their march. They had done well so far. They were into their fourth day behind enemy lines and the closest shave they'd had was when they'd had to slip into the sea to escape detection. There were also two lucky *Feldgendarmerie* who would never know how close they had come to death.

They heard the spotter plane fly over them later in the morning, returning from another fruitless patrol of the Kirkesfjord headlands. It was slightly to their right, closer to the peak of the hill along the side of which they were walking. The pitch of its engine changed suddenly, as the pilot took the aircraft into a tight turn.

"Get down!" snapped Carter, throwing himself onto the bed of pine needles below the trees. He shuffled his way forward, trying to get beneath the denser foliage.

"You think he's seen us?"

"I don't know, but something has made him turn."

The aircraft had reversed its course and flew back parallel to the tree line, as low as it dared go. Carter recognised the type from the silhouettes that they had seen pasted to the walls of the lounges on board the landing ships. It was an Fi 156, called a *Storch* in German, because of the spindly legs that held the landing wheels. It was ideal for this sort of work, having a top speed of only just over a hundred miles an hour meant that it could fly along the tree line at low speed, examining every feature.

"Shall I take it down?" Green asked, from his hiding place. "I reckon he's going slow enough for me to hit the pilot if he comes past again."

"No. It's the same as those two on the motor bike. If the aircraft crashes they'll send out a search party. If they find a bullet wound in either of them, they'll know it was us. Besides, he's got a radio. We may just be confirming what he only suspects right now and as soon as you shoot he'll be calling for help."

The aircraft had turned again and was making another pass along the tree line. The speed was so slow that Carter could make out the figure of the observer as he scanned the trees. Carter may have imagined it, but he thought he had even looked the man directly in the eye.

The aircraft climbed above the trees and went into a circular flight pattern, maintaining its position directly above Carter and Green. That was the worst thing he could have done, as far as Carter was concerned. It meant they were keeping the location under observation while they waited for ground troops to arrive.

What had given them away? Carter wondered. They had taken such great care to keep trees above them specifically to avoid being seen from the air. It had slowed them down considerably, as the pine trees grew so thick and close together.

But it didn't take much for a sharp-eyed observer. Perhaps just a glimpse of a rifle barrel or the shine of a face looking skywards. The remainder of their camouflage stripes had been washed away when they went into the sea and they hadn't repaired them. They lay still for nearly an hour, then the aircraft broke off its circling and flew off towards Holmvik.

"Short of fuel would be my guess." Green said, scrambling to his feet.

"Probably. Well, we've got until he refuels or until a truck load of soldiers arrives. My guess is they won't be far away by now."

"Which way?"

Carter did some quick thinking. Which direction would the Germans think most unlikely?

"Down the hill, across the road and keep going along the other side. The Germans will come from Groening, so we should be safe if we keep going. Meanwhile, they'll be busy searching up here and they'll take a long time over it. If anything comes along the road we'll hear it and have time to take cover."

He didn't wait for any objections. The decision was made and to reinforce it he pushed his way between two trees and headed downhill.

They had just crossed the road when two Mercedes-Benz trucks came around a bend, followed by a *Kübelwagen* carrying two officers. The trucks came to a stop and the *Kübelwagen's* driver pulled in to park behind them. One of the officers, probably the junior one, climbed out to take charge. Troops spilled out and formed up in ranks so that an NCO could start detailing them to tasks. The troops from the first lorry spread themselves along the road, establishing a barrier for anyone trying to cross it. The remainder formed into two files and headed to either side along the road before turning into the pine forest. It didn't take Carter any time to work out that they were forming a cordon around the area, which they would squeeze tight, forcing anyone inside to attempt to flee in the open direction, or surrender.

There was a lengthy wait until the *Storch* returned to provide eyes in the sky to tell the hunters if the prey fled out of the high side of the forest, then the troops on the road stepped into the trees and started to climb.

From a jumble of rocks on the opposite side Carter and Green could only lie and watch. How firm was the sighting? If the aircraft crew were only suspicious, then the search wouldn't be extended. If it was a definite sighting then they wouldn't leave until they had combed the surrounding countryside. Carter checked his watch. It was only eleven o'clock. Still four hours of daylight. Plenty of time for a search to conclude that they had moved on, which would result in the soldiers searching along both sides of the road. They couldn't avoid finding the two commandos if they did that. Despite a long-held doubt about the existence of a deity, Carter prayed for night to arrive.

* * *

The crashing of the hunters through the trees continued for a lengthy period, with the occasional shout or angrily barked order. Forming a cordon within a forest wasn't easy, especially trying to manage it so as to leave no gaps through which the prey might escape.

The officer in the *Kübelwagen* smoked cigarette after cigarette. He seemed nervous, as though a lot was riding on the success of this operation.

Carter had no sympathy. If he was doing his job properly he would be in the forest directing his men, instead of relying on the efforts of a subordinate.

The German got out of the car and paced up and down for a while, went and urinated into the edge of the forest, then climbed back into the *Kübelwagen* again.

When he heard the sound of the motorcycle approaching, Carter assumed it was the another *Feldgendarmerie* patrol, perhaps sent to assist the search. The engine's revs dropped fractionally, suggesting that the motorbike was slowing, but not enough to bring it to a complete stop. The machine appeared around the bend in the road, still travelling fast.

The first thing that Carter noticed was that the bike carried two people, but neither were wearing helmets. That wasn't normal for a military rider. The front one wore goggles, Carter could see that. Their clothes were wrong as well. They couldn't be soldiers.

The rider gave the throttle a blip and the bike gathered speed again. The officer in the *Kübelwagen* looked round, curiosity getting the better of him. What he saw made him panic, reaching for his pistol at the same time as he tried to throw himself out of the vehicle on the far side.

There was a sharp rattle of automatic fire and the officer slumped over the side of the vehicle. The driver, who had been unaware of any danger, just fell forward onto the steering column.

The bike roared away along the road, gone almost before Carter had realised what had happened.

"Holy shit! What was that?" Carter said, not making any effort to keep his voice low.

"That was trouble with a capital T." Carter replied. "I think we just saw the Norwegian resistance in action."

There was a lot of shouting now, from within the trees, as the hunters reacted to the noise behind them and a figure stumbled out onto the road, quickly followed by another. One ran to the front lorry and crouched down, taking aim along the road. The second figure did the same at the rear of the *Kübelwagen.* They were far too late to be of any use. More soldiers arrived and spread out along the road, using the drainage ditch as cover. A couple even crossed to the side of the road where Carter and Green lay concealed behind the rocks. Finally the officer appeared, going tentatively towards the occupants of the car to see if there were any signs of life.

The officer in the *Kübelwagen* was clearly dead, but the driver still had some life left in him. The officer lifted him so that he was sitting upright and started speaking. At first the driver was unresponsive then, gradually, he started to answer the questions that were being put to him. He raised an arm and pointed in the direction in which the motorbike had fled, before letting the arm drop again.

The junior officer gave some orders and the casualty and the corpse were lifted into the back of the nearest truck. Most of the troops clambered aboard but the officer detailed two of them to go in the *Kübelwagen,* one as driver and the other as escort. He climbed into the front of the nearest lorry, probably preferring the bumpy ride to the possibility of getting blood on his uniform.

The vehicles turned around in the road and headed back towards Groening. Seeing the ground troops departing, the pilot of the *Storch* also called it a day and turned his aircraft back towards the airfield.

"Brave types, weren't they?" Green said sarcastically.

"We're used to the mission taking priority, no matter what." Carter replied. "But these are garrison troops. They didn't even set up a defence in case of attack, which is basic stuff. They could have shot the rider off his mount well before he became a threat, but they had committed everyone to the search cordon. Everyone except that lazy officer and his driver. Far too over confident. Well, they paid the price. I'm guessing they've abandoned the search as a waste of time and gone back to get fresh orders, which gives us a chance to put some distance between them and us. So, let's use the opportunity."

Carter led them up onto the road and they jogged along it for a while. The sound of an approaching vehicle's engine sent them diving into cover on more than one occasion, but they were civilian vehicles that didn't represent any threat.

On the far side of the road the pine forest gave way to some empty fields and on the hill behind they saw the smoking chimney of a farmhouse. On their side the ground was broken, a mixture of tumbled rocks and moorland that stretched away towards the sea. Neither side of the road offered them much concealment if the aircraft returned, but there was no sign of it, so they just kept going. Carter thought they were about half way to their destination when darkness started to fall and he called them to a halt.

They were breathing heavily, but nowhere near the limits of their endurance. "We're going to need to find somewhere to lie up for the night." Carter said. "We can't use the road in the dark in case we stumble into a checkpoint and the cross-country route looks too hazardous with all those rocks. That looks like sedge grass over there and that means marshland. If we stumble into the wrong place we could find ourselves in trouble."

"Like we're not already in trouble." Green said. "There's plenty of farmland on the other side. We might be able to find a barn to lay up in."

"A pretty obvious place for the Germans to search. Remember them turning up at the logging camp. We got lucky there, we might not be so lucky again. I'd prefer a hedgerow or something. But there doesn't seem to be anything like that around here."

"What does the map show?"

"We're off the map now. They only issued us the one for the Kirkesfjord and Groening area. We're running blind now."

"Well, it's unlikely that the Germans will continue the search by night. Those *Kettenhund*[1] were sent to the logging camp because they were available. They were probably searching all the empty buildings in the area. All we have to do is find a place where we won't be seen from the road."

"True. Let's keep walking for a while and see what turns up."

What turned up was the ruins of an old building. It made Hamilton Farm look like the epitome of luxury, but its tumbledown walls provided some shelter from the wind. They daren't light a fire, but were able to get a hexamine stove working to make some tea, its small blue flame easily concealed from the road by their packs. Hot food was also out of the question, because of the aroma it would produce, but they each opened a can of fruit and ate them cold.

"What's yours?" Green asked.

"Peaches, I think."

"Mine's pears. I do like a nice juicy pear." Green chuckled.

Carter didn't rise to the bait. "I'll take first watch. You get some sleep."

Apart from the need to wake up and take turns doing sentry duty, the night passed without incident. The occasional vehicle passed along the road, but from late evening until early morning even that stayed silent. Before dawn they brewed more tea and shared a tin of sardines, which were easily identifiable from the shape of the tin.

Thinking that the Germans might have re-started the search for them, Carter kept them off the road, but shadowed its route on the marshy side. If they heard a vehicle approaching, the tall sedge grass provided them with some concealment until it passed. So far as they could see there was no military activity and they didn't see or hear the *Storch* either.

"I think they may have given up on us." Green suggested hopefully.

"Maybe, but we still can't take risks. It would only take one sighting and they'd be back out in force. They must know we're still out here somewhere. We're lucky that Norway is such a big country with a small population. The hills and fjords keep the communities spread apart as well. If we were in France we'd be tripping over people."

They came to a narrow side road, a small chapel built on the far side of it; more a roadside shrine, really. The door was closed but wilting flowers lay outside; someone's offering in the hope of a blessing of some sort. They checked the road in both directions for signs of traffic, then rushed across, taking shelter in the shadowy of the side of the chapel.

Without warning a man stepped out from behind the building, a pistol raised and aimed directly at Carter.

There was movement behind them and Carter turned his head to see a woman holding a sub machine gun; a British Sten gun to be precise.

The man was tall and good looking. He had a sardonic smile plastered to his face which Carter took an instant dislike to. He was dressed in typical Norwegian country fashion: woollen trousers topped with a thick jumper. To this, however, he had added a leather jacket. Carter recognised it at once as being the same the one the driver of the motor bike had been wearing the previous day.

Carter made no move to raise his hands in surrender. But at the same time he made no move to raise his own weapon, which he had been carrying in both hands.

"If you are the ones who shot that German officer yesterday, then I think we're on the same side."

"We are on our side, English. Everyone else is an enemy until proven otherwise." The man's English was good, if heavily accented.

"In that case, may I suggest we have a common cause, which is to defeat the Germans."

The man nodded, uncocked his pistol and slid it into a holster tucked in the waistband of his trousers.

The woman came around in front of them, but kept her gun levelled at them.

"I'm Lt Carter and this is my companion, Tpr Green. We're escaping from the raid that was carried out on Kirkesfjord a few days ago."

"I wasn't told your names, but I have been looking for you. You may call me Sven. It isn't my name, but it is better for me if you don't know my true identity. My friend here is Ingrid. That is her real name, but that doesn't matter because she is already known to the Germans."

"She doesn't smile much, does she." Green observed.

"Two weeks ago her brother was taken into custody by the Bergen Gestapo. He was tortured and then put in front of a firing squad as a warning to others. Her brother wasn't one of us. He was arrested only so the Germans could find out where Ingrid was. So Ingrid doesn't have a lot to smile about."

"I take it that she was the one behind you on the motorbike yesterday."

"She was. Now, I assume that you would like our help."

"If you are willing to give it."

"For the time being we are allies, if reluctant ones. When this war is over there will be a global revolution and I suspect that we will be on opposing sides. But for the moment, it suits us to assist you. I'm sure your government will be grateful."

Arrogant bastard, Carter thought. "By the looks of that gun they have already been generous."

"A pitiful gesture. We need money and we need more guns. I'm sure your government will be grateful for your safe return."

But not so grateful if those same weapons are turned on the Norwegian Royal Family at some future date, Carter mused. But he kept his thoughts to himself. Consideration of the wider ramifications of arming the communist Osvald Group was something that Carter was happy to leave to someone else.

"There are arrangements to be made. There is somewhere for you to hide while we do that. Have you paper and a pencil?"

Carter's hand went to the pocket of his battledress blouse and pulled out his notepad. Only it wasn't a notepad anymore. After his dip in the sea it was just a wad of half dried papier-mâché.

"Hang on." Green said. "Let me at your pack."

Carter turned his back and Green unbuckled his pack, pulling out a tin and ripping the label from it. he returned the tin to the pack and handed the paper over to the Norwegian. Carter offered his pencil.

The Norwegian scribbled some words in his own language then handed the paper to Carter. "Follow this road for half a kilometre, then you see a farm track to the right. At the end of the track you will find a farm. The owner is called Fredrick and he can be trusted. Give him the note and he will know that you have been sent by me. He will look after you until I come and get you."

"Do you know what happened to Olav and his family?"

"Are they the ones who sheltered you in Kirkesfjord?"

"Yes."

"I'll try to find out. One other thing. If you are captured before you get to Fredrick, destroy the note and don't reveal Fredrick's identity. If Germans come to Fredrick's place, try to get away so as not to compromise him. Now, go."

Carter and Green didn't argue, they just started walking in the direction that Sven had pointed. They heard the sound of a motor bike being kick started, then its diminishing roar as it headed along the road in the other direction.

"I didn't like him much." Green observed.

"Nor me. He's working in his own best interests, not ours. That means he'll abandon us if he thinks it necessary."

"The bird was a bit of alright though."

Carter didn't reply. Green was right of course, she was very attractive in a sad Nordic blond way. His thoughts turned to Fiona Hamilton and he wondered if he would ever get the chance to take her to the cinema.

¹ *Kettenhund* - Chain dogs; the derogatory nickname for the *Feldgendarmerie*, based on the gorgets they wore and the metal chains that hung them around their necks.

* * *

Fredrick's place turned out to be a modest sized farmhouse with a few outbuildings attached. They found him in the barn, where he was shovelling manure into a wheelbarrow. A dozen cows stood stamping and snorting, feeding from mangers bolted to the walls.

He was an old man, bent by the years. He was probably too old to be working a farm, but there didn't seem to be anyone else around who could take on the job.

Fredrick started with surprise as he heard the two soldiers enter the barn. He took the note warily, his eyes on the rifles that the two commandos were holding. He turned the note over. Examining the picture of the food, then looking meaningfully at the two soldiers.

Carter took the hint. He took off his webbing harness and opened his pack, taking out the remaining tins from within, including the one that no longer had a label. He laid them on the ground, then indicated that the man should take them. His demeanour changed at once, smiling as he realised that he wouldn't have to feed the two fugitives entirely at his own expense.

"We'll hang on to your food for the moment." Carter told Green while maintaining a stiff lipped smile. No one knew what the future held and they may need the other tins before they got back home.

Fredrick pointed and spoke a few words in Norwegian. "*Gå opp til hay loftet.*"

Carter recognised the word 'hay' and led the way up a rickety ladder. It wasn't perfect, but it was far better than the ruined building in which they had spent the previous night. The hay would provide insulation from the cold, while the animals below would generate heat which would rise to keep them warm.

"What about the smell?" Green said.

"They'll just have to get used to it." Carter replied.

* * *

It was the following evening that Carter heard the sound of a motor cycle engine. Despite being in Fredrick's care they had maintained their field discipline and continued to mount guard, two hours on and two off, turn about. Carter woke Green and they made their preparations to leave, just in case it was a *Feldgendarmerie* patrol.

Seeing the tall blond figure of Sven dismount, followed by the taciturn Ingrid, Carter relaxed. A few moments later Fredrick appeared to summon the pair into the house.

It was a spartan place, lacking a woman's touch. While it was clean there was a lack of a cared for atmosphere. The curtains at the kitchen window were threadbare and the table was covered by what might have been an old sheet. There was a total lack of decorative touches, not even a photograph.

Sven and Ingrid were sat at the kitchen table, Ingrid's Sten gun lying in front of her. Fredrick said something, then made himself scarce, knowing he wasn't needed.

"Good evening, English." Sven greeted them. "Has Fredrick been looking after you?"

"He has. The hay loft is warm enough and he has been feeding us well. We are rested."

"Good. It is time for you to pay for your passage to England."

"I'm sorry. We haven't any money to give you."

"We don't want money. Well, not the pittance you could afford. No, we want you to pay with your particular skills."

"I'm sorry, I'm not sure I understand."

"It is simple. There is a task we would like you to assist us with. If we are successful, you will be repaid with your passage home."

"And if we are unsuccessful?"

"You won't need a passage home." The sardonic smile was back on Sven's lips.

Carter considered the proposal for a moment. On the one hand they weren't under any obligation to the Osvald Group. They could collect their kit and try and make their own way home. On the other hand the assistance of the resistance would no doubt speed them on their way. They knew the country, they would know where to hide and who could be trusted.

"Tell me what you want, then I'll tell you if we will do it."

"There are some friends of ours under arrest in Ålesund, being held by the local Gestapo. We would like to get them out. You can assist in that."

"A frontal assault on a prison sounds like it could get us killed. Not just Carter and myself, but you as well."

"But if we don't then it is almost certain that my identity will be discovered. Then I will lose my freedom to move around. Besides, my comrades are important to us. We don't want to see them end up like Ingrid's brother."

"I'm not sure. It sounds high risk."

"Perhaps it would help if I told you who else was being held there. You asked me if I knew what had happened to Olav Andreaasen and his family. I made some enquiries. He and his wife and children were arrested. They were taken to Ålesund for interrogation and are still being held there awaiting transfer to the concentration camp at Ulven. You probably haven't heard of Ulven, but it has a reputation for brutality. Not many people live out a year there."

Despite the obvious moral blackmail and blatant manipulation, that changed things a lot. Olav had helped them to escape in the first place. Without his help, he and Green would probably already be on their way to a PoW camp. They might even be dead. He couldn't just let the man and his family be dragged off to a concentration camp. Although not much was known about the ones in Norway, compared to those opened before the war in

Germany, Carter was under no illusions about what might happen to the family once they arrived there.

"Can I confer with my comrade?"

"Of course. You are in this together, so I suppose he has a right to speak. In a true democracy, like Russia, all the people are involved in the decision making."

Carter doubted that but wasn't going to debate the issue. He took Green out into the farmyard.

"I can't commit you to this, Prof. You aren't under any obligation to obey an order for an irregular operation such as this." Carter told him.

"And let you go wandering off on your own? I don't think so, Lucky. Besides, I rather fancy that Ingrid. I don't want you nickin' her from under my nose."

Carter knew that Green was playing it for laughs for his benefit. He was probably as dubious about the idea of attacking the prison as he was himself. Green spoke again.

"It ain't right that Olav and his wife should go to a camp for helping us. If we can prevent that, then I'm in."

"OK, but I'm going to put some conditions around it. Just back me up on those."

"You're the boss, Boss."

They returned inside.

"Do you have a plan of attack?" Carter asked, when he and Green were seated again.

"Not yet. If you won't do it, then the plan would have to change, so I wanted your agreement before I risked anything."

"OK. Here's my conditions for taking part. Firstly, I'm trained for this, so I do the planning. That's not negotiable. Secondly, if I think it's too risky, we don't do it. Also not negotiable. Finally, if we get Olav and his family out, they go back to England[1] with me."

Sven and Ingrid exchanged some rapid Norwegian, before Ingrid nodded her head. "Very well, English. We agree to your terms. How do we proceed?"

"I'll need to get a look at the place, to see how it might be done. I think it's unlikely that we can simply charge in through the front door. If you can get hold of a floor plan, even a sketch map would do, it would help."

"That is possible. I called it a prison, but it's actually the town's police station. I'm sure I can find people who have seen the inside of it."

"That's good. Secondly, apart from the four of us, how many more people can you call on? I mean people who know one end of a gun from the other and who won't freeze if the shooting starts."

"We aren't strong in this area. Not yet. I rather hope that if we succeed in this operation it will help us to recruit. But I can probably persuade a few friends from further south to help us. It will take a couple of days for me to get them here. Let's say four more."

Eight people to assault a police station. It might just work.

"What sort of training have you had?"

"We train across the border in Sweden, though the Swedes don't know that. It is even more sparsely populated than Norway, for its size. We learn to fire a variety of weapons and the basics of sabotage and demolition. The rest is field craft specific to a resistance group. How to mount an ambush; how to communicate covertly; how to hide in plain sight; how to move around the country without being noticed; that sort of thing.

In many ways it wasn't that different to commando training, Carter thought. But he didn't want to give Sven a bigger head than he already had by telling him that.

"OK. That sounds good enough for what we need to do. When can we do a reconnaissance?"

"Tonight, if you wish. I'll leave Ingrid here with Green and you and I will take the motor bike."

"No, not tonight. First I need to see maps of the area and there are a lot of questions that need to be answered. We'll do the reconnaissance tomorrow night if you can get me the answers I need. Then we'll mount the operation the next night."

"That's *Nyttårsaften*, New Year's Eve."

"All the better. The Germans make a big deal out of New Year. With a bit of luck they'll all be drunk. But the Germans are looking for two people on a motor cycle, so isn't it a bit risky us going to Ålesund on the bike?"

"The Germans are predictable. We know where they mount their checkpoints and they're easy to avoid. We'll also be in a different command area, where they are a little bit more relaxed than the area where you attacked. We'll hide the bike on the edge of the town and walk in to the centre. You'll need to change your clothes."

"Not a chance. If I'm caught out of uniform I'll be shot as a spy. If I'm caught as I am, I'll be treated as a Prisoner of War."

"How very bourgeois. If you were in Russia you would just be an enemy of the people and it wouldn't matter if you wore uniform or not."

"Well, it's a good job that we're not in Russia, then."

[1] Up to and including the war years it was quite normal to use the term 'England' to mean the whole of the British Isles, so Carter isn't being chauvinistic. The terms Britain or United Kingdom were less popular at that time, except in official communications.

* * *

"It's going to be a lot more tricky than I thought." Carter said as he pored over the tatty map that Sven had provided. "You didn't tell me Ålesund is an island stuck right out here on the end of this peninsula. There's only one road in and out. If the Germans cut the bridge between the town and the mainland, we'll be stuck like rats in a trap."

"You think it can't be done?" Sven asked, stroking his chin thoughtfully.

"I didn't say that. I just think it's going to be a lot tougher than I originally thought. Where is the police station?"

Sven unfolded a street map of the town. "Here, just off Aspøya, the main road through the town."

"What about boats in and out."

"There's a fishing harbour to the west, here. It's also used by privately owned sailing boats." He pointed to the southern shore at the western end of the island. "But the ferries use this port here." He tapped the map to the north of the bridge that connected the island to the mainland.

"Could we get hold of a boat somewhere along here?" Carter tapped the older, small scale map, along the southern side of the fjord where there was another chain of islands all connected together by bridges. "If we could, then it's probably a more viable escape route."

"We could take a vehicle into the town and then steal a boat for the escape." Sven suggested.

"No. There's no guarantee that we could find one that we could start up. Besides, even the Germans wouldn't be so stupid as to leave that bridge unguarded. We wouldn't get into the town."

"It appears the Germans are that stupid." Sven corrected him. "I have crossed that bridge several times at night and never seen a single German. They stop traffic there during the day, but after curfew, never."

"I stand corrected, but I still don't like the idea of stealing a boat. Is there someone who could be bribed to take us across and then back?"

"Possible. I'll check that out tomorrow. If not?"

"Then I don't think we can risk it. We need a secure escape route and with that single bridge … no, it isn't viable."

"In that case I will make sure we have a boat, one way or another."

"You'll also need to check out the beaches on the south side of the fjord to see which one best suits our purpose. We'll look for landing sites in the town when we do the reconnaissance tonight."

* * *

Sven hadn't been lying. They walked across the bridge onto Ålesund island without being challenged. They had parked the motor bike up short of the town, hiding it in a ditch, and walked the rest of the way, keeping to the deep shadows where they wouldn't be seen. The ride had taken them two hours and Carter's face was still stiff from the cold.

The bridge was flanked by sandbagged defensive positions that were empty. The two men made their way along the main road, carefully picking their route so as not to expose themselves. The streets were totally dark, so as not to show any lights that might help approaching boats. The Royal Navy were known to carry out night time reconnaissance of the Norwegian coast, looking for shipping that they could target and keeping the town dark prevented them from identifying their location with any accuracy. Only the moon, now in its first quarter, provided a small amount of illumination.

The police station was an old Victorian era building. Outside stood an Opel staff car, probably used by the local Gestapo. There was also a car bearing Norwegian number plates, and a motor cycle, both marked '*Politi*', police.

Two sentry boxes protected by sandbag walls stood next to the main door, one on either side, but they were empty. In the thirty minutes they watched, no one had entered or left the building, though light showed around the edge of a window frame behind one of the sentry boxes. Sven led them through a couple of narrow lanes to the rear of the building.

The slope meant that they were now below street level, at the same height as the detention cells. A wall ran around the back of the police station, marking the perimeter of the exercise yard that was used by prisoners. It was topped by festoons of barbed wire. That could be cut, Carter knew, but they risked it rattling and attracting attention if they chose that route into the station. Besides, getting into the detention area didn't help them if they didn't have the keys to the cells and they had no explosives that would let them blow the locks on the doors.

Several of Carter's questions had been about the manning of the police station and had been answered by Sven's contacts in the town. Ålesund was a quiet, law abiding place. It made the word 'sleepy' sound frenetic. The cells were rarely used, except to allow the occasional drunk to sober up before being sent home. That was before the war, of course. Now they were put to more frequent use by the Gestapo. But the law abiding nature of the town meant that the police force was small. At night they could expect a maximum of two constables and a Sergeant on duty, the latter also acted as gaoler. If the constables were doing their job, patrolling the streets, the Sergeant would be alone. The two gestapo officers worked office hours. If they needed to make an arrest they called on the services of the local garrison.

"OK. I've seen enough." Carter whispered. "Let's take a look at the fishing harbour and the waterfront."

Most of the south side of the island was given over to boats and the businesses that supported them. There were fishing boats of various sizes tied up. They would only be allowed to put to sea with a German naval escort. That boat stood separate from the others, a trawler armed with an ancient artillery piece at the stern, with mountings fore and aft for a couple of machine guns.

What caught Carter's eye was at the very south end of the Island, where a sea wall jutted out into the fjord. Two E-Boats were tied up, a German sentry pacing along the top of the wall above them. What a tasty target they would make. The commando in Carter's heart made him yearn to attack them, but he had to be cautious. The objective was the release of the prisoners. Nothing could be allowed to distract him from that.

But more importantly, Carter found a suitable landing point not far from a lane that led up towards the police station. A rickety jetty sat rotting away next to what looked like it might be some sort of canning factory. Whatever it once was, it was now derelict. But its bulk threw pools of deeper darkness across the water; perfect for concealing a boat while its passengers carried out their mission.

"Right, let's get out of here. I've got an idea about how we can do this." Carter whispered to Sven. "But we have to have that boat and it has to be able to carry all of us. That's eight people in and fourteen out."

"You mean ten … Oh, sorry, I forgot about Andreaasen and his family."

Carter stopped and stared at Sven's retreating back. Was that just a slip of the memory? Or had Sven no intention of rescuing Olav? Well, Carter had every intention of making sure Sven kept to his side of their bargain.

* * *

The four extra members of the Osvald Group arrived in the middle of the next day. Three men and a woman. The woman was completely different to Ingrid. She was older and smaller, dark haired and dark eyed, but her expression was just as taciturn. But she carried herself with an air of authority. The three men seemed to defer to her. None of them spoke English, but between the six of them they managed to exchange names: The woman was Gudrid and the men Henninge, Ottar and Thobias.

Carter didn't like the idea of not being able to communicate directly with his team. Instructions often lost something in translation and the precise meanings of words often depended on context, which didn't translate so readily. Carter would have to keep that in mind and use language that was simple and difficult to get wrong, even with the worst translator.

Sven and Ingrid arrived shortly afterwards and Carter started his briefing at once. It would be a long night and to get to their objective and back in the dark they would have to start almost at once.

Sven brought Carter up to date with the situation regarding a boat, which was welcome news. He had found a fisherman who would do the job at a fair price. The man had reason to hate the Germans, which accounted for his co-operation. With that vital resource secured, Carter felt more confident about the feasibility of the operation.

"There are two Osvald Group members in custody at Ålesund." He started, "In company with the family of Olav Andreasson. Our mission is to release the Osvald Group prisoners being held in the police station in Ålesund." He started using the standard military format for briefings: situation, mission, execution, any questions and check understanding, abbreviated to SMEAC. Sven translated.

"Sven has brought a van in which we can all travel. He will also take his motor bike so that he can go ahead of us and make sure the road is clear." He waited for the translation to catch up.

"We will travel to this location here." He pointed, using his dagger tip to tap the map at a place marked Fyllingsjøen, which lay on an island on the south side of the fjord, directly opposite Ålesund. It was connected to the mainland by a series of country roads and bridges. "From there we will cross to Ålesund and land here." He switched to the street map of the town to indicate their landing point next to the old canning plant. "Two of you will remain with the boat to guard it. That will be Ottar and Thobias." The two men nodded their head to show their understanding. "If you are disturbed you will take the boat to this point here. He tapped the map at a location nearer to the bridge that connected the island to the mainland.

"The rest of us will go to the police station, enter it, get the keys to the cells and release the prisoners. The gaoler will be locked in one his own cells. I don't anticipate any sort of fight, but we will use force if we have to. Four of you will come directly back to the boat with the prisoners, but Green and I will go and create a diversion which I hope will cover your escape."

He paused while he moved his dagger tip to point at the sea wall at the far end of the town.

"Here there are two German E-Boats. We will take one of the cars from the police station and attack them and set them on fire. The Germans will assume that it is some sort of naval raid and will come to put the fires out and also to defend the boats. We will then take the car and head out over the bridge, creating a distraction which will allow the rest of you to escape in the boat. We expect them to give chase, but it will take them time to get organised. Most of the garrison seems to be in bed at night and of course it's also New Year's Eve. We think that the Germans will probably all be drunk, so I don't think we are in any danger of being caught. We will keep going until we reach this point here..." He switched back to the small scale map and pointed to a hamlet by the name of Valle, "… Where we will hide the car and we will lie up until you can come and collect us as you go by. With you having to cross by boat, we'll be there before you."

"Why don't you let us attack the boats?" Sven asked.

"Because, ultimately, we are expendable. You are needed to get your friends into hiding; that's something we can't do. If we don't make it, we rely on you to get Olav and his family out of the country, or at least to a place of safety."

There was an exchange of Norwegian between Sven and Gudrid, which made it clear that the woman was confused about something. Sven made a short jerky gesture with his head towards Carter, saying something in an angry tone, and the woman fell silent.

I wonder what that was about? Carter mused. Clearly some sort of disagreement, but what about? Was it because Carter was taking such a prominent role, or was it because she disagreed with the plan as a whole? There had been a clear clash of egos there. But it was something that Carter couldn't interpret, which meant it remained a mystery.

He ran through the briefing a second time, then answered a couple of questions put to him through Sven. Carter checked his watch. "I have one more thing to do." He said, "Then we go."

9 – E-Boat

The van belonged to a baker and the heady aroma of fresh bread made Carter's mouth water. Unfortunately the baker hadn't seen fit to leave any of his product inside, so the lengthy ride to Ålesund was turning into something akin to torture.

Sven had been surprised to see the two commandos climbing into the back of the van carrying all their equipment with them. "Why do you need all that? Surely just your rifles and ammunition would be enough."

"Are you familiar with the Boy Scouts?" Carter asked.

"You mean that bourgeois organisation aimed at brainwashing young children into propagating the Capitalist tyranny?"

"Yes, that would be them. Do you know their motto?"

"Of course. It's 'Be Prepared'."

"Precisely. We also adhere to the spirit of that motto. While I am sure that my plan will work, we have to consider the possibility that it might not. If that is the case and we have to go on the run, it won't serve us very well if our equipment is back here, out of reach. So, when we travel, we take everything that we will need to keep us alive."

"It seems an unnecessary waste of effort, if you ask me." Sven dismissed the notion.

Thank goodness that I'm not responsible for your life then, Carter thought, heaving himself into the back of the van and settling himself into a corner.

The van was fitted out with uprights with runners screwed into them, into which bread trays could be slid. It meant that it was difficult to find a comfortable position, so in the end Carter just sat with his legs half crossed, back bent, his arms across his knees, his rifle lying on the floor in front of him. It would need a good cleaning, afterwards, he mused. Flour and bread crumbs would get into it and clog it up. Fortunately the German rifle was a simple weapon, not dissimilar to the Lee Enfield three-oh-three that Green was cradling. After tonight, of course, Carter might not need it again and he might be able to just drop it into the North Sea and forget about it.

The van lurched onwards, with Sven flitting up and down the road, bringing news of what lay ahead. 'Nothing', was the most common report, as the Germans settled down to enjoy *Silvester*, the name they used for New Year's Eve. Carter made a mental note to try and find out why the name had been adopted[1].

The van did pause for a while, hidden along a side road, as a German lorry rumbled past, heading in the opposite direction, but it was the only unplanned diversion.

The journey was a lengthy one as the road switch backed up and down the side of fjords. The four men and one woman in the back bounced off the sides at each twist and turn of the road. At one point Gudrun was sent sprawling onto Carter's lap. As she pushed herself back into her place she gave Carter a look that suggested he was at fault.

The Norwegian coastline didn't offer many opportunities for the building of straight roads, and it was too difficult to build through the steep hills and mountains without tunnelling. Perhaps the Norwegians would do that one day, if ever their nation became wealthy enough. There was little chance of that, Carter thought, with an economy based on fish and forestry. Mineral wealth, that was what they needed, but there wasn't anything much to be had in these mountains. The harvest from the North Sea may be bountiful, but it would never make them a wealthy nation.

At last the van lurched to a halt and the back doors were opened. Carter and Green went into their familiar routine, dashing to find cover and letting their two key senses, hearing and smell, tell them if there was any danger about. The resistance fighters watched on with some amusement, but it was Carter who had the last laugh. He stood up from his hiding place and returned to the van, ordering everyone into silence with a whispered command.

"There's someone down there." He whispered to Sven, pointing into the darkness. "Are you expecting anyone here?"

Sven shook his head emphatically. He gabbled some Norwegian and his comrades spread out along the side of the road, finally falling silent.

Carter ordered Green forward to see what might be in front of them. In the distance he could hear the gentle hiss of the sea on the gravel beach. Behind it was swathes of long salt grass, reaching all the way to the road.

Carter's nerves jangled. There was no reason for there to be any Germans here, he knew. They didn't know about the raid, so they couldn't have anticipated that the group would use this beach as the departure point for their boat … unless someone had betrayed them.

But that didn't make any sense. If any of the group had betrayed them, there were plenty of places where the Germans could have mounted an ambush. They didn't need to wait until they got to this point. It wasn't even the best place for an attack. It was too open and offered too many opportunities for escape in three directions. The sea blocked only the fourth escape route. The only advantage the Germans would have was that they were on an island, where they could cut off any fugitives simply by closing the bridges. But the same applied to several other places along their route.

Green returned, a big grin on his face. "A bloke and his bird making whoopee in the grass over there." He pointed. "Looks like they came by push bike."

"On a cold night like this, they have my total admiration." Carter replied. "Did they see you."

"Lucky… please." Green was clearly affronted by the idea that he might have been detected.

"I'm surprised that they didn't stop when the van pulled up." Carter continued.

"When you're in the middle of what that lad's in the middle of, you don't stop for anything. I reckon it would take a team of horses to pull him off of her right now." Green chuckled.

"OK, that'll do thanks Prof." Carter reproved him before scuttling across to tell Sven what Green had discovered.

"Besides, the wind is blowing in from the sea. It would muffle the sound of the vehicle engines." Green finished his report.

"What do we do?" Sven asked.

"We wait for them to leave. If we stay quiet, they won't even realise we're here. The van is a bit of a problem. Do you think your men can push it along the road a bit?"

"Which way? We don't know which direction they are going."

"Which way are the nearest houses? They've probably come from them."

"There's a small place, no more than half a dozen houses and a couple of farms. About three kilometres that way." Sven pointed.

"They're only on bikes, so the chances are that's where they're from, so push the van in the other direction. It only needs to go about a hundred yards … I mean metres."

Sven gathered his men around him. Leaving Green to keep an eye out for the copulating couple, Carter leant his shoulder and they moved the van out of the way as silently as they could.

The pair of lovers stayed only fifteen minutes longer, before emerging from the grass, half carrying, half dragging their bicycles. However they may have been dressed when Green had seen them, they were now bundled up in coats, hats and scarves. They giggled and whispered their way back to the road before mounting their bikes and cycling off in the direction in which Sven had indicated the nearest dwelling lay, oblivious to the fact that they had been under reluctant observation.

Green went ahead as scout, while the remainder of the group stumbled their way through the grassy tussocks to the shore line. Sven took out a torch and flashed it into the darkness three times, receiving an identical signal in return. A few minutes later an ancient fishing boat crept in towards the shore. It was flat bottomed, making it suitable for inshore work.

The boat's skipper might have stepped straight off the label of a pilchard can. He was big and bearded, a woollen cap pulled down as far as his bushy eyebrows, thick grey hair sticking out from underneath it at random angles. His legs were clad in oilskins, and he wore a waterproof jacket, buttoned tight against the weather.

Since the raid on Kirkesfjord, the light winds had been from the south, keeping the air unseasonably mild, but that morning the wind had turned to the north and now blew in icy blasts across the fjord. Although the numerous islands prevent the growth of large waves, the wind did whip up smaller swells which were rocking the boat as the eight waded out through the shallows to board.

"This is Peder and you are on his boat. I have paid a not inconsiderable sum for him to be here." Sven translated the introduction he had already made in Norwegian. Carter and Green shook hands with the elderly fisherman, who eyed their shoulder flashes with interest.

"Here are the materials you requested." Sven indicated some objects that were laying in the well, behind the tiny wheelhouse. There was a wooden crate of screw top bottles, a large can and a small heap of rags. "May I ask why you want these things?"

"When you did your training, did they not teach you to make petrol bombs?" Carter asked.

"No, but I think you are about to."

Carter suppressed a smile. Every day's a school day, he thought.

"These were first created during the Spanish Civil War as a quick and easy explosive device that could be made from readily available materials. The fuel doesn't have to be petrol. Any flammable liquid will do. Let me show you."

Carter lifted one of the bottles from the crate and unscrewed the cap. He shook it next to his ear to make sure it was empty, then placed it on the ground. Lifting the can he unscrewed the cap from it and sniffed, to make sure it contained petrol. Satisfied, he carefully poured some of the contents into the bottle. "You only fill it half full, so that when you put the wick into the bottle it doesn't soak up any of the contents." He demonstrated by tearing some of the rags into smaller sections and stuffing one of the pieces into the neck of the bottle. "Make sure that you dry any of the petrol that gets on your hands," he admonished, "and don't be tempted to soak the rag in petrol. If you do, the bomb will go off early and smother you in burning petrol. Now all you need to do is set fire to the rag and throw the bottle against something hard. The bottle smashes and the fuel explodes. Simple."

He removed the rag and screwed the cap back onto the bottle, before bending to fill as many of the bottles as he could before he ran out of petrol.

"Always carry the bottles with the caps screwed on so that the fuel doesn't spill out and catch fire accidently. You can use them against vehicles, buildings, people or, as in my use for them tonight, two E-Boats harboured up in Ålesund."

"That was very informative, thank you Lieutenant. So, it will take about sixty minutes to cross the fjord, if you want to keep the engine noise low. We can go faster if you wish, but the boat will make more noise."

"Sixty minutes will be just fine, thank you." Carter felt the soft smack of snow flakes on his face, just a light flurry, but enough to make him smile with satisfaction. Lucky by name, lucky by nature it seemed. Snow would help them, providing cover and also keeping the Germans tucked up in front of warm fires, drinking their New Year's schnapps. "Do you have a bag in which I can carry the petrol bombs? I'll wrap the rags around the bottles to stop them clinking together and they will be easier to carry than in the crate." He had only filled half the bottles, so the crate was too big for his purposes.

"I'll see what Peder has." Sven wandered off to speak to the skipper, who was in the wheelhouse.

The small boat rocked alarmingly as it hit a bigger wave, but Carter could see Peder swaying with the motion rather than trying to fight it. A couple of the other resistance members were looking unhappy at the disturbance, but for himself and Green it was as familiar as walking down the high street, after all the time they had spent on board landing craft in far worse weather, while training for Operation Absolom. Carter found himself a spot in the lee of the wheelhouse where he was out of the wind and snow and crouched down. Green came and joined him.

"Do you think this will work, Lucky?" Green asked quietly, a hint of anxiety in his voice.

"As far as the attack on the police station is concerned, yes. I could take that place with a Brownie pack. The risky part will be getting ashore and getting back to the boat again. Going in shouldn't be too bad as we'll have the element of surprise. I hope the snow stays with us, it will help to conceal our approach and discourage the Germans from going out onto the streets. But the escape is dependent on us creating a diversion to draw the Germans in two directions. The E-Boats are in one direction and we will be making a lot of noise going across the bridge so they chase us. That should give the boat a good chance of escape."

"And if we get caught?"

"Unlikely. We should be able to stay ahead of any pursuers, but if necessary, we go to ground again and make our own way back to Fredrick's place."

"Where did you go after you finished the briefing?" Green asked.

"Just to use Fredrick's radio. I wanted to get the shipping forecast on the wireless. That's how I knew the snow was coming." The weather was a vital part of Carter's plan, so he'd had to use the wireless to get a weather forecast. Neither the BBC nor the Germans broadcast the weather forecast, not since the start of the war and it had taken Carter some searching of the short-wave frequencies until he had picked up an Irish station that gave him the necessary information in English.

"Won't that be a problem with leaving tracks?"

"Not the way I plan to do things." Carter replied enigmatically.

"You want to brief me in on that?"

"When the time comes. I promise you, Prof. You're going to love it."

Green gave a wry smile and shook his head. It was going to be another 'Hamilton Farm', obviously, so trying to get the boss to give up the goods before he was ready was going to be a waste of time. Green could only hope that he lived up to his nickname.

The boat lurched onwards into the night then started to slow. Peder had brought them unerringly to the old jetty. What navigation markers he'd used, Carter couldn't guess at. The snow had dwindled to a few brief flurries, which improved visibility, so he assumed that Peder had been able to pick out the signs he navigated by.

The hull of the boat ground against the pilings and Carter didn't know which was in the most danger of collapse, the jetty or the boat. As it happened, both managed to stay upright, at least long enough for everyone to disembark. Thobias remained on board, nonchalantly holding a pistol, just in case Peder got cold feet, while Ottar took up a position in the shadows of the crumbling factory, a Sten gun in his hands.

The remaining six hurried through the silent streets. Ålesund was remarkably lacking in any New Year's spirit. Carter could understand that. The Norwegians were under curfew from ten o'clock until six the next day and the Germans would be confident that the law and the weather would combine to prevent them needing to patrol the streets. The snow was already melting and the pressure of their feet left few footprints and those that they did leave were already forming into shapeless puddles.

They crammed into an alley across the road from the Police Station, Carter and Green at the front, observing silently, looking for any signs of danger. The same three vehicles were parked there, the only change being that the Opel was now the middle of the three.

Carter raised his hand, indicating that they should cross the road. There was a mad flurry of running feet and the six of them threw themselves into the shadows of the sentry boxes, three on either side of the door. Carter crept around the one on his side and gently tried the door handle. It turned easily. Sven was on the other side, his Sten gun at the ready. There had been a brief whispered argument, with Ingrid unwilling to relinquish her prized weapon, but Sven had pulled rank and won possession. He would go through the door first, the gun saying all that needed to be said to whoever was inside.

Carter pushed the door open hard and heard it slam back against the wall. Sven dashed through, shouldering the door aside as it tried to close itself under the impetus of its own recoil. He fired a short burst of automatic fire into the ceiling of the police station, making sure that he had the attention of whoever was there.

Carter winced at the sudden noise. It had been unnecessary and could raise the alarm. Sven had watched too many gangster movies.

The only person inside turned out to be the police Sergeant, dozing behind the tall desk and now trying to clear his befuddled mind as he woke to the sound of the gunfire.

"*Ikke prøv noe dumt.*" Sven barked, producing a negative shake of the head from the Sergeant. "*Hvor er nøklene til cellene?*"

The frightened gaoler scrabbled to open a drawer and produced a ring with five large keys on it. From the floor plan of the police station, Carter knew that there were only four cells, so the fifth key must either give access to the holding area, or to the exercise yard at the back.

"Ask him for the keys to the vehicles." Carter instructed. Outside Green and Ingrid covered the street, making sure that they weren't surprised from behind, while Gudrid and Henninge squeezed into the small entrance area and added their firepower to threaten the already frightened police officer.

"*Bilnøklene også.*" The Sergeant dipped into the drawer again and came out with three keys, placing them on the counter next to the cell keys. Carter swept up the three small keys while Sven took the keys to the cells.

"*Hvor er konstablene?*" Sven asked.

"*Hjemme. Jeg sendte dem hjem tidlig.*" The Sergeant replied in a shaky voice.

"He says he sent the Constables home early. That means there should only be him here."

"In that case I'll leave you to it. When you see the flames from the E-Boats, make a run for the jetty and get out of here as fast as you can. We'll see you at Valle in a couple of hours."

"Good luck, English." Sven gave him his sardonic smile.

"Please, don't call me English." Carter said as he left. "Call me Lucky."

As he emerged, Green trotted down the police station steps after him, the sack full of petrol bombs slung over his shoulder. Carter identified the key for the Opel and tossed it to his companion. As soon as the car's engine coughed into life, Carter threw the two remaining keys behind the sentry boxes where they would lie until daylight revealed their location. It would only delay pursuit by a few minutes, as any police officer worth his salt would be able to hot wire the other car, but every minute counted.

Carter folded himself into the small interior of the Opel. The local gestapo obviously didn't hold sufficient rank to warrant a larger vehicle. Carter's webbing and pack added bulk to him, making the front passenger seat even more cramped. The snow had started to fall again.

"Ok, Prof. Change of plan." Carter said as Green pulled the car out of the centre of the three parking spaces.

"As if I hadn't guessed." Green replied, his teeth glinting in the dashboard lights.

Carter laughed. "We're still going to the harbour, to the E-Boats, but we're only going to burn one of them. The other one is our transport home. Before you ask, there's no time for questions. If we get away, I'll be happy to tell you why." And if we don't get away, explanations won't matter, he thought.

Green shrugged his shoulders. Carter was right, this wasn't the time for explanations. Following the instructions that Carter recited from memory, Green drove them through the blacked-out streets to the west end of the island, where the harbour wall projected out into the fjord. The two E-Boats were still tied up securely to it. The clouds were broken, scudding along under the north wind, allowing a small amount of moonlight to shine through intermittently. The sentry was just about visible, a dark figure against the slightly lighter sky, huddled inside his greatcoat. He looked around, hearing the car approaching, unslinging his rifle from his shoulder and holding it across his body.

Seeing the Opel the sentry stiffened. He would recognise the vehicle as belonging to the Gestapo, but that didn't mean it was friendly. In fact, it could mean just the opposite. "Stop about ten yards short of him and keep the headlights on full beam." The headlamps had been reduced to thin slits as part of the blackout precautions, but the extra candle power of the main beams would destroy the sentry's night vision.

Carter felt at his belt, finding what he needed and holding it in his left hand, resting on his lap. Winding down the passenger side window Carter extended his right hand and made a beckoning motion. They say that at night all cats are grey, so Carter hoped that the sentry couldn't make out the khaki of his battledress sleeve.

The sentry answered the summons. Carter was unsurprised. You don't disobey a summons from the Gestapo. He was *Kriegsmarine*, not *Wehrmacht* Carter noted, Navy not Army.

As he approached, Carter crooked his finger, beckoning, as though he wanted the sentry to look inside. Obediently the German lowered his head. With his right hand Carter grabbed the collar of his greatcoat, pulling him further down, while with his left hand he stabbed upwards with his commando dagger, catching the sentry cleanly in the neck just below the strap of his helmet. Hot blood gushed over Carter's hand out of the severed artery in the man's throat; or was the jugular a vein? Carter thought idly. He withdrew the knife and the German collapsed to the ground, releasing his grip on his weapon and clasping at his throat, as though he could stem the red tide that was flooding across the cobbles that paved the top of the sea wall.

Carter pushed the car door open, finding it difficult to climb out as the sentry's body got in the way. "Help me get him over the side." Carter ordered. Green climbed out of the driver's side and between them they grasped the body, Green at the feet and Carter holding the arms. He found himself looking down into the pleading eyes of the German, desperate not to have his life ended but it was already too late for that, Carter knew. Most of the sentry's blood was now making the cobbles slippery under Carter's feet. The knowledge that he had inflicted a mortal wound in cold blood disturbed Carter. It was different in training. Then the daggers were rubber and the victim got up afterwards and went for a mug of tea. He couldn't look the German in the eye and had to avert his gaze. They dropped the body into the sea with a splash and Green returned to the pool of blood and picked up the German's rifle, pitching it after the body. They heard it hit the water, then the only sound was the low burbling of the Opel's engine.

"OK. Bring the car forward to the first E-Boat and get the petrol bombs onboard." Carter ordered, pulling his rifle from behind the passenger seat and jogging away along the wall.

As soon as he drew level with the E-Boat he slowed and looked for any signs of life. There were none. Now, the problem was, how did he start an E-Boat? Did it need keys? Could it be hotwired? Could the two of them sail it by themselves? He realised that he hadn't really thought this part of the plan through. But if they couldn't start it, they could still revert to Plan A and fire bomb both boats before heading for the bridge. The island was barely a mile long. They could be there in little more than a minute.

He crept along the narrow gangway and stepped onto the deck behind the low superstructure. He felt gentle vibrations under his feet. The boat was under power, perhaps an auxiliary motor of some sort, keeping batteries charged and the heating and ventilation systems working. Lucky Carter! Lucky, lucky Carter.

He climbed a short ladder and found himself in a small wheelhouse. In the centre stood the wheel, not one of the big, spoked affairs of the movies; it was barely the size of the Opel's steering wheel, though the brass it was made from glinted in the faint light. In front of the wheel was a dashboard, much bigger than that of a car but serving the same purpose. To one side were three throttle handles set close together, side by side so that they could be operated one handed. On both sides of the dashboard there was a profusion of dials and switches, below which were two buttons, one red and one green. Black plates were engraved with white letters to announce their purpose, as if Carter needed telling: '*Motoren Starten*' and '*Motoren Anstahlen*'. Engines start and engines stop.

He heard footsteps behind him and saw Green gently placing the sack of petrol bombs on the deck.

"Back onto the wall and undo the mooring lines." Carter hissed, pointing fore and aft. Green hurried to obey. A few seconds later there was a muffled thumping as the bow line was thrown onto the fore deck, then a similar sound from the rear as that rope, too, was thrown inboard. Green pulled the gang plank up onto the wall, then dropped onto the deck, landing with a thud of boots.

Carter pressed the green button and there was a muffled roar as the three marine diesels sprang into life. Turning the wheel slightly to steer the boat away from the wall, he nudged the centre throttle handle forward a fraction. The boat moved slowly, edging away from the wall. Once it was clear and in no danger of colliding with the other boat, just a few yards away, Carter returned the throttle leaver to the neutral position and went down to join Green on deck.

Green had already removed the screw caps of the bottles. Carter picked one up and stuffed a length of rag into the neck. They worked quickly, preparing all six bottles. When they were all ready, Carter held one in each hand and tilted them towards Green. He fished in his pocket and found a box of matches. Striking one, he lit the rags in the bottles. Pulling his arm back, Carter threw one bottle in an arc towards the E-Boat that was still held against the sea wall. He then transferred the other bottle to his right hand and threw that as well.

The first bottle crashed into the deck of the E-Boat halfway between its superstructure and a pair of ventilators that stood in the middle of the deck. Another bomb, thrown by Green, arced towards the boat even as Carter's second struck it. They exploded in a satisfying whoof of igniting petrol. Carter's third bomb was directed towards the aft of the boat, where a pair of twenty millimetre machine guns stood on a tall mounting. Green sent the last two bombs towards the foredeck, which they were just drifting past. One landed between the life rafts, while the other crashed against the mounting supporting the forward twenty millimetre machine gun. Flames were spreading as paint and other flammable material caught fire. Soon the boat would be alight from stem to stern, but Carter had no time to wait for that. He doubted that the fires would do any permanent damage. The metal of the hull wouldn't burn too well, but the insulation on the electrical cabling would burn through and that should be enough to put the boat out of action.

"Prof, do you think you can fire those two machine guns?" Carter asked, pointing aft to where they stood pointing through a sheet of armoured metal.

"Shouldn't have too much trouble working it out, Lucky." He replied.

"OK, keep them aimed at the sea wall. If you see so much as a stray cat up there, you let fly." With the fire illuminating the sea wall and the water around the burning boat, if the Germans arrived they would be clearly visible, while their E-Boat would be hidden by the darkness.

He returned to the wheelhouse and peered through. The snow was back with a vengeance and he had difficulty seeing through the windows. He wondered what the German for 'windscreen wipers' was but didn't have time to work it out by trial and error. Instead he nudged the middle throttle handle forward a little once again, to give the boat some forward momentum and steered it away from the wall and into the navigable channel. He turned the wheel gently to the left, clearing the wall by a safe margin and peered into the night, trying to make out the lights of the safe channel.

During daylight he would have been able to make out the green painted buoys on the left and the red ones on the right, the opposite way round to the way they were viewed when approaching harbour. Before the war each buoy would have been brightly lit with a flashing light of the appropriate colour, but that was no longer the case.

Then he saw one. A tiny glimmer of green on the blackness of the sea. The markers were still lit, but with far lower wattage lights. They would have to be, Carter realised, or the harbour wouldn't be usable at night and that was when the Germans moved a lot of their shipping, keeping it invisible to the RAF.

The light was in the correct place, but he couldn't make out its opposite number on the right. No matter, so long as he kept the green ones in sight and on the left of the boat he didn't run any risk of hitting any rocks. The map he had studied told him that he had to go east before he could turn back to the west, to get around the island of Hessa, which was joined to the end of Ålesund by another bridge. Then he could turn west and pass between the islands of Godøya to the north and something unpronounceable to the south. Only after that would they be in the open sea.

Carter looked around the cabin for the radio, finding it mounted above the windows, just in front of the throttles, probably where the captain stood, right next to the helmsman. It was a simple enough looking set, a VHF ship-to-shore radio and he didn't need to be a genius to identify the on/off switch. It took a minute or so for the set's valves to warm up, then the wheelhouse filled with a jabber of noise. There was the definite sound of panic in the words he was hearing as the Germans on shore sought to find out what was going on. It was too distracting, Carter decided and it told him nothing. He switched the radio off again.

The two islands at the mouth of fjord would be fortified to protect shipping, just like at Moyland, Carter suspected. He could only hope that the snow kept up, rendering them invisible from the shore. He knew the local telephone lines would now be buzzing with hastily issued orders. Soldiers and sailors would be being roused from their beds by panicking NCOs and berated for their slowness getting dressed. Carter gave a self-satisfied smirk as he imagined the garrison commander having to explain to his superiors how he had let an E-Boat be stolen from under his nose. But they were far from out of the woods yet.

He picked out the next green light, further to the right than the last one. That marked the start of the turn in the channel that would take them around the eastern end of Hessa and through one hundred and eighty degrees to the exit of the fjord.

He was frustrated by the slow speed, but there was nothing he could do. If he went too fast he might miss the next channel marker and run them aground on the opposite shore. It might even result in the boat sinking under them. He couldn't risk that.

Behind him he heard the loud bark of the twin twenty mm machine guns. Someone must have arrived to investigate the flames. Green kept up a controlled rate of fire, just a few rounds in each burst, picking out targets as they silhouetted themselves against the burning E-Boat.

A freak wind lifted the curtain of snow momentarily and Carter made out the sweeping arc of twinkling green along with the red lights that were now closer on the right hand side, then the snow closed in again. But it had given him some idea of the route they would follow. There was still a lot of curve in the marked channel. He had to keep the speed low. Once they were on a straight course, heading between the two islands, he would open the throttles wide and take them up to top speed. He wondered just how fast the boat could go. More to the point, how far could they go without refuelling? Was it far enough to get them to Scotland? Carter had to hope so.

He scanned the dials, looking for the ones that would indicate fuel levels. In the army they refuelled their vehicles every time they stopped, so that if they had to make a run for it, they would do so on full tanks. Did the Navy do the same? Particularly the German Navy? He found two dials that had the word 'Ltrs x 100' engraved on them. They must be fuel gauges he thought. The needles of both were resting reassuringly on the right hand stops.

Carter looked behind him as he heard feet on the wooden planks of the wheelhouse's deck.

"We're out of range of anything other than a really good sniper, or artillery." Green informed him.

"They may have some of that on these islands." Carter replied. "We'll have to hope that the snow masks us."

"Was this the plan all along?" Green asked.

"Sort of. The snow was the final element. We couldn't risk it without that. Snow will keep the Luftwaffe grounded in the morning, so they can't carry out an aerial search for us. E-Boats work in flotillas of between five and a dozen boats, so we would have to assume that there are others tied up along the coast who would come out to try to chase us down. But in this weather, they could pass within a hundred yards and not see us."

"You didn't trust Sven to keep his word and help us to get away."

"Not really. I was pretty sure he had already lied to us."

"How so?"

"It was when he told us about Olav and his family being in Ålesund. He told us that the town was in a different control area. The Germans may be many things, but one of them is that they are sticklers for the chain of command. Olav wouldn't have been taken to another area for interrogation. In particular he wouldn't have been taken to such a small town as Ålesund. It only has two Gestapo officers, for goodness sake. I think they'd have been taken to Bergen. It's the biggest city in this region. I didn't pick up on it at first, but when we did the reconnaissance, Sven seemed to have forgotten that there should be fourteen of us on the return journey and that made me think. He said there would only be ten. I had to correct him."

"Would he have killed us?"

"I don't think so, but he would have played us off for his own purposes. Maybe tried to persuade us to carry out more raids for him, or maybe used us for leverage to get more guns or money from the government. Anyway, I didn't trust him to get us home any time soon, so I took the opportunity when it appeared."

"But you decided not to tell me."

"Yes, sorry about that. I wanted to, but if anyone had overheard us, Sven would have found a way to stop us. We only had his word for it that none of the others spoke English, including Fredrick. His radio was tuned in to the BBC Home Service, I had to retune it to an Irish service. I'm guessing Frederik new at least a little bit of English."

"It was a risky plan, Boss."

"Yes, but he who dares, wins." Carter liked the sound of that. It had a certain ring to it. Someone should turn that into a motto, he thought. Maybe he'd suggest it for 15 Commando.

"Pity about poor old Olav and his family."

"Yes. I'm a bit cut up about that. Helping us will probably cost the lives of him and his family."

"Are the concentration camps really that bad?"

"Everything I've heard about them says they are. If you aren't a Nazi then you're not worth keeping alive, as far as the Nazis are concerned. It will be worse for Olav. He aided an enemy. I wish I hadn't given him that tin of bully beef now."

"You thought you were doing the right thing. For all you know it wasn't the bully beef. Maybe it was someone else from the village. One of them Quislings."

"Yes, but as they say, the road to hell is paved with good intentions." Yes, thought Carter. It might not have been his fault that their presence in the village had been revealed. It could have been down to nosey neighbours who were also disloyal. It was a thought he had to hang onto if he wanted to ease his torment.

Green must have sensed his anguish. "They might not have found that bully beef at all. Maybe we gave ourselves away, you know, showed a light or something."

Carter fell silent, troubled by his own thoughts about the loss of innocent lives. War is Hell. Who had said that? Carter wondered[2]. He thought it might be an American but couldn't be sure.

The boat gave a lurch as a larger roller came in, propelled by the strong northerly wind. It meant that they had moved out of the lee of Hessa and into the more open waters of the fjord. He couldn't see them, but ahead were the two islands that he had to navigate between. If he got the course wrong who knew what would happen.

Another gap opened up in the snow and Carter saw a line of tracer ammunition stitching its way across the sky. It was a long way away, several kilometres probably and didn't pose any sort of threat, but it did give him some sort of idea where one of the islands lay. The Germans were just firing blind, hoping against hope to hit something. The snow closed in a round the E-Boat once again, forming a reassuring blanket.

"They must have some charts around here somewhere." Carter said. "Take the wheel. I'll go and have a look."

He had spotted a doorway beneath the windows on the right hand side of the wheelhouse, so he crossed to it. He opened it and found a short flight of stairs leading into a closed-in room. It didn't have any windows. Scrabbling around the entrance he eventually discovered a light switch. He covered his eyes as protection against the sudden light and flicked the switch.

The sudden light didn't come. Instead there was a dim red glow. Good old Navy, Carter thought. They had thought about protecting the night vision of the crew. A tiny chart table sat on the opposite wall, rulers and protractors sitting in brackets above. Below the table was a suite of drawers which held the charts. The only other features were a hard backed chair in front of the table, an empty ashtray and a tin of German cigarettes sitting on a shelf, held in place by a thin wooden batten. This must be the Captains hidey hole, where he could smoke without showing a light above deck.

Carter looked at the chart that was held in place by a couple of metal clips. As he had hoped, it was the one that allowed the navigator to guide the boat between Ålesund and the North Sea. On it was drawn a straight line that marked the normal course. Pencilled in alongside it was a number: two six zero; ten degrees south of due west.

Carter returned to the wheelhouse and checked the compass, which sat directly in front of the wheel. The number on the compass card adjacent to the red mark on the housing was two seven zero. They were heading due west, fractionally too far north.

"Turn left a little." Carter said, deciding that non-nautical terms were better, considering the circumstances. He wasn't that sure of the correct naval commands anyway. They had been given plenty of training in boat handling and navigation, just in case the Navy crew of their landing craft ever suffered some injury or even death, but the Navy had tried to use laymen's terms wherever possible, concluding that trying to re-educate the Army was too great a challenge.

The compass swung in response to the turn of the wheel and when it was just short of the required bearing, Carter told Green to stop turning. The compass settled on the two six zero mark, varying a little to either side as the boat was buffeted by the waves.

He nudged the other two throttles levers forward a little, to match the centre one and felt the surge of power through the boat. He had expected the bow to rise, as it did in a speed boat, but the E-Boat stayed more or less level.

"It feels powerful." Green said, seeming to enjoy himself in the role of helmsman.

"That's only a fraction of what it can do." Carter replied. "I'm only using about a quarter throttle at the moment. We call these E-Boats, I have no idea why[3], but the Germans call them S Boats. The S stands for *Schnell*, which means fast."

"*Was ist los?*" A voice came from outside the wheelhouse.

Carter and Green exchanged surprised looks. So that was why the boat had power applied. There had been a sentry aboard. But how had it taken so long for him to realise that his boat was being hijacked?

"*Was ist los?*" The shout came again. Whoever it was must be shouting up from the deck.

"*Frohes neues Jahr.*" Carter shouted back, using one of the only two German phrases he knew, taught to him on a drunken night out by a fellow student. Happy New Year. He had a feeling that the other phrase '*Entschuldigung, Fraulein, mein Freund denkt, sie sind sehr hübsch. Darf er dir einen Drink kaufen?'* wasn't suitable for the occasion.

"*Er … Frohes neues Jahr.*" Came the reply, followed by the sound of cautious footsteps on the wheelhouse ladder. Carter moved silently to one side of the door. It swung open and the barrel of a rifle poked through. The figure could see Green's stiff back silhouetted against the wheelhouse windows.

"*Wer bisen sie?*" The German asked.

"Evenin' Fritz." Green called over his shoulder.

The German stepped fully into the wheelhouse and opened his mouth to speak again, which was when Carter sent his left fist flying straight into the middle of the German's face. The German staggered backwards, missed his footing on the ladder and fell onto the deck below. Carter leapt through the door after him, landing astride the prone figure. The German had dropped his rifle as he tried to save himself and Carter bent over and swept it up. Raising it above his head he drove the butt down into the side of the German's head. He lay still.

Carter threw the rifle overboard, the howl of the wind preventing him from hearing the splash as it hit the water. Where had he come from? Where had he been hiding? Perhaps not hiding, just asleep somewhere warm. To the right of the wheelhouse ladder he saw a door. It was closed against the wind. He turned the handle and it swung open, though Carter had to fight the wind to get it wide enough to dog it back, using the clip fixed to the deck. He peered inside. A short flight of steps led downwards, beneath the wheel house and also beneath the chart room. The lights were on and Carter could make out a cabin area, bench seats ran along both sides, in front of which were two tables and another pair of long benches flanking a central aisle. The crew's dining area, Carter concluded. That meant there would be a galley of some sort further forward and possibly even bunk space somewhere.

Carter returned to the comatose German and grabbed him beneath the arms. Dragging him through the door he bumped him down the stairs and into the cabin. Two schnapps bottles rolled across the top of one of the tables, as the boat hit another wave. One was empty and the other was almost empty, its cap missing, allowing some of the remaining alcohol to spill out before it rolled back across the table again to come to a stop against the fiddle, the wooden rail that ran along the edge of the table to stop things sliding off in heavy seas.

So that was why they hadn't discovered the German before. He'd been out for the count. But even the most drunk person would eventually respond to some stimulus and somewhere deep in the sailor's mind something had told him that the boat was moving when it shouldn't have been. If he had been completely sober, he might have taken more care in approaching the wheelhouse.

Carter searched the cabin but there was nothing suitable for restraining the sailor. He went forward and found that there was a tiny galley there, but that held nothing suitable either. Returning back through the mess deck he saw another door to the right of the cabin steps, a lighter wooden one.

Behind the door was a sleeping cabin, just room for a bed, a locker and a small desk. To use the desk it would be necessary to sit on the bed. This must be the Captain's quarters, Carter thought. The bed was made up with clean sheets and a single blanket. Stripping the top sheet off, he hacked at it with his dagger, cutting it into lengths which could be used to secure the sailor's hands and feet.

Satisfied that the sailor wouldn't be bothering them again, he returned to the wheelhouse. Carter told him what he had found.

"These Jerries don't deserve to win the war, getting drunk on sentry duty like that." Green offered his opinion, contempt heavy in his voice.

"Complacency. He knew he had a mate outside patrolling the wall, so he thought he'd have a little drink. He probably only meant to have one or two, but you know how things are sometimes."

"Well, for him the war is over. The only question is whether it will end in a PoW camp or at the bottom of the North Sea, if the Jerries get their act together and find us."

"They'll know where we're headed. If the snow stops we'll turn the boat round and head for a fjord, one that doesn't have any towns or villages in it. The wonderful thing about Norway is that there are plenty of places to hide a boat. Did you know that the Germans have got battleships hidden up here that the Navy and the RAF have been looking for since the Spring of 1940 and still haven't found?"

"I'd heard that."

The sea began to get rougher, long, slow swells that told Carter that they were now in the open, with no land protecting them from the power of the northerly wind. The snow also seemed to get thicker and heavier, forming a white wall around them that was impossible to penetrate with the eyes.

"Well, it's true. Now," Carter took hold of the throttle levers, "I think it's time we found out how fast *Schnell* really means."

He pushed the levers forward and the boat seemed to leap like a horse that had just received a crack from a jockey's whip. This time the prow of the boat did lift a little, but still not as much as expected. They heard the thrum of the wind against the glass of the windows and the boat seemed to bounce from wave top to wave top.

The waves were coming from the rear right hand corner of the boat. Carter tried to recall the language used in the Hornblower books he had read before the war, reaching into his memory for the correct terminology. 'Aft starboard quarter', he decided after a while. It probably wasn't right, but there were no sailors present to correct him. He remembered the cool condescension that he had been greeted with when he had referred to the heads as the toilets when they were on board the Prince Leopold. It made no difference when he pointed out that the signs on the door in English, French and Flemish, also said toilet, in deference to their pre-war landlubber passengers.

He remembered that when a boat's motion became too uncomfortable, it could often be reduced by slowing the boat down. He eased back on the throttles a little and found that it worked. But he doubted that any pursuing craft would slow down. The chase would undoubtedly be on.

[1] *Silvester* - When the Gregorian Calendar was reformed in 1582, the result was New Year's Eve moving to the same day as the feast of St Silvester, a 4th century Pope. This also happened to coincide with a far older pagan festival. With the date having a double significance for the Germans they retained the name. Over time, the "Saint" part was dropped, leaving New Year's Eve with the name "Silvester". Noise was a particular feature of the festival and is probably the reason we set off fireworks on New Year's Eve which, in Germany, predates the use of fireworks to welcome in the New Year in other parts of the world (except for China, of course, where fireworks were invented).

[2] War is hell - General William Tecumseh Sherman. General in the Union Army during the American Civil War and, later, the Commanding General of the United States Army.

[3] E-Boat - The E stands for 'enemy'.

10 – Beaufighter

"If you don't mind me asking, Prof, why didn't you join the army with a commission? Don't feel you have to answer, we're just chatting here." Carter handed Green the cup of tea he had just made down in the tiny galley, using up the last of their precious stock of leaves.

"No big secret, Lucky. Just the Great British Class System at work. You probably know that my dad was big in the trades union movement in London. He did a lot of organising for the Labour Party and that earned him a peerage from Ramsey MacDonald when he was in government. I did get a scholarship to a Grammar School, but that bit of prestige helped me to get a place at University, the first ever in our family. It was great, at first.

There were loads of Labour Party supporters amongst the undergraduates, so I had plenty of people to talk to and debate with. But I soon realised that I wasn't getting the invites to the sherry parties or the dinner invites from the Dons. It didn't worry me too much, I was too busy studying and when I wasn't doing that, I was organising anti-fascist marches. Then war broke out. I'd just graduated and decided that I wasn't going to let that bastard Hitler run free around Europe, so I decided to volunteer.

I went down to my local recruitment office in Deptford and the Sergeant didn't even look twice at me. He asked me if I needed any help filling in the form. I think he thought I might be illiterate. There it was, all over again, only this time it was from my own class. The only question he asked me after that was if I wanted to join the West Kents or the London Regiment. I said West Kents. Then he looked at my form, just to make sure I'd filled it in right and he wouldn't believe I had a degree. I had to go home and bring the certificate in to convince him. Even then a commission wasn't mentioned, so I thought 'Fuck em' and got on with it."

Carter nodded his head in understanding. He'd seen the same thing at his own university, with the middle class lads not wanting to mix with the ones that had fought against the class system tooth and nail to get in. He wondered if he was guilty of the same prejudices and decided that it was quite likely.

"If you joined the West Kents, how come you ended up with the Huntingdons?"

"That was a bit of an accident. After training I was sent to join the battalion in France. It was still the phoney war then, of course. Anyway, the Germans invaded Belgium and Luxembourg and my platoon were sent to defend a bit of woodland until the rear guard came through. We became separated and that was the last we saw of the West Kents, at least in France. The rear-guard was provided by the Huntingdons, as I'm sure you know, so our platoon officer just attached us to them.

When we got to Ramsgate, there was transport waiting for the Huntingdons to take them up to their depot, but nothing for us West Kent lads, so the acting CO said we should go with them and they'd sort us out later. Anyway, long story short, I liked being with the Huntingdons, so I asked if I could stay with them. Someone must have done the paperwork, because I was allowed to change cap badges and that was that. Then they shipped us off to Wiltshire because there wasn't enough room at the depot for us and that's where you found me."

"What made you volunteer for the commandos, if you liked the Huntingdons so much?

"Boredom! I probably shouldn't say it, but I enjoyed the fighting in France. It provided me with challenges that I'd never faced before. I couldn't stand garrison life, that endless round of parades and inspections and route marches. I wanted something more, so when I saw the request for volunteers, I thought 'why not?' What about you? Why did you become a commando?"

Carter decided not to mention the comments that the battalion CO had made after Green had been dismissed from his interview. "Same thing. I was bored out of my skull. I hadn't thought about it before, even though I'd seen the call for volunteers, but when I saw your application form on my desk, I thought 'Why not?' as well. The rest you know."

"Turns out we'd have got all the action we wanted if we'd stayed with the battalion. They're in Malaya now, fighting the Japs."

"Yes. I wonder how they're getting on. Well, we've got several hours still to go, so may as well get some sleep." Carter fished around in his ammunition pouch and pulled out a bullet. He put his hands behind his back and shuffled it between them, before offering two closed fists to Green. "Pick a hand." He said.

"Left."

Carter opened his left hand to show that it was empty, then his right hand to show the bullet. "I win, so you get first watch. That switch there," he pointed, "marked *Autopilot*, is the automatic pilot. If you need to leave the wheel, just switch it on and the boat will maintain its course and speed until you switch it off again." He looked at his watch and then at the wheelhouse clock, puzzled to see that there was an hour's difference between them. He hadn't had cause to use his watch much over recent days and no chance to make a comparison with other timepieces, but an hour's difference was a bit strange. Idiot, he thought. That clock is on Berlin time and his watch was on GMT. "Wake me at six thirty, by that clock." Carter instructed him.

He made his way down to the Captain's tiny cabin and stretched himself out on the bed. It felt unusual after days of sleeping rough. But despite that, he was asleep within seconds.

* * *

At eight thirty by the bridge clock, they were changing shift for the second time, with Carter just about to go for another sleep. In the dawn light the snow had cleared as though someone had used a switch to turn it off. Behind and to the left Carter could still make out the almost solid wall of the storm stretching across the eastern horizon, but now they were pulling away from it under a cloud base that must have been ten thousand feet above them.

"It won't make any difference to us." Carter said. "So long as the snow is covering the coast the Germans won't send up any aircraft.

"What's that then?" Green said, pointing at a dot just above the distant horizon, to the south west of them, almost exactly above the prow of the E-Boat.

"Must be one of ours." Carter replied. He reached for the big naval binoculars that sat in a custom-made holder within easy reach of the wheel. With the boat pitching and yawing Carter decided to go up onto the flying bridge to get a better view.

On the course that the boat was taking, coupled to its speed, the northerly wind could barely be felt. He leant his elbows on the bridge railing to steady the binoculars, then dropped to one knee so that he could put his eyes to them. Adjusting the focus, the dot took on the shape of an aircraft.

Carter could see that it was a twin engined plane, but it only had a single tail plane, so it wasn't an Me 110. For the same reason it also couldn't be a Dornier, but could be either a Ju88 or a Heinkel He111. Carter ruled out the Heinkel, as it didn't seem to have the 'greenhouse' glass nose that made up the front of the German bomber. So it was probably a Ju88 or something British, he concluded. It could be a Beaufighter. He had seen a couple of them quite close up over Kirkesfjord and the shape seemed to be similar.

Whatever it was it must have spotted the E-Boat, because it went into a turn and flew towards them, losing altitude as it came so that it could take a closer look. A couple of minutes later it flew over the boat from fore to aft, at about a hundred feet, it's RAF roundels clearly visible on the under sides of the wings.

"We're safe now, Prof." Carter said. "They'll report our position and the navy and will come and get us."

Carter was proven wrong almost before the words were out of his mouth. The aircraft made a tight turn that took it out onto the E-Boat's beam, giving the crew a side-on shot and came back at them, four twinkling lights beneath its nose indicating that it had opened fire with its cannons. Spouts of water stitched their way towards the E-Boat and something struck the metalwork at the aft of the boat with a loud clang. The aircraft roared over their heads before starting another turn that would bring it back on the other beam to rake its target once again.

"Bloody ''ell!" Green said, "If that's what our friends do, I'd rather take my chances with the enemy."

"All he sees is a German boat!" Carter snapped. "Where's the Very Pistol? They must have a flare gun somewhere."

"Over there. Lucky. By the chartroom door."

Sure enough, a flare pistol lay on a shelf next to the door, boxes of flares of various colours sitting alongside it. Carter grabbed it, broke it and inserted a cartridge in one smooth movement, snapping it closed once again before he climbed back up onto the flying bridge.

Already the aircraft was back within cannon range and the spouts of water were stitching their way towards the boat. There was another loud bang and the E-Boat started to slew to the right as the starboard engine lost power while the centre and port engines drove it onwards. Green tried to correct the turn by reducing the power on the other two engines, at the same time battling with the wheel to counter the turn with the rudder.

A cloud of smoke was rising from the engine room ventilators. Carter prayed that the designers had seen fit to install automatic fire extinguishers, because there was no hope of either him or Green having the opportunity to get down there to fight the fire.

The aircraft was completing another turn and was on its way back, spouts of water again marking the strikes of the cannon shells on the sea. Carter fired the flare gun and a green light burst above and behind them. But the twinkling lights ceased as the crew puzzled over the meaning of the signal. The aircraft overshot them once again, Carter waving his arms frantically to attract the crew's attention. The crew were bound to be confident they could resume their attack on the E-Boat whenever they wished.

Carter returned to the wheelhouse door and threw the flare gun to Green. "Keep firing flares. Doesn't matter what colour, so long as they get the message that we're trying to communicate." He slid down the stairs and ducked into the crew quarters. Green gave up the fight to try to control the direction of the boat, instead pulling back on the throttles and leaving them in their neutral position. The E Boast slowed and wallowed in the long North Sea swells.

Carter returned a few seconds later, the bottom sheet from the Captain's bunk crumpled up under his arm. Taking hold of a signal halyard he knotted one end to a corner of the sheet, then the other end to the other corner. Hauling hard on the rope he sent the makeshift flag of surrender up the mast to the yard arm.

The Beaufighter had just completed another turn and was again heading in for a low pass over the E-Boat. Seeing the white sheet streaming across the port side, blown by the northerly wind, the pilot waggled the aircraft's wings twice. Message understood.

"That was close." Green said, dropping the flare pistol back onto the shelf. "With his firepower we were goners."

"It didn't occur to me that we would be seen as the enemy."

Carter opened up the centre throttle so that they could move forward without having to fight the power of an asymmetrical thrust from the port engine. They would be a lot slower now, but with an airborne armed escort Carter was no longer worried about being discovered by German sea patrols.

"What's he doing now?" Green asked, craning his neck to try to see the Beaufighter. Carter looked back through the wheelhouse door.

"Climbing and circling. I think he's going to keep us under observation until they can get a boat here to check us out."

Sure enough, the Beaufighter began to describe large circles in the air above the E-Boat, each circle overlapping the previous one as it edged south west, keeping pace with the E-Boat's forward motion.

"He'll get dizzy going round in circles like that." Green chuckled.

"Prof, can you check out that engine fire, make sure that we're no in any danger of sinking."

Green located the hatch down into the engine space. His ears were assaulted by the hammering of the two remaining marine diesels, big engines that could provide the massive amount of power needed to propel the E-Boat through the water at high speed. Either the fire had burnt itself out or there had been automated fire extinguishers. Carter reported back that there was a gaping hole in one of the starboard engine's cylinders where it had been struck by a cannon shell. The matching hole in the side of the boat wasn't letting in any significant amounts of water; just the odd slop when a wave struck the side of the boat at the same time as the boat rolled in that direction.

They scanned the dashboard to see if they could make out a control that might switch on the bilge pumps, finding one marked *Bilgenpumpen*, switching it on and hoping for the best that it meant what it seemed to mean. Carter blessed the fact that so much of the English language shared a common root with German. Or was it that the Germans had borrowed so many words from English?

"You not going for a kip, Lucky?" Green asked after a while. "I've got this."

"Hardly seems worth it. We must be pretty close to Scotland by now and the navy will have patrols out covering Invergorden and Scapa Flo. A ship is bound to be on its way to investigate, so it can't be long before it gets here."

The speed indicator was showing ten knots, which was the best they could hope for in the heavy seas and only using one engine. It was frustrating for them after having travelled at between thirty and forty knots before that. Carter did try opening up the port engine once again but found the strain of having to keep steering to port to counter the thrust was too much and he shut the engine down again.

"Well, if you're not going to sleep, we've got time for something to eat." Green dropped a heavy-handed hint.

Carter took the hint and headed down into the tiny galley. He found a store cupboard filled with tins. None had labels, but they did have their contents printed on their tops. Carter chose two that said *Hühnersuppe*. He had no idea what a *Hühner* was, but *suppe* had to be soup. He opened them up and poured them into a large saucepan. It turned out to be chicken soup.

Once hot he took the saucepan, two large bowls and two spoons back to the wheelhouse and served up their first hot meal for twenty four hours.

After about an hour the aircraft dropped down to about five hundred feet, flew across the E-Boat's bow and waggled its wings, before climbing once again and heading off to the west.

"Where's he off to?" Green asked.

"On his way home for tea and medals, I would think. He's either short of fuel, in which case we can expect another escort aircraft soon, or he's seen the navy and knows he's not needed any more."

Green picked up the powerful marine binoculars and scanned the horizon from south to west. "I can't see anything."

"From down here we probably can't yet. If there's a ship there he's probably still below our horizon. But from up where the aircraft was he would have been able to see further."

"So we don't know if help is close or not."

"Not for certain, but the aircraft crew would have been under orders to make sure we don't slip away, so he must feel confident that wouldn't happen."

"I'd feel a lot more comfortable if we could actually see a ship."

"I'll go up to the flying bridge. Maybe the extra height will help."

Carter left the wheelhouse and climbed the ladder to its roof, the binoculars hanging from their strap around his neck. As the boat reached the top of a swell he raised them to his eyes and scanned the horizon. Still nothing.

He turned to descend again and something caught his eye. Returning to the top deck he raised the binoculars to his eyes again, braced himself against the rolling motion of the boat and scanned the eastern horizon. Nothing.

He shook his head, worried that he was starting to imagine things. But better safe than sorry. He raised the binoculars again. Just as he did so, a tiny shape appeared on the crest of the swell, so narrow he wasn't sure if he was seeing it or not. It disappeared again, but was replaced by a second shape, slightly to the left of the first.

They could be British MTBs, Carter mused. They were so far away it was difficult to make out their shapes. But equally they could be E-Boats like the one on which he was standing. All he could say for sure was that they both had white bones of frothing water in their teeth, indicating that they were travelling at considerable speed.

Carter threw himself down the ladder and back into the wheel house. "We've got more company, two boats going flat out. At their speed they'll be up with us in minutes."

"I take it they're not friends." Green said.

"I've no idea. The trouble is, we can't afford to wait until they're close enough to find out. If they're E-Boats they'll have us outgunned and we can't outrun them on two engines. They'll split up, which means we can't turn, so there's only one way we can go."

Carter threw the port engine throttle wide open and the boat at once speeded up, at the same time as it slewed to the right. Green fought the turn, the tendons on his neck standing out as he strained to the hold the E-Boat on a south westerly course. Their only hope lay in reaching the coast or, better still, running into a Royal Navy patrol.

"I'm taking that sheet down." Carter said, leaving the wheelhouse. While he was happy to surrender to the RAF, there was no way he was going to surrender to the *Kreigsmarine*. He untied the signal halyard and let the sheet fly overboard on the wind, where it settled onto the surface of the sea.

"OK. Do you want to go on the machine guns again, or shall I go this time?"

"I'll let you go, Lucky. Not being rude or anything, but this wheel is pretty hard to hold onto and I'm a bit stronger than you."

Not wanting to get into an arm wrestle to prove Green wrong, Carter dropped down to the deck and made his way to the centre of the aft deck where the two 20 mm machine guns stood behind their flimsy armour. The deck felt terribly exposed. Ammunition belts trailed from boxes mounted next to the guns. A quick check revealed that they were three quarters full after Green's defensive fire, when they had been navigating clear of Ålesund.

He scanned the deck, looking for ammunition lockers but couldn't identify anything that looked as though it might contain bullets. Perhaps the ammunition was stowed below decks.

Spare torpedoes were lashed to the deck on either side of the boat and the thought did cross Carter's mind that they were probably the best way of countering this new threat, but he had no idea how to arm, aim and launch them. The machine guns would have to do the job.

The boats were clearly visible now, about two miles distant. Still too far away to open fire. He wasn't sure what the range of the machine guns was, but two miles seemed too long. Besides, the Germans weren't yet firing and they would know the range of their weapons. He returned to the flying bridge and viewed the boats through the binoculars once again. There was no doubting their identity now. Their profile was recognisable, but through the binoculars Carter could also see a red flag with a black cross, a swastika in the middle, that flew from the top of each boat's mast, blown across to Carter's right on the northerly wind. There would be a second one flying from the jack staff at the rear of the boat, but that was obscured by the superstructure of the boats.

The Germans had been really lucky to find them, Carter thought, or he and Green had been very unlucky. But then again, had they been?

The Beaufighter had been circling above them for an hour, acting like a beacon for any surface vessel in the vicinity. Perhaps that was what had given away their position. The two boats wouldn't have wanted to attract the attention of the aircraft, for exactly the reasons that Carter and Green had experienced, but if they had hung back, sitting as low on the horizon as they could, waiting for the aircraft to leave, that would explain their arrival now. It was a little bit coincidental otherwise and Carter didn't believe in coincidences.

The Germans were the first to fire, the left-hand boat sending out a stream of machine gun fire from its single forward gun. It fell well short. Carter peered through the binoculars once again, now able to make out the pale white blobs of the faces of the gunner and his loader. He raised the glasses slightly and made out the crew on the flying bridge. Two figures stood, wearing thick white jumpers as a protection against the cold. One wore the peaked cap of an officer while the other wore the brimless navy blue hat of a sailor. From the accommodation below the decks of their own boat, Carter estimated that there were between twenty and thirty other crew members that he couldn't see.

But the E-Boats were closing fast, their three engines able to deliver considerably more thrust than the two remaining engines on Carter's boat. The left hand boat fired again, this time getting some strikes in, sending splinters and paint chips flying.

Carter returned to the main deck and made his way back to the twin machine guns. He tucked the butts of the two guns into his shoulders and placed his hands on the triggers. These weren't weapons of great accuracy, the pitch and toss of the sea prevented that, but put enough bullets into the right area and you were bound to hit something, Carter concluded. He squeezed the triggers and the weapons leapt under his hands, sending a twin stream of bullets skimming across the surface of the sea, whipping small spouts of water from the surface. He raised the elevation of the guns a little and tried again, aiming at the figures on the bridge. He must have hit something because the two figures dived for cover.

Tracking downwards he picked out the gunner and let loose another stream of bullets. Sparks danced from the metal deck but the German gunner continued firing.

More rounds were hitting Carter's own E-Boat now and the second German boat had joined in the action. They hadn't yet got close to him, seeming to concentrate their fire on the wheelhouse. Green was vulnerable up there.

A bullet pierced the flimsy armour of his gun mounting, wrenching the guns to one side on their swivel. Green wasn't the only one who was vulnerable. What the fuck was he doing here? Carter wondered. He was a soldier, a commando, he should be somewhere where he could put something solid between him and the enemy. Something like a house, or a rock or even a blade of grass. Instead he had a quarter inch of metal plate in front of him which was about as much use as a bully beef can. The armour didn't even protect his legs properly.

Settling the circular sight of the machine guns on the bridge of the left hand boat once again, Carter fired another burst. Again he saw sparks striking off metal, but he had no idea if he was doing any serious damage.

Switching his aim, he poured a stream of fire into the right hand boat. It started to turn, pulling away to one side. At first Carter thought he had done enough damage to cause the boat to slew, but then he realised that the two boats were splitting up. Once in position they could pour fire into the E-Boat from both sides, but Carter could only fire on one boat at a time.

Carter was startled to hear the sound of a tearing sheet above his head. Instinctively he looked up, but there was nothing there. A boom echoed across the water. At the same time a great gout of water was flung up from the sea in front of the right hand E-Boat. The boat ploughed straight through the middle of it, emerging in a cloud of spray.

It took Carter some time to work out what was happening and it was only when a second tearing sound, followed by another boom, assaulted his ears that he realised that he was hearing artillery fire; rather it was naval gunfire. And, more importantly, it wasn't being aimed at him, which made it friendly naval gunfire.

The right hand E-Boat disappeared in another cloud of seawater and when it re-emerged it was already slowing. Smoke billowed across the water, evidence of a serious wound. At once it began to fall behind as Carter's own E-Boat continued at the same speed. It took the rattle of bullets hitting the hull of his own boat to remind Carter that the stricken boat hadn't been alone.

Carter swung his machine guns to the left and opened fire once again. Able to concentrate on a single target his twin guns were able to inflict more damage than the German's single gun. But they were gradually being overhauled, which would mean that the German would soon be able to bring his aft guns into play as well. Carter had no intention of allowing that to happen.

Almost as the thoughts scuttled across Carter's busy brain, the two machine guns stopped firing with a final click as the bolts fell on empty chambers. The two machine guns were useless to him now unless he could locate the ammunition lockers. Unless he brought the forward machine gun into play.

He sprinted forward and threw himself up into the wheelhouse. "Prof, get down onto the forward machine gun and whatever you do, keep it firing."

Grabbing the wheel, Carter pushed Green to one side.

"Don't you mean the aft guns, Lucky?"

"No, I mean the forward gun. Now don't stand around arguing, or it won't matter which gun I mean."

Green didn't need telling a second time. He slid down the stairs and a few seconds later Carter saw him reappear at the forward machine gun. He heaved back on the cocking handle, then turned the gun to aim as far to the rear as possible. But he didn't have a clear field of fire, so he looked up at Carter with a puzzled look on his face.

Carter released the wheel and at once the boat went into a turn to the right. When the wheel stopped spinning Carter helped to speed up the turn until, looking through the side widows, he judged it necessary to start straightening the course before he overshot.

The forward machine gun started to chatter as Green was able to locate a target, then Carter was able to pick out the bow of the pursuing boat, then its wheelhouse and then its profile started to narrow as Carter's E-Boat was steering straight at it.

"Ever played chicken?" Carter whispered to the other E-Boat's distant Captain. To be truthful, Carter had never played the game himself, only read a reference to it in a book. It was usually played with cars, not E-Boats, but the principle remained the same.

Both E-Boats were heading towards each other at a closing speed in excess of fifty knots. Green pretty much kept his finger on the machine gun's trigger, sending hundreds of rounds into the hull and superstructure of the other boat. If he was worried by what his officer was doing, he showed no sign of it.

But it was the German who blinked first, or at least whichever German was manning the wheel. The boat slewed to the side, allowing Green to send a raking stream of fire along the boat's length as they passed each other. The forward machine gunner was last seen crawling away from his position while the aft gunner slumped down, blood spurting in great gouts from a terminal wound.

But gunners could and would be replaced and the other E-Boat was heading away from them at a considerable pace. It wouldn't be long before it started to turn. Carter had to reverse his course as well, or he would have the German back on his tail once more.

But then something wonderful happened. The E-Boat started to turn, but then headed away on a course that would take it to the north east, away from Carter's boat. As he slewed his boat across the top of a roller, he saw why. A much larger boat was bearing down on them, foam flashing from its bows as it headed for them at full speed. It wasn't a big boat, a corvette Carter guessed, but it was the most beautiful boat Carter had ever seen. It must have been the source of the artillery fire which had crippled the second German boat. It was also big enough to make the captain of the remaining E-Boat turn tail and run for home. The corvette sent it on its way with some more heavy calibre shells, but there was no sign of any striking home as the E-Boat's commander zig zagged his boat in a series of evasive manoeuvres.

Carter eased back on the throttles and turned towards the crippled boat. They had no option but to surrender and Carter could accept that on behalf of the naval crew. As they approached, A rating went to the mast and lowered the Kriegsmarine ensign, while at the jack staff a second rating did the same. Green kept his machine gun aimed on the E-Boat's bridge, where a stiff faced officer stood, a cigarette in one hand, but there was no longer any real threat.

"I suppose that means I've got to go back to calling you 'Sir', now that we're back within the fold." Green said, arriving back on the bridge, a hint of humour in his voice.

"Yes, I'm afraid that's the way of the army. You call me 'Sir' even if you don't mean it and I call you Tpr Green so that the blokes don't think I showing you any favour."

"That's OK by me. The blokes hate it when officers have favourites. It makes them think that tales are being told behind their back. But could I ask a favour, just this once?"

"If I can grant it I will."

"Can you put in a good word for me. I think I could be on a fizzer for disobeying an order and going looking for you. Or maybe for going AWOL[1]."

"I'll certainly give it my best shot. I doubt I could have made it this far without you and that deserves some credit." There was a risk of the conversation taking an embarrassing turn, so they fell silent and watched the approaching corvette.

It swung to the north and made a slow approach towards them, using its larger sides to create a wind shadow in its lee. Carter eased his boat into the side ship's side, where a scramble net had already been rigged.

Ratings lined the rails, aiming rifles and Lewis guns down at them, suspicion on their faces. A Sub Lieutenant leant over the rail and called down to Carter, who was standing on the flying bridge.

"What the hell is a pongo[2] doing out here on a German E-Boat?"

Carter cut off his desire to call the sailor a fish head in retaliation for being addressed as a pongo. Politeness was probably a better course of action under the circumstances. "It's a long story and one best told over a G&T in the wardroom." Carter replied.

"I think the Captain is going to want something a bit more formal than that." The officer laughed, nodding his head towards the front of the ship.

Carter followed his gaze to where a head wearing a peaked cap stood on the bridge wing, looking back towards him.

"Happy to oblige." Carter replied.

"Well, leave all your weapons and equipment on the boat. We'll look after it for you."

You mean you don't trust us, Carter thought. But it made sense. Until their credentials had been checked out, they must remain objects of suspicion. Carter shrugged out of his webbing and laid it on the deck. "Oh, by the way, there's an unconscious German on the mess deck, trussed up like an oven ready chicken, if you could look after him. He'll probably need medical attention."

"Will do. Now climb up the netting and I'll take you to meet the Captain."

As he climbed over the rail, the Naval Officer's nose wrinkled in distaste and Carter realised that it had been over a week since he had last bathed. No wonder Gudrid had given him such a filthy look when they had been in the back of the baker's van.

[1] AWOL – Absent Without Official Leave. It is a lesser offence than desertion which implies a permanent absence, but it is still a serious offence.

[2] Pongo – A derogatory word for soldiers used by the Navy and the RAF. It probably originated in 19th century Musical Halls. At that time it was normal for soldiers to wear uniform when off duty, making them easy to identify in the audience. Traditionally an army on the march, accompanied by draft animals and live animals for slaughter, as well as using latrine pits, was quite a smelly

organisation. A comedian could always guarantee a cheap laugh with the line 'Where the army goes, the pong goes'.

11 – Aftermath

The door to 25 Gillies Street was opened by Mrs Bliss. Carter was shocked to see how she had aged in the few weeks in which he had been away. She seemed to be at least twenty years older.

"Are you OK, Moira?" he asked, slipping his webbing off and setting it on the floor in the hallway.

"As well as can be expected, Steven." She said, her tone heavy, her voice sounding listless. She glanced sideways into the dining room. Carter followed her gaze and saw the framed photographs of Moira's sons, standing on the sideboard as they always had. Except that one of them was now draped with a black ribbon.

"Your son …" Carter didn't know what to say, reluctant to jump to the obvious conclusion in case he was wrong.

"He was on board the Repulse. Apparently it was bombed by the Japanese and was sunk, along with the Prince of Wales. My son was amongst those killed."

"I'm sorry. I had no idea, Moira. We've been away …"

"I know where you've been, Steven and the whole town is proud of you. The whole country is proud of what you boys did. Captain Turner, before he went on leave, told me you were missing, though. Presumed dead yourself."

"Officially I was. I've just got back. It was quite an adventure. But you … is there anything I can do for you?"

"There's nothing that can be done, Steven. My boy is gone and there's an end to it. He wasn't the first in this war and I'm sure many more mothers will lose their sons before it comes to an end. Now, you get yourself sorted and I'll put some dinner on. I wasn't expecting you, so there isn't much in. Would mince and tatties be OK?"

* * *

Two hours previously, Carter had stood in front of Lt Col Vernon's desk, reporting his return to his unit. He threw up a smart salute.

Vernon rose and came round the desk, grasping Carter's hand and shaking it firmly, pumping the hand up and down as though trying to extract water. "Welcome back, Steven. Am I pleased to see you! We'd given you up for dead."

"Well, if 6 Troop had had their way I might be." Carter laughed. "But I've got a thick head and I survived."

At last he released Carter's hand and returned behind his desk. "Well, take a seat. I want the whole story, beginning to end and don't miss anything out."

"Of course. I'll be writing a full report, but here goes." Carter took him through a blow by blow description of his and Green's adventures. Occasionally Vernon interjected with a question, but mostly he was content to say 'my, my', or 'incredible'.

"Then we were put ashore at Invergorden and there were a couple of Redcaps[1] waiting for us. It seemed odd, but they were very polite. Said that there were some people in Edinburgh that wanted to talk to us and it was their job to see us safely there. We weren't allowed to carry our weapons, which seemed a little bit strange. They went in the boot of the car. I'd expected just to be given a rail warrant and a lift to the railway station, but we were to get a car all the way there."

Tea had been delivered by one of the commandos who doubled as a clerk and Carter took a sip of his, enjoying the flavour.

"Anyway, we were taken to the Castle and interviewed by a bloke who said he was Intelligence Corps. But if he was a soldier I'll eat my hat. It was more like an interrogation than an interview. It went on for two days. They didn't seem to accept that Green and I were who we said we were, and it wasn't until the 2IC turned up and vouched for us that they believed us. If he hadn't shown up I've a feeling we might be locked up in the Tower of London by now."

The Colonel laughed. "Yes, we heard you'd been taken to Edinburgh and couldn't work out why, so I sent Teddy Couples over to find out what was going on. Pretty much everyone else is on leave at the moment. But you know how suspicious everyone is these days. There are rumours of spies everywhere, so when a couple of people turn up out of the blue in a German E-Boat, claiming to be British commandos, you can see their point. But still, all's well that ends well and here you are now.

I've had a couple of interesting signals come in about you. First of all there's one from HQ Combined Ops, thanking you for the donation of two German E-Boats. I had no idea what they meant by that until you just told me. Congratulations on that. The second was from some outfit calling themselves the Special Operations Executive. They thank you for the service you did while in Norway, but don't say what that was. I assume it was the attack on the Police Station."

"Probably, Sir. I probably shouldn't talk too much about that. Careless talk costs lives and all that."

"Quite right. I promise not to tell anyone what you've told me. Anyway, if you write up that report of yours, I'll pick the bits I need from it. I think I can probably work it up into a DSO^2 for you. Now, what about Green?"

"If I could ask, Sir, that you exercise a bit of leniency for Tpr Green. After all he was only trying to …" Carter stopped talking as Vernon raised his hand.

"I have no idea what you're rabbiting on about Steven. Green acted with the bravery and initiative we expect from commandos, to go to the aid of his officer, that is to say you. All I want to know is if he did anything that could earn him a gong."

Carter almost laughed, partly out of embarrassment and partly out of relief that Green wasn't in any trouble for coming to find him in Kirkesfjord. "Of course, Sir. Silly of me. Yes, I think there's probably a case for a Military Medal for what he did in fighting off the German E-Boats when they caught up with us."

"Good. You write up the citation and I'll sign it off."

"What was the casualty rate for the raid?" Carter asked. The 2IC hadn't said much on their journey from Edinburgh, just commenting that it was probably up to the CO to fill him in on what had happened.

"Not too bad, all things considered. We lost two officers and fifteen ORs killed. Five officers and forty eight ORs wounded. Most of those were minor wounds, thankfully, though there were some nasty burns to the men in Molly Brown's landing craft. Colin Foggerty will have a story to tell his grandchildren. He got half his ear shot away. Lucky it wasn't a fraction to the right or he wouldn't have lived to tell the tale. As it is he'll be in hospital for a while."

"If I could get my hands on the pilot of that …"

"Don't be too harsh on the RAF, Steven. That aircraft was shot down and the crew is listed as missing, though no one saw any parachutes so it doesn't look good for them. The RAF paid a heavy price for covering our backs and our casualties would have been a lot higher if we'd have had to contend with the Luftwaffe as well. They lost eleven aircraft all told, with all the crew listed as missing, presumed dead."

"I'm sorry, Sir. I didn't know."

"No, very few people do. The casualty figures have been kept hushed up. After all, we don't want to take the shine off our victory. We're the talk of the country right now, ever since the news-reel footage was shown in the cinemas."

"But we didn't take any cameramen with us."

"It's amazing what you can do with some footage shot during training, edited with a bit of archive stuff. There was a stills photographer with us, of course and he got some very good shots. The public will see some brave British commandos storming the enemy shore and blowing lots of stuff up. It may not be us they're seeing, but they will believe it is. And it isn't really a lie because that's exactly what we did. And I have a personal telegram from the Prime Minister congratulating us for doing it, if proof is needed."

"What sort of damage did we do?"

"Well, we blew up the three fish oil factories, of course. We also took ninety eight prisoners. We have no idea how many Germans we killed but it was a fair few. There were a dozen or so

Quislings arrested, including the Mayor. By a stroke of luck we also sank ten German ships. Five were anchored along the fjord towards Groening, but another five just sailed straight into the North Channel, right onto the guns of the two destroyers that were guarding the approach. It would have been good to capture some of them, but the ones we didn't sink the Germans scuttled to prevent them falling into our hands. Everyone is very pleased with us, as I said."

He took a sip of his tea before continuing. "With the casualties and a couple of other personnel changes, we've had to move people about a little. Don Donaldson of 6 Troop has been promoted to Major and he's off to the Middle East. So Molly Brown has been promoted to Captain to take his place, which means you're now the senior Lieutenant in 4 Troop. I have to say I thought I was going to have to replace you as well, so you've saved me a problem there."

"Do we know who's replacing Molly?"

"Not yet. We're waiting for a draft to come down from Achnacarry to replace all of our casualties, officers and ORs. They'll be with us within the month. Which brings me to the subject of leave. Everyone else has been sent home for a fortnight, of which they've got a couple of days more to go. But of course you and Green have to have your two weeks as well."

"If you've no objection, Sir, I'd like to take my leave up here."

"As you wish. Any particular reason?"

That was an awkward question. On the one hand Carter didn't want to mislead his CO, but on the other there was no reason for Vernon to know about the strained relations between Carter and his family. In the end he compromised with the truth, even if it wasn't the whole truth.

"There's a young lady I promised to take to the cinema. Now would seem to be the best time, before we get back into training again."

Vernon gave Carter an amused look. "Well, enjoy yourself while you can. You've earned it. There's a new Humphrey Bogart film at the cinema, something about a falcon in Malta. Not my cup of tea but you know how the ladies love Bogart."

"Thanks for the suggestion, Sir. Sounds just the sort of thing. By the way, how goes the war in the Far East? Have we sent the Japanese back home to lick their wounds?"

"Sorry, I keep forgetting you've been out of touch. I'm afraid it isn't looking good. The Japs are everywhere. They're advancing down the Malay peninsula and already Singapore is under threat. It makes the fall of France and the Low Countries look like a side show. I dare say your Huntingdons are in the thick of it. The Japs are also attacking Indonesia and Indochina. The Americans are preparing to defend the Philippines and there's even been Japanese ships seen off the coast of New Guinea."

"It all sounds a bit gloomy. Is there any likelihood of commandos being sent out there?"

"It's a possibility, but we haven't heard anything so far. I dare say the powers that be are too busy fighting the conventional war to bother with ideas about raiding forces yet. The big threat is to India. If the Japs decide to turn north out of Malaya and attack through Siam[3] and Burma ... well, who knows what might happen. OK, well, you cut along now and reclaim your billet before someone else does. Mrs Bliss has something of a reputation as a cook. We start training for a new op in a couple of weeks, so get all the rest you can, because you're going to need it."

"Where's this one, Sir?"

Vernon tapped the side of his nose. "All will be revealed in due course, Steven."

[1] Redcaps - Royal Military Police, so called because their peaked caps have a red cover. For a similar reason, RAF Police are nicknamed 'snowdrops'.

[2] DSO - Distinguished Service Order. Awarded for "Distinguished services during active operations against the enemy."

[3] Siam - Although Siam officially changed its name to Thailand in 1939, it was often still called by its old name. Changing its name back again between 1946 and 1948 extended the colloquial use of the old name until quite late in the 20th century. On maps in the 1950s/60s it was still being shown incorrectly as Siam.

* * *

The view was as he remembered it, the January sun twinkling off the Firth of Clyde, a halo of cloud sitting above the Isle of Arran. He heard her feet behind him and turned to greet her.

The first thing he noticed was that she was dressed differently. Although she still wore 'country' clothes, they were considerably more feminine. Her flat cap had been replaced by a Robin Hood style hat made popular by the pre-war Errol Flynn film. The pony tail was gone and her hair had been curled up and pinned into place. Unlike their previous meeting she was now wearing make-up. Not a lot, but enough to make it clear that she had taken some care over her appearance. A tweed jacket and skirt replaced the farmer's trousers and weather proof jacket and she wore brown brogues instead of wellington boots. Between her ankles and the hem of her skirt Carter could see that she wore silk stockings. Those were a rarity at a time when silk was in short supply and used only for making parachutes. They must be a pair that had been set aside for special occasions. He felt flattered that she had decided to wear them to meet him. The only things that hadn't changed were the horn handled walking stick in her hand and the black and white collie that trotted at her heels.

"Hello." She greeted him with a smile. "I thought I wasn't going to hear from you. The rest of your unit returned nearly two weeks ago." Carter wondered how she knew, then remembered that Troon was a small town. The return of three hundred and fifty soldiers wouldn't go unnoticed and news travelled fast in small towns.

Remembering the distress his mother had felt when he had telephoned her to tell her he was safe, Carter decided to avoid a true account of his adventures. His mother had been overjoyed to hear his voice, of course, having been notified by the War Office that her son was missing in action. But the fact that he was still a serving commando was something with which she struggled to cope. He reminded her that if he wasn't a commando he would now be fighting the Japanese in Malaya, but it didn't mollify her. He wanted to avoid similar conversations with Fiona Hamilton if at all possible.

"Sorry, I had some business to attend to after the raid."

She gave him a look that suggested she didn't believe a word of it, but didn't pursue the matter

"You're all officially heroes now. Are you sure you want to be seen with a stay-at-home country girl like me?"

He blushed. "Quite sure. In fact, I'd like to honour my promise to take you to the cinema., Apparently there's a Humphrey Bogart film showing."

"Yes, The Maltese Falcon. They say it's quite good. As it happens, I'm free this evening."

"This evening suits me fine. I'm officially on leave for the next two weeks."

"You'll be going home then." She sounded resigned to his absence once again.

"Actually, I was thinking of staying up here. Could you use an extra pair of hands around the farm? I have nothing else planned."

"It's hard work. Are you sure you're up to it?"

He wasn't sure if she was serious or just teasing him, then she saw the smile she was trying to suppress. "I'm sure I can manage, so long as you don't ask me to milk a cow. I don't know how to do that."

"That is something I can teach you. Why don't you come for tea and we can discuss it. Mother insists and she promises ham sandwiches."

"That would be delightful." He turned to walk down the hill and she stepped in close beside him, linking her arm with this. He liked the intimacy of the gesture.

"So, tell me. What's Norway like at this time of year?" She asked, as they strode along the field, the collie darting about in front of them.

He wanted to say 'dangerous' but that would open up a can of worms, so he stuck to 'cold'.

This ends the first story in the "Commandos" series.

Historical Notes

The Army commandos were established in June 1940 on the direct orders of Winston Churchill. It was he who recognised that to maintain the war effort until victory could be achieved, he needed to maintain the morale of the British people following the disaster that had been the evacuation from Dunkirk. The skilful use of propaganda had turned that defeat into a sort of victory, but genuine victories, however small, would be needed if he was to convince the British people that the war could be won.

It would be the commandos that would provide those small victories. Often the targets of their raids were insignificant in military terms but, on occasions, they had a far greater impact than could ever have been imagined. For example, following successive raids on Norway, Adolf Hitler became convinced that they were the prelude to an invasion of that country as a stepping stone for invading Denmark and then Germany itself. No such plan existed, but Hitler ordered 300,000 additional troops to be sent to Norway, where they remained for the rest of the war, along with additional Luftwaffe and naval units. The fact that the invasion of Norway never came about was proof to Hitler that his strategy had worked. Had those troops been available at Stalingrad, El Alamein or in Normandy in 1944, who knows how the outcomes of those battles might have been affected.

15 Commando is a fictitious unit. The Army commandos were numbered 1 to 14 (excluding 13). 50, 51 and 52 commandos were formed in North Africa. The Royal Marine Commandos weren't formed until 1942 and took the numbers 40 to 48. Unlike the Army commandos, only 40 (RM) Cdo was made up of volunteers. The rest were just Royal Marine battalions that were ordered to convert to the commando role. For this reason the Army commandos tended to look down on them, but once they had proved themselves in combat they became part of the commando family.

No 2 Commando did undertake training to become Britain's first paratroops, doing their training at Ringway airfield in Manchester, which would eventually become Manchester Airport. In late 1940 they were split off from the commandos and in 1942 they became 1st Battalion, the Parachute Regiment. No 2 Commando was re-established in 1941. Battalions of the Parachute Regiment and the commandos would work together many times during the course of the war, especially in France and Germany. They built up a fierce rivalry which continues today.

No 10 (Inter Allied) Commando was made up of members of the armed forces from occupied countries in Europe who had escaped. There were two French troops, one Norwegian, one Dutch, one Belgian, one Polish, one Yugoslavian and a troop of German speakers, many of whom were Jewish. They often accompanied other commandos on raids to act as guides and interpreters, as well as carrying out raids of their own. On Operation Absolom I have sent Norwegian commandos with them, which was the case for the real raid on which Operation Absolom is based. Major Martin Linge, Commanding Officer of the Norwegian troop, was killed in that raid.

Quislings were the supporters of Vidkun Quisling, the puppet Prime Minister of Norway while it was under German occupation, who co-operated with the German authorities. When the commandos captured any known Quislings, which was on almost every raid against Norway, they were taken back to Britain and put on trial by the Norwegian government in exile.

If you wish to find out more about the Army commandos there are a number of books on the subject, including my own, which details my father's wartime service; it's called "A Commando's Story". I have provided the titles of some of these books at the end of these notes. These also provided the sources for much of my research for this book.

Achnacarry House is the ancestral home of Clan Cameron and it was taken over by the War Office to become the Commando Training Centre. The original occupants of the house moved into cottages in the grounds. During the course of World War II over

25,000 commandos were trained there, plus their American counterparts, the Rangers, who were modelled on the commandos. Originally each commando was responsible for providing their own training, before the first training centres were set up at Inveraray and Lochailort, in late 1940, before moving to Achnacarry.

Although in use from 1940 onwards, Achnacarry House was a holding centre for volunteers for special service before becoming a formal training school in March 1942. I have allowed myself a little bit of poetic licence to provide commando training for Steven Carter and Archibald Green a little bit earlier than that, in the summer and early autumn of 1941. It isn't too far from the truth as informal training was carried out at Achnacarry before 1942, as part of the commando selection process. Achnacarry was used to select both commandos and paratroops, as there was no difference in the selection procedures at the time.

The march from Fort William to Achnacarry was the traditional greeting for volunteers for the commandos and was an early test of fitness and determination. If you couldn't survive the march it was unlikely that you could manage the rest of the training, which was extremely physically demanding. The singing as the squad marched through Spean Bridge is my own invention, but it is quite likely that the soldiers did sing as they marched as a way of keeping up their spirits. The pipe band escort over the final two miles, however, was real. The band was staffed by commandos of the Demonstration Platoon, whose main job was to demonstrate commando techniques and tactics to the trainees and to provide the 'enemy' during training exercises. Also part of the weeding out process was the run up Ben Nevis, which was carried out regardless of the weather or the season. Whether or not the run was completed while wearing boots, I have no idea, so please forgive my poetic licence if it wasn't.

There was a line of crosses at the entrance to the camp, but they weren't real graves. They served as a warning to commandos never to forget the lessons they learnt, with inscriptions such as 'He showed himself against the skyline' and 'He failed to take cover during a beach landing'. But the sight of the crosses did shock new arrivals into the realisation that the work they were going to undertake would be dangerous. There were a number of real deaths in training at Achnacarry and many trainees suffered injuries.

The school's commandant, Lieutenant Colonel Charles Vaughan of the Buffs (East Kent) Regiment, was a real person and he took command of the school in 1942, so Carter couldn't have met him, but he was a colourful figure and I didn't want a mere historical fact to get in the way of him appearing in this book. He had risen from the rank of Private, which was almost unheard of in the army at that time. He served with Nos 7 and 4 Commando before taking command at Achnacarry. However, the words I put in his mouth are from my own imagination. Some of the events described did take place, including the blowing up of the tree and the poaching of the buck.

Two other characters drawn from real life are Eric Anthony Sykes and William Ewart Fairbairn. Both had served in the Royal Marines during World War I, after which they joined the police. They then went to Shanghai and served in the Shanghai Municipal Police. Shanghai was a pretty tough city at that time and while in China they literally wrote the book on street fighting and how to counter it. When World War II broke out they returned to the UK to enlist, but found they were too old for service in a combat unit. Instead, their skill sets were found to be very attractive to the commandos, who embraced them and employed them providing unarmed combat training. They also trained agents of the Special Operations Executive (SOE) who were parachuted into occupied Europe to work with resistance groups and to gather intelligence. Sykes and Fairbairn's other claim to fame is that they designed the Sykes-Fairbairn Fighting Knife, otherwise known as the Commando Dagger, the weapon that became synonymous with the commandos, the image of which was incorporated into their shoulder flash, where it remains today with the Royal Marine Commandos. Again, the words spoken by Sykes and Fairbairn are from my own imagination.

Should you ever travel to that part of Scotland you will find a small museum to the Commandos at the Spean Bridge Hotel. At least, it was there the last time I visited. If you continue to drive north along the A82 for a couple of more miles you will come across the Commando Memorial, unveiled in 1950. You can't miss it, it's 17 ft tall. If you have time, please stop for a moment to remember the men who trained in that rugged countryside. Some of them, including my father, have memorial plaques lodged there in the small memorial garden.

The idea for providing rock climbing training for commandos came from an officer of 3 Commando, Lt Algy Forester. He trained an enthusiastic Australian officer by the name of Lt Bill Lloyd and between then they started training the rest of the commando. Later, a climbing school was established at Glen Coe where soldiers from each commando would be trained as instructors before returning to their units to pass on their training to their colleagues.

I have changed the names of most of the Royal Navy vessels that are mentioned in this book, but not those of the first commando landings ships: HMS Prince Leopold, HMS Queen Emma, HMS Prince Charles and HMS Princess Beatrix. These were Belgian and Dutch cross channel steamers converted for war use. Landing craft would be slung from the lifeboat davits and were lowered to deck level to allow the commandos to board. They would then be lowered until they skimmed along just above the surface of the sea as the ship approached its landfall. When the final order was given for the landing craft to be launched, they would be lowered into the sea, their propellers already turning and then the falls would be released, so that the landing craft could be launched without the need to stop the ship and turn it into a sitting target.

I have also retained the names of HMS Repulse and HMS Prince of Wales, which were sunk off Singapore in a Japanese air attack on 10th December 1941, along with four destroyers. Over 800 sailors died in the attack.

Operation Absolom, which forms the centre piece for this book, is a fictitious operation, but is loosely based on Operation

Archery, a raid on Maloy and Vaagso which took place on 27th December 1941. My father took part in that as a trooper in 3 Commando and was wounded when a Hampden bomber of the RAF accidentally dropped a phosphorous smoke bomb on his landing craft, setting it alight. Two soldiers were killed and several more seriously wounded. My father escaped with minor burns but was still hospitalised for six weeks, such was the nature of medical care in the 1940s. I have borrowed that incident for use in this story. The level of casualties suffered by 3 Commando and the RAF are the same as those I have described for Operation Absolom.

Also wounded during the raid was Lt Dennis O'Flaherty, who did have half of his ear shot off, as well as suffering other injuries. He was hospitalised for two years but was awarded a DSO for his actions at Vaagso. He later returned to active service. During the Korean War he was awarded the American Bronze Star while serving with the Royal Artillery. He retired from the Army in 1975 as a Brigadier.

Major "Mad Jack" Churchill was 2IC of 3 Commando and did go ashore on the island of Maloy playing the bag pipes, another incident that I have appropriated for this book. The tune was reported to be The March of the Cameron Men. While he had intended to be the first man to attack the artillery battery there, he was hampered by having to find somewhere safe to deposit his pipes and then draw his traditional Scottish broadsword (no, I'm not making this up).

Churchill was the last man in the British army to kill an enemy using a longbow, which he did during the fighting in France in 1940. After being promoted to command 2 Commando, Churchill was taken prisoner in September 1944 while operating behind enemy lines in Yugoslavia. He then escaped from a PoW camp in northern Germany and made it to the Baltic coast at Rostok before being recaptured. Along with about one hundred and forty others he was sent to the Tyrol under SS guard and feared being executed under the infamous "Commando Order"[1]. After an appeal to Wehrmacht soldiers, the SS were forced to hand over their prisoners, who were then released when the German soldiers withdrew from the area. Churchill walked about ninety miles south to the Italian city of Verona, where he met up with an American Army unit. As if this was not enough, Churchill was then posted to Burma to join the commandos fighting there. Fortunately the war had ended by the time he arrived.

Churchill's was just one of a remarkable number of true stories that came out of the Army Commandos of World War II which actually makes it difficult to write novels about them. The truth of what they did is often far more remarkable than any fiction that could be written. They attracted the bravest and, sometimes, the most foolhardy soldiers of the British army; I can only attempt to reflect their bravery and inventiveness.

Again appropriated from fact was the discovery that Vaagso was playing unwilling host to an additional fifty soldiers of an elite German infantry battalion over the Christmas period, 1941, doubling the size of the garrison. However, they were not SS troops, as I have made them.

The raid on the Lofoten Islands in March 1941, code named Operation Claymore, was genuine. The commandos took over 90 German soldiers prisoner without suffering any casualties, destroyed several fish oil factories and sank a significant amount of shipping in the harbour. Many Norwegian men volunteered to return to Britain with the commandos, to join the Royal Norwegian Navy. One Norwegian woman who also tried to volunteer had to be put ashore, protesting vociferously. The number of prisoners taken in that one raid was greater than the number taken in France during the entire period from the outbreak of the war until the evacuation of Dunkirk. Operation Anklet saw the Lofotens raided again on 26th December 1941, as a diversion for Operation Archery.

For those readers that think that it is unlikely that the Germans would leave a town such as Ålesund so poorly defended, even at New Year, I have to say that once again the truth is often stranger than fiction. When 3 Commando carried out the very first commando raid, on Guernsey (Operation Ambassador, 14th July

1940), they couldn't find a single German soldier, despite the island having a garrison of two hundred and fifty. The only person they encountered was a rather surprised stockman, on his way to work to do the morning milking. When he was asked where the Germans were, he replied that they returned to their barracks every night and went to bed. The commandos had to withdraw without firing a shot, or being fired upon. The Germans only knew the commandos had been there at all because they cut the cables to the telegraph station before they left. In distant Norway it is quite feasible that the Germans wouldn't have learnt the lesson of that raid.

Although I have been very disparaging about Lieutenant Llewelyn in this book, I do not wish you to think that I regard the Guards as being bad soldiers or officers. When No 8 Commando was formed it was mainly made up of volunteers from the Brigade of Guards and the commando served with distinction in the Middle East. David Stirling, founder of the SAS, was an officer in the Scots Guards before joining 8 Commando. I did, however, want to show Lt Col Vaughan's genuine intolerance of officers with over inflated ideas of self importance, so I created Llewelyn.

Towards the end of the book I refer to Carter and Green being taken to Edinburgh Castle. I use this location again in the second book in the series. The castle actually ceased to be a military facility in 1905, but remained a 'Royal Castle' and continued to be guarded by the army, just as it is today. Although no longer officially a military base, I can't see it having been left unused during the Second World War and therefore have incorporated it into my narrative. The castle is a UNESCO World Heritage Site and is one of my favourite places to visit when I'm in Edinburgh.

In the fictional world, Lieutenant Carter and Trooper Green have been reunited with 15 Commando, but they are destined, like my father, to have many more adventures before the war comes to an end.

[1] The infamous Commando Order or *Kommandobefehl* was issued on the instructions of Adolf Hitler on 18th October 1942 and stated

that all commandos/special forces personnel who were captured, even those in uniform, were to be executed without trial. Over a hundred suffered that fate, including some who were just ordinary soldiers, sailors or airmen.

Further Reading

For first hand accounts of Commando operations and training at Achnacarry, try the following:

Cubitt, Robert; A Commando's Story; Ex-L-Ence Publishing; 2018.

Durnford-Slater, John, Brigadier: Commando: Memoirs of a Fighting Commando in World War 2; Greenhill Books; new edition 2002.

Gilchrist, Donald: Castle Commando; The Highland Council; 3rd revised edition, 1993.

Scott, Stan; Fighting With The Commandos; Pen and Sword Military; 2008.

Young, Peter, Brigadier; Storm from the Sea; Greenhill Books; new edition 2002.

For a more general overview of the commandos and their operations:

Saunders, Hilary St George; The Green Beret; YBS The Book Service Ltd; new edition 1972.

Preview

1 - Edinburgh

Lt Col Vernon found Carter doing PT with his troop down on the beach, running through sand up to their ankles to increase the resistance. Carter had only just returned from leave following his escape from Norway and had some catching up to do with his troop. As well as the shouts of welcome at his safe return back to the unit, he had also been greeted with a few ribald remarks and references to the smell of cow dung. It was the price he had to pay for spending his leave on a local dairy farm.

"Got a phone call just now from Edinburgh, asking if I could send you over sometime today. It was posed as a request but sounded like an order. Do you know anything about it?"

The puzzled look that Carter gave said more than his words. "Not a thing, Sir. Did they say what time they wanted me?"

"ASAP, apparently. Better go and get changed. I'll see if I can arrange a car to take you. If not I'm afraid it will have to be the train." Like all the commandos, they didn't have an allocation of transport. Being considered a mobile hit and run force meant that no one thought that they might need vehicles just to get around the local area. Fortunately, there were enough sympathetic transport officers in other units for vehicles to be borrowed from time to time. Not the good, new, shiny vehicles of course; just the ones that were already on their last legs.

"How was your leave?"

"Very pleasant, Sir. I spent it with the Hamilton family. They're local famers."

"Yes, I know them. Got a very pretty daughter, so I've been told."

Carter blushed bright crimson. "Well, I have to say that you have been told correctly. I learnt to milk a cow."

Lt Col Vernon permitted himself a smile. "I'm sure that is a skill that will stand you in good stead while you're in the commandos." The CO chuckled. "Should I be picking myself out a hat?" Seeing Carter's face, he hurried to explain himself. "For the wedding, I mean."

"Oh, I think that might be a bit premature. We've only just met, really."

"That may be the case, Steven, but you shouldn't let that get in the way. Things are different these days, as you have better reasons than most to know. Now, you cut along and get changed. If I can get you a car, I'll send it to your billet. If not, I'll send someone around with a rail warrant for the journey."

Carter handed over command of the troop to the Troop Sergeant Major and jogged back to his billet, cooling off after his exertions. He had a quick bath and changed into his battledress, strapping on his pistol belt with its Webley. He decided he wouldn't need anything more for a visit to Edinburgh Castle. After about half an hour a driver wearing the cap badge of the Royal Army Service Corps arrived at the door to collect him.

The journey to Edinburgh was uneventful. Carter took the opportunity to read the newspaper that the driver had brought with him. Dropping him outside the gate of the castle, the driver went off to find himself some lunch while Carter marched over the ancient drawbridge and through the narrow barbican and reported to the guardroom inside. An orderly arrived to escort him along the narrow winding road up into the upper ward and into the offices situated in the old granite building at the rear. The route was familiar to Carter, having walked it only a fortnight before on his return to Scotland from Norway. He was ushered into an office to be greeted by the man who had interviewed him on his previous visit. The man who wore the uniform and insignia of the Intelligence Corps but who, Carter was pretty sure, wasn't a soldier, despite introducing himself as Major Nigel Warriner.

For a start soldiers in the British Army didn't wear neatly trimmed beards. Not unless they were Sergeant Farriers in the Life

Guards, the cavalry regiment that provided the personal escort to the monarch.

He was also wearing pilots' wings, but those issued by the RAF. He wasn't old enough to have served in the Royal Flying Corps or to have been awarded the three medals whose ribbons were displayed on his chest. On his shoulders he wore the crown of a Major. However, looks can be deceiving so Carter paid him the due military honours before sitting in the chair proffered by the officer, on the other side of the bare desk that was the only other furniture in the room.

"Sorry to drag you up here on such short notice, Carter, but I've a need for a man with some special talents and you were the first to come to mind. By the way, I'm not based here. I've come up from London specially to see you."

That made Carter wonder why he had chosen to come to Edinburgh. If he just needed an office in which to hold a meeting, they could have used the 4 Troop office in the old sweet factory in Troon that 15 Commando was using as its headquarters. Carter wondered if he should mention that but found he didn't need to.

"I know you're thinking I could have saved both of us some time by going to Troon, but I needed to be in a place where we wouldn't be overheard. The walls in this part of the castle are over a foot thick. The only way to hear what is going on in here would be to listen at the door and I've got a Redcap[1] posted outside to make sure that doesn't happen."

"It all sounds very mysterious, Sir."

"If I tell you what this is about, you'll see just why. But before I tell you a thing, I have to ask you if you want to volunteer for the job. Now, I know you commando types will do just about anything if it smacks of a little bit of adventure, but this is different. There is a real chance you won't make it back. It's a high-risk proposition and one that the War Office thinks hasn't much chance of success."

There was an obvious question for Carter to ask, so he asked it. "In that case, Sir, why is anyone even thinking of doing it?"

"Because we have to give it a shot. The lives of thousands, probably tens of thousands, of men depend on it. We have to take the chance; it's the very least we can do."

"And what if I say 'no'?"

"Then we will have to find someone else. There's bound to be someone mad enough to do it."

"If it's insanity you're looking for, then I probably qualify." Carter grinned.

"It's no joking matter, Carter. This is a matter of national importance. The whole of the war in North Africa may depend upon the outcome. Churchill himself has given it the go ahead."

"Well, Sir, I can hardly refuse the wishes of the Prime Minister."

"Thank you, Carter. I knew you were the right man for the job. The reason I asked for you is that this operation involves you working behind enemy lines for a few days. That's the experience you've got that I need."

"It was probably more luck than judgement that I got away, Sir."

"That's as may be, but luck may play a part in this operation as well." He lifted a briefcase off the floor and opened it up. From it he withdrew a plain buff folder. "Don't let the colour of this fool you." Warriner said. "The contents of this folder are Top Secret[2]. But if this briefcase was to be stolen, I didn't want the thief to think they had anything of importance inside it." He put the briefcase down and opened the folder. The top item was a head and shoulders photograph of a soldier. Upside down it wasn't easy for Carter to make out any of the detail. Warriner handed the photo across so Carter could take a closer look. It was of a man in his mid forties, wearing full dress uniform and although the photograph was black and white, Carter didn't need to be told that he was wearing the red tabs of a staff officer at his collar and that the band of his peaked cap was red.

"That is Major General Walter Gillespie who, until recently, was on the staff of General Auchinleck, Commander in Chief of the Eighth Army. He was on his way back from Cairo for a personal meeting with the Chief of the Imperial General Staff on a matter so delicate that it couldn't be trusted to anyone else. What that matter was, we still haven't found out, though The Auk has now sent a replacement representative, considering what has happened."

"What has happened, Sir?"

"Sorry, getting ahead of myself a bit. Gillespie was travelling on a Royal Navy destroyer, HMS Cape Inch, along with a couple of aids when they got a bit too close to the French coast. From what we can understand the need for speed was such that they took the shortest route, which took them close to the Brittany coast, cutting the corner just west of Ushant so they could sail a straight-line course for Portsmouth. Unfortunately they ran afoul of a U-Boat and the destroyer was torpedoed and sank.

Now, here's the thing. The survivors were taken to Brest, along with the General's two aids, but of Gillespie himself there is no sign. Then, a couple of days ago, we received word from Jersey that security around the airfield had suddenly been increased."

"And you think the General has been taken there."

"Yes. But more than that, we think that the Cape Inch wasn't just unlucky. We think that she was being shadowed, which means that the Germans knew who was on board and understood the significance of the journey. This view is strengthened by the fact that surface vessels arrived pretty quickly to pick up the survivors, as though they had just been waiting to be told where to go."

"If you don't mind me saying so, that's a big leap of logic, Major."

"I don't mind you saying so, because it's true. But normally when the Germans capture an officer of general rank, they can't wait to get his picture on the front pages of the *Völkischer Beobachter*[3]. The propaganda value of such a high value prisoner is significant. But not this time. There hasn't been a peep out of their newspapers. And before you say it, the Jerries would be just as vocal if Gillespie had died in the attack, so we are pretty confident that he's still alive. Which brings me to your role in this ..."

"You want me to go to Jersey and bring the General home."

Warriner smiled. "There's no fooling you, is there Carter?"

Carter was getting a bit annoyed with the continued use of his last name, as though he were of a much more junior rank. A Major would normally address a Lieutenant by his Christian name. It was another reason that he suspected that Warriner probably wasn't a soldier.

"The conversation was heading in that direction, Sir. What else could you possibly need me for? But why take him to Jersey?"

"Because it's an island. It's easy to defend and difficult to escape from. We suspect that they're keeping him there so he can be interrogated about the reason for his journey to England. Whether the interrogation has started or not we can't be sure, but we think not. This is a specialist job and there have been no reports from our informers of any transport planes arriving from the mainland. That would signal the arrival of the interrogation team. It is also possible that they're going to fly him off the island direct to Berlin for interrogation. But the weather over that part of the Channel has been pretty poor these last few days.

Nothing is flying from Calais as far as the Bay of Biscay. The cloud cover is too low. No doubt if there was an emergency, they'd make an attempt, but if they have the General safe, they've no need to take any risks. So it looks like they're waiting for the weather to improve. That gives us a window of opportunity."

Carter nodded, "But with no guarantee how long the weather will play ball, Sir."

"Exactly, Carter… and that means time is of the essence. We want you on the island within the next three days. According to the Met Office boffins, that's about as long as we can expect the current weather situation to last." Carter nodded again, as Warriner continued.

"Even if trained interrogators arrive in the interim, we think that the General could probably withstand interrogation for that long. It's unlikely they would start in with physical torture straight away and Gillespie will try to give them useless information to start with, just to delay things while they go away and cross check it. Once you're on the island, you'll have to get the general out of wherever they're keeping him as soon as is humanly possible, then get him off the island. We'll keep a submarine on standby each night for seven nights. If we haven't heard from you by then, we'll assume that you're either dead or a prisoner yourself."

"And what if I can't release the General, or we can't make it to the rendezvous point?"

"If you have to, you use that." Warriner pointed to the holstered Webley revolver at Carter's waist.

"You mean you want me to kill him? A General in the British Army?"

"If it silences the General, then yes. I hope it doesn't come to that, but it may do. And before you ask, yes, Churchill does know that it's a possibility."

Carter sat silently for a moment, contemplating his options. Just because Churchill knew of the possibility of the General having to be killed, it didn't constitute an order from the very top. He had killed before, only a couple of weeks ago. He had done it without giving it another thought. It was what he had been trained to do and it had been necessary in order to preserve his own life and that of Tpr Green, who had been with him in Norway. But this would be murder. Not the killing of an enemy in self-defence or as an act of war, but the murder of someone on his own side. Could he do that? Carter sincerely hoped that he never had to find out.

"Do I go in alone?"

"You can take up to three men with you. Handpicked by you. They must know as little about the mission as possible until you're briefed at Weymouth, but you can tell them how dangerous the mission is. They have the right to know that before committing themselves."

Who could he ask? Carter wondered. Tpr Green, of course. he had shown himself to be resourceful and utterly loyal. But who else? O'Driscoll perhaps. He was a good commando, he had shown that in Norway. Maybe Glass. He was very good at field craft and an expert at hand-to-hand combat. Yes, if silence was an essential, Glass would be the ideal candidate. He would give the matter some more thought on the journey back to Troon.

"There's obviously no time for training for this one. I need you down in Weymouth by tomorrow night so we can start briefing you. Can you manage that?"

"I should think so. How do we go in? The same submarine?"

"No. We've got an MTB for the insertion. A submarine has too deep a draft and you would have to paddle a long way to land. With the coastal currents that could end up with you on the wrong beach and maybe being captured before you even get ashore. After stealing that E Boat you'll feel right at home" Warriner allowed himself a half chuckle at his own joke. "For similar reasons it has to be a submarine for the extraction. We can't risk an MTB sitting off the coast of Jersey from dusk till dawn for seven nights. If it's discovered it will point to something happening on the island, not to mention the risk to it getting there and getting away again each day in broad daylight."

"What's the plan once we get on the island?"

"That will be up to you, but essentially it's the same mission as you carried out for our friends in the Norwegian resistance. Attack the location where the General is being held, get him out and get him to safety, We'll give you as much intelligence as we can to help you, but you won't have any help from the islanders. We have some informers there, but no one who has the skills you would need. Also, it's the sort of place where one half of the island is either married to the other half or related to them. We don't think you would be betrayed, but the risk is from gossip. We know that the Germans use paid informants in the occupied countries so there is the real possibility that they are doing so on Jersey as well. We don't know who they might be, so we have to keep the islanders from knowing anything about this operation, just in case."

"How big is the German garrison?"

"We can't be sure. We know there are several anti-aircraft artillery units there and there are also coastal batteries to prevent us invading, not that we have any plans to do so at the moment. We're guessing about two thousand troops and that would include the Luftwaffe personnel at the airfield. There aren't any aircraft permanently based on the island, but the Germans sometimes use it as a temporary base to provide air cover for German coastal shipping."

That brought furrows of thought to Carter's face. Four men against two thousand was hardly healthy odds. Even given that the four men were commandos didn't help the odds that much.

"This sound more like a job for the SSRF[4] than it does for an ad hoc team, if you don't mind me saying so, Sir."

"I would agree with you, except they're just like the rest of you in that they're trained for quick 'in and out' operations. You are one of the few commandos to have operated behind enemy lines for any significant period. That makes you almost unique in the British Army. What we do plan to do is mount a diversionary operation on one of the other islands using the SSRF, on the night you go in. That should draw away naval and air units chasing after them."

It wasn't a convincing argument, as far as Carter was concerned, but knowing that there would be a diversion was comforting. But it could also be counterproductive. If it put the Germans on Jersey on the alert, it might lead to them being discovered. "If it's all the same to you, I think I'd rather not have the diversion, Sir. The quieter the better for us, if you don't mind."

"If that's the way you want it."

"It is, Sir. And I'd also like complete control of the plan. I'm sure that your people would do a good job, but if I'm to sell it to my men I'm going to need complete faith in it, which means having devised it myself."

"If you say so. Given that you could die on this operation, the least we can do is give you the right to choose how you do it."

"Thank you, Sir. That's very comforting."

[1] Redcaps - Royal Military Police, so called because their peaked caps have a red cover

2 Top Secret - There are five grades of classification used by the British military: Unclassified, Restricted, Confidential, Secret, and Top Secret. Documents are held in folders coloured and marked in accordance with the classification of the highest graded document; buff for Unclassified and Restricted, green for Confidential, pink for Secret and crimson for Top Secret.

3 *Völkischer Beobachter* -The official newspaper of the National Socialist (Nazi) Party. The title means 'The People's Observer'.

4 Small Scale Raiding Force. Also know as 62 Cdo. A group of about fifty five commandos established in 1941 to carry out small raids, several of which were against the Channel Islands. They were disbanded in 1943 as the commando's role started to shift towards operating as spearhead units for regular military operations.

- END OF EXTRACT -

And Now

Both the author Robert Cubitt and Selfishgenie Publishing hope that you have enjoyed reading this story.

Please tell people about this eBook, write a review on Amazon or mention it on your favourite social networking site. Word of mouth is an author's best friend and is much appreciated. Thank you.
Find Robert Cubitt on Facebook at
https://www.facebook.com/robertocubitt and 'like' his page; follow him on Twitter **@Robert_Cubitt**

For further titles that may be of interest to you please visit our website at **selfishgenie.com** where you can optionally join our information list.

Printed in Great Britain
by Amazon